BOMBS
& BELIEVERS

A NOVEL
KEN SONENCLAR

This book is a work of fiction. Although certain real places and institutions are named, their descriptions, geography, topographies, configurations, architecture and work rules have been altered to accommodate the story. All characters are creations of the imagination. Any resemblance to real people, living or dead, is purely coincidental.

Published by Tunix Books
© Copyright 2013 Ken Sonenclar. All rights reserved.
ISBN 978-0-9888423-1-1
For more information about this book, see
www.bombsandbelievers.com

For Sheryl, Liana, and Charles

*But there is neither East nor West, Border nor Breed
nor Birth,
When two strong men stand face to face, though they
come from the ends of the earth.*

Rudyard Kipling
The Ballad of East and West

Prologue

Istanbul: July 4th

Felix Maurer wiped his cut and bloodied hand across his forehead. "Hold on!" he screamed to the buried voice as he lifted a chunk of stone and mortar and heaved it aside. "I'm almost there. Talk to me!"

It had been a glorious evening. Clear and warm, with twice as many stars as you normally see through Istanbul's lignite haze. The 1,500 American sailors packing the open-air concert in their honor had risen for *The Stars and Stripes Forever*. Their rhythmic clapping had given way to a patriotic roar as fireworks illuminated the domed mosques on the edge of the city's old Moslem quarter. And then hell burst its seams.

Maurer wasn't dead because the seamen and their officers had filled every seat and more. He'd been consigned to standing room along with the diplomats, far to the rear. Still, the explosion had flattened him like a mule's kick.

Those around him were shocked and battered. Spread before him was a sea of death and anguish. Overhead, red, white and blue fireworks flanked a spiraling funnel of acrid smoke and radiated a splash of light. Sirens wailed.

He circled along the only path not clogged with debris or bodies, tracking a cry for help to a pile of stone and twisted metal. He dropped to his knees and ripped away at the mound. The voice was coherent and strong. Michaels was his name, from Evergreen Shores, he said, on Michigan's Upper Peninsula. The kid sounded heartened when Maurer said he'd summered near there as a boy.

But Maurer hadn't heard anything for five minutes now. Their exchange had dwindled to a pleading monologue. "Hold on, buddy. I'm almost there, I swear!" And a few seconds later, "Come on, Michaels! We're going fishing off Mackinac, dammit!"

The two guided-missile cruisers and the destroyer that had brought the sailors to Istanbul were bound for maneuvers in the Black Sea following their stopover. But how many were dead now? Hundreds, he was sure.

His aide at the consulate had reached him on his cell to say it was a truck bomb, and apparently part of a synchronized attack. Less than two minutes before the blast, a suicide bomber leveled the recreation hall at the NATO base at Incirlik, near the Syrian border. At least 75 dead.

"Michaels!" He dug furiously and finally saw fingertips. He scooped away more dirt and gravel. The boy's arms were stretched out, like a swimmer reaching for the shore. Maurer grasped the thin wrist. He held his breath and shut out the hysteria swirling around him.

He prayed for the faintest beat.

There was none.

He stood and crossed himself. It struck him that he never even saw the boy's face. He bent down again and took Michaels's hand. It was still warm. He squeezed the palm and held it, raging that he couldn't rub life into it. It was all the mourning he could muster. He surveyed the chaos for a place to help. He needed to find the living. Tomorrow Washington would have just one question for him. Who did this?

Part I

This blessed plot, this earth, this realm, this England.

William Shakespeare
Richard II

O sages standing in God's holy fire
As in the gold mosaic of a wall,
Come from the holy fire, perne in a gyre,
And be the singing-masters of my soul.

William Butler Yeats
Sailing to Byzantium

Chapter 1

Linus Hart Crane fidgeted with excitement at the rear of the empty auditorium. He'd finally managed to wire his laptop to the projector and sync the remote, letting him run through his slide show. Normally one of his grad students would have worried about the technology—after all, he was the James C. Loeb Professor of Archaeology, not Computer Science—but they were scattered at digs around the world or teaching summer school back at Harvard.

He adored lecturing in this clunky old hall in the bowels of the British Museum. The sight lines were poor, the acoustics impenetrable, and the A/V system would no doubt fail at the first opportunity. But the room swelled with history: Einstein had spoken here, and Churchill of course, and hundreds of other icons from Darwin to Lennon. He loved being part of this great institution that refused to march to the drumbeat of progress. He was picturing himself at the podium tomorrow morning, the place jammed with know-it-alls, jackasses, and other full professors who wouldn't drag their tenured bones out of bed before 9 a.m. for anyone in the field but him.

Crane slid the dimmer-switch down, easing the hall into darkness except for the projector's beam and its reflection off the wall-sized screen. He sped through his presentation, lingering on each slide just long enough to mumble bits of narrative. He had no notes and didn't take any now. He never wrote or memorized a speech. He was famous for the impromptu tangents he'd follow before weaving his way back to his presumed topic. His less spontaneous colleagues found him maddening. His students revered him.

The door behind him opened and Finn Sorenson, the conference chairman, stepped inside. Sorenson stared at the screen, trying to make sense of what he saw. He was a United Nations bureaucrat from Denmark, not an archaeologist. But Crane did not hold that against him. He had trained at Georgetown's School of Foreign Service, and his years in America had left him more open-minded than the striped-pants cookie-pushers that run most U.N. agencies and make doing good work so difficult. When Crane phoned him a week ago asking his okay to scuttle his prepared remarks—already published in the proceedings for this special U.N. conference, "The New Barbarians: Ancient History, Modern Plunder"— and speak instead about something extraordinary he'd come across in his latest field work, Sorenson gave his approval without probing further.

"Looks fascinating, professor," Sorenson said. "Have you a title yet? You're on in nine hours, you know."

"Yes," Crane said, smiling. "It's called, 'A Funny

Thing Happened on the Way to the Conference.'" He waited for a laugh but saw only Sorenson's confusion. "Don't worry, Finn, I won't let you down."

"I'm sure not. That's why I have invited all the important newspapers and TV networks."

Crane was concerned. "You haven't tipped them about my subject, have you?"

"How could I? You haven't told me anything."

"Right," Crane said, as Sorenson retreated.

Crane watched the door close behind the Dane and wondered whether he should even bother going back to the hotel. He was too revved-up to sleep. He hadn't felt this anxious since defending his Ph.D. thesis to a trio of calcified naysayers nine years ago when he was just 21. And since then he'd certainly gotten used to the spotlight: a full professorship at 26 to keep him from bolting for Stanford, two best-selling histories of the ancient world, a highly rated PBS series, frequent contributions to *The New Yorker*, and his first novel just delivered to his publisher, the movie rights already auctioned to DreamWorks. Even his colleagues who viewed him as a vulgar popularizer—and there were more than a few—admitted privately that he was the brightest and most inventive classical archaeologist of his generation. But his latest work—discovery would be a more apt description—would elevate him to a new level altogether.

Before long he was down to his final slides. He figured he was running about 15 minutes over his allotted hour without even leaving time for questions. He would trim as he went along tomorrow, but when his audience heard what he had to say they'd let him talk all day if he wanted.

The door opening again interrupted this thought. He turned, expecting Sorenson, but instead saw a young woman in a yellow sundress and gold sandals. She closed the door behind her. A canvas carryall emblazoned with a *Huffington Post* logo was slung over her shoulder. An Oxbridge grad student, Crane guessed.

"Hope I'm not disturbing you," she said, apparently noting the surprise on his face.

He couldn't place her slight accent. Perhaps Israeli. She certainly looked it: satin-like olive complexion, long brunette hair, coal-black eyes. Her beauty pushed him a little off-balance. "No, not really. But it's so late I didn't think anyone else was here."

"You are Professor Crane, right?"

"Yes," he said, unconsciously standing straighter and tucking in his shirttail.

"I wanted to get a copy of your presentation to read tonight, if that was possible."

"I'm sorry, Miss, uh..."

"Please call me Sherin."

"I'm sorry, Sherin, but there's nothing on paper. You're welcome to take notes tomorrow."

"There's nothing at all?"

"No. Just what I'll be projecting from my laptop here." He tapped the machine, which had fallen into *sleep* mode. Crane reached for the switch to turn up the lights.

"That's okay," she said, with a smile that put him at ease. He watched her dig into her shoulder bag. When she pulled out a sleek, Sturm Ruger pistol and leveled it at his chest, the sight was so out of sync with his initial impression of the girl, that she killed him before he could even raise a hand.

Chapter 2

Detective Zander Blake stared out at Santa Monica Boulevard through the bronze-and-glass picture window of "Demarest's New World Treasures" art gallery. With no customers in sight, he banged the Stickley desk usually occupied by the man he was impersonating today: Henry Demarest.

Zander knew he had less than an hour to wrap this sting up and get on the freeway to LAX. Otherwise he could kiss his flight good-bye. Forget London, forget the conference, forget his speech, forget everything. He would embarrass the department and look inept—he didn't need that now.

He glanced at his watch. Just after 3 p.m. There was still enough time, he reassured himself, if only his patsy would show up. Still, Zander wondered why he was surprised to be in this situation. The days he left town always ended in bedlam.

• • • •

The morning's odd commute had lulled him into

thinking today would be different. Instead of the usual race and crawl—already inducing a premature loss of tooth enamel, according to his dentist—traffic from Manhattan Beach into downtown had barreled along at 45 miles per hour. When he rolled into the LAPD's Parker Center headquarters, no one had cursed or threatened him before 7 a.m. for the first time in months.

The quick ride left him time for a cup of coffee, which he gulped down after jogging up the echo-filled stairwell to the third floor. He tossed his empty cup into the trash beside his battered desk and scanned yesterday's "To Do" list, realizing that despite a 12-hour shift he couldn't scratch off any of the 15 items, all of which had seemed critical 24 hours ago.

Today would be different. All he needed right now was business cards for the trip. He opened a drawer and grabbed a fistful.

Detective Zander Blake
Head, Art Theft Detail
Los Angeles Police Department

He slipped into his chair and thumped the pile of resumes on his desk. Two weeks ago he'd told his captain he'd have no problem filling the Detail's junior slot before this trip. But the days had vanished and now he was grateful the captain had left for vacation without requesting an update. Besides, Zander was still raging at his last partner, who had sat across from him for 18 months and sucked him dry of a career's worth of insights into the art business, then called to say he was moving to Seattle as the VP of Security for an online art auction house. "A hundred-sixty large. How could I say no?" the son-of-a-bitch had asked. "Plus stock," he added, before Zander could tell him how to say no. Not that Zander begrudged him the opportunity—he had rejected the offer himself first—but the timing was wrong. He was just putting Jessica's betrayal behind him.

His best candidate now was a 28-year old woman coming off three tough years in CATS, the department's special unit for battling auto-theft rings— the ones with more efficient assembly and distribution operations than Ford. At least he wouldn't have to put her through basic training. She claimed she was bored tracking illegal boatloads of fenders to Indonesia. Zander tried to convince her that tracking a cache of stolen Roman coins to Kuwait was no less tedious, but he could tell she didn't believe him. Which was okay, since he didn't believe it either. She also shrugged off Zander's warning—though he saw it as a bonus, not a handicap—that the Art Detail was an isolating job. You might not talk to your pals down the hall all week, but every day you were texting cops in New York, Washington, and Paris. She knew nothing about art— nothing useful, anyway—but neither had he seven years ago.

He skimmed through his email and printed out a bulletin from Interpol, which highlighted a theft of Laplandic ivory carvings from an Oslo museum. He Googled "Lapland," unsure where it was, and then stuffed the bulletin inside a folder he knew he'd probably never open again.

People imagined the Art Theft Detail only traced stolen Renoirs and raided studios churning out bogus

Jackson Pollocks. But the masterpieces—the cases that made the papers—were rare, by definition. Zander spent most days on things as likely to turn up at estate sales as museums: Disneyland posters, Gold Rush photos, Bullwinkle animations, Hemingway first editions, Gary Cooper autographs, Prussian coins, Victorian ball gowns. And even the paintings were rarely Old Masters. His favorite open case involved half-a-dozen missing Red Skeltons, mostly sad-faced clowns that the sad-faced comic had dashed off in the 1960s. They looked to Zander about as artistic as poker-playing dogs, though he knew no one was paying him for his opinion. And whether you called these things art or collectibles or garbage, as he often did, more and more people were buying them, and more and more people were stealing them or forging them. With the murder rate down and art theft skyrocketing, Zander was continually begging for more budget. But California's gaping deficit made a joke of that.

He had calculated on his ride in that to run his sting, make his plane, and still keep his blood pressure within AMA guidelines for a 40-year-old male, he had to cut out by eleven. He scrolled through his open investigations. This would be his first extended absence without any human backup—after London he was off to Cairo for a crash course in smuggled Egyptian artifacts. But he felt satisfied—pretty much—the center would hold until he got back.

He emailed his itinerary to his captain's assistant and was surprised with the almost instantaneous response. "What are you bringing me back?" the message asked.

"Sorry," he wrote. "I already promised my

daughter a pyramid."

• • • •

Despite the afternoon's looming disaster, Zander savored days like this.

Going undercover beat the hell out of lecturing the Q-tip clients of another bank trust department about security and bunco artists.

He had slapped the gallery operation together after Demarest, southern California's preeminent dealer in Native American art, reported that an eager young man had phoned to solicit interest in "the most amazing Indian artifact you've ever seen." The gallery owner said that his antennae shot up when Mr. Smith, as he called himself, sidestepped questions about his source. Zander appreciated the tip, though he had no illusions that the dealer was any sort of Boy Scout. In fact, Zander was sure Demarest's basic instinct was to grab the artifact no matter how hot, and flip it within an hour at an 800-percent markup. But since returning from 18 months in a Federal cage for receiving stolen property, Demarest was working hard to suppress such urges.

The dealer had gotten to know Zander while performing a thousand hours of community service. Demarest had sworn that he would rather clean the streets with his tongue than go back to jail, and he had tried to prove it by becoming one of Zander's best resources, happy to play teacher or stoolie. Still, Zander could count the truly reformed ex-cons he knew on the fingers of one hand. And he wasn't ready to add Demarest to this pantheon. The dealer still spent too much time in the shadows. Though in his late sixties, he traveled half the year visiting clients, curators, auction houses, all flavors of middlemen, and many remote archaeological digs, some authorized, Zander guessed, but most not.

Zander had Demarest invite Mr. Smith to the gallery, even though there was no proof that he was guilty of anything more than a lack of imagination in picking an alias. By his own choice, Demarest was staying in the background. He was a tiger of a negotiator, but had no stomach for confrontations. Zander would stand in for him, pretending to be Henry Jr. in case Smith had seen Demarest's photo on the web.

To play his part, Zander had unearthed his sharpest suit: a nine-year-old Hugo Boss, steel gray with pinstripes. He looked good in it. Since splitting with his wife he'd spent a lot of evenings at the Y, losing his stomach and regaining his chest. But like most men who don't dress up for a living, his accessories betrayed him. His shoes were scuffed, his socks resembled a lint farm, and what had once been a power tie had fallen limp.

Smith's appointment was for 1:30, leaving Zander plenty of time to squeeze him, if he was indeed a black marketeer, and still breeze to the airport. But Smith had called just before his ETA to say something had come up and perhaps it might be better to reschedule. Demarest was all too happy to put things off. But Zander made it clear with a sharp finger to the sternum that the dealer must tell Smith it was now or never. Postpone, Zander knew, and the guy would never show. Smith finally agreed to come by no later than 2:30. That was half an hour ago.

Zander fretted about missing his plane. He was a

highlighted speaker at a United Nations conference on "The New Barbarians." The London meeting had been called to hatch fresh strategies for smashing the global alliance of thieves, shady dealers, and corrupt officials trafficking in stolen and smuggled antiquities. Zander had a prime slot and had worked hard on his speech.

"Looks like our friend got cold feet," Demarest said while straightening the centerpiece of the gallery's current exhibition: a wall-sized wood screen dominated by a fire-breathing eagle sitting atop a whale. Zander could only roll his eyes when he saw the $350,000 price tag.

"He'll be here," Zander shot back, knowing he had no basis for such confidence. He watched the dealer move behind him to dust a wall of photos. Each featured a smiling Demarest shaking hands with the President—every President since Nixon. Zander thought he had aged well. "No party preference, Henry?"

"If you mean Democrats and Republicans, none at all, Alexander." Demarest was the only person since his grandmother to call him Alexander. "I only distinguish between winners and losers, and I give generously to the winners."

Zander could only smirk at Demarest's politics, though that was hardly the right word for his gift giving. Zander returned to the business at hand. "So what do you think Smith's bringing in?"

"I wish I knew," answered Demarest. "I love the mystery of it all."

"No guesses?"

"It was obvious from our chat," Demarest said, "that Smith is devoid of any sophistication. I'm sure whatever he's got he found himself. It could be anything: weaponry, a headdress, a cave painting. You never know," he added while rearranging a window display, "what you'll find if you dig in the right place."

The sound of the door at 3:15 spawned new hope that the day might be salvaged. A stunning blond in a chic olive suit strolled in. Against all the facts, Zander wondered if this could be Smith. She circled the gallery, looking at a few pieces without genuine interest. Zander caught her eye, but if she returned his smile he didn't see it. When she opened the door to leave, though, she stood aside for a tall young man carrying a black cello case. The closed door rattled behind her as the cellist shuffled to the desk.

"Mr. Demarest?"

Zander stood. "Mr. Smith?"

Zander looked into an innocent, college-age face. A dark suit couldn't hide his rail-like chest and arms. His heavy-framed glasses only clinched Zander's notion that he did his surfing on the net, not at the beach. Harder to reconcile was Smith's deeply tanned face and his callused hands. Holden Caulfield working on a chain gang, Zander thought.

Smith followed Zander into the back office. Demarest was on the phone, flicking a pencil in place of the Macanudo he'd been ordered to give up. Zander pointed to a sofa opposite the desk and Smith sat down.

Zander nodded toward Demarest. "This is my father, the gallery's founder."

Smith and Demarest exchanged nods.

"You have a first name, Mr. Smith?" Zander asked.

"Uh, Joe," Smith said, glancing around the office as if he were looking for an emergency exit.

Zander saw that he needed to put Smith at ease. "So you play the cello, Joe?"

Smith stared back blankly. Then he glanced at the case and caught on. "Oh... no," he grinned. "This was the easiest way to carry it."

Zander looked at his watch. The sweep-second hand seemed to be spinning like a propeller. "Not to rush you," he said, "but I'm running very late."

"Oh sure, sure," Smith said. He cradled the case between his legs, flipped up the latches, and opened it to reveal what looked to Zander like a big, tattered Kachina doll. Its head brushed the base of the case's neck. Zander couldn't believe he might miss his plane over a long lost toy and was about to drop his cover and bolt when Demarest came out from behind the desk.

"My God," Demarest said in a reverent voice. "This is the finest Anasazi mummy I've ever seen."

Zander winced as he understood he was looking at a little girl, no more than three or four. He glanced at Smith, whose smile suddenly repulsed him, and wondered what his own kids were doing at that moment. The Indian traits were obvious, and the skin, which Zander feared might crumble at his touch, was mud brown and tough as parchment. Only wisps of black hair remained. The most striking feature was the set of large white teeth. The girl was wrapped in a ragged blanket whose pattern, perhaps bold once, was now a dull rust. The skin had decayed on the forehead and right cheek. He'd seen plenty of gore in the streets, but this still spooked him.

"What do you think?" Smith asked.

"Startling," Zander said, wanting to press Smith, but also curious about the little girl. "When did she live, uh… Dad?"

"It's difficult to be precise," Demarest said. "A thousand years ago, give or take a century."

Zander tuned in and out of Demarest's mini-lecture on Anasazi history while considering his next step. There was nothing criminal per se about carrying a mummy around in a cello case. If a crime had been committed it had to do with digging up the mummy. "Can I ask you where you got this, Joe?"

"Is that important?"

Another time and place, Zander would have played Smith with some finesse. But with his plane already pre-boarding, Zander pulled out his badge. "Yeah. It is."

Smith needed only a few nanoseconds to catch on. "Oh, fuck."

"I'm Detective Blake, LAPD."

Smith sank into the couch, his thin chest turning concave. "Oh fuck."

"Mr. Carter over here is actually Henry Demarest," Zander said. "And your name.... your real name is..."

"David Reeps."

The young man looked ready to drop whatever he'd eaten for lunch on the antique rug. Demarest grabbed Reeps and tried to drag him to the bathroom. "Not on my Sarouk!" he insisted.

Zander pulled Demarest away and pushed Reeps back onto the sofa. "Henry, I don't have time for your crap. Just sit your ass down." He grabbed Reeps by the shoulders and got him to breathe slowly. "Okay. Now where did you get the mummy?"

"I'm not supposed to say," he whispered, the effort seeming to drain him.

"You seem like a nice kid, David. You don't want to come down to jail with me, do you?" Zander wanted to take Reeps downtown even less than Reeps wanted to go.

"You won't arrest me?"

"Not if you tell me what I need to know."

"Okay," Reeps began, getting his land legs back and sitting forward. "I'm a senior at San Diego State. These men came to campus looking for students who wanted to work outdoors and make some good money. It sounded great. We're digging near Laughing Wells, in the desert. Me and seven other guys."

"Where you found some virgin tombs," said Demarest.

Zander felt this came out of Demarest's mouth with a tad too much enthusiasm. He glared at the dealer.

"But I didn't know it was gonna be that way until we got there," Reeps continued. "I swear."

"So why are you here with the mummy?" Zander asked. "Freelancing?"

"I guess so. There's so much stuff."

Zander took a pen and pad off Demarest's desk and handed it to Reeps. "I want the name of everyone out there. The organizers and the students." Zander grabbed a highway atlas from the shelf. "And show me exactly where this dig is. You can give me the precise coordinates if you've been using a GPS. Then I want you to get the hell out of here and you're to have no further contact with the dig. Kapisch?"

"My friends will wonder where I am."

"You'll see them in September."

• • • •

It was 4:15 p.m. Zander was sure he'd cut it too close. Demarest was still admiring the mummy, his eyes spinning like a slot machine. "Don't even think about it," Zander said.

"I don't know what you're talking about."

"Tell me something. You have customers who would take this?"

"It's a specialized niche, but I wouldn't have any problem."

Zander shook his head, revolted by Demarest's confidence. "I've heard archeologists talk about a fine line between death and art, Henry, but this isn't a gravestone here, it's a little girl. It's twisted."

Zander appreciated Demarest not arguing with him. He took the pad again, wrote a few notes and slipped them into the cello case. "I want you to deliver this yourself to Steve Drinkwater at the UCLA museum."

"Today?"

"By 6 o'clock."

"I'd like to study it a little."

"By 6 o'clock, Henry."

He slapped Demarest on the back and bolted out the door, sensing the dealer cursing at his heels.

• • • •

Twenty minutes later Zander was in his Manhattan Beach apartment. It looked like a maid had just been through, but he kept it neat all by himself, neater than he'd ever been in his marriage. He decided soon after the break-up that he wasn't going to slide down civilization's slippery slope. He'd seen it happen to too many of his newly single buddies. Piles of clothes, filthy kitchen, empties everywhere. Oscars without

Felixes.

Last night he had pulled out a suitcase with the best of intentions, but didn't pack, cracking open a few Coors instead and watching the Dodgers trash the Giants.

Now he made a point of locking away his 9mm Glock, relieved that he was getting out of harm's way. He wasn't sure if his Scotland Yard buddy Figgis, who had invited him to the conference, even carried a gun.

Now, with no time to piss, let alone pack, he filled his bag like a contestant in a supermarket giveaway, stopping only because it was full. He grabbed the bag and bolted downstairs.

Chapter 3

Helen Vandameer's breathing grew shallow as she rode the elevator up to the Goodge Street tube stop, a short walk from the British Museum. Rarely anxious, she was meeting a man she knew only from a brief phone conversation. She felt like a character out of a le Carré novel when she spotted him by the station newsagent, flipping through a copy of *The Economist*, a stuffed briefcase at his feet. As promised, a blue-and-white-striped umbrella, superfluous on this clear night, dangled from his arm.

"Mr. Hazim?" she asked.

He nodded but said nothing. They strolled in silence down Tottenham Court Road before cutting up Bayley Street and into a deserted Bedford Square.

This was Helen's second night in London, the eve of the U.N. Conference she had flown in to attend. Now 28, she'd just celebrated her second anniversary as curator of Ancient Near Eastern Art at the Metropolitan Museum in New York, the youngest department head there in 75 years. Her expertise encompassed 7,000 years of art history and most of what is now called the Middle East.

She'd spent yesterday selling the National Gallery on her idea for a joint blockbuster: "The Wrath of God: Golden Idols in the Biblical World." Afterwards, already calculating the merchandising possibilities of Golden Idols, Helen had a late supper with Peter Sloan, an old boyfriend and Princeton classmate of her brother's. Now an economic attaché at the American embassy, he showed his good manners in not mentioning the fiasco she'd happily left behind in New York. He also confirmed for her what she'd heard just before she left: a handful of Middle Eastern diplomats in London, unsure how the Arab Spring's turmoil would ultimately affect their careers, were selling priceless artifacts. Some were doing it to buy food and medicine for their families back home, others just for the cash. He even passed along the card of Jaffar Hazim, a Syrian cultural official who had approached him at a recent World Bank reception. "Do *not* call him at the embassy," Sloan said. "This is a private matter and he'd be severely compromised if his compatriots got wind of this."

She had returned directly to her hotel and phoned Jaffar Hazim at his home. Mentioning Sloan's name was enough for the diplomat to understand why she called.

Looking him over, Helen thought Hazim was probably 35, but it was hard to tell. He was a handsome man, with powerful shoulders that filled out his dated suit. His hair and mustache were jet black, but his heavy eyes and the lines around his mouth betrayed his weariness.

She was surprised that he barely glanced at her. No one would call Helen a great beauty, but she was tall and thin, and suffused with the confidence of doted-upon daughters to the manor born. Her family had been ensconced among the Manhattan elite since Christiaan Vandameer, in exchange for underwriting a colony of 50 men and women in New Netherland, had received the title of Patroon in 1634, along with a bountiful chunk of what is now Westchester County.

Helen was growing antsy with Hazim's silence. "You wish to engage in some sort of exchange, Mr. Hazim?" she said, sensing the diplomat's need for ambiguity.

"Yes," he said. "But you must understand why I am here. I am a loyal citizen and I love my country."

She found confessions from friends uncomfortable, but from strangers they were presumptuous and ill mannered. "I'm sure you are," she said, thinking that supporting Hazim was the easiest way to move on to their business.

"But my government's recklessness," Hazim continued, "has led—"

"You don't have to explain yourself to me," Helen interrupted and then smiled, hoping Hazim would see she had no interest in judging him.

"But you must understand," Hazim continued, growing more agitated, "the chaos can return any time."

Helen wanted to grab the frazzled Hazim by the shoulders before he spun completely out of control, but she knew this would be crossing a cultural bridge too far. Instead she stared him straight in the eyes, raised an open hand, and took a stern but reassuring tone. "I understand, Mr. Hazim," she said. "Truly, I understand." Her steadfastness seemed to calm him.

Hazim reached into his case and came out with

something draped in cheesecloth, the size of a large flashlight. He unwrapped it slowly, revealing a carved ivory statue of a young man, perhaps a Nubian prince. Helen knew immediately it was nothing special.

"It is Assyrian," he said.

"No doubt," she said, irritated by Hazim's assumption she didn't know. She waited for Hazim to hand it to her.

"It is 3,000 years old," he said

"More like 2,800." Helen cradled the ivory and ran her palm over its length. It was a good, solid piece, but the delicate face, handsome and less stylized than others from the period, had degraded from exposure. It would make a minor addition to the collection, but she wouldn't even bother if this were all he had. She brought it to her nose and smelled it. "It's nice," she said, thinking that her evening might have been better spent in the West End.

"This ivory has always brought good fortune to its owner. I deeply regret parting with it."

"Anything else?" she asked.

"One other." Hazim dug deeper this time and pulled out a leather case, shaped like a thin cigar box. He handed it to Helen and took back the ivory.

The box was missing a hinge and the lid slid off as she lifted it open. Inside was a necklace of gold beech leaves on strands of lapis and carnelian beads. Helen's head snapped back in surprise and she was sure Hazim noticed. She recognized it as Sumerian, perhaps 5,000 years old. She remembered a similar strand at the Oriental Institute of the University of Chicago, where she'd earned her doctorate, though theirs—with several broken leaves and a chain with blatantly modern fixes—was far inferior. Hazim's necklace was flawless and obviously royal. She ran a finger across an eyebrow and pictured how it would look draped around her neck. Jewelry had always been a strength of her department, but this was truly magnificent and she wanted it. This piece would draw a crowd. She cleared her throat and took a moment to collect herself. Art and beauty aside, this was still a negotiation.

"It was excavated at Ur and belonged to Queen Pu-Abias," Hazim said with a tone that was more used-car salesman than university lecturer.

Helen traced the gold leaves with her fingertips. She wondered where Hazim had gotten his hands on a piece of this quality. "I have to ask, Mr. Hazim, this wouldn't have come from Baghdad, would it?" Much Iraqi treasure, looted during the long war, had supposedly found its way to Damascus. "Because I couldn't possibly…"

"No, never," he insisted. "This has been in my family for many generations."

She doubted the necklace was a personal heirloom, but knew when to stop asking questions. She pulled a jeweler's eyepiece from her bag and examined the strand for imperfections that might suggest a forgery, but found none. "Exquisite," she said, thinking that while the ivory might be worth a few thousand, this necklace would easily fetch a half-a-million at Christie's. And that was the problem. Her budget was shot for the year. "How much do you want, Mr. Hazim?"

The Iraqi closed his eyes as if searching for his courage. "Thirty thousand?" he asked, his voice suddenly very faint.

Only the thought that Hazim was joking kept Helen from jumping in the air. "Pounds or dollars?" she asked, thinking it hardly mattered.

"Dollars," he said, the quiver in his voice undermining his determination.

"Dollars," she repeated, forcing a frown.

"But I must have the money *now*," he added, his voice regaining its timber. "I cannot meet with you again. And you can take the ivory as well."

"But Mr. Hazim," she said, her shoulders contracting from a pang of anxiety. "You can't think I'm carrying that kind of cash."

"Of course," he said, and surprised her before she could speak by opening his clenched hand to reveal a business card.

'Bank Julius Bär & Co., Zurich,' it read, with a hand-written account number. She laughed to herself. "You're a regular Eagle Scout, Mr. Hazim."

It was still only 4 p.m. in New York. She took out her phone and called her banker. She relayed Hazim's account information, insisting that the transfer be executed immediately. Less than a minute later a text confirmed the wire. "The money has been sent," she said, with no more concern than if she were paying for a pair of pumps at Bergdorf's. "Would you care to call your bank to confirm?"

Hazim held up his hands. "That is not necessary." He handed Helen the rewrapped ivory and the box.

She slipped it into her briefcase. "I'm at the Connaught," she said, ready to burst. "Please call if you have anything else."

Chapter 4

Whether jet-lagged and unable to sleep or just eager to grab the free breakfast, delegates to the U.N. Conference began filling the British Museum's lobby moments after the doors opened at 7:30 a.m. Badges, proceedings and coffee were waiting.

The chief of the museum's AV department edged his way through the crowd and headed downstairs to prep the auditorium. He pulled open the scratched maple doors and flipped the master light switch, bringing the cavernous, windowless hall to life. He took the clipboard from under his arm, checked the box alongside "main overheads" and headed toward the front. He climbed the three steps onto the stage and pushed the lectern into position. He made a note to get a new set of clean water glasses and gazed out at 40 empty rows of faded, blue-cloth chairs.

The sight of Linus Hart Crane, lying crumpled and bloody at the foot of the soundboard half way up the center aisle, did not register for a second. But the AV operator then bounded off the stage. He stopped a foot short of the body, unsure what to do. Feel for a pulse?

Run upstairs? He glanced around to assure himself he was alone, and not the next victim. Then, nervously slapping at his sides, he remembered his walkie-talkie and called Security.

• • • •

Zander Blake's plane arrived from Los Angeles on schedule, just after noon. He'd only managed to sleep two hours, and decided in the taxi line to catch a quick nap before going to the conference. "Bertrand Hotel," he told the driver.

He leaned back and flipped through the advance agenda. He caught his own name and could barely believe he was sharing the stage with people he'd been reading about for years. He was especially sorry he had missed Linus Crane's keynote and hoped the professor would stick around afterwards. They'd never met, but Crane had generously spent hours on the phone with him last spring, explaining the subtler points of three Attic vases that had turned up on the credenza of a Beverly Hills movie agent after disappearing from the Boston Museum of Fine Arts. Most academics Zander had encountered—including those with far more free time than Crane—would not have bothered. His conversations with Crane had even opened a rare dialog for Zander with his son Josh, who was a fan of Crane's TV series and was impressed to hear that his father was buddies with a celebrity. Zander wanted to thank him even more for that.

The taxi crossed the Earl's Court Road, closing in on downtown. Zander leaned forward to read the meter when his eye caught *The Mirror's* screaming headline on the seat beside the driver: "PROF MURDERED AT

BRITISH MUSEUM."

Zander asked the cabbie to pass him the paper. He ripped the tabloid open to find the story and shuddered with disbelief when he saw Linus Crane's name. He read the brief account, hoping to find some rational explanation. "Hey!" he shouted at his driver. "Forget the hotel. Go to the British Museum."

Chapter 5

It was almost 7 p.m., the evening sun still high in the muggy summer sky. Zander slowed his pace as he neared St.-Martin-in-the-Fields, where a memorial service had been hastily arranged for Linus Crane. He peered into one restaurant after another and longed to sit down to dinner and a bottle of wine even if it was only mid-morning in L.A.

It had already been a long and frustrating day. Zander had rushed to the British Museum, desperate for some credible information about Crane. Stymied there, he headed to the University of London, where the conference had been moved, but arrived only after the day's session had adjourned. A Google search on his phone turned up nothing beyond what he'd read that morning. When he finally reached his hotel to check in, he had no luck getting through to his buddy Figgis at Scotland Yard.

Too wired to nap, he called his ex-wife Jessica, hoping to catch his kids. She surprised him by answering the phone. If neither Layla nor Josh picked up she usually let the machine take it. Zander assumed she was expecting her agent to call with news about some part, though he wouldn't give her the pleasure of asking. He cut it short after learning that Josh was camping at Bear Lake and Layla was still asleep. "Just remind them where I am, please, so they don't think I've abandoned them." However brief their conversation, it drained him, letting him fall asleep for a couple of hours.

He was late for the service by design, having taken a circular route to St. Martin's that swung him past the law courts at Lincoln's Inn, onto a bit of Fleet Street and around Covent Garden. He wanted to pay his respects, but that desire was partially checked by his distaste, bordering on dread, for anything to do with death and dying. This included memorial services, funeral parlors, burials, wakes, hospitals, assisted-living communities, and medical tests that did not return instantaneous results. He never knew what to say to the bereaved, and his tongue flagged at the mention of the terminally ill.

None of this infringed on his conduct in the line of duty, for which the department had commended him 11 times. In fact, he showed little regard for his own safety, taking chances he'd talk someone else out of. But sickness and death made him uncomfortable in a way that he realized he'd never outgrow.

Zander climbed the stone steps to St. Martin's columned portico and waited at the closed doors. A wave of laughter from inside surprised him, easing the tightness in his chest.

The only other person on the covered walkway was a beautiful young woman leaning against one of the columns. She seemed oblivious to the passing traffic, pedestrians, and him. A pair of black-and-maroon striped harem pants and a black tank top accentuated her lithe figure. He was watching her when she seemed to reenter the real world and looked at him. Her eyes were red from crying.

"You all right?" he asked, noticing that her tissue had been reduced to a ball the size of an aspirin.

She took a deep breath before answering. "I'll survive."

"I'd offer you a handkerchief," he said, digging through every pocket, "but I don't have one, of course."

"Don't worry about it."

"Would you like a sleeve?" He extended an arm and elicited a smile just as more laugher erupted inside. "Someone's telling some funny stories."

The woman nodded. "If they only knew."

"Knew Crane, you mean?"

When the woman nodded, it finally struck him that she was American.

"Was he a friend?"

The woman sighed. "Friend, boss, mentor, not to mention thesis advisor."

Zander pursed his lips. "You're Penny Theobald."

The woman glanced at her chest as if to check for a name tag.

"We've spoken. Zander Blake, with the LAPD. You and Professor Crane helped me on a case a few months ago."

She nodded. "I remember. The Attic vases. Detective Blake. Why are you here?"

"I'm speaking at the conference tomorrow."

"Really? That's wonderful," she said, her voice sinking with her mood.

"This must be horrible for you," he said. "Have you heard anything? The papers claim it was a robbery."

"Right." Her voice was thick with sarcasm. "They also imply that Linus put up a struggle, which I can tell you without the tiniest doubt that he would never do. I had to badger him into thumb wrestling."

"Well, trigger-happy thieves don't need any provocation."

"Maybe in Los Angeles." She brushed away some hair that had fallen across her eyes. "But not here. Anyhow, you didn't settle for simple explanations when you called about the vases."

"That's true." Zander was embarrassed it had taken this long to see that this woman wanted answers, not consolation. "It's an odd spot for a robbery."

"I'll say."

"And if it was murder—"

"I think so too," she interrupted.

"Whoa! I didn't say I thought he was murdered."

"But what else could it have been? He was a cream puff."

Out of a mix of chivalry and longing, Zander did not want to let her spirits sag again. "Listen, I've got a friend on the force here. I can let you know if he's heard anything."

"I'd appreciate that."

Zander pointed to the entrance. "You going in?"

"No. I can't listen to a bunch of hypocrites who were probably ripping Linus apart an hour before he died."

"You said he was a cream puff."

"That doesn't mean people weren't jealous."

Zander watched a tear roll down her cheek as the doors burst open and the crowd poured out, moving down to the sidewalk like an army brigade. "Where's everyone off to?" he asked a strutting older man.

"Conference dinner."

Zander looked at Penny and read the indecision in her face. "You should eat something," he said.

"Or at least drink," she shot back.

Five minutes later they were in a grand banquet hall around the corner. Zander's attention drifted to a fleet of seraphim gliding across the blue sky of the ceiling, and then down to the suits of armor standing sentry between tapestries of a medieval hunt and a gluttonous feast. It reminded him of a producer's home where'd he'd gone to investigate a slashed Rembrandt.

"This is a wonderful re-creation," Penny said, apparently noting Zander's curiosity.

"Of what?"

"Of the original building here. This whole part of town was leveled during the Blitz. The few pieces that survived are over at the Victoria and Albert."

"I see," Zander said, happy to hear Penny dispense her insight without the condescension he encountered at most turns in the art world. No one had to remind him he wasn't on the faculty at Yale.

He left Penny on the buffet line for what turned out to be a 15-minute expedition to the cash bar. Weaving his way back through the subway-dense crowd, he saw Penny locked in an intense conversation with a well-tailored, broad-shouldered man, who embraced her and departed before Zander got close enough to see his face.

"Who was that?" he asked, handing Penny her vermouth.

"Bulent Ozbek," she said with a dreamy look that bothered Zander for no rational reason.

"Should I know him?"

"Not really. He sponsored Linus's work this summer. Linus was filming a series of Young People's Lectures on ancient history, sort of like what Leonard Bernstein did decades ago to get kids interested in music. You remember that? It was before my time."

"Mine, too," Zander mumbled, wondering how old he was looking these days.

"Ozbek's Turkish," Penny continued. "He lives in Istanbul. But he keeps a place in London and he flew in as soon as he heard about Linus. He was devastated. I could see it in his eyes."

He wondered if she'd blow him off if he suggested they ditch the crowd and grab a quiet dinner. "How did Oswald get involved with Crane?"

"Oz-BEK," she said slowly, "Bulent Ozbek—"

"Excuse me. Ozbek."

"Bulent was at Harvard last year endowing a chair in Turkish Studies."

"Just one?"

"So far. Anyway, after the ceremony he was visiting some old haunts. He got his MBA there. As it happened, that was the day Linus heard that his National Endowment grant for the Young People's series was being cut in half. But after spending an hour with Linus, Bulent pulled out his checkbook and we were fully funded again."

"A regular fairy godmother," Zander said, wondering how he could compete with this guy. One-on-one hoops?

"He is. He's set up rural schools across Turkey,

he's underwriting all sorts of bioagricultural research there, and he's building a museum at ancient Troy, which makes sense since he's supposedly got one of the greatest private collections of ancient art in the world." Penny dropped her voice to a whisper. Zander leaned in. "He also happens to be the Prime Minister's brother."

Zander scanned the room until he found Ozbek chatting with a slender woman, who was leaning into him like a palm tree in a hurricane. "Don't you know that brothers like that are always idiots? Bill Clinton's brother, for instance."

"Hardly," Penny said, clearly enjoying deflating him. "They say his brother isn't well and that he's got his eye on the P.M.'s job for himself."

"Miss Theobald?" a voice with a drawl grabbed their attention. Zander turned toward a wide-eyed American who could have been an undersized tackle for Alabama. He was about 35, in a dark gray suit, white shirt and rep tie. His blond hair was short and neatly combed. Zander did not need any ID to know where he was from.

"I'm Dean Goodrich, Miss Theobald, Assistant Legal Attaché with the Federal Bureau of Investigation here in London."

"Yes?" Penny said, with a skeptical look. "I thought you guys were called agents."

"Yes, ma'am. Special Agents. Back home we are, but overseas the Bureau gives us a more exotic designation."

Zander introduced himself. To his surprise, Goodrich seemed happy to meet him. Most agents Zander encountered suffered a congenital dislike for local law enforcement. Goodrich, on the other hand, looked relieved to learn that Zander was with the LAPD. "Hey, that's great," Goodrich said, pumping Zander's hand. "I spent my youth at D.C. Metro. I loved it, but I couldn't afford it anymore. Washington was so broke I had to buy my own vest and pay my own cell-phone bills. Lucky for me I got an offer from the Bureau."

"I used to think I'd wind up at the Bureau someday myself. I even managed a year of law school." Zander hadn't mentioned this to anyone in years and wasn't sure what the point was now. He blamed the competitive enzymes that Penny had stirred up.

"Maybe it's not too late," Goodrich said. "We should talk sometime. But I need to speak with Miss Theobald right now."

"Don't let me stop you." Zander kicked himself for not getting Penny out sooner.

"I'm not investigating the death of Linus Crane in any formal capacity," Goodrich told her, "but the Bureau gathers background whenever a high-profile American like the professor is killed overseas. So I'd like to ask you some questions."

"Sure." Penny grabbed Zander's arm. "I'm gonna crash soon. Could we have lunch tomorrow?"

"Of course," he said, his spirits lifting again.

"Great." She took a few steps with Goodrich before turning back. "I want to hear what the police know about Linus."

• • • •

The Met's Helen Vandameer recognized Bulent Ozbek the moment he entered St.-Martin-in-the-Fields.

She had made overtures through official and unofficial channels to get to him for a year, hoping that she and the Met could curate the first public exhibition of his collections. But neither professional, diplomatic, nor family connections had opened the right doors.

She spent the memorial service planning her approach for the dinner, and making contingency plans in case Ozbek didn't show. She wondered what good fortune might come her way from Linus Crane's death.

Helen had watched Ozbek with Penny, making a mental note to find out who this woman was that deserved such special attention. She pounced as she left. Ozbek didn't seem to mind.

"I had no idea such a charming and beautiful woman wanted to meet me, Dr. Vandameer," he said. "My aides can be overzealous in guarding my time. How can I help you?"

"I want to show your collection at the Met."

Ozbek chuckled. "That's a big request."

"The only one worth making."

"I agree. But we should discuss this in a more private setting."

"I'd love to." She pulled her phone from her purse, ready to fly anywhere and cancel any conflict. She hoped he would suggest something in the next three months, Thanksgiving at the outside. "What would be good for you?" she asked, tapping the calendar icon.

"Right now."

Helen looked into Ozbek's ebony eyes. "I'm all yours," she cooed.

• • • •

Zander finally reached the buffet as Bulent Ozbek

passed him on his way out. A busboy had just deposited a stack of fresh plates, but the buffet itself had been picked clean. "Son of a bitch," Zander mumbled. "They're worse than cops."

He snatched a limp piece of celery and swept it through some speckled dip. He was wondering if he could still get room service at his hotel when a hand tapped his shoulder. He turned. "Figgis, you bastard!"

"Come on," Figgis said, "I wouldn't feed this crap to my dog," and he led Zander out to the street.

Chapter 6

Zander hadn't seen Figgis in almost a year, but their friendship wasn't built on the minutiae of each other's daily lives. They exchanged plenty of e-mail, but it was case-related and rarely personal. In person they picked up wherever they had left off. Figgis was a good listener and understood Zander's frustrations as no one at the LAPD could.

Figgis was Deputy Detective Chief Inspector of Scotland Yard's Art and Antiques Squad. They were an elite group, taught by legitimate dealers who wanted to clean up the business, and recognized as the best in the world. Still, the Art Squad had its share of enemies, both in and out of the Yard. They were disbanded under Thatcher and it took five years of clamoring by honest dealers and curators to get them reassembled. More recently the Yard's Organized Crime Group had tried to absorb them. Top brass at the Yard and the occasional parliamentary oversight committee didn't like that these cops jetted off to Jerusalem and Rio and New York. But with a third of the world's stolen art passing through

Britain, there was no other way to do the job.

After a short cab ride, Figgis led Zander down a dimly lit street and into La Stella, a neighborhood trattoria where Figgis was greeted like royalty.

"So how've you been, big guy?" Zander asked after Figgis toasted his safe journey with the first glass from a bottle of Barolo. Zander wasn't sure he wanted the answer. His elation at having Figgis rescue him from the decimated buffet had waned on the drive over. In the dim light of oncoming traffic Zander thought Figgis looked god-awful. He'd always been a big man, broad and solid across the chest. But that firmness now sagged, his nose resembled a page from Rand McNally, and the gray once confined to his temples traversed his scalp.

Figgis slapped his belly. "Put on a few pounds."

"You look fine."

Figgis ordered in Italian for both of them without consulting the menu.

Zander watched the waiter scurry to the kitchen. "Sounds good," he said. "Now tell me some news."

"We snagged a beautiful El Greco last week. Biggest recovery in a while. Christ on the Cross. Very moving. You might recall it went missing three years ago. Caused a stir. Cheeky bastards left a note thanking the gallery for its absent security."

"I remember."

"They weren't the brightest bulbs. Surveillance got clean shots of their faces and their Mercedes."

"But they knew enough to lay low for a few years."

"Maybe," Figgis said, as the waiter made room for a gargantuan salad. "More likely they finally realized the picture would always be too hot to fence. Story started circulating among the local bottom-feeders that it might be available at a fire-sale price. We put out word about a buyer willing to pay half a million. And I wound up with the task of meeting the buggers at a seaside resort in Brittany."

Zander smirked. "Probably like a postcard there."

"Yes, it was." Figgis's tone was wistful. "Seems like the only time I get someplace romantic is when I'm alone. Anyway, couple of hours after I arrived the idiots dropped by my room and exchanged the Greco for handcuffs." Figgis picked up the wine to pour refills, prompting Zander to cup his hand over his glass.

"I'm speaking tomorrow morning."

"You think you'll make more sense if you can see?"

"It's possible."

"Then let me finish with Brittany," Figgis said, filling his own glass. "After our boys led them away, I'm alone in the room and I take a good long look at the picture." Figgis held his hands out, as if grasping a frame. "There's something about El Greco."

"His stuff always strikes me as sadistic. Like everyone's been on the rack."

"Exactly," said Figgis. "So I'm looking at this tormented Christ, and I feel this blind rage welling up."

"At who?"

"I don't know," Figgis said. His hand shook as he held his thumb and index finger an inch apart. "But I came this close to punching a hole through our dear lord and savior."

Startled to see Figgis's eyes close and his breathing grow labored, Zander reached for his friend's arm. It felt tense, the muscles taut beneath the sleeves of his coat. "Hey, relax," Zander said. "You okay?"

Figgis stared off into space and gradually his breathing slowed and returned to normal. "Zander," he said, "I didn't intend to drop this on you, but it's been a hell of a year. Maggie left me in February."

"You're kidding," Zander said, shocked. "What happened?"

Figgis lifted his blotchy face. "Slight indiscretion on my part."

"Really?" Zander asked, never having pictured Figgis as Don Juan.

Figgis downed his glass. "Don't be so surprised. I've had my share."

Sad and humiliating images of his break-up with Jessica filled Zander. He ground his teeth and forced his attention back to Figgis. "How'd your wife find out?"

"Friend of hers saw us weekending in Cornwall. Reported back like some fucking Gurkha scout."

"And you admitted it?"

"What could I say? Maggie was waiting for me like a sniper when I got back. I was supposedly on a stakeout. Caught me off-guard. Threw me out then and there."

"Who was the girl? Someone from the squad?"

"No no. Smart little gallery number. But that's gone by the boards as well."

"Maybe Maggie'll take you back."

"Don't think so. Says she could never trust me again."

"I suppose not." Zander emptied the bottle into his own glass. He needed it to digest the news, but he also hoped to slow Figgis down. It didn't. Along with a veal platter the waiter delivered a new bottle.

"Then last month," Figgis continued, "the Detective Chief Inspector of the squad retired. The job was supposed to be mine. I was first in line, length of service in the squad and at the Yard. But the gods thought otherwise. Don't know how I offended them, but they jumped Maidstone over me." Figgis growled like an angry bear. "Dumb bastard can't find his own pecker if someone doesn't point to his fly. But he won't have any help from me. So I put in for early retirement end of the year. I'm a 20-year man. But I'll tell you, Zander, I'm scared. Pension'll barely pay the gas bill."

"Christ." Zander looked for the lever to lift his friend's spirits. "You're still young. What are you? 51? 52?"

"I'm 46."

"Even better, then," Zander blubbered, thinking that as far off the tracks as he felt his own life had veered, Figgis seemed on the verge of careening out of control. Zander watched his friend nervously spin the wedding ring he still wore, but also noticed the frayed shirt cuffs, something the old Figgis would never have tolerated. "You'll hook up with one of the security consultants that have been hounding you. They must pay better than the Yard."

"Yes, well, they haven't been returning my calls." He shrugged. "Hope I've not ruined your evening. You still skipping out on us in a day or so? Cairo, right?"

"First thing Sunday morning, assuming the place doesn't explode like Turkey. The State Department still has its travelers' advisory for the whole Middle East. Not that you have to go that far to get yourself killed, of course. I'm sick over this Linus Crane business."

"He helped you crack that Boston case, didn't he?

Those vases?"

"Yup. Very decent guy. He deserved better. Can you tell me anything that hasn't made the papers?"

"Well, this decent guy got someone upset. Shot point blank with no struggle. Might have known the shooter. Then again, guards and conference staff say Crane was carrying a laptop and wearing a watch, neither of which were on his property list."

"Which supports this botched-robbery theory?"

"Can't be ruled out."

"Not yet, anyway."

"And maybe not at all. But it's a bit more complicated.

"How so?"

"Well—and this bit is not for broadcast—the good professor's hotel room was burgled last night."

"You're joking."

Figgis's expression made clear he wasn't.

"Before or after he was killed?"

"Ninety percent certain it was before."

The notion that someone was hunting Linus Crane focused Zander's attention through the alcohol buzz. "Any leads from the hotel?"

"Not yet. But the best in the Yard is working the case."

Figgis's news only thickened the fog around Crane's death. Whoever shot Crane knew where to find him and wouldn't be deterred. But was killing him the plan, or the last exchange in an unintended argument? Did the killer come to collect a debt, finally settling for a few pennies on the dollar with the watch and computer? Zander didn't see Crane as a gambler. Just as easy to imagine a spurned lover pocketing Crane's things as a simpleminded misdirection for the police. And was this a local score being settled? Or something from back home?

Zander straightened himself up and pushed his chair back from the table. He took a deep breath and nodded at Figgis, who was dipping a last almond cookie in his cappuccino. Only one other table was still occupied. Zander watched the bartender wipe down the long expanse of dark wood while some shouting in Italian drifted from the kitchen. "Let's walk a little," he told Figgis, hoping the night air might let him make some sense of Crane's murder.

Chapter 7

Bulent Ozbek's limo pulled up in front of his townhouse just off Belgrave Square. Helen Vandameer knew there were few private homes left in the area, most having been converted to embassies or merchant-banking boutiques.

She took a moment to survey the block as Ozbek headed straight for the door. It was not late; the last remnants of twilight lingered, but the street was quiet, disturbed only by the diesel chug of a taxi ambling away. She couldn't imagine what the wide, four-story limestone home might have cost. The perfection was marred only by the silver sheen of a gum wrapper lodged at the base of the black, wrought iron fence that fronted the property.

She fell a few paces behind in the palatial entry hall, dropping her normal, seen-it-all demeanor in the face of the Louis XVI giltwood furniture, a Beauvais tapestry depicting the life of Alexander, and a towering triptych mirror whose frame, Ozbek volunteered, was carved by Bernini for Pope Urban VIII.

The scene repeated itself in the sitting room. While

Ozbek waited under an immense Rembrandt portrait of Amsterdam's elite—striking a pose, Helen noticed, virtually identical to one of the 17th century mercantilists—she hung back to appreciate a glorious pair of Canalettos offering complementary views of Venice, and the mesmerizing inlaid wood ceiling, modeled on ancient Islamic floral designs.

They soon settled down to drinks and hors d'oeuvres. Helen had learned at the memorial service about Ozbek's connection to Linus Crane. She was touched to see Ozbek's animation drain away and his eyes glass over when he recalled his fondness and respect for Crane. Few men she'd known, especially successful ones, let their guard down like this. He had begun to tell her about his last meeting with Crane when the butler called him away for an urgent phone call.

Helen took the opportunity to stroll the room from one treasure to the next: a gold and enameled snuff box covered in miniature views of Istanbul; vases with painted harem scenes; flawless polychrome pottery; a mother of pearl chest; and a wall of intricately carved daggers and swords.

When an apologetic Ozbek returned, she was caressing a blue-and-white porcelain sprinkler bottle, letting the light play off its dozen inlaid rubies.

"It would look beautiful on your vanity," Ozbek said.

"I was thinking the same thing," Helen laughed, not surprised that Ozbek enjoyed having his collection admired.

They moved to the dining room and sat catty-cornered at one end of a Louis XIV table that could accommodate 30. Ozbek was still subdued and he seemed happy to let Helen enjoy the art, a panorama of life under the Sultans, which ran floor-to-ceiling all around them: Streetscapes of children at play, a traditional wedding, the chaos of the bazaar, the Ottoman army in battle. One wall was devoted to court portraits: narcissistic men with delicate hands and ice in their veins, Helen thought. Far more engaging to her was the portrait above the mantelpiece of a seated odalisque, kicking off her shoes and gazing indolently across the room. Helen returned her own gaze from the woman to Ozbek, bringing him back to life.

"Collecting draws a very rough crowd these days," he said. "When I was young I enjoyed nothing better than a day at Sotheby's. But today the auctions attract only vultures."

Helen grinned. "The great collectors I've known take comfort in the art, find a release in it."

"As I do. But it's more than that. To me the objects are magical."

"They have a transcendent power," she agreed.

"Exactly. When I find something that was touched or perhaps even owned by a general or a statesman, I feel a connection, I draw their strength and wisdom, whether it was Amenhotep or Mencius or Augustus or Muteczema."

"Men who changed the world," Helen said.

"Vision like theirs is gone today," he said, his eyes widening. "Vanished! The empires they ruled and the worship they inspired fall beyond our understanding. And you might think the monuments they left behind were delivered from outer space."

Helen smiled. "Some believe they were."

"And why is that? Because we seem puny alongside these men. Our deeds compare like the flailings of children in a sandbox." Ozbek sat forward, his hands gripping an invisible sphere. "Having the treasures these giants left behind is a source of tremendous energy for me."

Though she thought the food splendid—French refinements of Turkish classics, including warm eggplant and garlic, and lamb dumplings—Helen lost herself in the force of Ozbek's intelligence and the meal seemed to pass in a flash. Most so-called collectors she dealt with never thought beyond the ROI of their latest purchase. Their understanding of what they owned was thin as a coat of varnish. Ozbek, she realized, was a world away from that lot. While they sipped coffee, the butler brought Ozbek a marquetry humidor.

"Do you mind if I indulge?"

"Do you mind if I join you?" She motioned toward the odalisque, who clutched the mouthpiece of a tall bronze water pipe.

Enjoying Ozbek's approving laugh, Helen examined her San Jose Corona. "From Miami, right?" she said. "I'm surprised you're not smoking Cubanos. You can get them, I assume?"

"Yes, of course. But I refrain out of friendship for the United States. My brother has devoted his career to building ties between Ankara and Washington—"

"A policy," Helen interrupted him, "that you may have the opportunity to shape even more directly, from what I hear."

Ozbek smiled, apparently pleased with Helen's suggestion.

"I've been to Turkey many times," she continued,

"but how is it there now for Americans, with the bombing and—"

Ozbek cut Helen off with a raised hand. "Don't even say it. That horror will never be forgotten. But always remember that you were one of the first to learn that the murderers were captured. That was my brother on the phone with the good news. Six jackals were arrested this evening."

Helen felt a chill of excitement that she was party to such inside information. "Is that all of them?"

"We are quite confident."

"Who were they?"

"At least three of them are Kurds, which is no surprise. They despise everything good and beautiful in the world. But outsiders undoubtedly financed them. An operation like this is well beyond them."

"You mean al-Qaeda?"

"Possibly. There's no love lost between Kurds and Arabs, but they both hold the tribal view that the enemy of my enemy is my friend. Some of these Kurdish swine even trained at bases in Greece, and we shall see where that trail leads. It is only natural for a people to rally together after a tragedy such as this. You saw it in America after 9/11. It is the same in Turkey now. We are putting our differences aside to fight the enemy. And we have never stood closer to Washington than today."

"Then can I make a suggestion?"

"Please."

"Could there be a finer way to solidify Turkish-American friendship than allowing the Met to bring your magnificent collection to New York?" Helen sat back and let her request echo. She watched Ozbek lift his head.

"You don't beat around the bush, Dr. Vandameer."

"You didn't get where you are by beating around too many bushes. And please call me Helen."

"Then let me be blunt, Helen. I normally wouldn't consider dealing with someone whose resignation was demanded on *The New York Times* editorial page."

She couldn't help but wince at the remark, but she was glad it had finally come up. Part of her always dwelled on this past spring's debacle, when it was revealed that the centerpiece of her "Age of Bathsheba" show—a jewel-encrusted silver goblet—was confiscated from a prominent Czech-Jewish family by the Nazis. She understood now that her big mistake wasn't procuring the piece, despite its shaky provenance, but in holding out so long against a mountain of evidence and media scrutiny. She was proud she'd weathered the storm, holding on until the press lost interest, and she was grateful the trustees had stuck by her. Still, she knew she'd tarnished the museum, as well as her dream of someday winning the Directorship of the Met. Now she felt almost a compulsion to do something stupendous for the museum. Something breathtaking, even shocking.

"I've made my *mea culpas* on that."

"Yes, so I've read," Ozbek said.

"Besides," she added, "*no one* will defend your collection against the inevitable attacks from overwrought politicians or simple-minded academics as vigorously as me."

Helen was silently elated to see Ozbek nod his concurrence.

He stood up. "Let me show you a few things,

Helen."

She took Ozbek's arm as they ascended the townhouse's winding mahogany stairway. "I keep only a handful of items here. The bulk of my collection is in Istanbul. But I'll be disappointed if you don't care for one of my favorite pieces." She followed him into a small gallery with an entryway guarded on each side by a lion relief in glazed brick. Helen knew they could only have come from the royal palace of ancient Babylon.

Ozbek flipped wall switches, throwing a spotlight on a stone pedestal that held an 18-inch ivory carving of Baal, the Phoenician fertility god. In full beard and mustache, toga and crown, Baal was seated—a king holding court.

"May I?" she asked. Ozbek seemed happy to hand her the god. She held him at eye level, brushing a fingernail across his underside. The joy of clutching such great beauty never waned for her. Her eyes lost focus for a moment as they swept across the flawless figure. "Obviously you know how rare a Phoenician ivory is. And in this condition." She turned it around to search for some break or imperfection or hint of forgery. "I'd kill to get this into a show."

"You know," Ozbek said, running his gaze over Helen, "I think you might.

It makes me wonder what you would do for something new I'm adding to my collection. Something with a pedigree that would take your breath away."

"Really?" Helen said, startled at Ozbek's suggestion. "Tell me more."

"Not now," he smiled. "Maybe never. But before we discuss any agreement I need to feel completely comfortable with you." He opened his arms to embrace the whole room. "These are my children. And I don't let just anyone take charge of them. Perhaps we can meet when I'm in New York this fall. If that's agreeable, I'll have my driver take you to your hotel."

Helen's joy fell away. Was he sending her home like some schoolgirl up past her bedtime? "We absolutely need to know each other better," she said. "But why wait months when we're here now? It's still early." She stroked his cheek. "What would you like to know?"

"Everything." He kissed her curled fingers.

• • • •

Dean Goodrich, Jr., Assistant Legal Attaché in the FBI's London "legat" office, pressed the headphones to his ears. He was cramped in the rear of a brown-and-white Fiat van, parked down the block from Bulent Ozbek's townhouse. The "GeoGuard Security" van was crammed with electronic gear. With his hands by his ears and long legs scrunched up near his chest, Goodrich looked like he was practicing a duck-and-cover drill. But he endured his discomfort because the payoff for his four-hour shift was approaching. He listened to the husky voice deliver its cool message: "Perhaps we can meet when I am in New York this fall. If that's agreeable to you, I'll have my driver take you to your hotel."

"Playing hard to get tonight?" Goodrich chuckled to himself. He wondered what tactic the girl would take. Did she want him bad enough? It didn't take long to find out: "We absolutely need to know each other better. But why wait a few months when we're here now? It's still early."

Goodrich grunted. "Reeling her in like Hemingway with a marlin," he said, miming Papa landing the big one. "He's playing her, giving her just enough line."

"What?" asked Ed Crockin, the legat's techno wizard, lifting his face from the *Herald Tribune*. He was not wearing a head set.

"Sshhh!" Goodrich heard what sounded like a long, soulful kiss and the raspy swish of a dress being hiked over nylons. "Son of a bitch."

"Hold it," she blurted through the headphones. Goodrich tightened with concern. Was she snapping the line? "Can we find someplace more comfortable?" she asked. Goodrich relaxed.

"Of course," the Assistant Legal Attaché lip-synched to Ozbek's reassurance. He faced Crockin and pulled off his headphones. "This guy gets more poon than George Clooney."

"Can we go home now?" Crockin asked.

Goodrich put the headphones back on. "We can't leave before the evening reaches its climax," he said, winking at Crockin. "And I need to pull the hard drive with his phone calls. Ozbek told this bitch they nabbed six motherfuckers in Turkey tonight for the bombings. That's the goddamned best-kept secret in the world."

Chapter 8

Just after 10 the next morning a police truck made a sharp right off of Cambridge Street and into the alleyway behind Harvard's Sackler Museum, home to the university's Departments of Ancient and Asian Art. The size of an old paddy wagon, the truck was bright white except for the "Cambridge Police" stenciled in blue letters on both sides. The patrolman at the wheel, his sergeant yawning beside him, backed up to the museum's shipping dock. When the truck stopped, another patrolman raised the louvered rear door from inside and jumped to the ground. He held an armful of unassembled corrugated boxes.

The trio marched around the corner to Broadway and entered the museum's main doors. While the patrolmen loitered between a pair of huge allegorical statues of "Day" and "Night," the sergeant approached the front desk. A thin blond sophomore sat behind it, sheltered by racks of postcards and exhibition catalogs. She kept a wary eye on the cops, true to the city's historic distrust of authority.

"We're going up to Professor Crane's office," the sergeant said.

The woman pointed across the lobby to a young man who was perched on a stool behind a lectern. "You have to talk to him," she said. Although a laminated card labeled "Security" hung from his jeans, the *Boston Globe's* sports section had his full attention. The sergeant tapped his knuckles on the lectern to get Security's attention and repeated his intention to get to Crane's office.

"Uh, sure," the young man said. "Any news about the professor?"

"No, nothing," the sergeant grumbled.

They found Room 316 in the middle of a right-angle extension at the end of a carpeted hallway. The sergeant was happy to see that only a bulletin board covered with newspaper clippings and study-abroad programs separated it from the loading-dock elevator. This would be easier than he expected.

There was no nameplate on 316, only a sign that said, "Curator of Ancient Art." But the sergeant had no doubt this was Crane's office. A small shrine had accumulated there. Flowers, letters, and photographs were tacked or taped to the door or lying on the floor. A few candles in Crane's memory had already burnt down to lumps of wax.

"Don't disturb this stuff," the sergeant ordered as he carefully moved the offerings onto a black-leather bench beside the door. "Wait here," he told the officers, and walked to the end of the hall and knocked on the Department Office. It was empty and locked.

The sergeant returned to Crane's office and dug a single key out of his coat pocket. "Let's be quick," he said, leading the others inside. They closed the door and set to assembling the boxes.

The room was narrow but deep, with almost every inch of wall space covered with books and journals. A small metal desk hugged the far wall below the only window.

One of the patrolmen sighed. "You said this would be fast."

"It will take as long as it takes."

"Everything goes?" asked the other cop, still piling up boxes.

"Everything but the furniture."

The three grabbed books off the shelves and stuffed them into boxes. They emptied the file cabinet, careful to keep Crane's papers in order. Despite the air conditioning, all three were soon sweating.

Everything was packed in less than an hour. The two patrolmen carried boxes onto the loading-dock elevator while the sergeant sat and checked the desk drawers one last time. He glanced behind him to see a student in the doorway.

"What are you doing?" asked the young man, bouncing nervously from foot to foot. He was wearing jeans and a grey Michigan T-shirt.

The sergeant stood and turned. "Stay back, please, son. This is a crime scene."

"What are you talking about? Professor Crane was killed 4,000 miles from here."

"We all know that. But we're assisting with the investigation here."

"You can't just take everything. The field notes and work papers for my thesis are in here. Do you have a warrant?"

"Son, the professor is the victim, not a suspect."

"But you've got my stuff!"

"It will all be returned to you, I promise."

The student started into the office.

"I asked you to stay back."

The student stopped a foot from the sergeant. He pulled a pad from his pocket and wrote down the sergeant's name and shield number.

"Well, if you don't mind, uh, Sergeant Denton, I'm going to make a call."

The student turned to leave but the patrolmen blocked his way. "Hey, what is this!" he protested, and was looking to squeeze between the officers when the sergeant grabbed him with his left arm and quickly snapped his neck.

"Get the last box," the sergeant said.

Chapter 9

"Fuck!" Zander woke with a jolt, afraid he had slept through his only reason for coming to London: his 10 a.m. speech. He squinted at the alarm clock and thanked God it was only 8. He recalled planning a morning run through Hyde Park as his head fell back onto the pillow. Tomorrow, he swore.

His mouth tasted as dry as the papers being delivered at the conference and he lurched to his feet to pop a couple of migraine-strength Excedrin. Dinner with Figgis drifted into focus. If he felt this awful, he figured Figgis might be dead.

Somehow his friend had managed to drop him back at the hotel. He remembered flopping onto the bed and calling the UCLA Museum to insure that Henry Demarest had delivered the mummy. The director's secretary told Zander that he could have spoken to Demarest if he'd called 10 minutes sooner. The dealer had just dropped off the cello case.

His head eased when he thought about lunch with Penny. Then his mood faltered. He didn't know where she was staying, and she didn't say she'd be at the conference. How was he going to arrange it?

He hung his suit in the bathroom and cranked the shower to scalding, hoping to steam out some of the creases. Meanwhile, he fell onto the narrow bed in a button-down shirt, underwear and socks, and flipped on CNN. A khaki-clad correspondent announced that six men had been arrested for the Turkish bombings that had killed 500 Americans just weeks before. Zander felt a wave of satisfaction—almost as if he'd led the investigation himself—though he feared that countless more were ready to follow these half-dozen radicals over the barricades.

The local update led with Linus Crane's murder. Officially the crime remained a bungled robbery. There was no mention of the hotel burglary. But there was some news, or at least a rumor the police refused to confirm: a witness had supposedly told detectives they had seen someone running from one of the museum's emergency exits about 11 p.m. On top of this, the London Harvard club was offering £25,000 for information leading to a conviction; and Bulent Ozbek was establishing a Linus Crane Fellowship at London University with an initial £100,000. Zander wondered if Ozbek had told Penny. He was also amazed how, in the course of 12 hours, he'd gone from never having heard of Ozbek to feeling like he was tuned into some bizarre cable channel: all Ozbek, all the time.

Zander slipped on his refreshed suit and was heading for the elevator when the phone rang. He rushed back in. It was Penny. "How'd you find me?" he asked, ecstatic.

"You were clutching your Bertrand key with your change when you brought me my drink last night."

Good eye, he thought. "So where are you?"

"Here at the Bertrand. Isn't it great?"

Zander looked around his storage-locker-with-bed. "Which Bertrand are you at?"

"The one where they gave me a suite at no extra charge because they didn't have any single rooms left."

Zander glanced around what was evidently the last of the single rooms. "Is it big enough for two?"

"Two? You could fit the Red Sox in here."

"Then you might have a roommate later," he said with a laugh.

"That might be interesting," Penny said, laughing in turn.

Zander pulled the phone from his ear and stared at it, as if this might clarify Penny's comment. "So you still up for lunch?"

"Absolutely."

"Great, but I haven't had a chance yet to pick a place."

"No worries. Let's meet at Munstead's. 12:30. You can get directions at the front desk. But what did your police friend tell you about Linus?"

"He didn't know much more than what I just heard on the TV, except—"

"Except what?" Penny said.

"Except that Crane's hotel room was burgled the evening he was killed."

"Ha! I *knew* it."

"Knew what?"

"That Linus didn't die because he wouldn't hand over his Timex. Now it's starting to make sense."

"How?"

"I'll tell you at lunch."

. . . .

Zander vaulted onto the stage to the applause generated by Finn Sorenson's introduction, which had downplayed his gun-toting day job while hyping his membership on the President's Advisory Commission on Antiquities. The commission only took him to Washington every few months, but Sorenson knew what would impress his audience.

"The astounding generation of new wealth," Zander began his speech, "has sent an almost unlimited supply of money chasing a very limited supply of masterpieces, pushing prices up and up and up. And it's not just dealers and auction houses that see opportunities here. Criminals read the papers, too— criminals who are smarter, better organized, and better financed than ever before. The best of them have embraced state-of-the-art communications and information technologies and gone international, either on their own or in alliance with groups such as the Cosa Nostra, which, by the way, is integrating art theft into its traditional money laundering, gambling, and drug rackets."

To illustrate his point, Zander laid out the annual report for Art Crime, Inc., a company he'd whipped up in his latest failed attempt to boost his LAPD budget. The company's financial statements showed a better return on equity than Google.

Zander felt the audience warming to him, the faces relaxing and even smiling. But that was as sympathetic as he was going to get. "And I don't have to tell you," he said, reaching toward the front row, "how many art crimes are never reported, since you're the people who don't report them." Zander paused, waiting for this jab to connect. As he expected, the smiles disappeared. "You curators and museum directors don't want to scare off potential donors or broadcast that your security might be lax, since you've convinced yourselves that this will only attract more thieves and vandals." Zander sensed animosity overtaking the high-ceilinged room, like clouds drifting in front of the sun.

"Let me ask you," he said, watching some latecomers scan the packed room for empty seats, "What's the difference between an antiquities dealer and an illegal immigrant?" He held the room in silence for a beat. "The illegal immigrant doesn't mind having his trunk searched."

Zander took a moment to scan the 40 gently ascending rows for any familiar faces, especially Penny's, but he found no one he knew. "I find it startling how many antiquities collectors prefer swallowing a loss—either from being swindled or robbed—just to keep the government from looking too closely at what they're up to. And I'm not talking about nickel-and-dime stuff here. Serious fraud goes unreported every day."

Zander heard three or four notebooks slam shut. He thought of likening clever dealers to insects who adapt to new environments and even thrive on some pesticides, but that might be pushing too far. Instead, he invited questions. A tall, rugged man wearing a blue blazer over a yellow silk polo shirt called for a microphone.

"Detective," the man boomed in a Boston accent under a full head of polar-white hair, "I can't tell you how far off the mark you are." Zander heard applause, but kept his eye on his Brahmin adversary. "However, instead of rebutting you point by point, let me say simply that this conspiracy you've concocted that blames everyone in this room for the rise in antiquity theft is a fantasy. And even if there were some truth to your paranoia, the bottom line is that the artifacts you contend are turning up illegally in America and elsewhere are far better off there than in the hands of the unqualified, uneducated, and unfunded local thugs and institutions who would otherwise control them. Do I have to mention anything more than how the Taliban machine-gunned the priceless ancient colossal Buddhas under their control?"

Zander gathered his thoughts amid the stormy applause. "Look," he said. "I'm not here to defend the Taliban. They were savages. But let me put this in a perspective you might understand better. Let's say that you own a vintage Jaguar, an XKE. And let's also imagine that your garage is full of other cars—Beemers, Mercedes, and an Aston Martin maybe—so full that the XKE is sitting outside. Now, I come along and, because my garage is half-empty and because I know a lot about old Jaguars, I say you should let me have that great XKE because you don't know how to take care of it. It's out in the rain and the smog, plus it's easy prey for passing thieves. I can absolutely guarantee that Jag will last much longer if you let me have it."

"What is your point?" the man demanded.

"You can act as the world's protector and savior if you want. I might even agree with you on some level. But until the law changes, I'm gonna do my best to put you in jail."

Zander wondered how many felons were sitting and facing him. The mention of prison had apparently cowed any other questioners, so he thanked the audience and stepped aside for Finn Sorenson. His warm welcome had deteriorated to a silent good riddance, which was fine with him. He had wanted to touch a nerve and he had.

Figgis appeared as Zander left the stage. Zander was surprised how good his friend looked: almost healthy, not to mention unaccountably cheery. Maybe spilling his guts last night was what he needed.

"Brilliant, Zander my boy," Figgis said with great sincerity. "Just super." "Thanks." He turned toward the crowd, which had dispersed into murmuring groups. "Just glad I don't need car fare from any of them."

"Fuck 'em if they can't take a joke." Figgis pulled Zander farther aside. "I have an update about Crane."

"About someone running from the museum last night? I heard it on the news this morning. It's true?"

"Indeed. Cabby phoned it in. But that's the least of it. The driver watched this person toss a set of clothes— women's, it turns out—into a dumpster." "A woman," Zander said, surprised despite enough years on the force to have lost count of the female killers.

"Maybe," Figgis said. "The driver couldn't say if he saw a man or woman. Could have been a disguise, of course. They're running forensics on the outfit and there may even be some usable prints."

"That's a helluva lot more than they had last night," Zander said, excited to hear that the ring was tightening around Crane's killer.

"And maybe even more," Figgis said, lowering his

voice a notch, "though it's pretty wild and I couldn't confirm it."

"What?" Zander asked, eager to get to lunch and relay the news to Penny.

"They supposedly found a conference name tag in a pocket of the jacket pulled from the trash."

Chapter 10

Penny rose awkwardly enough to show she was excited to see Zander when he reached her table at Munstead's. He was tickled that she had primped for him. Her hair was back in an elegant weave, her nails glistened ruby red, and her short, floral-patterned dress wasn't left over from any dig. Zander watched half-a-dozen heads turn her way.

They ordered a glass of wine. "I'm impressed," she said.

"With what?"

"Your speech. You were tremendous up there today."

"You were there?" he asked, uncomfortable as always with a compliment. "I looked for you."

"I was hiding in the back. But what's this thingamabob Commission you're on?"

"You mean the *Presidential* thingamabob?"

"That's the one."

Zander sat back. He rarely talked about the Commission back home and no one ever asked. In fact he was beginning to think it was causing more trouble than it was worth. One commander had recently questioned how much time he was devoting to it, while another seemed to think Washington should be funding part of his detail's budget. "Three years ago," he told Penny, "I shut down a ring trafficking pre-Columbian carvings. Big, beautiful pieces coming straight from tomb robbers in Guatemala. Two Americans and a German were trucking the stuff up through Mexico and across the border near Mexicali. The bust got two inches in the *L.A. Times*, but it made a big splash in Mexico. For some reason the Mexican president took an interest."

"Probably wanted a piece of the action."

"Maybe," Zander said with a laugh, "But he mentioned it to *our* president a couple of weeks later. It happened there was an opening on the Commission, so I was appointed. One of the 11 seats is saved for a cop."

"Who are the others?"

"A couple of academics and museum types, but mostly hot-shot dealers and collectors. Half the time I think I'm there to keep an eye on the other commissioners."

She leaned in, obviously intrigued. "And what do you all do?"

"We advise the President on smuggling—and other crucial matters of national security."

"The President attends the meetings?"

"Of course," Zander said, unable to stop himself. "He generally sandwiches them in between briefings on Iran and education reform." He watched Penny's eyes open wider. "No," he continued. "I've never met the man."

"Well, if he ever stopped by you'd give him an earful."

"Meaning I went too far today?"

"Are you kidding?" she said with a hardened smirk. "That crowd gets its collective butt kissed every day. They needed to have it kicked."

Zander swigged half his glass. "Not that it's going to change anything."

"You can't be sure."

Zander marveled at her mix of cynicism and clear-eyed naiveté. "Well, nobody came up afterwards for an autographed picture."

"Doesn't matter. They'll remember what you said. Probably the only thing they'll remember from the whole conference. You should celebrate."

"Sounds good to me. Maybe we could kick around town tomorrow."

"I'd love to," she said. "Except that I'm flying back to Sicily at 7 a.m."

"For what?" he asked, ripping a chunk of bread in his frustration.

"My summer project. I only came up to learn what I could about Linus. I felt so helpless down there when I heard the news."

"What are you going back to?"

"I'm doing restoration work at Piazza Armerina."

"The Roman villa?"

"You know it? I'm impressed again."

"Only from pictures. But I know they've had trouble there."

Penny nodded. "Three break-ins in the past year. One nut poured paint and tar on the mosaics. Another one smashed a few with a hammer."

"Typical Mafia subtlety."

"The people I work with don't like to talk about it."

"You'd better be careful," he said, wondering if she had enough sense to avoid trouble. "Antiquities are just another commodity to the mob, no different from heroin or guns. Nobody gets in their way."

"I'm steering clear," she said. "I'll send you some pictures."

"That'd be great," he said, feeling less restrained since resigning himself to a one-meal relationship. "Maybe one of you in that dress. Wallet size would be fine."

"I meant of the mosaics," Penny said, shaking her head but smiling while she recrossed her bare legs.

Zander signaled a waiter and they ordered lunch.

"Tell me your theory about Crane," he said after the waiter retreated.

She took a manila envelope from a carryall she had stuffed under her chair. "It's more of a show-and-tell." Penny pulled out a pair of large color photographs but then froze, her attention drawn to something over Zander's shoulder. Using him as a shield, she pointed toward a couple seated behind him. Only a fountain with a spigot fashioned like a unicorn's head separated them. "I saw that woman corner Bulent Ozbek last night," she whispered. "She latched onto him like a shark."

Zander stole a peek. "She left with him, too." He tried to read Penny's reaction to this news—jealously or professional rivalry? "What's the big deal?"

The woman turned toward them and waved. Zander watched a wire-thin smile cross Penny's face. "Nothing," she whispered like a ventriloquist.

"You know her?"

"Nope," Penny said with what sounded like total disinterest. Zander thought for a moment of probing further but instead picked up the photos.

"Hold them like this," Penny said, overlapping them slightly to show they offered an extended view of a single, complex mosaic.

"Nice," Zander said. "From Sicily?"

"No."

"Then where?"

"I can't say for certain."

Zander rubbed the corner of one photo. The pictures had been generated on a mediocre color printer. "I hope you're not asking me to ID them."

"No, but look at this," Penny said, handing Zander the printout of an e-mail message. "'Don't quit now,'" he read aloud. "'I've got something more enticing than OUR DEAD FILMS.'" He looked at Penny. "What the hell does that mean?"

• • • •

"I almost couldn't make it here today," reported Helen Vandameer's lunch date and occasional boyfriend, Peter Sloan. "Bomb scare shut down my subway line."

"Any explosion?" she asked, glancing around Munstead's crowded tables.

"No, thank God. That's all we need. I was just talking to a colleague in Turkey. The consulate staff has been working 24/7 since the bombing there two weeks ago. Notifying next of kin, helping with the cleanup, fending off reporters, and on and on."

"They caught the terrorists there," Helen said,

recalling Bulent Ozbek's elation when he relayed the news. "Six of them."

"You're on top of things," Sloan said.

Helen shrugged, seeing no benefit to disclosing her sources.

"Actually," Sloan continued, "that reminds me of something closer to home. You should know that your friend Hazim—"

"What?" Helen interrupted, "Has he got more to sell? I got the most lovely piece from him."

"More? No no. Mr. Hazim has gone out of the retail business." Helen's attention had drifted across the fountain to her left, where a couple was examining two large photos.

"Shhhh!" Helen hissed, as she looked at Sloan but trained her ears toward the other couple. She had done her homework and knew that the woman, who had had Ozbek's attention before her last night, was Penny Theobald, the dead professor's graduate assistant. Helen also recognized Zander from the conference. She'd been impressed with his knowledge of the business—for an outsider.

Sloan slapped the glass table, forcing Helen's attention. "Did you hear me?"

"I'm sorry, Peter. Give me just a minute."

Sloan, however, could not wait. "I said that a squad of secret police from the Syrian embassy ushered him onto a plane for Damascus yesterday morning. And we believe that two hours after he arrived he was sentenced to 30 years at hard labor."

"My God," she said, but still saw that Penny and Zander had stopped talking and were now inspecting the pictures. She pulled a pen and paper from her purse and scribbled some notes.

• • • •

Zander watched Penny absent-mindedly folding the paper napkin she had pulled from under her glass of wine. He was waiting for her to explain Crane's note but her attention had drifted back to the woman and her companion at the far table. Zander did not want to turn around again.

"What are you doing?" he asked, trying to distract Penny by pointing at the napkin, which she had now creased and doubled over onto itself into what looked like a tiny swan.

"Nothing," she said. "Just a nervous habit."

Zander put the paper swan aside and cupped Penny's hands in his for a moment. "Hey!" he said. "They can't hear you. Don't worry. Just eat something and tell me about Professor Crane."

Penny nodded at Zander and picked up her fork. "Linus e-mailed me that message with the pictures just three days ago," she said, picking at her salad. "I printed them at the Bertrand when I got here. I have no doubt it's Byzantine, which makes sense since Linus was spending his summer in Turkey. And it's clearly the work of a master. The technique and coloring are both brilliant. But the design makes it hard to pinpoint. It's unique, as far as I can tell, which is extraordinary."

"How so?"

"Because virtually every significant mosaic from antiquity through the middle ages follows very strict guidelines in iconography, structure, and characterization. Unconventional designs are more rare than hen's teeth. And," she continued, "I think there's a link here to Linus's murder."

Zander took a deep breath and rubbed the back of his neck, which had felt tight since the flight. He was happy to follow Penny's zigzagging logic about mosaics—and plenty of other things, for that matter. But not about murder. "First things first. Tell me about the inscription."

"The back is a message for me. Linus wrote 'Don't quit' because I resigned from his program three weeks ago."

"Why?"

"It's a long story."

"I've got 'til 7 tomorrow morning," he said.

She drained her wine glass. "Quite simply, I'm just burned out on academia. The rigidity of it, the intensity of it, the pettiness of it."

"Sounds like me talking about the force. You still want out?"

"I don't know. Linus's death throws everything up in the air."

"I'm sure it does." He pointed to the handwritten message again. "But explain 'our dead films.'"

"Okay. But first understand that Linus loved games."

"Like what? Grand Theft Auto? Madden?"

Penny laughed. "No, I mean more mental games. Linus was constantly playing with words. He said it was a way to fight the tedium. He'd sit through a department meeting and not take a single note, but manage to fill page after page with anagrams and jumbles."

"So 'our dead films' is a word puzzle?" Zander asked.

"It has to be. We didn't sit around watching *Casablanca* together. So I ripped it apart and came up with *famous riddle*, which makes perfect sense."

Zander stared at Penny. "Perfect," he said. "Now explain it to me."

Penny smiled. "It's the kind of mythological reference Linus loved. The implication is that solving some big new famous riddle would have huge consequences."

"My mythology's a bit rusty. What's the *old* famous riddle?"

"The riddle of the sphinx, as Sophocles told it. It goes like this: what creature walks in the morning on four feet, at noon upon two, and at evening upon three?"

Images of something he once saw on a porno site flashed through Zander's head. "No idea," he finally said.

"The answer is man, who crawls on all fours as a baby, strides erect as an adult, and in old age walks with a staff."

"Okay. But why was that the riddle of the sphinx?"

"Because the sphinx, which was a monster with a woman's head and bust and a lion's body and wings, stopped people on the road to Thebes and asked them the riddle. The sphinx destroyed them if they didn't know the answer."

"Sounds like some reality TV show."

"However," Penny continued, ignoring him, "Oedipus solved the riddle. And as a consequence, the sphinx destroyed itself, and the people of Thebes made Oedipus their king in gratitude."

"This is the same Oedipus who…"

"Who killed his father, slept with his mother, and poked out his own eyes? Yeah. But that's another story."

Zander held up the pictures. "So Crane was suggesting there's something royal and powerful and maybe invaluable waiting for whoever figures out some new riddle?"

"Right," Penny said, her voice quivering.

"So assuming for argument's sake that Crane was murdered," Zander said, "you think it was because someone else wanted this mosaic?"

"That's my theory. But I still swear Linus didn't have an enemy in the world."

"If you don't buy that Crane was a random victim, which I don't, then he had at least one. My buddy from Scotland Yard told me this morning they recovered a set of women's clothes in a dumpster outside the museum that the killer may have discarded."

"You're kidding! My God. A woman. I can't believe it."

"They're not saying that yet. There was a wig in the pile too, so who knows? But Figgis was adamant the Yard's best people are working the case." Zander was about to ask Penny if she wanted coffee when he saw that she was looking past him again, presumably at the woman she'd noticed before. He turned and found the woman just inches behind him now and stealing more than a casual glance at the photos.

"Hello. I don't think we've met formally," the woman said. "I'm Helen Vandameer, with the Metropolitan Museum in New York."

Zander introduced himself while Penny slid one picture under the other and folded her arms over them.

"This is Penny Theobald," he said, while Penny offered only a tepid smile. "From Harvard, by way of Sicily."

Helen continued, "I couldn't help noticing those breathtaking mosaics when you held the pictures up before. They're fabulous."

Zander thought he could actually see the hair rise at the base of Penny's neck.

"I'm sorry," Helen went on, seemingly unperturbed. "I didn't think you'd mind if I came over for a closer look. Can you tell me where they're from?"

"I wish I could," Penny said. "But it's a mystery right now. I couldn't even guess."

"But they're your pictures, right?"

"Yes."

Helen frowned.

Penny said, "Why don't you leave me your card. If I find anything out I'll shoot you an e-mail."

Helen extracted a monogrammed case from her purse and handed a card to Penny. "I'll look forward to hearing from you."

Penny crumpled the card as soon as Helen turned her back. "I don't like her and I don't trust her," she told Zander. "And I want to tell Scotland Yard about these pictures."

Chapter 11

Zander had gotten the name of Norman Parrish, the Detective Chief Inspector heading the Crane investigation, from Figgis. Parrish told Zander on the phone he was eager to hear from people who knew Linus Crane and agreed to meet Penny at the conference hall at the University.

There was no sign of the DCI when they arrived, so Zander gently pulled open the auditorium door and poked his head inside. The air smelled a little stale, not surprising for the middle of the afternoon, and the crowd had thinned, but more than half of the red cloth chairs were still filled. On stage, the director of the Bulgarian State Museum was detailing the wholesale looting of his country's national treasures that began with the fall of the Communists. A beefy man sporting a goatee and a winter-weight gray suit, the director insisted he was no fan of dictatorship. But Zander sensed a painful nostalgia for life under the old regime, famous for enforcing the sanctity of the country's historical endowment with a rigor that made the Koran seem forgiving.

When Zander glanced back at Penny, she was introducing herself to Parrish. His tall bony frame, elongated ears and bristly hair suggested a Wisconsin dairy farmer to Zander, not one of Scotland Yard's elite.

Penny was probing for news about the investigation when Zander joined them and shook the DCI's hand. Parrish was gracious and forthcoming, his intelligence manifest in the sharp focus of his deep-set blue eyes. He mentioned the dumpster before Penny asked. "Our lab confirmed Crane's blood on the dress—a size 6 from Harvey Nichols department store. We're checking their inventory system for when it was sold and who the salesman was. If we get that, we'll jog some memories for a description of the buyer."

"What about the break-in at Professor Crane's hotel room?" Penny asked.

Parrish raised an eyebrow. "How do you know about that, Miss Theobald?"

Penny looked like a ninth-grader caught smoking in the girl's room. Zander was about to take the heat when she volunteered she'd read it in a newspaper.

"You wouldn't recall which one, would you?"

"No, I don't think so."

Parrish shook his head but carried on. The guy clearly knew what was important and what wasn't, Zander thought. "We're looking into it, but at least one other room at the Westbury was broken into that night, so it's not as useful as it first appeared."

"The department store connection sounds promising," Zander said.

"I hope so," said Parrish. "And what have you got for me, Miss Theobald?"

Penny hesitated for a minute. "Can we find some privacy?"

Zander led Penny and Parrish to the speaker's lounge. They sat around a circular table where Penny placed the pictures and laid out her suspicions connecting Crane's death to the mosaic. She started forcefully, but quickly grew hesitant, either cowed by relating her story to the authorities or losing faith herself.

She was barely speaking above a whisper when she finished, and the DCI made his lack of interest clear by setting the pictures aside and asking her about Crane's recent health. Zander could see that Penny felt foolish for taking the inspector's time.

She was mentioning Crane's occasional asthma when Finn Sorenson knocked on the open door and joined them inside. The conference chairman, who evidently had already spoken to Parrish, told Penny that the director of her Sicily project had called and needed to speak to her. Sorenson took Penny's hand and offered his condolences. Penny stood and embraced him.

The shock of Crane's death descended on Zander all over again, his lungs feeling the same pinch as when he read about the murder on the cab ride into town. Sorenson started edging toward the door but stopped after glancing at the mosaic pictures. He rubbed his fingers across them as if he could feel the texture of the tiles. "Dr. Crane's presentation."

"What?" Penny asked. "This was part of it?"

Sorenson nodded.

"Did you see the rest?" Zander asked.

"I'm sorry, no. Just this."

Penny was breathless. "Did he say anything about it?"

"No. It was all a big secret."

As Sorenson left, Parrish scooped up the pictures for another look. He was studying them when his cell phone rang. The detective listened intently, barely saying a word until he muted the microphone. "Miss Theobald," Parrish said, "Do you know a woman named Nina Chahine?"

Penny's eyes widened as a small gasp escaped her lips.

• • • •

Helen Vandameer stared at the gabled facade of the Bertrand Hotel from a shaded bench in the park across the street, contemplating the path of least resistance to Penny's room. With a plan starting to percolate, she crossed the street to the hotel, found a house phone, and asked the operator to connect her with Penny Theobald.

She hung on for 20 rings, happy the hotel was too dated to offer voicemail, and then got an envelope and stationery with the Bertrand logo from the concierge. She wrote Penny's name on the envelope and sealed it with a blank sheet inside. She strolled over to the front desk and handed it to clerk, telling her that Penny Theobald must receive this envelope as soon as possible. The clerk took it and called Penny's room. When no one answered, she slipped it into the mail slot right behind her for Room 567.

Helen returned to the house phone and called housekeeping. "This is Miss Theobald in 567. I asked for extra towels an hour ago!" She heard what sounded like a book slamming shut.

"I'm sorry. I'll send someone right up."

"Pronto!"

Helen rode the elevator to the fifth floor, exhilarated as a general whose first assault has broken the enemy line, and waited. Standing in the hallway, she found herself absent-mindedly extending a leg and brushing her toes across the carpet, the residue of 11 years of ballet training. Three minutes later a maid with an arm full of towels arrived at the door. She knocked and, when no one answered, entered the room. Helen followed. "Are those my towels?"

"Yes, ma'am," the maid said.

"Just leave them on the bed."

"Yes, ma'am." Helen slipped a pound coin into the maid's hand as she retreated. "Thank you, ma'am."

• • • •

"Yes," Penny said after glancing around the room. "I know Nina."

"How?" Parrish asked.

"Through Linus. They dated... well, I should say they lived together. She was one of his first grad students, but she was finishing up when I first got there."

"Would you consider Miss Chahine hostile to Professor Crane?"

"Look," Penny said, her tone rising. "I don't want to point a finger at anybody. I haven't seen her in years."

Parrish nodded and scooped up the mosaic pictures. "Miss Theobald, I need to review some test results at our lab, and I'd like our specialists to analyze your photos. I hope you don't mind coming down to answer their questions?"

"As long as we can do it today," Penny said.

"All the better," Parrish said. "Where are you staying?"

"At the Bertrand."

"I'm at Holborn Police Station. It's a short walk from your hotel. If you can stop by in an hour or so I'm sure we can finish straight away."

• • • •

"Where does a grad student get the money for this?" Helen wondered when she saw that Penny's room was a suite. She found it even odder that the oversized dresser was empty and the two walk-in closets held only a single white cardigan.

The object of her desire—Penny's laptop—was sitting atop an Edwardian desk. Helen powered the machine up and immediately found what she was looking for: a folder labeled "Linus's Mosaics." She clicked on it, and the left half of the mosaic appeared. She shook with excitement; it was even more spectacular than she recalled from the restaurant. The other picture was equally crisp.

She pulled a thumb drive from her purse and inserted it into the machine's USB port. Three seconds later she had a copy of the files.

• • • •

Penny led Zander at a fast pace back to the Bertrand. "I can't believe Nina Chahine killed Linus," she said. "How did they come up with her?"

"I can guess."

"How?"

"Figgis told me this morning that they found a conference name tag in the jacket pulled from the dumpster. I didn't mention it because I don't think he believed it himself. But perhaps it was Nina's tag."

"Incredible!" Penny said, throwing her arms up.

Zander grabbed her elbow. "Who is she?"

"Wow. Where can I begin? She's this Egyptian beauty. Slim, dark hair, olive skin, incredibly sexy. A real siren. But brilliant too. She runs the Egyptology Department at the Sorbonne. Anyway, like I told the Inspector, she was one of Linus's first grad students."

"And this young girl became his live-in lover?"

Penny laughed. "She was a good two years older than him."

"How long did it last?"

"Three years, maybe. They were breaking up just when I got there. It was awful. I remember a lulu of a fight right in the department office."

"Physical?"

"No, which was good for Linus. She could have destroyed him."

"She didn't want it to end?"

"That's how it seemed to me. But it had to be more complicated than that. It always is, right?"

Zander slowed his pace. "It always has been with me." Merely speaking the words triggered the vision of one particularly disturbing shouting match with Jessica in their back yard, both Josh and Layla covering their ears. Only Penny's tap on his forearm brought him back to London.

"Hey. Did I say something?"

"You? No. Just some marital echoes kicking around my brain." Zander shook his head. "Sometimes you just wonder how the hell you ever got yourself into things."

"I was married," Penny said.

"You're kidding. You look barely damaged."

"It only lasted six months. Married my college boyfriend the day after graduation. Neither of us had any notion of what we wanted to do, so we moved to Berkeley and did nothing. By Christmas I was sick of it. He wasn't. I came back East. For all I know he's still there."

"Did you think he'd follow you?"

"Maybe… probably," she said, staring down at the narrow street's medieval cobblestones. "Thankfully there were no kids," she added, looking at him again. "That changes everything."

"For most people," Zander said.

"Linus didn't talk about Nina," Penny said, as if understanding an old memory for the first time, "but I'm sure he had regrets. He never had a serious relationship after her."

Zander pictured the pale, angular Parrish questioning the dark Egyptian beauty, video cameras running. "He may be interviewing this Chahine girl right now. He'll use you to corroborate or contradict her answers, at least some of the historical stuff. And I suppose he'll see if he can make any connection to the mosaic."

Inside the Bertrand, Zander was surprised when the desk clerk, an eager young man desperate for orthodontia, handed him a message that his captain had called. Zander pulled out his Blackberry, which he realized he'd silenced before his morning speech. His captain had called there too.

"Trouble?" Penny asked.

"Who knows?"

The same desk clerk now handed Penny a sealed envelope, her name written in an expressive script. She ripped it open at the end. "That's odd," she said, after finding only a blank page.

Zander took her envelope and asked the clerk if he knew anything about it. He said he didn't and checked his computer, which showed no messages had been logged in under either Penny's name or room number.

Zander nodded toward a nook near the men's room. I have to call L.A."

"I'll meet you in the tea room," Penny said.

• • • •

Helen flew down to the lobby with a rush of victory. She dropped into a club chair by the elevator bank, pulled out a well-worn address book and rang an Oxford University number on her cell. She was connected to Horace Lloyd-Walker.

"Dr. Lloyd-Walker, this is Helen Vandameer."

"Helen Vandameer! Yes, yes. Of course. Helen Vandameer. How are you, my dear?"

"I'm well, professor, but in an unfortunate hurry. I'm in London and I've got something to show you, a mystery I need your help to unravel."

"Then by all means bring it right along, dear girl. Can't say I've got much else to do. They let me keep a small office at the Ashmolean. Meet me here?"

"I'll be on the next train."

• • • •

No more than 20 feet away but behind a wall of

plants, Zander listened to his captain berate him because a small Rembrandt had been stolen from Cameron Diaz's mansion, and he had no specialist to send over because Zander still hadn't recruited a new partner. Zander offered to call the actress if that would smooth things over, but was told the Chief was smoothing things over personally. Zander stifled a laugh and was about to assure the captain he had some strong candidates and would make one an offer the moment he returned from Cairo, but the captain cut him off to take another call.

Zander hurried down the hall, but found the tearoom empty except for an old American couple parked in the far corner, finishing up a plate of cucumber sandwiches. Penny's bag sat on a chair two tables from them. He thought it odd for her to go to the ladies room and leave it in plain sight, but he sat down and picked up the brief menu.

"Are you waiting for the young lady who left that bag?" the old man asked.

"Yes. Why?"

"Because a very rude fellow escorted her out before you came in and I'm not sure she wanted to go."

Zander rushed across the lobby, suddenly crowded with traveling students. He pushed through the revolving door and stopped to scan the sidewalk and street. He was hoping the old tourist was either exaggerating or simply mistaken when he saw a thickset man shoving Penny toward a taxi waiting near the corner of the park. An arm from inside flung open the rear door. Zander took the hotel's stone steps three at a time and cut across the street, missing a speeding Toyota SUV by inches. He saw the barrel of a gun pointing at Penny from the back seat and cursed himself for leaving his pistol at home.

Zander reached the cab just as the back door slammed shut and the heavy man pivoted to face him. He lowered his shoulder, intending to knock the goon aside like a tackling dummy and rip open the door, but at the moment of contact the back of Zander's skull ignited like it had been scorched by fire. His head whipped forward and his knees buckled. Before he hit the ground he saw Penny through the taxi's window, her eyes bulging and a dark hand covering her mouth. Her muffled scream was the last sound he heard.

Chapter 12

Helen caught the 4 p.m. train for Oxford out of Paddington station. She found a pair of empty seats, set her bag next to her to ward off an unwanted seatmate, and placed her big-screen MacBook Air on the tray table. She opened the stolen photos after quickly copying and erasing them from her thumb drive.

Now that she had the time to dwell on the mosaic, she was dazzled by how deftly the artist had woven together a curious array of Greco-Roman and Christian themes and characters. One central scene, played out under the watchful eye of a saint, depicted an ancient sea voyage. Jason and the Argonauts was a possibility. Maybe the mosaic was the artist's effort to show that the classical myths, taken as literature and not religion, were no threat to Christianity. She focused on the dirt and debris around the edges. This, plus the photos' poor lighting, left no doubt that the pictures were taken *in situ*. She was certain this was a recent discovery, almost certainly the fruit of an illegal dig, most likely from a long-forgotten cave or a tomb. Nothing could explain the astonishingly fine condition.

At Oxford station, Helen grabbed a taxi for the Ashmolean Museum. She sighed in frustration when she saw she had missed the 5 p.m. closing by 15 minutes. She was reaching for her phone when a plump, middle-aged woman pushed open the main doors.

"Dr. Vandameer?"

"Yes."

"Please come with me. I'm Sheila Witherspoon, Dr. Lloyd-Walker's assistant."

Helen followed her guide inside, up two wide flights of stone stairs that almost cost her a heel, down a long empty hallway and finally into a cozy anteroom. Sheila Witherspoon pointed to the inner sanctum. There, waiting for her, stood Horace Lloyd-Walker, all five-foot-one of him. Helen thought he must be at least 90 by now. Atop a creased face that only a Shar Pei would envy sat a striking mop of white hair.

As she leaned to kiss his cheek, Helen recalled hearing that during World War II Lloyd-Walker had parachuted into northern Greece for British intelligence. One persistent rumor—that no student ever had the nerve to ask him about—was that he'd married some beautiful resistance fighter who was killed by the communists in the Civil War. Whether this was true or just a romantic fiction, his affection for Greece was legend and he stayed on through the mid 1950s to run the British Institute for Classical Studies in Athens. For decades now he had been the chief advocate—the chief nuisance, most thought—in Britain for returning the famed Elgin Marbles from the British Museum to Athens. He found appointments for countless students, though not Helen, since her interests led her out of his orbit.

She sat and took a moment to look around the dormered office, crammed floor to ceiling with books, journals, newspaper clippings, prints, and maps. A small statue of Vishnu on his desk reminded her that he'd grown up in India, the son of civil servants. He claimed to have hunted tiger and elephant. Now he was shorter than most big guns.

They spent a few minutes catching up, but Helen was eager to unravel her mystery and quickly dispensed with the chit-chat.

She pushed an open journal aside to place the laptop right in front of him. "This shouldn't take much of your time, professor."

"No need to rush on my account. I've got nothing but time, my dear."

Helen opened the first of the mosaic photos. Lloyd-Walker grasped both sides of the screen with his gnarled hands and pulled it closer.

Despite her excitement, Helen was unprepared for Lloyd-Walker's reaction. If he were younger, she thought, his hair would have turned white.

He stared at her. "Helen, can I ask you where you got this?"

"I'm happy to share what I can," she said, leaning forward with a conspiratorial air, "but I'm afraid it isn't much. And anything I say must remain in confidence."

"Yes, of course."

"A prominent dealer—you'd recognize his name instantly if I could mention it—came to the Met this week, offering this piece." She paused to consider where she was taking this, buying time by bringing up the second photo on the computer and resizing them together to show the panoramic effect. "The seller wants a commitment of at least $20 million in the next 72 hours. We're interested, naturally, but—"

"A bargain, I should say, in this day and age," Lloyd-Walker interrupted. "But isn't this outside your field?" he asked.

"Yes, it is," she said, swallowing hard in an effort to suppress her excitement. "But the unique nature of the offer makes it an all-hands-on-deck situation for the Met. We assume the seller is shopping it around and we want to move decisively if we're interested. Since I was already in London, I was asked to gather some intelligence here. Our people have their own ideas about it, but we want the very best outside expertise as well, particularly yours."

"Very kind of you to think of me, my dear. So very few do. I'm sure that when my obituary runs in *The Times* most readers' first reaction will be, 'Dear God, I thought he passed 20 years ago.'"

"Don't be silly, professor."

He focused on the laptop. "Now tell me, how do you read this?"

"As you said, this is outside my area. I'm exclusively ancient Near East now, plus I'm really squeezed for time and need to get back to London."

The subtle pressure focused him. "My impressions? Yes, that is why you're here, isn't it? Hold on just a moment." The don spun his chair around, shuffled to the nearest bookcase, and pulled an oversized volume down from a shelf just within his reach. Helen moved the laptop off to the side. He opened the book to its title page, respectful of it. Helen saw that the book was in German, the title in elaborate medieval script. She caught a publication date of 1881 and "Berlin" before Lloyd-Walker turned to a list of illustrations. "Ah ha!" he said when he reached page 79 and turned the book to face Helen, keeping a hand over the caption explaining the picture. "Look familiar?"

"Yes, of course," Helen said, running her fingertips across the heavy page. "It's a drawing of Athena, very similar to the one in the mosaic."

"Correct. Beautiful, isn't she? Goddess of wise counsel, heroism, and skill in battle. The goddess of the brilliant eyes."

"Very impressive," Helen said, anxious to get show-and-tell over with. "And in the mosaic she's been brought as a talisman on board the ship. If not Jason's, then someone else's."

"Yes," he said. "I can almost see how you would think that. But your mistake is in seeing Athena as an adjunct to the story, when in fact she *is* the story."

"And what if she is?" She realized how indifferent she was to the mosaic's iconography. What she wanted were his insights into a presumed provenance, especially his hypothesis as to where it might be today.

"What if she is?" Lloyd-Walker repeated. "Well, that certainly depends."

"On what?"

"On whether the story depicted in the mosaic of an incredible lost treasure is true," Lloyd-Walker said with a grin.

Helen's voice rose half an octave with anticipation. "Lost treasure?"

Chapter 13

The woman who reached Zander first called the police from her cell phone. Zander lifted his bloody head in groggy confusion as two bobbies and an ambulance arrived. He wanted to stand but the emergency medical workers kept him horizontal while the police searched his wallet for ID. One of the cops jumped into the ambulance for the ride when he discovered that Zander was a fellow officer.

The back of his head pounded like a blacksmith was shoeing it. "Lay back, friend," was all Zander heard as traffic parted before their siren. He wanted to take the story from the top, sure he could make everyone understand, but he passed out again just before they rolled down the Emergency Room ramp into University College Hospital.

• • • •

Horace Lloyd-Walker looked at Helen bemusedly "I know the Greeks are not your strong suit, my dear, but I'm sure you're familiar with the Athena Parthenos."

Of course she was. "It was the grand cult statue inside the Parthenon."

"Just so. It was commissioned by the great Pericles and built by the ingenious Pheidias shortly after he completed the Parthenon. Dedicated around 440 B.C. The greatest statue of the ancient world. Perhaps the greatest statue ever sculpted by man." He jabbed a finger at the goddess's imagined recreation in the antique German book on his desk. "From what we can tell, she stood over 30 feet tall and was, except for an internal timber support, constructed entirely of gold and ivory. But sad to say we don't know much more than that. Pliny the Elder, who later succumbed to Mt. Vesuvius at Pompeii, recorded seeing it around 50 A.D. And Pausanias, the Guide Bleu of his day, visited it about a hundred years later."

Helen laughed to herself. She appreciated Lloyd-Walker's complaint about a lack of hard data. But he at least was citing sources with names, people who'd written books that survived to our day, people whose births and deaths were known and recorded, people who themselves were noted in other ancient literature. It was a cornucopia compared to the guesswork and mysteries that she had to deal with in her own specialty. "And after that?" she asked.

"After that, plausible sightings grow even sketchier. A minor Greek historian named Zosimus observed the statue being worshipped sometime around 375 A.D. As to its condition, he didn't say. I don't have to tell you how frustrating it all is. You'd give anything to shake the buggers by the shoulders to get some details."

"You think Zosimus was mistaken?"

"No. He probably saw the Athena, as did the others. But how did it compare to the statue Pericles knew? Around 295 B.C. a tyrant named Lakares seized power in Athens and, some suggest, stripped the gold from the statue to pay his troops. In fact, the gold was designed for easy removal in case of emergency, though whoever used it was obligated to restore it."

"Did he?"

"Once again, we don't know. Though I have always suspected it was returned. We do know that Lakares paid dearly for demeaning the goddess. He was murdered shortly afterwards."

"By?"

"Perhaps his own men. Perhaps by the goddess herself."

Helen cocked her head and gently smirked at what she took to be an old teacher's toying with a student, but then saw how serious he was. "You're not suggesting Athena exacted her own revenge."

"No," the professor said, his milky eyes widening. "The gods rarely killed directly. They normally enlisted others to wield the dagger or spear for them, or lured their victims to their own demise. Certainly Lakares deserved his fate. The gods always resent neglect and insults to their honor. Whether he disrobed Athena or not, we have multiple accounts of Lakares trying to steal a fantastic trove of gold battle shields that Alexander the Great had affixed to the Parthenon to honor the goddess. Lakares should have known better, but I think perhaps he was not a believer—like you."

"Well, professor, it's a bit hard—"

"Dismiss it if you like, but the goddess brought great power to those who honored her, and disaster to those who disparaged her. Before Lakares, the tyrant Demetrios dishonored the goddess by turning the Parthenon into a home for himself and his mistresses. Not only did he plunder Athena's stored riches, but he violated the taboo against fornication on the Acropolis. He too suffered for his sins, as did all Athenians, some of whom joined his orgies that defiled the Athena. The penalty for this desecration, when he was finally ousted, was bloody civil war."

Helen leaned back. She knew better than to argue with a true believer. And besides, she hadn't come to hear fables about angry gods. She wanted facts. "But as for the statue itself, that's all we know?"

"No, there's a little more, and it's most interesting because it ties in with what you've shown me on your, uh, fliptop here."

Helen inched forward in her chair again. She felt she was finally getting what she came for.

"A philosopher named Proclus claims he witnessed the statue being removed from the Acropolis sometime between 450 and 500. That's significant because this oversized and rather grave-looking figure here"—he stopped to point to the screen—"is actually the Byzantine emperor Zeno, who ruled for a good part of that same period. Greece, of course, was part of Byzantium by then. So if the statue was carried away at that time, then the mosaic—which I read as telling the story of the statue's removal from the Acropolis— perhaps has some veracity."

"But is that the end of it?" Helen asked. "Nothing after 500 A.D.?"

"There are other stories—perhaps myths would be a more apt description, since they don't carry even the

minimal documentation of what I've already told you—
that have the statue turning up in Byzantium later in
time."

"You don't believe them?"

"No. Because no eyewitness account survives from
anyone we can trust. There's a Byzantine coin from
around 900, in the Louvre, that depicts a statue much
like the Parthenos standing in the Forum of Constantine
in Constantinople. Is that a reliable source?" There was
a hint of disdain in his voice, as if Helen had suggested
it might be. "There's even a legend that the Parthenos
stood at the entry to the harbor of Constantinople in
1204 when the city was pillaged by the Crusaders. One
version has it that the statue was in fact destroyed by
rioting locals who blamed it for attracting the Crusaders
in the first place."

"So it could have lasted that long and been
destroyed."

"It would be fascinating to find out. If the statue
were recovered it would be priceless on many counts:
as a link to a lost world, as a work of art, and for the
gold."

"How much gold are you talking about?" she
asked.

"If it were all there, well in excess of a ton."

"My God," Helen said, as she pictured the grand
Athena commanding the Met's cavernous Great Hall
facing Fifth Avenue.

"In fact, so much gold was used that the people of
Athens didn't believe Pheidias had put it all into the
statue. He was charged with keeping some for himself
and thrown in jail. They released him after a few
months when they did an accounting."

Lloyd-Walker seemed to ponder Pheidias's plight for a moment, but then picked up a pencil to help narrate the mosaic. "Right here, the Parthenos is being removed, and here it is being loaded on a ship, crossing some body of water. But after that I can't say until I see more."

"More?" asked Helen.

"I assume you know that there's more to this mosaic than you're showing me?"

Helen pondered what she was in for if she admitted her ignorance. "There may be more but that's all we've got."

"Then your dealer either doesn't have the remaining segments or isn't showing them, at least not to the Met. Perhaps he hopes to sell them later on. In any case, we can't even guess the rest of the story without them."

Helen sighed.

"Why so glum, child? What you've shown me is more than worthy of the Met. It would dominate even the finest collection."

"No doubt," she said, considering whether Penny Theobald knew any more about this. Certainly if she had other pictures they would have been on her computer and Helen would have them now.

"And the remainder may still be buried," the professor said.

"That's true," Helen agreed, her enthusiasm returned like the tide. "Then if you were going to follow up on this, professor, where would you go?"

"Well, if this ancient body of mine allowed, I'd set off for Turkey. And assuredly Istanbul itself. The workmanship is far too good for the provinces." Lloyd-

Walker tapped the screen with the eraser end of a pencil. "A work of this size and beauty was most likely a royal commission. When Constantinople fell in 1453, the Ottoman Turks probably concealed it. The Muslims, of course, don't go in for idolatry. And despite the lunacy we see from their zealots today, Muhammad said that sacred objects are to be spared when a people are conquered. So when the Turks took Byzantium, instead of destroying the Christian art they covered it up—quite civilized of them actually. Better than we would have done with theirs. I would guess that some Muslim cleric mistook the good emperor Zeno here for a saint and plastered him over." He leaned close enough to the computer that the screen fogged from his breath. "In fact, the plaster on the far right side suggests to me that the balance of the mosaic remains hidden."

Helen had survived Lloyd-Walker's jabs and she felt some of her swagger returning. More importantly, though, the old man had confirmed the mosaic's status as a masterpiece, and his observations about the work's condition—and the possibility that more remained buried—jibed with Helen's notion that it was only recently uncovered. Plus there was the giant, golden Athena. The goddess would make Lord Elgin's Parthenon marbles look like weatherbeaten miniatures. This was cover-of-*Time*-magazine stuff, she thought. Was it possible? Well, she had a place to look, or at least a starting point.

A little while later, Lloyd-Walker led Helen out. She thought he looked every one of his 90 years as he clutched the banister on the way to the lobby.

"You're not leaving yet?" she asked as he held the door for her.

"No, I've a bit more puttering to do. That's what we fossils specialize in."

She clasped the archeologist's right hand in both of hers. "Thank you again, professor. You've been wonderfully helpful."

"Yes, well I hope you're not traipsing off to Turkey now."

"As a matter of fact, yes, I probably am," Helen said, confused by Lloyd-Walker's tapered enthusiasm. "You're not trying to discourage me, are you?"

"Well, my dear, it's just that the likelihood of actually finding anything is remote indeed. I mean, even if the story in the mosaic is true, and not just some artist's fancy, and supposing we are interpreting it correctly, you must still find the remaining segment to see where the story leads. And if you get that far, and do figure out where the Parthenos was taken, the odds of it still being there are too long to calculate. You must have better things to do with your time."

"I appreciate your concern, professor, but I've got to follow this up."

"My goodness," Lloyd-Walker said, taking on a more paternal air. "I feel responsible for sending you on a wild goose chase. But if you must, then stop by the State Archeology Museum. It's a wonderful place to get your bearings in old Istanbul."

"I'll remember that," she said and walked to a waiting taxi.

• • • •

Horace Lloyd-Walker followed Helen with his eyes until she had driven away, and then trudged up the stairs to his office. He massaged his temples for a moment before picking up the telephone. "Miss Witherspoon, would you ring the Greek Foreign Minister for me?"

The phone rang back a minute later. "Hello? Panos? Yes, quite well, thank you. But I feel I must alert you to a potentially disastrous situation."

Chapter 14

The ER staff at University College Hospital cleaned and shaved the bloody mess on Zander's head, and closed his wound with 23 stitches. Doctors checked his pupils and poked his extremities and finally took an MRI, which confirmed what he already knew: he had a concussion. The good news, he was happy to hear, was that beneath the midnight blue blemishes across his torso, his ribs were only bruised, not broken.

He was asleep in a private room by 7 p.m. Detective Chief Inspector Parrish arrived half an hour later. The bobby who rode with Zander in the ambulance had called the DCI, having made out the words, "Call Norman Parrish."

He opened his eyes to see Parrish standing over him. "Don't tell me," Zander said, raising himself on one elbow in search of a comfortable position, "Linus Crane's girlfriend is no longer a suspect."

Parrish snorted. "The Harvey Nichols saleswoman is positive the girlfriend didn't buy the outfit pulled from the dumpster. She gave us a vague description of the woman who did and we're reviewing the in-store video. But she paid cash, so no ID."

"And the name tag in the jacket?"

"Turned out the conference organizers had tossed a pile of misspelled tags in the garbage. Miss Chahine's unfortunately got snagged to the jacket. How do you feel?"

"Like shit thrown from a race car."

"Doctors say you'll be fine."

Like an asthmatic, Zander yearned to take a deep breath but couldn't. "You still can't tell me this is unrelated to Crane."

"No, I can't say that anymore." Zander couldn't tell if the DCI was sincere or if he was just humoring an injured friend of the victim. He had done that more than once and now realized how despicable it was.

Without prodding, Zander poured out his recollections, embarrassed and angry he had so little to offer. He had only glimpsed the thug who forced Penny from the hotel, and any telling detail had been lost in the beating. Beyond that, he got no license plate and never saw the gunman in the cab or the driver. He suggested talking to the hotel staff and finding the old couple in the tearoom.

Parrish told Zander the doctors wanted to keep him for a couple of days, so he was posting one of his men outside his door. Zander was too tired to protest.

• • • •

The Gulfstream taxied less than a minute after touching down. The flight had been long but comfortable. Penny had been treated well, almost pampered, although she hadn't touched the steak dinner.

They had driven her straight from central London to some small airport. It had seemed like a long ride, but she was too stunned and distressed to say for sure. At the airport they pulled up alongside the bright white jet, giving her no chance to fight or scream for help.

She was left alone in an overstuffed leather seat. Her captors—the thug who had taken her from the hotel at gunpoint and the smaller man who had hauled her into the back of the cab—barely spoke to her or each other. She was too frightened to talk, though both men had kept their pistols holstered. They looked Middle Eastern to her and the few words they exchanged after blindsiding poor Zander sounded like Arabic. She was sure her abduction was connected to Linus's death. How could it not be? What had she ever done to merit being kidnapped? What had Crane done?

Penny stepped out onto the gangway moments after the plane rolled to a stop, trying to figure out where she was. It was hot and clammy, but also late and very dark. A control tower and a pair of terminals rose up in the distance, lights blinking red and blue. But the jet had parked in a remote corner of whatever airport they were at, far from any identifying markings. Her abductor poked her, "Move please!" Penny eased down the metal-grill stairs to the tarmac. A helicopter was waiting. She felt another shove to move ahead, turned to say she'd had enough, but saw her kidnappers retreating back inside the jet.

A door opened on the helicopter and a woman with short black hair jumped to the ground. "Please, Miss Theobald," she said, extending her arm like she was welcoming Penny to a fine restaurant.

Hearing this stranger say her name chilled her. She

climbed inside the helicopter.

The woman sat beside Penny. The copter rumbled as the rotor gained speed. Penny was resigned to being kept in the dark until she reached her final destination, wherever that was. She jumped when the woman spoke.

"We have only a short flight," she said, and handed Penny a blindfold. Her unsmiling face made clear that "no thanks" wasn't an option.

Penny's senses sharpened with the blindfold in place. Despite the copter's din, she thought she heard the rasp of an envelope being ripped open. Then a jab to her forearm, and everything went black.

• • • •

Zander's eyes popped open just as Figgis dropped a note on the nightstand. The soon-to-retire detective was wearing the same sharp suit he'd worn that morning, but his shirttail was bunched up in back, his collar was unbuttoned and his tie hung loose.

"I see you're enjoying your stay in safe and friendly London."

Zander winced as he hoisted himself to a sitting position. Figgis smelled like he'd had a pint or two on the way over.

"Sit down already," Zander ordered his hovering friend. "You're making me nervous." He pointed to the closet. "And could you get my watch?"

Figgis handed it to Zander. The crystal was gone and the hands bent.

Zander shook his head. The watch had been a gift from his ex on their first anniversary. He smirked thinking that now it looked more like a fair depiction of their relationship.

"What's so funny?" Figgis asked.

"Nothing," Zander said. "What time is it?"

"Ten."

"How'd you find me? Did I make the papers?"

"No. Afraid you'd have to die for that. Parrish called me. Thought I'd like to know my friend had been clobbered strolling through Bloomsbury."

"They took Penny," Zander said, a pulse of anger and guilt surging through him like an electric shock.

"I know."

Zander heard his guard in the hallway checking someone's ID. A moment later a nurse with a stream of jet-black hair in a tightly wrapped ponytail walked in. She was carrying a paper cup full of pills.

"Hello, Mr. Blake," she said through a light accent Zander couldn't place. "You should be getting some *sleep*," she added in words clearly meant for Figgis.

Zander tossed the pills back, followed by a sip of water.

"I woke him so you wouldn't have to," Figgis said with a smile that elicited a scowl from the nurse.

"Any news at all, Graham?" Zander asked as his blood pressure was taken.

"Not that I've heard. Sorry."

"Christ." Zander's scalp started to throb.

"Relax," Figgis implored.

"How can I fucking relax?"

Figgis pulled a folded sheet of paper from his jacket pocket. It was a "Kidnapping Alert" from Scotland Yard that featured Penny's photo.

"Where'd they get the picture?" Zander asked.

"From her bag at the Bertrand. She hadn't checked out yet."

Zander studied this face he barely knew but felt responsible for.

"What did you tell Parrish?" Figgis asked. "Did these apes leave anything to follow?"

"You know, the whole thing happened in a nanosecond. Penny was inside the cab by the time I got out there. I heard some yelling what sounded like names, but all I can remember sounds like gobbledygook."

The nurse slipped an electronic thermometer under Zander's tongue.

"What did you hear?" Figgis asked.

"I thought one of them was called Charbook Al."

Figgis leaned toward the bed. "Say again."

"Please don't talk," the nurse said, motioning Zander to sit back.

Zander pulled out the thermometer. "I said Charbook Al. And then one of them said, 'Have an Alan, Oona.'" He wasn't surprised that Figgis looked confused. So had Parrish. "I know," said Zander. "Sounds like a demented Damon Runyon."

"Did you say *Oona*?" asked Figgis.

"Yeah. *Oona*. But he said the oo more like Al Pacino when he played that blind colonel. The one who drove the Porsche."

"Probably saw better than I could last night."

"No doubt," Zander said, surprised that their drunken dinner was just last night. It felt like a month ago. "But does it mean anything to you, Graham? Have an Alan, Oona or Charbook Al?" Zander stuck the thermometer back in his mouth.

"What's an *Alan*?" Figgis asked. "A brand of cigar?"

"How the hell do I know?" Zander said, throwing his arms up but then pulling them back because it felt like someone had jabbed his side with scissors. "Goddammit!"

"You can't blame yourself for not remembering more. You were barely conscious at that point."

Zander nodded with exasperation, finally quiet as his nurse removed the beeping thermometer. "Have an Alan, Oona. Charbook Al," he heard her say while she read the display under the light.

"That's it," Zander said, startled by the sound of the words in their original intonation. "That's what I heard."

"Those are not names," she said. "Did what you hear sound like, 'Havaalanina çabuk ol?'"

"Yes, yes!" Zander said. "That's it exactly."

"It means, more or less, 'Get to the airport and hurry.'"

"In what language?" Figgis asked.

"Turkish."

"Turkish?" Zander asked, looking at the nurse. "Are you—"

"Yes," she answered, scribbling on his chart. "And you," she pointed at Figgis on her way out. "Two minutes."

"Well that's fucking great!" Zander said, pounding his fist on the sheet. "She's in Turkey."

"What?" Figgis said and stood up. "That's a bit of a jump."

"Why? You don't go to an airport to sit in the lounge, Graham."

"Of course not. But there are Turkish communities all over Europe. There are two million Turks just in

Germany. And these hooligans could be working for anybody."

Zander nodded. Figgis was right. Who knew where they'd taken Penny? But this was something. He straightened up and the pain had abated, thanks to nurse Feelgood. "You'll call Parrish with this?" Zander asked.

"Of course."

"What airport would a private plane use here in London?"

"Stanstead for the most part. But what are you thinking? Aren't the doctors keeping you here for a few days?"

"How do I get there?"

"You need to rest!"

Zander glared at him. "Are you going to help me or not?"

Chapter 15

Zander slept fitfully after Figgis left. Light-headed and queasy, he eased out of bed at 8 a.m. He shaved, dressed himself painfully, and signed out.

He bought a baseball cap to conceal his scalp—no need to scare anyone, he thought—then treated himself to a taxi to Liverpool Street station, where he caught the train to Stanstead. A cab to the airport would have been easier on his brittle body, but he decided to save his cash for lubricating any reluctant memories.

He bought a copy of *The Herald Tribune* and spread it out across two seats, forgetting his own problems for two minutes while he read that five of the six terrorists arrested the day before for the Turkish bombings had confessed. To top it off, the sixth man, the supposed ringleader, had hung himself in his prison cell. Zander examined the blurry photo, taken off a TV screen, of one of the bombers. The poor sap's swollen jaw confirmed that the Turkish police didn't dispense Miranda warnings.

He tossed the paper aside and the Scotland Yard alert with Penny's picture from his shirt pocket. It was a candid shot of her leaning against the base of a fallen column, wearing a sweet half smile, as if to ask, "Why are you wasting this picture on me?" If Penny was in Turkey, he thought, the police there—the ones who had tracked down the terror bombers, anyway—could find her before sundown. He'd ask Parrish about alerting the Turks. Her hair was the same style she'd worn this week so he assumed the photo was recent, probably from Sicily. If anyone at the airport had seen her they'd recognize her.

Zander limped the length of the Stanstead terminal with Penny's photo. But two hours of questioning every skycap, baggage handler, ticket taker, and maintenance worker he could corner yielded nothing.

With no one to pocket his bribe money, Zander took a taxi back to town. He slept for the hour ride and dragged himself into the Bertrand lobby. The heat and humidity had wilted him like stir-fried spinach and his head was pounding. It was only 4 in the afternoon, but he couldn't remember feeling so exhausted since he'd marched around his house for 16 hours straight, cradling his infant son in his arms, soothing a double ear infection.

He called Figgis but hung up on voicemail. Parrish's phone rang a dozen times before the detective picked up to say they'd drawn blanks at all the London airports. Logbooks, Parrish said, showed no private jets leaving for Turkey around the time in question, and Penny's picture hadn't produced any leads at the commercial or private terminals. Zander was glad to hear that Parrish had already contacted both the Turkish police and airport authorities. But his mood was tempered when the DCI warned that such requests rarely turned up anything useful.

"What next, then?" Zander wanted to know.

"We'll go back to Heathrow and Gatwick, and probably widen our ring to a few more remote airports. Nothing to lose, but frankly I'm leaning toward turning the photo over to the press. We have no live leads. Of course we'll keep working the Crane investigation for anything that points toward Miss Theobald. What about you?" Parrish asked. "Staying in town? Going home?"

Zander thought for a few seconds. "I don't know."

Zander called home as soon as he finished with Parrish. It was early in L.A. The phone didn't even ring before he heard Layla's bold hello. She was only eight, but somehow had always known how to speak on the phone.

"I was waiting for you, Daddy," she said.

"Really, honey?"

"Yes, I knew you were going to call."

His daughter's certainty surprised but pleased him.

"Mommy's waiting in the car to take me to camp," she reported.

"She can wait a minute longer." Zander told Layla about London, omitting little but his trip to the hospital. "You'll come here with me someday," he said, thankful Layla was still young enough not to question his dreams, unlike 10-year-old Josh, who demanded specifics.

He fell silent, though, when she asked about the pyramid he had promised to bring back. "I'm working on it, honey," he said, not wanting to disappoint her.

Hanging up left him desolate and he dragged himself to the lobby bar where he downed two Heinekens and nibbled on pretzels. What should he do?

He wasn't helping anyone, including himself, in London. He thought of going to Turkey, but it seemed absurd. What would he do there? He didn't speak the language. He didn't know anyone. He had no leads for the police. But he couldn't go on to Egypt either. That seemed superfluous now.

• • • •

Helen Vandameer's taxi dropped her at the American embassy in Grosvenor Square. Pigeons picked at breadcrumbs that a woman tossed from a plastic bag onto the sidewalk. Across the square, past the statue of General Eisenhower, a police whistle competed with a lorry driver leaning on his horn. Her visit was a surprise, but Peter Sloan was happy to put aside his extended analysis of EC-Russian trade patterns and escort her upstairs.

"God, how dreadful," she said when they reached Sloan's crammed cubicle. "You deserve something nicer, Peter. At least with some natural light." She pulled a cigar box-sized package wrapped in brown paper from her shopping bag. "I need a favor," she said. "Can you take care of this? It's what I bought from Mr. Hazim the other evening. A necklace."

"Why? Where are you going?"

"Well, that's the other thing I need to tell you," she said, holding her breath before revealing her news. "I'm off to Istanbul for a few days."

"But," Sloan said, his mouth turning down in disappointment, "I thought we were going to the Lake District. I've gotten the time off and booked a room. We were lucky to get it. It was only because of a cancellation."

"I'm really sorry, Peter. Some work has come up."

"What work? You said you were free when the conference ended."

"I was. But I've gotten a lead on something quite extraordinary. I've spent the whole day arranging my trip."

"But the inn's paid for already. And it's not refundable."

Helen ran her hand down his cheek. He seemed much younger to her, all of a sudden. "How about this? Tell them you don't want a refund. You just need to postpone. For a week. We'll go when I'm back. I promise."

"I don't have much of a choice, do I? But forget the Lake District for a minute. Don't you realize how dangerous Turkey is right now?"

She shook her head. "I'll be fine."

"The Department has issued a high-risk advisory for all Americans."

"Is it illegal for me to go?" she said in soft voice, not wanting to be heard by anyone lurking beyond the half-height gray walls.

"No. But the group that did the bombing..." Sloan fished a memo off his desk. "'Allah's Revenge for the Martyr Krekar,' they're called. It's not even clear what they want yet. There could be more trouble at any time."

Helen looked deep into Peter's eyes, trying to convey the confidence she felt without explaining why. "They won't be making any more trouble," she said.

"How do you know?"

"I have my sources."

"Better than the United States government?"

"Peter, I appreciate your concern. I really do. Now, you'll hold this until I get back?"

Sloan took the box. "Of course I will, but is this all you got from him?"

"There was a trinket, too, but I'm taking it with me. Hazim said it was a good-luck charm."

"Well, *his* luck certainly ran out."

"Mine will be better," she said, kissing him softly on the lips. She lifted a corner of his limp smile with a finger. "Cheer up. You know how much I was looking forward to our weekend. So you can imagine how important this trip is."

• • • •

The blare of the hotel phone startled Zander like an unexpected foghorn. The curtains were drawn and he felt it must be 3 a.m., but it was only 8:30 in the evening.

"Zander Blake?"

"Yes."

"This is Dean Goodrich Jr. I'm with the FBI here in London. We met a couple of nights ago at the service for Linus Crane."

Zander cradled the phone between his shoulder and ear while he rubbed his eyes awake and dredged up Goodrich's surfer-boy face from memory. "Yeah, of course."

"As far as I'm concerned, this call is not happening."

"So you're not calling to recruit me?"

Goodrich snorted a chuckle, but there was no humor when he spoke. "And it would be best if you felt the same way. Am I making myself clear?"

"Yeah, sure. What's up?"

"Maybe you already know that the Bureau, for national security reasons, occasionally undertakes surveillance of representatives of foreign governments."

"Keep going," Zander said, intrigued by Goodrich's cloak-and-dagger tone but wondering what this had to do with him.

"But you might not be aware that it's a Federal violation to disclose information gained from such surveillance outside the Bureau. Which is why this conversation is not taking place. We're still clear on that?"

Zander perked up at the prospect that Goodrich's paranoia might lead to something. "Couldn't be clearer."

"Good. Do you know Bulent Ozbek?"

"Only for the past couple of days. Why?"

"Some information has surfaced that Ozbek has been inquiring into the disappearance of Penny Theobald, and he may have turned up something."

Zander sat up now, wide-awake. "Like what?

"I don't know."

Zander squeezed the phone to stop from cursing out the FBI agent. "I'm not up for games, Goodrich."

"No games. It's just that if you've ever worked this type of source you know you don't get to ask questions. So it's not clear, other than the fact that she appears to be in Turkey."

"Well, Jesus Christ. That's more than the police know right there. Have you told anyone? The State Department or, uh, I don't know, the CIA, maybe?"

"Like I said, the law prohibits disclosure of information gained from surreptitious surveillance of foreign officials."

Zander slapped his hand on the night table. "That's so ridiculous it's probably true, but then why are you telling *me*?"

"A number of reasons. Number one, Miss Theobald seemed like a real nice gal. I'd like to think that if my girlfriend was snatched off the street and you had a lead you'd pass it to me." Zander was about to say that Penny was not his girlfriend, but why undermine Goodrich's largesse? "Most important, though," he continued, "speaking as a former cop, I know you'll *do* something with the information. If I pass this to any of our Foreign Service officers here, even underlined in red ink, they'll scratch their nuts for a month deciding how to handle it. And in the end they'd wind up compromising me as their source."

"I appreciate your trust. But I don't understand why your rules cover Ozbek. He's not a government official, is he?"

"Because his brother is the Turkish P.M. he travels on a diplomatic passport. He's essentially a minister without portfolio. And some people think he's in line to be Prime Minister himself."

"I assume you were not eavesdropping to find out about Penny?" Zander said.

"Let's say that's outside the Bureau's interests right now."

"A kidnapped American is outside the Bureau's interests?"

"That's not what I mean."

"Then why are you bugging him? I thought he was legit."

"As far as I know he's completely legitimate."

"Then why the tap?"

"Turkey is a tinderbox right now," he finally said. "You watch the news, don't you?"

"Of course. I just thought you were pulling on some special thread."

Zander waited but heard nothing. "All right. I'll wait 'til it's in *The New York Times*."

"That's a good idea."

"Tell me at least where I can find him. You've obviously got his address."

"He left for Istanbul this morning."

"Christ," Zander said, angry that the chance for some quick answers was gone. The disappointment seemed to squeeze his aching ribs.

"Listen. The Bureau doesn't keep a permanent office in Turkey, but there are 70 agents there now investigating the July 4th bombings. Not that he can help you out, and I'm not sure how much longer he'll be there, but one of them is a demolitions expert buddy of mine named Ned Nolan."

"He knows what you're up to?"

"No. And mentioning it would ruffle a lot of feathers. But he's a good guy and if you get down there you should look him up."

Zander dropped the phone into the cradle. He grabbed his cell, tapped feverishly on the virtual keyboard, and five minutes later was booked to touch down in Istanbul by early afternoon.

Part II

It hath fallen out sometimes that both Papists and Protestants, Jews and Turks may be embarked in one ship.

Roger Williams
Letter to the Town of Providence

Foolish is the mortal who sacks cities, temples, tombs, and the sacred places of the dead.

Euripides
The Trojan Women

Chapter 1

Zander arrived in Istanbul on an Alitalia flight through Rome. From the airport he checked into a two-star pension near the Topkapi Museum mentioned in a guidebook he'd bought at Heathrow. His room was surprisingly pleasant, spacious and sun-filled with high ceilings and antique furniture.

He did not unpack before heading for the American Consulate, where his token supply of patience was expended hurdling fortress-like security—the aftermath of the bombing, he was told. Perched atop an arid brown hill, the consulate complex looked to Zander like a cross between Alcatraz and the Dalai Lama's palace in Tibet, all surrounded by a concrete barrier wall that could run alongside any California highway. Once past the Marines, metal detectors, and database checks, he flashed his LAPD badge to the receptionist and demanded to see the highest-ranking person at the consulate "about a delicate matter."

This subterfuge got him to the executive foyer, where he now shared a couch with a rail-thin man sporting a grey-specked goatee who glanced his way every now and then. The man's left arm was in a sling, but he deftly scanned *Time* by resting it on his crossed leg and flipping the pages with his good hand. When he finished he offered Zander the magazine.

"No thanks," he said, instead standing up to tuck in his shirt and try to look as serious and presentable as possible while wearing a green baseball cap. He pulled a folded sheet of instructions from his breast pocket. It was something a nurse had handed him when he'd checked out of the hospital. He hadn't looked at it before but now saw it was a list of warning signs for "Post Concussion Syndrome": Headache, dizziness, apathy, difficulty concentrating, depression, anxiety, and impaired memory. He crumpled the sheet, knowing that the only cure for his symptoms was rest, which was the one thing he couldn't do. He was tossing the paper into the trash when the secretary waved him into the executive suite.

Zander marched across the sizeable office to shake hands with his host, who looked like a college student dressed for a Wall Street interview.

"Gary Durkin," he said. "I'm special assistant to the ambassador."

Zander took a deep breath. "Detective Zander Blake, LAPD. "No offense, but I was expecting someone a bit… uh…"

"More senior?"

"Exactly."

"Well, that leaves us even. I was expecting a *Turkish* policeman."

"Yeah." Zander felt no regrets about the mix-up. "I can't say it was unintentional."

"Okay, now that we've got that straight, rest assured I speak with full the authority of the ambassador. And you're here on police business?"

"Unofficially."

Durkin slumped like a movie producer cornered by a down-and-out screenwriter. "Well, you're in," he said, glancing at his watch. "I can give you three minutes."

Zander warned Durkin that his story was a strange one, and prefaced it with credibility-building details about his tenure at the LAPD and on the President's Cultural Property Committee.

"Go ahead, detective, I see you're not here on a whim."

Zander recounted the highlights of his London misadventure. He focused on Linus Crane's murder—which Durkin said he'd read about—and Penny's kidnapping, and then on the tip about getting to Bulent Ozbek.

Durkin didn't seem to care that Zander ran well past his three minutes. But instead of probing for details, Durkin finally asked what he wanted.

"I need an introduction to Ozbek. I thought the ambassador could help."

"The ambassador probably could, but he's not in the country. You might know there's a G8 summit under way in Italy this week, up on Lake Como. The ambassador is there, briefing the President on the aftermath of the bombings here. I expect him back Friday. But the Secretary of Defense is returning with him, which will keep us all running around non-stop. I'll be happy to bring this up as soon as the Secretary leaves, though."

Zander's stomach churned with disappointment. "But that could be four or five days from now. Maybe a week."

"I'm afraid it could."

"That's too late."

"I wish I could tell you otherwise."

Zander turned to leave in disgust. "I wish you could, too."

• • • •

Felix Maurer leaned back in his desk chair, ergonomically customized for the back he had twisted early in the Afghan invasion. The CIA station chief pressed a button on his phone to route all his calls to voicemail, then slipped the headset off while he massaged his neck. He was tired, having gotten up at 4 a.m. to plant the fresh bug in Durkin's office. The consulate was swept once a week for listening devices, but the cleaners worked for Maurer and he took care of the ambassador's wing himself.

He had listened attentively to Zander Blake's story, probably with more interest than Gary Durkin. Must be some piece of ass to chase her halfway around the world, Maurer thought. He had no doubt Bulent Ozbek could find her if he wanted to. Nothing got by him. The cop's biggest worry, Maurer thought, was that if Ozbek found her he might want to keep her for himself—for a while, anyway. He created a reminder on his PC to run Blake through the Agency's database. If the cop checked out and still needed help in a few days, maybe he'd lend a hand.

• • • •

Durkin caught up to Zander in the waiting area and approached the goateed man on the couch, who was now reading *Der Spiegel*. He was about 35 and dressed in an ill-fitting suit and scuffed wingtips. When he saw he was the focus of Durkin's attention, he tossed the magazine back onto the table and lifted himself up.

"Yucel," Durkin shook his hand, "This is Detective Zander Blake from the Los Angeles, California, Police Department."

"Rodney King," the goateed man chirped as he grasped Zander's hand.

"A long time ago," Zander said, struck by the association but not offended, given the stranger's warm smile.

"Zander," Durkin said, "This is Yucel Goktepe. Yucel is one of the best journalists in Istanbul and very well connected. I'm sure that if he can't personally get you what you want, then he knows people who can, and faster than we can do it here."

"That would be terrific," Zander said. He'd been about to ask Durkin for at least Bulent Ozbek's address but felt relieved he'd found some help. "I'd appreciate it."

Durkin turned to the journalist. "I know we have an appointment but I have to beg off until next week. Meanwhile you take care of my friend Zander here, all right?"

"As a favor to you, of course," said Goktepe. "But have you done anything about what we discussed last time?"

Zander watched the diplomat consider lying—a look he'd seen in the interrogation room a thousand times. "No, not yet," he said, already halfway back to his office, "but I promise I'll get to it the moment the Secretary leaves." He closed the door behind him.

"So how does Gary think I can help you?" the journalist asked as they headed out.

"I need to see Bulent Ozbek." Zander watched Goktepe's eyes widen.

"Are you going to arrest him?"

"Why?" Zander asked. "What's he done?"

Goktepe looked at Zander as if he'd just asked the stupidest question he'd ever heard.

Chapter 2

Yucel Goktepe's beat-up Jetta, littered with loose papers, crushed soda cans, newspapers, and unopened mail, smelled like an ashtray on wheels. The journalist apologized for the mess and dumped the clutter from the passenger seat into the rear.

Zander dug out a seat belt from between the stained cushions, but found the buckle decapitated. He wouldn't have minded, except that he normally didn't drive with a stranger who operated a stick shift and steered with the same hand.

The Jetta's broken air conditioning forced them to keep the windows down. It was too noisy to talk, so Zander sat back to enjoy the breeze blowing across the Golden Horn and admire the domes and minarets that overshadowed the otherwise low-slung skyline. When traffic came to a halt past the bridge, Goktepe navigated a maze of narrow backstreets like a madman. They finally sped to a stop at a waterside cafe in the Sultanahmet, within earshot of Zander's hotel and the journalist's office.

Goktepe yanked the parking brake. "Not exactly L.A."

"You're right," Zander said. "The smog is actually worse here."

Zander followed Goktepe out to the sunshine of the cafe's patio. They sat at a wrought-iron table perched at the edge of a 15-foot drop to the water, far from a handful of other patrons. Zander maneuvered his chair so he was shaded by the table's umbrella and slipped on his sunglasses to relieve the glare. His host, who wore clear, wire-rim glasses, did not seem bothered.

While Goktepe flagged down a waiter, Zander took a hard look at the journalist. He was easily six-foot-four, but stick thin, giving his body a rubbery quality, like a ship's mast bending in a storm. His oval head was topped with a mop of straight brown hair cut short, balancing his goatee. Bags so heavy they looked like lampblack weighed down his eyes.

"You've been to California?" Zander asked when the waiter had deposited two coffees.

Goktepe lit a cigarette and laid the pack on the table. "Once. About seven years ago. I was working for PricewaterhouseCoopers."

"Really?" Zander asked, struggling to picture Goktepe in a three-piece suit.

Goktepe nodded. "I was the firm's first forensic accountant in Turkey. PwC flew all the forensics from around the world to a meeting in Los Angeles. I got to see the city, and Hollywood. I even went to a baseball match," Goktepe nodded at Zander's cap.

"What did you think?"

"Very, very slow until the end. Someone named Green hit the ball into the crowd and the players all walked off the field. It seemed arbitrary."

"Right," Zander said with a nostalgic smile, thinking he would explain the rules another time. "But tell me, when you did your forensics, you were trying to save the companies or doing autopsies after they went belly up?"

"We always tried to save them first. We would go in and figure out who's embezzling or laundering money or stealing goods, if that's what was happening, so the company could be resuscitated and the criminals caught."

"But you gave it up?"

"I always wanted my own business, so I quit PwC. But that really wasn't for me either. Worrying about paying my staff gave me an ulcer. Meanwhile, I'd written some letters to one of the newspapers to explain a financial scandal they had misreported. When the editor offered me a job, I closed my firm and took it."

"And you're still with them?"

"No." He dropped two spoonfuls of sugar into his coffee. "I lasted a year. Here in Turkey the big newspapers are part of the same corporations I was investigating. My success made my editor's life miserable, so I left for The Express. It's a weekly with a tiny circulation and the salary's terrible, but it's not owned by anyone with anything to lose. So I do what I want."

"No regrets?"

"Not at all. Now what's your interest in Bulent Ozbek?"

Zander listened to the water lapping at the sea wall and wondered how much to tell Goktepe. Three years ago he gave a reporter at the *Orange County Register* some background about a fraud ring that was snookering high-profile residents of the Malibu colony. The reporter had agreed their chat was off the record, but the paper printed it all the next day, blowing a month's investigation. Zander complained to the guy's boss and got an apology. The last he heard, the weasel was with the *National Enquirer*.

"A friend of mine," he started, "an archaeology grad student, was kidnapped off a London street last week by some Turkish thugs, who left me with this." Zander removed his cap so Goktepe could inspect his stitches. "Ozbek knows this student, and while I can't say for sure that she was brought here, I'm certain Ozbek is trying to find her and may know where she is."

"What makes you think he didn't kidnap her himself?"

Zander leaned forward. He had no interest in trying to decode the journalist's comments. He needed clarity. "That's the second time you've suggested Ozbek is a criminal. Are you serious or is this some kind of Turkish inside joke I'm not getting?"

"This is nothing to joke about."

• • • •

Gary Durkin felt particularly satisfied. The ambassador's assistant had not only freed himself up to focus on the Defense Secretary's imminent visit, but he'd helped out that California detective by sending him off with Goktepe.

Barely half an hour had gone by, though, before the 25-year-old was interrupted by the one person in Turkey who made him regret turning down Georgetown

Law for the Foreign Service: Felix Maurer, the CIA's Istanbul station chief.

Maurer and Durkin were the same height, just under six feet. But while Durkin had the lean physique of a runner, the station chief carried himself like a weightlifter. His shoulders were broad, his neck strained against his shirt collar, and he radiated a compact energy. Durkin imagined that he had cruise missiles tattooed on his forearms. His close-cropped hair was just blond enough to hide any gray. Durkin had studied his face and concluded that though Maurer could easily pass for 35, he must be at least 50, given his stories of far-flung Agency escapades.

Storming into Durkin's office without knocking, the station chief, wearing an eggshell poplin suit that Durkin thought would look appropriate on a coffee plantation, dropped into a tufted leather chair opposite the desk.

"Yes?" Durkin asked.

"Just wondering why you're still doing business with Goktepe."

"How did you know he was here?"
"Saw him loitering outside your office. I've told you before. He's a plagiarist and a troublemaker who has no love for the United States."

Durkin's impression of Goktepe couldn't have been more different. He'd told Maurer this before and didn't want to bother again, especially now. Durkin assumed that lying was part and parcel of the spy trade. But it made him wonder if Maurer was some sort of sociopath, which scared the hell out of him because the station chief was one of the smartest people he'd ever met. It wasn't just the megabytes of history and geopolitics Maurer could spew at will. In fact, despite his Ph.D. from Hopkins, he sometimes seemed barely literate. But there was an intensity about his intelligence that wore an opponent down like prolonged exposure to carbon monoxide. It left Durkin wondering why the spy side of the business attracted people who, though often lacking a solid core, seemed to revel in their work, while the diplomatic service was overrun with dolts.

He saw Maurer glance down at the daily press digest. This morning's issue was twice its normal size, devoted to the unexpected arrest, trial, conviction, and sentencing of the five surviving bombers—all in the last 48 hours.

Durkin decided to take the offensive. "Your job just got a whole lot easier," he said, tapping the digest for emphasis. Maurer had been a passive observer to these stunning events, a role Durkin was sure he loathed. Despite the air of mystery Maurer cultivated, it was known around the consulate that he was Washington's point man on the bombings. The White House had promised revenge the day of the attack, and rumor had it the President was pummeling the Director of Central Intelligence on a daily basis, demanding a bulletproof answer to a simple question: Who financed and trained the terrorists? Was it an al-Qaeda cell or an independent group? That pummeling was being passed down the intelligence line, with Maurer the final punching bag. Durkin didn't see Maurer every day, but the assignment was obviously taking its toll. Normally a poster boy for clean living, he looked to Durkin like the subject of a sleep-deprivation study.

He watched Maurer's eyes and mouth narrow. If the station chief had a tail it would have stopped wagging. "You know, whenever you say something like that it makes me want to call Yale and see if you actually went there. Or did you just sit around Davenport and smoke weed for four years?"

Durkin was sure he'd never mentioned living in Davenport.

"Maybe," Maurer added, "I'll order up your transcript."

"Afraid only I can do that," Durkin shot back, content in his certainty.

Maurer laughed. "Right!"

He wasn't sure how, but Durkin felt his back to the ropes again.

"If," Maurer continued, "you're referring to this morning's news, the reality is that my task is now infinitely more complex. Besides, I'm amazed you're not out picketing the death sentences."

"Under most circumstances, I would be. And I can't believe I'm saying this, but they deserve whatever they get."

Maurer picked a gold Cross pen off Durkin's desk and spun it like a baton. "My young friend, you have picked the wrong time to become a hardass."

"What do you mean?"

"I'll give you even money those dumb bastards had as much to do with the bombings as you did."

"But they all confessed," Durkin insisted.

"And Lee Harvey Oswald was a lone gunman."

Durkin was jarred by Maurer's tone. "You don't believe their confessions?"

"Why should I? I didn't interview them, and neither did any other American."

Durkin knew this was true. An army of FBI

counter-terrorist specialists had arrived right after the attack, but the Turks had limited them to forensics at the bombsight. No direct contact with the suspects.

"Before the sun was up yesterday, while you were getting your beauty rest, I was parked outside Bayrampasa prison watching those five poor schmucks get packed off to the court house. They say the security forces here are trying to use *evidence* as the basis for charging terrorists, as opposed to confessions. But I don't think they tried very hard here. Not that I'm an expert in torture—"

Durkin laughed and was surprised when Maurer smiled back.

"But from what I could see of them—gimpy gaits, blank stares, shriveled lips, not to mention rope burns on their wrists—it was obvious they'd been savaged. Bottom line is, these guys were ready to cop to crucifying Jesus."

The image of the torture constricted Durkin from his stomach to his testicles. "And what about their leader, Mazari? He didn't kill himself?"

"Suicide?" Maurer roared, "That story stinks worse than the Ganges in August. And here's something to break your bleeding heart. I met Mazari's sweet mother outside the prison gates. She was there to collect her boy's remains, but they turned her away."

"Why?" Durkin asked.

"Well, I have it on good authority that Mazari resembled Texas road kill before they slipped the sheet around his neck. I wouldn't count on an open casket."

"And this group they were part of? 'Allah's Revenge for the Martyr Krekar?' That's a total fabrication?"

"Mehdi Krekar was a doctor who got drummed out of the Turkish Army 20 years ago on account of his pro-Kurdish views. He surfaced in Teheran as a religious figure and a poet and lived there until he died last year. As to this supposed group using his name, it's a new entry in my database."

"So you think the Iranians are involved?" Durkin asked, knowing that Maurer's conclusions would largely decide who got bombed back into the Stone Age.

"I don't know yet who's involved. I'm questioning every connection. The only proof of outside influence I've seen is the bomb trigger the FBI is piecing together. Originated in Afghanistan. But it's no surprise if the bombers are veterans of Afghanistan—or of Chechnya or Bosnia or Iraq or wherever. There's even a story being floated that there's a Greek connection."

"Greek?" Durkin didn't understand.

"You heard me," Maurer said. "One of the few verifiable facts we've got is that three of the six fuckers are Kurdish. The Greeks, you should know, though you obviously don't, have longstanding ties to the Kurds. Strange bedfellows, you might think, but they share a very deep and very ancient animosity for the Turks. And besides loathing the Turks for a millennium, Greece has more America-bashers than anyplace in Europe."

"All the more so since the economic collapse," Durkin conceded.

"Absolutely," Maurer snapped back, smiling like a teacher suddenly impressed by an ordinarily slow student. "In fact, the Greeks make the French look like our greatest fans. Meanwhile, way too many Kurds have never forgiven us for abandoning them to Saddam Hussein after the first Gulf War. And since we took out Hussein, they think we betrayed them by not letting them turn the north of Iraq into an independent Kurdish state."

Durkin waited a moment for Maurer to top the theory he was building with a damning accusation, and felt oddly disappointed when the station chief backed off. "Then again," he finally continued, "the other three bombers aren't Kurdish, so I don't know where these puzzle pieces fit. Or if they're legit pieces at all."

Maurer stared down at the floor and shook his head, betraying a hint of the despair. "If there is a Greek connection, of course, you can put a fork in NATO, since it would be the end of the alliance and probably trigger a full-scale war across the Aegean, not just some skirmish over grazing rights for donkeys on Cyprus. And if it's the Iranians—well, if the prospect of some Ayatollah with his finger on a nuclear trigger wasn't enough, we can add this to the list of reasons to go in. Of course, a bunch of home-grown Islamic fundamentalists could be behind it all, which is maybe the worst prescription. The last thing the Turks want to admit is that their own fundamentalists are eating away at the country like a cancer."

Durkin had a million things to do and he knew arguing with Maurer was pointless. But he couldn't help himself. "I don't know how you can say Turkey is going fundamentalist. This place gets more American all the time. Fries and Coke everywhere. I even saw a Dunkin Donuts yesterday. They'll all be dead from heart and gum disease before they turn against the West."

Maurer smirked. "You've got to look below the surface, my friend. I'll give you five-to-one that the asshole driving the truck bomb was wearing Levis and Nikes and just ate at Burger King."

• • • •

Zander had no time for implications. He needed direct answers. "You're telling me Ozbek is capable of kidnapping?"

Goktepe craned his long neck to see if anyone was listening. "I am sure he is capable of far worse."

"People are capable of a lot of things. But you have some proof?"

"The facts speak for themselves. You know, of course, that Ozbek's brother is the Prime Minister. The Ozbeks come from a middle-class Istanbul family. Not poor, but far from wealthy. Their father was a lawyer and occasional municipal official. The Prime Minister has spent all his adult life in politics, and hasn't made any money. And Bulent, from the time he returned from business school in America until his brother became P.M., was involved in numerous private ventures, most of them failures, and none which earned him much money.

"However, since his brother became P.M. five years ago, he's made a fortune as a consultant—I use the term loosely—during the privatization of certain banks, steel and petroleum companies, the state airline, and the state television networks. Anyone who wanted a piece of these deals had to cut Bulent in. No tribute, no business. Now he's the person to go to if you want a digital cellular franchise. God knows what he's pocketing to guarantee the winning bids. Meanwhile, he's invested his money around the globe. So from his base as a marginally successful small businessman prior to his brother's victory, he is now worth $1.1 billion, at least according to Forbes magazine."

Zander sat back, fingering the brim of his cap. The journalist did not strike him as a liar or a kook. He had no trouble keeping his gaze and his tone was calm and measured, like an accountant's. But unless Goktepe's worst fears were true—and Zander wondered what Penny would make of these accusations—Ozbek's business shenanigans, even if he were the Jeff Skilling of Turkey, were irrelevant. Still, he needed to press Goktepe. "Don't be offended, but how the hell do you know all this?"

Goktepe apparently expected the question. "You remember All the President's Men? Deep Throat told Robert Redford, 'Follow the money.' That is good advice for accountants and reporters."

"For cops as well," Zander added.

"And can I tell you that this is not the worst of it?"

"I'm still listening."

"Ozbek has funneled much of his extorted money into businesses all over the world. Most are totally legitimate, but some are dirty. I don't have enough documented proof yet, but I have no doubt there's a direct link between what you could call organized crime and certain politicians and their associates, including Bulent, which is fitting since he wants to move into the Prime Minister's office himself. I believe that in exchange for the politicians looking the other way at drug or arms deals or money laundering, the criminals handle certain problems for them."

"What kind of problems?" Zander asked, but

giving Goktepe only half his attention. He had turned the balance inwards in a squall of self-pity. An hour ago, sitting confidently outside the ambassador's office, Ozbek had seemed within his grasp. Now, the more Goktepe revealed, the more foolish he felt. He slipped his sunglasses off and squinted at the brilliant sky, amazed at his own naiveté. This kind of shit, he told himself, was probably going on here while dinosaurs were still falling into the La Brea tar pits.

"Mostly protesting students and nosy journalists," Goktepe replied. "I'm embarrassed as a Turk to say that a dozen reporters have died mysteriously in the past 15 years. Some have drowned; others have had packages explode in their hands. But not one case has been solved."

"But you're still here. And there can't be anyone nosier than you."

"A degree of notoriety has protected me." Goktepe flexed his sling-bound arm. "But that hasn't stopped them from issuing a warning,"

"You didn't get that playing basketball?"

"No. A flight of stairs I did not go down voluntarily."

"The police are no help?"

"I do not want you to think I'm paranoid, but these people own the police. Ozbek first among them. But if you still want that introduction I'll call my former editor and he'll arrange it."

"Christ!" Zander snarled, pushing his chair back. He grabbed a cigarette from Goktepe's pack and lit it. "This is shutting off the one possibility I had. It's the only reason I'm here."

"Have you talked to the police?"

Zander could tell from the journalist's tone that "yes" was the wrong answer. "I haven't myself, but Scotland Yard contacted the officials here when they first suspected a Turkish connection to my friend's disappearance."

"Then the chances are good Ozbek already knows you are here. And if he knows you're looking for him he'll contact you—if he wants to see you."

"No, he couldn't know I'm here. That wouldn't have come up."

"As you say. But I do not recommend going to the police."

Zander nodded, but the notion that the police—not just a bad cop but the entire police force—couldn't be trusted was frightening. "Do you know where Ozbek lives?"

Goktepe pointed across the water. "You can see it from here. This is the Sea of Marmara and those are the Princes Islands. Ozbek has built himself a compound from several Ottoman mansions. I'm told there hasn't been anything like it since the time of the last Sultan."

The journalist pulled a business card from his jacket pocket. "Take a look at the Express website. I have built a very deep section on Ozbek's business networks there. It's not for public use, but enter your last name as a password. I will set it up for you."

Zander tucked the card into his breast pocket.

"Good luck," Goktepe said, shaking Zander's hand. "I met Ozbek years ago, when I was an accountant and before he got involved in any of this shady business. He didn't seem like a bad fellow. I haven't talked to him since, but I'm told now that he's so uh—what's the word?—so *grand*, like a pasha, that he just takes whatever he wants." Goktepe paused for a moment, his lips pursed, seemingly searching for the right words.

"What is it?" Zander asked.

"Do you suppose that your friend has something Ozbek wants?"

Zander pulled the brim of his cap down in the face of a gusting wind. He scanned the streaming barges and the islands beyond them and wondered if he was looking at Penny's prison. "I don't know," he said, but guessed she might.

Chapter 3

A piercing screech rousted Penny from her narcotic sleep. It took only a moment to find her visitor's probing black eyes through the open window. He raised his fierce head and hooked beak: a big, sleek bird with a fan of white and ochre feathers. Some sort of eagle, Penny thought, watching it rock on a pine branch. "Go!" she hissed at her tormentor, who jerked his head forward but then flapped his wings and disappeared.

She scanned the sun-drenched room from her four-poster bed: its dark wood paneling, inlaid ceiling, and marble slab floor softened with an ancient kilim. A peek beneath the blanket confirmed what she sensed: she was naked. Anxiety simmered in her stomach and she struggled to remember where she was. She had no recollection of arriving, of undressing, or climbing into bed; only the fuzzy image of boarding a helicopter on a darkened tarmac.

Perhaps she'd been drugged, though she wasn't sluggish or woozy. If anything, she felt hyper-alert. Not seeing her clothes anywhere, she wrapped herself in the blanket and searched a mahogany wardrobe and walk-in closet. Both were empty.

She retreated to the bathroom, and emerged five minutes later wearing a silk robe, startled to find the bed made and everything she'd been wearing yesterday—black jeans, T-shirt, bra, panties, socks, and sneakers—laid out for her, cleaned and pressed.

She dressed and brushed her hair before trying the door. It was locked, which didn't surprise her. Standing beneath the open transom, she heard a violin playing Bartók over distant speakers.

Breakfast had arrived along with her clothes, set out on a small table between the tall windows: melon, orange juice, rolls and cheese, an omelet on a glass-lidded silver plate, a bowl of assorted berries, and tea. A note card was propped against a crystal vase holding a magnolia cutting: "Please join me when you are ready."

Her appetite surprised her. At first sight the meal had seemed a ludicrous addition to an absurd room, but she hadn't had a bite since lunch yesterday and wound up devouring everything, doing her best to reconstruct the prior 24 hours as she ate. She could barely fathom strolling through Bloomsbury yesterday afternoon. It felt like weeks ago. She shuddered at the memory of those animals beating Zander, his head and face a bloody mess.

She was still sipping her tea, her stomach churning at the prospect of leaving this seemingly safe cocoon, when a key turned in the lock, and a short, bald man in a butler's uniform entered. He bowed and motioned for Penny to follow him. She steeled herself and her silent escort led her down a corridor that hugged a courtyard.

The Bartók was growing more exuberant.

She followed the butler up a double flight of marble stairs. At the top of the landing she stopped and stared through an oversized entryway in shock. There, under the center of a towering rococo dome, mesmerized by his own playing, stood Bulent Ozbek.

Something, perhaps the intensity of her glare, broke Ozbek's concentration. He lowered his bow and handed the instrument to the butler, who departed with it down the stairs. Ozbek turned an expressionless face toward Penny and held up a finger to signify, "One moment." He filled a ceramic bowl with water from a blue-glazed pitcher, washed his hands and gently dried them with a white towel.

Penny held her spot on the wide-plank floor, just beyond the fringe of the carpet. Ozbek was dressed casually and seemed at ease. Penny, on the other hand, felt her fury rise with Ozbek's every step closer. He stopped three feet away.

"Bulent," she said, her voice quivering. "*You* kidnapped me?"

He did not say anything, but just stared into her eyes, a tight smile turning up the corners of his mouth.

"And don't give me some damned silent treatment."

"No, Penny, no silent treatment."

"Then where the hell am I and what am I doing here?"

"You're in Istanbul. At my home."

"But why?"

"That's more complicated, but you'll understand shortly."

"I don't want to hear *shortly*," she fumed. "Tell me

what's going on!"

She was on the ground before she took another breath. Ozbek had slapped her, hard, across the face. She stayed down, her arm drawn defensively across her cheek, terrified that he might strike her again. She had no illusion this was a dream, but she was numb with the feeling that some kind of cosmic error had placed her here. She didn't deserve this.

She raised herself up on one knee, rubbing her hand across her mouth. Part of her wanted to spring at his legs and take him down. But she knew he could overcome any momentary advantage she might enjoy. One good shot wasn't worth a pounding. She didn't see or taste any blood, but the left side of her face was on fire. She'd never been hit before in her life. Not like that.

"Get up," he said, not as a command, but in a tone a parent would use after disciplining a child. He extended his hand. She stood on her own. Ozbek reached for her cheek, apparently to soothe the pain, but she pulled away.

"What do you want?" she finally said.

"Please," Ozbek said, "your anger is not helpful. All I need is your cooperation and you'll be on your way back to London or Sicily or wherever you want. Now let's go."

She followed Ozbek out onto a broad slate terrace. She approached the edge and leaned over a waist-high stone wall, beyond which the manicured property dropped off into a wilderness until it reached the sea. The Istanbul skyline rose on the horizon. For the first time she understood she was on one of the Princes Islands, and she turned around to examine her prison. It was a yali, a grand summer home of the Ottoman gentry, built by a member of the Imperial court whose fortunes rose and fell in tandem with the Sultan's. It made sad sense to her that Ozbek saw himself as a modern incarnation of such a man. She looked out over the boats plying the sea-lane between the island and the city. Seeing civilization so close reassured her. She leaned further over the wall to measure the immediate drop and for a moment she contemplated leaping the wall and taking her chances on reaching one of those boats.

Perhaps Ozbek was reading her mind, for he grabbed her elbow and led her in silence along a gravel path to a second yali, painted yellow and with a red ceramic roof. It was smaller and plainer than the main house, but still grand. A guard stood aside as Ozbek entered a security code that opened a sliding glass door.

The building had been reconstructed to accommodate his collections. The ground floor was devoted to Egyptian and Mezo-American statues, jewelry, and wall paintings. She wanted to stop and examine several seemingly flawless pieces, but she would not flatter him. More than once she yearned to grab an ancient stone and drive it into his skull.

"I thought seeing this would put you in the right frame of mind for the work ahead," he said.

What work? she wondered, unable to imagine any skill she had that a thousand others couldn't provide willingly.

They were passing a wall of royal Egyptian gold when Ozbek directed her through another glass door. Inside the lights were dim and the chill raised goose bumps on her arms. Ozbek examined a thermostat, which seemed to meet his approval. Penny realized they were inside a gallery of antique death. There were mummies and statues of underworld gods as well as funerary masks and artifacts from a dozen ancient cultures on six continents. On a raised platform rested three skeletons—a father, mother and child—partially encased in hardened volcanic ash, the parents' faces raised toward heaven in a death shout as lava incinerated them. Penny couldn't help peeking into a finely carved Roman sarcophagus, the lid pushed off center. A face—half skeleton, half parchment-like skin—smiled back at her, touching off a memory of a daytrip she'd taken through the Palermo catacombs with Linus Crane. Still disoriented from Ozbek's blow, an appalling image of Crane's own decomposing face settled atop the ancient Roman's neck.

"Come look at this," Ozbek implored, jarring Penny from her morbid fantasy. She came around the sarcophagus and looked through a glass covering. Repulsed at first, she stared closely at what looked like something that had spent eons trapped in a peat bog. It was, he explained, a young woman who lived 30,000 years ago in what is now Denmark. Her brown, leathery skin and her hair were largely intact, preserved by a glacial flow. She lay on her side, tucked in a fetal pose. Ozbek grinned. "It's more anthropological than archaeological, but I couldn't resist."

His glee sapped Penny's interest. "You must be crazy if you think I care about any of this. Just tell me what you want."

Ozbek led her out of the museum building and they walked further along the gravel-covered path, passing another beefy security guard, his vigil fixed toward the property's perimeter wall.

They approached yet another mansion, this one far larger than the museum. A pair of stone lions slept by the doors. She stopped in her tracks, unwilling to contain herself. "Do you know what happened to Linus?"

The question did not seem to faze Ozbek, who folded his arms and took a moment to look Penny up and down, as if deciding whether she was old enough to hear the answer. "Professor Crane reneged on an understanding."

Penny took Ozbek's response as a provocation. "What understanding?"

"I suppose there wasn't any reason for you to know."

"Know *what*?"

"When I met with Linus at Harvard last year.... you recall, you were there. The day I replaced his lost funding."

"I remember."

"It was not an insubstantial sum. Four-hundred-and-fifty-thousand dollars."

"Yes, I saw the check. From one of your foundations. It seemed very generous of you," she acknowledged.

"And I was happy to do it. It is rare one gets the opportunity to underwrite someone so deserving as Linus Crane."

"And you reached some understanding that day?"

"Indeed. Something very simple. I asked that if he came across any important pieces in the course of the summer's work that he turn them over to me for disposition, and that he not disclose their existence without my approval."

"That's preposterous," Penny insisted, understanding now that Ozbek was nothing more than a well-dressed tomb robber. "Linus would never agree to that!"

"Why do you say that?"

"Number one, because it's against university policy," she said, not sure if it was or not. "And besides, doesn't the Turkish state own all antiquities no matter who finds them?"

"True. But the state can dispose of its property as it chooses." His wink clenched Penny's jaw. "As for Harvard, Linus was important enough to make his own policies."

Penny thought about the mosaic. Was it the source of the dispute? "So you're saying that Linus found something he wouldn't turn over to you?"

"That's right."

"I'll know you're lying if you tell me he kept something for himself."

"No no, not at all. Linus Crane wasn't capable of such a thing any more than you. But he made clear, unfortunately, that what he uncovered was too important to put into my hands. You'd think he'd found the Holy Grail. And then he took off for London to make what would have been a rather dramatic announcement. Of course, I couldn't let that happen."

"Then how could you look me in the eye and offer your condolences?" she asked. She raised her fists to pound his chest but he grabbed her wrists. "What kind of monster are you?"

Ozbek's eyes tightened and his nostrils flared. She was certain he was going to hit her again and she braced herself. Instead, he opened the door to the building, which had been refurbished as modern office space. They passed an unattended reception desk and headed to the end of a well-lit, empty corridor. They stopped outside a closed door.

"You and I are going to have our own understanding," he said.

She heard the words and appreciated the threat but felt too defeated to face him.

Ozbek opened the office and flipped on the overhead lights. Penny looked in the doorway and trembled.

Chapter 4

Extrapolating from Horace Lloyd-Walker's conjectures, her own deep archaeological knowledge, and the history of Constantinople she now immersed herself in, it did not take Helen long to construct a profile of the building she believed might house Linus Crane's great mosaic. In fact, the more she read and hypothesized during her British Airways morning flight to Turkey the more optimistic she grew.

Just before going to bed, she had phoned the Met's vice director, her nominal boss, to let him know she had learned of a phenomenal piece coming to the market in Istanbul. The chief didn't ask any questions and Helen didn't offer any details, especially that the object was outside her realm. Met departments guarded their turf like Cerberus at the gates of hell and there was no way either Medieval or Greek and Roman would let her chase down something for them. But she felt better checking in, since at least she could honestly say she was representing the Met.

In some ways, Crane's mosaic, magnificent as it

was, had become only a stepping-stone. Her goal was the Athena Parthenos itself. The possibility that the gold-and-ivory goddess had long ago been stripped like an abandoned Corvette on the Van Wyck Expressway, its vandalized carcass hauled away for scrap, she dismissed out of hand. The Parthenos *had* to exist, and if it didn't she would will it into being. Bring it back to New York like King Kong, Helen thought, and the Met was hers. She felt as if her whole life had been spent in preparation for this.

She had briefly considered recruiting Bulent Ozbek to her cause in the midst of packing, but had decided against it and remained confident in her decision. Even though his knowledge and contacts would be invaluable, he would push her aside and take control if they got within sniffing distance of the goddess. Her father had always told her there's only one lead dog on any team.

Despite Istanbul's vastness—with more than 13 million people it is larger than any city in Europe, and half the city lies east of the Bosporus Strait on the Asian mainland —Helen was confident that the clues already in hand made a potentially unwieldy hunt manageable. The fact that the mosaic was Byzantine sharply narrowed the search. Though Istanbul is an ancient city, relatively few Byzantine structures survive, including fewer than 30 churches. What's more, the old Byzantine city was largely confined within a fortified fifth-century wall on the European side erected by the Emperor Theodosius II to turn back Attila the Hun and his Golden Horde. All the places she held suspect—select churches and public buildings— were in this section of the city, which the residents call

Stamboul. She could cover Stamboul in three days.

She also felt it was safe to skip the most famous buildings, such as Saint Sophia, because a discovery of the magnitude suggested by Linus Crane and Horace Lloyd-Walker couldn't possibly remain secret in such heavily trafficked spaces. And since Crane had evidently seen the mosaic within the past few weeks, it must be accessible, though certainly not in plain sight.

Taking Horace Lloyd-Walker's recommendation, Helen's only stop before hitting the streets was the scholars-only archive in the State Archaeology Museum, which was housed in a neo-classical limestone hall on the fringes of Topkapi, not far from her hotel. She was dressed comfortably but was weighed down by her oversized carryall. Beyond her normal daytrip paraphernalia—make-up, sunglasses, pepper spray—Helen had her laptop, maps and guidebooks, camera, her "good luck" Ivory Nubian from Hazim the unfortunate Syrian, and pictures of Linus Crane clipped from the London newspapers. The best clue, she figured, might be a caretaker or cleric who recalled seeing the professor recently. She also carried $8,000 in cash, mostly for greasing palms. She knew from digs in the Anatolian hinterland that "whole ones," as greenbacks were known on the black market, were the preferred form of *rusvet*. The booming illicit trade in antiquities had made sophisticates of even ox-worshipping villagers who happened across a rarity in their dung-covered fields. No more buying Manhattan for wampum, she knew.

She parked herself in a corner of the archive's sub-sub basement with the facsimile edition of a thousand-year-old map and several Latin and Greek texts. She was disappointed, for while she found numerous mentions of the Parthenos, they added nothing to what Lloyd-Walker had told her at Oxford.

Helen closed her eyes and the front page of *The New York Times* appeared: below the fold, a tall picture of the Athena Parthenos, a photo of herself inset at the goddess's feet, and the four-column headline: *Met Curator Finds Greatest Ancient Treasure*. She smiled at the vividness of her own imagination and sank further into the cushioned seat.

The next sound she heard, she could tell through closed eyes, was someone tiptoeing around her table. She didn't even recall putting her head down. She opened one eye just enough to make out the form of a man—fortyish, short, angled features and one extended eyebrow—before springing up like a rattler. "Yes?"

"I'm sorry to disturb you." The man took a nervous step back.

Helen checked her watch. It was 5:30. She'd been asleep a half-hour.

"I'm Busra Kazan, head of the Archive." He proffered his hand, which Helen shook without interest. "You've hidden yourself away down here."

"I prefer the quiet."

"You are our first visitor from the Met in some time and I only came to offer my assistance." She wanted to shoo him away, but thought he'd depart on his own after sniffing around for a minute. When he gave no indication of leaving, Helen closed the lid on her laptop and was about to get up when his demeanor changed from curious to amused.

"What's so funny?"

"I'm sorry," Kazan said, calming like a pot of

boiling water that's been taken off the burner. "We get one or two a year."

"One or two what?"

"People searching for the Athena."

Helen's poker face deserted her. How long had this idiot been here before I woke up? she wondered. Had he scrolled through her computer? She smiled. "Assuming that's why I'm here, what can you tell me about it?"

"What would you like to know?"

Helen saw no reason to dance around the issue. "Has anything been found?"

"Has anything been found?" Kazan repeated, blushing. "No, of course not. Don't be silly. There's nothing to find."

"Thanks for your help, Mr. Kazan. I'll be sure to return the favor next time you need the Met's assistance."

He reached for her arm. "Please forgive me. I'm only trying to save you time and trouble."

"How could you do that?"

"Come upstairs with me."

Helen's curiosity overtook her desire to leave Kazan worrying that he'd joined the Met's "enemies list." She threw her loose items into the carryall and followed the director upstairs to the spacious periodical room. Racks of professional journals surrounded foursomes of club chairs. Kazan led her to the only occupied seat, where an elderly, white-haired man in a pinstriped navy suit sat ramrod straight reading the *Times of London.*

"You look well, my friend," Kazan told him as they shook hands.

"Of course I do. Why shouldn't I?"

Kazan introduced Helen to Odysseus Simonedes.

"Simonedes here is on the trail of the Parthenos," Kazan told her. "And I believe Dr. Vandameer shares your interest, Odysseus. I shall leave the two of you alone."

"Ah. A goddess in search of a goddess."

Helen felt calmed by Simonedes's charm and Kazan's departure.

"He's an idiot," Simonedes said, winning Helen over. "Would you care to sit?"

"I'm really running late."

"You've got much to do?" he asked.

"Quite a lot. Yes."

"Kazan doesn't believe the Parthenos exists."

"But you do?"

"Of course. Who could destroy anything so beautiful? I assume you agree? Or is Kazan having some fun at my expense?"

"If he were, I assure you I wouldn't be party to it."

"I hope not," he said, patting Helen's hand.

"You're Greek."

"Yes, but my family has very deep roots in Turkey—more than a thousand years. Besides, who else but a Greek should find the goddess?" Simonedes slapped his chest. "Every Greek carries the breath of the ancients in his soul. We would all sacrifice to regain Athena's glory, which is why I am here. Do not let anyone tell you different. There is a hole in the heart of every Greek that will only be filled by her return."

The depth of Simonedes's feeling startled Helen. His hunger was palpable.

"Do you share any Greek blood?" he asked.

She smiled. "I'm afraid not. But do you think you're close?"

"I have no doubt. Very close indeed."

Helen finally sat.

Chapter 5

Zander used hand signals after Goktepe left the cafe to order another cup of the jet fuel they called coffee, along with a platter of lamb in yogurt sauce. When the salt spray sent a chill up his arms he pushed back from under the umbrella's shade and into the sunlight. Lack of sleep and Goktepe's portrait of Ozbek had deflated him. He felt pale and withered and needed the sun to recharge.

His lunch tasted better than it looked. Zander stared at the island where Goktepe said Ozbek had his estate. The narrow sea-lane looked as chaotic as the Long Beach Freeway, jammed with pleasure cruisers, garbage haulers, ferries, tankers, and sailboats. Splotches of color dotted a waterfront village on Ozbek's island. The possibility that Penny was only a motorboat ride away was almost calming. Maybe the haystack wasn't so big after all.

Zander questioned how he had come to consider Ozbek his ally. Everything he knew about him was second hand at best. But the guy was more revered than

Mother Theresa. Penny praised his generosity, intellect, and compassion. Could she have been duped? Harvard took his money. Were they taking donations from criminals? And the Bureau endorsed him. Goodrich would have told him if the guy was either bent or dangerous.

Zander forced himself to consider that Penny was working some angle. True, he barely knew her. But he couldn't believe his instincts were that wrong.

He paid his bill and started walking back to his hotel, sticking to the main road that hugged the water. No doubt there was a faster route, but he was sure he'd get lost.

Heavy traffic crept along beside him, fouling the air. But between the noxious clouds, a cool sea breeze blew in, tempering the overheated cement and macadam. Just after turning toward Topkapi—his North Star—he stopped beside a wall of large tiles patterned like a gold-hued Oriental rug. A pipe at the base shot out a stream of crystal water, like an oasis in a concrete desert. He bent down and splashed his face.

On the move again, Zander wondered what proof Goktepe had against Ozbek? Was his newspaper nothing more than the Turkish *National Enquirer*? Not long ago Goktepe and Ozbek were both young professionals on the make. Now Ozbek was rich and Goktepe was driving a piece-of-shit VW. Was it simple envy? Zander knew that tune. It was a side of himself he didn't care for.

With his hotel in sight, he passed through a crowd of tourists taking turns posing with a trained bear being led around by a chain through its nose. The sight left Zander depressed; he felt he had about as many options as the bear. Even if Goktepe was right—that Ozbek was merely a thug hiding behind a veneer of money and political access—Zander still had to get to him. He would call Goktepe to set it up.

Nobody was minding the hotel desk, but from the back room Zander heard the patter of a Turkish DJ somehow segueing between The Carpenters' *Close to You* and Miles Davis's *All Blues*. He rapped on the counter, noticing that several mailboxes held message, including his. When no one emerged he grabbed the slip of paper from his cubbyhole and was excited but concerned when he saw Norman Parrish's name and "Skotland Yard—URGENT."

Chapter 6

Penny squirmed at the touch of Bulent Ozbek's hand on her shoulder. "Go ahead," he said, pushing her inside the office.

She lurched ahead and stopped to look around the high-ceilinged room with its old fluorescent fixtures. A pair of tall windows consumed the far wall, both open but barred outside. Ozbek left the door open, letting a breeze blow through, but the white walls still smelled of fresh paint. Metal shelving crammed with books and journals covered one long wall. On the opposite side, beside a lumpy couch, cardboard boxes overflowed with loose papers. A badly scratched wood desk and three folding chairs were bunched near the windows.

She moved along, running her hand over the books like a priest offering solace to a crowd of mourners. Her insides plummeted as her eyes settled on volumes once handed to her by Linus Crane. "Are you some kind of ghoul?" she asked, her despair leaving her oblivious to his rage. "How did you get all this?"

Ozbek stretched. "How this got here is trivia. *Why*

it is here is the question."

A grossly overweight young man ambled inside, his wide face and chin sitting atop his shoulders as if he'd been assembled without a neck. "This is Hikmet," she heard Ozbek say, but her eyes were fixed on a laptop with a Bugs Bunny decal the young man was opening and booting up.

"That's Linus's computer," she said, picturing him at his Harvard desk, laughing as he answered the scores of emails that arrived daily from around the world.

Ozbek closed the door. "Very observant."

Penny looked past Ozbek, through green latticework to a flower garden and, further back, a pine forest. She shivered at the prospect of staying in this room.

Ozbek gripped the back of Hikmet's chair. "Let me spell things out for you. The last conversation Linus Crane and I had, he insisted that no one country, let alone one man, could ever possess what he'd uncovered. The heritage of all mankind, he called it."

Penny felt her anxiety ebb. She was drawing sustenance from Crane's courage and Ozbek's anguish. "If that's what Linus thought, no doubt he was right."

Ozbek slammed the desk. "I'm sure you think so. In my view, though, ignorant bureaucrats and small-minded academics are the last people on earth to control such a wellhead of power, not to mention an object of sublime beauty and majesty. Something that Linus Crane felt was worth his life."

Penny wondered how much Ozbek actually knew about what Linus had found. On the one hand, she felt she already knew more than him. If he had Linus's photos of the mosaic he probably would have stuck them in her face. On the other hand, this powerful and majestic object he described couldn't be the mosaic, could it? What had Linus told him? She did not even want to ask a question, fearing she would give too much away and compromise what little leverage she might have.

"He knew the implication of the choice he made," Ozbek continued. "And his dilemma is now yours. In this room and on this computer is everything Linus Crane left behind. That includes his London presentation. I'm sure you're aware that Crane kept his notes in some sort of gibberish shorthand."

"And you think I can figure it out?" Penny asked, understanding at last why she'd been brought to Turkey. "What if I can't?" she added, afraid to pose her true question: what if I won't?

Ozbek ignored her reservation. "I said before that you and I would reach an understanding, and this is it: you will analyze what is on this computer, with all of Crane's resources at your disposal, and you will tell me what he did not." Ozbek nodded at his associate. "Hikmet is at your disposal. He's an MIT-trained computer scientist and speaks half-a-dozen languages." He headed toward the door. "You have 48 hours."

Chapter 7

Helen scooted out of the periodical room, leaving Odysseus Simonedes to his *Times*.

Hearing him say he was close to finding the Parthenos had raised her competitive hackles. Still, why not piggyback on some of his work, she thought. "Do you mind if I ask how long you've been looking?" she had asked him.

But the question seemed only to trigger a wave of reveries for the old man. He lost his focus and lifted his head high, as if he wanted the gods to hear him. She wondered if his claim was a delusion. He seemed sweet and well-intentioned and in need of a sympathetic ear, but she had no time. Not today.

Helen jumped into a taxi and told the driver to head for the furthest outpost on her itinerary: Kariye Mosque, known before the Ottoman conquest as Saint Savior in Chora.

It felt good to be on the move, no longer simply preparing. She reminded herself that despite the archivist's skepticism, she had a piece of the puzzle they had never seen. Winners rise above the riffraff, she reminded herself.

Helen gritted her teeth at the row of motor coaches stretching off toward the church. A mass exodus of silver-haired Germans—the women outnumbering the men four to one—forced her to wait outside. She could see that the church was thick with seniors, stooped with age and HD camcorders, following their guides around like attentive third-graders. Helen cursed the rabble under her breath and grabbed a pamphlet from a box alongside a glass case that held a medieval manuscript open to display an exquisite Byzantine calligraphy.

The temperature dropped a few degrees when she finally made it inside. Historical claptrap ricocheted in 10 languages off the ancient squinches and arches, fusing into an indistinguishable din. Still, the noise couldn't undermine the encompassing beauty. She realized that scrutinizing Saint Savior might consume the day. The church was covered with mosaics and frescoes: Two domes packed with Christ's ancestors from Adam onwards; scenes from the life of Jesus; an apocryphal life of the Virgin; the lives of the saints; a study of Christ's infancy. Nook after nook begged for attention.

Iron railings kept crowds away from the walls. Helen maneuvered like she was walking the length of a packed subway, scanning up and down, back and forth, straining her neck in case a mosaic was sitting atop a poorly lit arch, or even using the long lens on her digital Nikon as a telescope. On three occasions a niche that called to mind something in the Athena mosaic prompted a second look, but nothing more. She drew an X on the church map as she left each section. When she had crossed out everything, she tipped a guard to let her peek behind rusty gates that protected a few royal tombs, but saw nothing special.

The only thing she found unusual was a tall, hard-bodied young man she bumped into while craning her neck toward a distant Madonna. She excused herself, felt a wave of deja vu, but kept on going. She tried picturing him in something other than his Bermuda shorts and polo shirt, but still couldn't place him.

She left Saint Savior disappointed. A beautiful sunset was overtaking the city. She flagged a taxi and told the driver to head toward the Hyatt, wanting to see one more structure, something near the hotel. Two of the city's ancient underground reservoirs were on her list. Helen chose the Cistern of a Thousand and One Columns.

The caretaker there, a small man with a narrow face and delicate hands, said the cistern was closed to the public. Helen said she understood and peeled off a $20 bill, but the caretaker started closing the door nevertheless. He stopped when she pulled out a hundred and stuck a picture of Linus Crane in his face. Helen couldn't tell if he was wondering why she was showing him the photo or if he was trying to recall if he'd seen this person before. She pulled a different shot of Crane out of her bag and the caretaker's eyes lit up. This excited Helen and she signaled that she was ready to see the cistern.

The caretaker waved her off to the side. She watched him pull back a beat-up rug they'd been standing on and lift a large trap door.

Helen stared into the black hole. Musty air blew past her from underground, reminding her of the basement of her parent's 18th century weekend house in New Paltz. Frigid, damp, and dark even on the hottest summer day. Her stinking brothers had once tied her up down there. She shivered at the memory. The caretaker opened a rusted metal panel on the wall and flipped two switches. Dim lights illuminated a deep stone stairwell. She thought about saving her inspection for the morning, but knew that wouldn't make a difference. The cistern existed in perpetual night.

The caretaker gestured for her to go down. She nodded yes, but stood still. "Any snakes down there?" she asked with a nervous laugh. When she realized he didn't understand, she held her breath and clambered down.

Chapter 8

Zander spooned sugar into his coffee and then angled the computer monitor to cut the late afternoon glare. He'd passed the Blue Crescent Internet Café on his walk back from lunch with the journalist Goktepe and now he'd returned to make sense of the news he'd gotten from London. But some internal alarm clock, a mystery of his brain chemistry, had gone off the moment he'd sat down, reminding him Layla was turning seven today. He'd never been away for his daughter's birthday before and it emptied him. He shook his head at the strangeness of everything around him, feeling like his only anchor was the memory of Layla's smile and the curl of her fingers. Without that he might float away forever. But knowing that the sun was just now rising in California and that she'd wake up to see his email first thing cheered him. And she wouldn't know it had taken him half the day to remember. He missed her more than anything in the world right now and he told her exactly that.

Clicking "send" brought him back to Istanbul. His

conversation with Scotland Yard had taken barely a minute. Parrish explained that his crew had widened its airport search yesterday and had found a ground worker in Southampton who recognized Penny from the police photo. Unfortunately he provided nothing useful about her abductors.

"But they took her to Istanbul," Zander had said.

"That's the flight plan they filed," Parrish confirmed.

Zander gulped his coffee and typed in the address for the Express newspaper website. He typed "Blake" when it requested a password and was thankful for Goktepe's efficiency. A few keystrokes later he was staring at Ozbek's empire.

Zander was amazed, though no longer surprised, as he panned up and down and across an astounding array of holding companies, operating units, and subsidiaries spread across 60 countries. Chemicals, construction, telecommunications, mining, pharmaceuticals, agriculture, and even the odd charity. Almost as amazing, he thought, waiting for a copy of the schematic to print out, was the journalist's meticulous information gathering.

"That son of a bitch," Zander grunted when he saw what he hoped to find in the recesses of Ozbek's corporate web: Anatolia Airlease. Parrish had told him that the plane out of Southampton had been registered to Anatolia Airlease. He clicked on Anatolia, which linked him to some aeronautical website.

Zander waved to the café's director, who was holding his Visa card for security. The young man, in black plants and black T-shirt with close-cropped hair, hurried over, apparently happy to get out from behind the front desk.

"Would you mind translating something for me?" Zander asked, glancing at the lopsided name tag that identified him as Taner.

"If I can," he said, peering over Zander's shoulder while nervously tugging on his single earring.

Zander pointed to the paragraphs under the Anatolia Airlease heading.

"It's just a list of assets for this airline," he said, mumbling to himself for a moment before offering a summary. "It says the company is the biggest lessor of business jets in Turkey—350 planes all together."

Zander slumped back in his seat. "Thanks," he said, as Taner scrambled back to the desk to answer the phone. This, he realized, was no smoking gun. Anatolia was most likely a completely legitimate business. And with such a huge fleet, he had no way to tie this one jet directly to Ozbek. Any of the airline's clients could have held the lease. If he were home he'd be on the phone with the prosecutor's office about getting a search warrant and impounding files. But he wasn't home and he needed to use the few tools he had at hand.

Chapter 9

Helen pressed the toe of her right boot into the packed dirt floor of the Cistern of A Thousand and One Columns, and let her eyes adjust to the dim light. She was near a corner, looking off into a forest of unfluted limestone columns, each easily 40 feet tall, supporting a segment of the endless vaulted ceiling.

The air was not as musty as she'd anticipated, but a faint farm stench hung in the air. Shallow mud puddles reflected off the floor. More than half the bare dusty bulbs in the towering brick walls were burnt out. She thought she could see the far corner maybe 300 feet away.

The place was dank and frightening and she was eager to get back up, but what better spot could there be to find something Crane had uncovered, hiding in plain sight? Helen made out some wall decorations toward the rear of the cistern and headed toward them.

She kept close to one of the walls since it would be easy to lose direction in the sea of columns. An occasional cigarette butt or silver gum wrapper told her that most visitors followed the same path. She let her hand drag across each column, like a kid who steps on every crack in the sidewalk to ward off the bogeyman.

She had moved about a hundred feet into the cistern when she thought she heard shouting from upstairs. She stopped to listen, but after a moment assumed the caretaker had simply turned on the television she saw in the cottage's corner. She resumed her slow march. But a frightening crash of dishes or glass stopped her again. More breaking glass, more shouting, and the crunch of smashing furniture. There was a full-scale brawl going on up there. The fight ended with a thump, a moan, and then quiet. Her stomach tightened into a fist when the cistern's few miserable lights blinked out and she heard someone descending the stairwell.

She ducked behind a column, caught her breath, and then peeked back toward the stairs. All she could make out was the outline of a man carrying an oversized flashlight. She stood, watching the blazing white beam scan the entire complex. As silently as possible, she reached into her bag for her pepper spray.

She realized she needed a diversion, so she pulled a few Turkish coins from her pocket and flung the heaviest one down a row of columns. As the man followed it, she inched toward the sliver of light that shone from the caretaker's cottage.

She had advanced no more than 15 feet before the stranger circled back. Light hit her like a splash of red paint and she barely had time to lift her hand before he was on her. The beacon shot directly in her eyes just as she sprayed his face. He yelped and swung his arms out, knocking the can from her hand.

Helen was exultant that she had saved herself, but she was effectively blind. Yellow blotches and black spots left by the xenon beam froze her in place. She heard the stranger staggering, slapping at his own face, gagging. She retreated by feeling her way between pillars. Eventually she found a wall.

Even as she tried to rub sight back into her eyes, her heart beating like a 12-cylinder engine, Helen was pleased to hear her attacker's agony. She thought he had vomited, but now his whimpers were diminishing. She stood flat against a column, her sight slowly returning. But her pursuer had recovered enough to retrieve his flashlight, which now beamed back and forth across the cistern. As far as Helen could tell, he was inching down an aisle close to the center.

At last Helen could make out the light from the cottage again. She thought she was closer to the steps than he was, but she wasn't sure she could outrun him. Besides, Helen thought, after the pepper spray he was probably ready to rip her to pieces.

Confident that the angle between them would let her move unseen, she dashed to the next column, then the next, and then a third, all toward the stairs. Each time she moved with all the grace that a dozen years of ballet class allowed. But a careless step let her bag scrape roughly across a column. In the awful silence of the cistern it carried like a dinner bell. She had maybe 10 yards to go, but she heard him turn. She froze. The flashlight continued to crisscross the chamber. He was moving quickly now. Helen was certain he would emerge any moment.

The only weapon she had left was surprise. Her

breathing had grown shallow as a yogi's and the darkness seemed to amplify her hearing. She sensed his every step. Now she was sure. He was coming down the aisle next to her, less than three columns away. The flashlight's beam brushed the wall in front of her. The closer he came the more noise he made, masking the sound of Helen sliding the shoulder bag down her arm. She gripped the strap in her right hand and wrapped it around her wrist, as though trying to pull a powerful dog on a leash. A second later, as he stepped between the last two columns, Helen whipped the carryall across her body like an Olympic hammer. The bag landed squarely in the man's face. Something broke. No doubt her Nikon. Once again the flashlight fell to the ground, the beam illuminating the area like a spotlight. Helen jumped in front of the man as he staggered backward, blood pouring through his cupped hands. She was stunned for a moment to see it was the hard-bodied man who had caught her eye at Saint Savior! She stepped forward and shot her right leg up like a missile, delivering her boot directly into the crotch of his Bermuda shorts. The stranger doubled over in a swamp of agony. Helen heard him collapse to the ground as she raced for the stairs, taking them two at a time.

She emerged into the cottage to find the caretaker bleeding from the head but already reviving. She kept on running, out the front door and into the dark night.

Her thundering heart calmed slightly as she moved into the middle of the noisy crowd in the public square outside the cottage. Old and young strolled by, many hand in hand, even as children dashed among them, playing tag. Men who looked old enough to remember the last Sultan relaxed on wooden benches, some slicing cheese or sausage onto crusts of bread. She took a deep breath and was about to ask a passing couple to point her toward her hotel when she was startled to spot a familiar face across the square.

Chapter 10

Zander called the American Consulate the next morning. He had decided to track down Ned Nolan, Dean Goodrich's buddy on the FBI's terrorist task force. The Bureau was his only potential path to find some cops in Istanbul he could trust—national, local, or provincial, he didn't care, as long as they could act as a lifeline for whatever mess he got into tracking Penny. The urgency he felt the evening before doubled when heard on CNN that the five convicted terrorists had been hung overnight. He was used to inmates on California's death row lingering for a decade on appeals before taking their final injection. Weren't the bombers arrested just the day before yesterday?

The consulate's receptionist said she didn't see Ned Nolan in her directory, but connected Zander to an unidentified official who let him explain that he was a police detective and had been directed to Nolan by an FBI agent in London. The official put him on hold for almost five minutes before coming back to say that Nolan had given his okay to stop by the bomb site.

Zander grabbed a taxi right outside his pension and 15 minutes later found Ground Zero hidden behind a curtain of black tarpaulins draped between telephone poles and suspended from wire 75 feet up. American military police stood guard at the seams. Flashing his LAPD shield as I.D., the M.P. Zander approached phoned for an escort. A sergeant named Rivera led him inside.

Focused solely on Nolan, Zander had given little thought to what he would find behind the tarp. "My God," he said aloud, never having seen such devastation in person before. "I had no idea."

"Yes, sir," Rivera agreed. "It's hard to believe until you see it."

They ambled across the 150 yards encircled by the hanging tarps. Zander listened intently to Rivera's account of the rescue efforts that followed the bombing, his tone a roller coaster of reverence for the dead and fury at the enemy. The sergeant said that the temporary morgue had already been removed, though two large tents they walked past were still functioning as forensic laboratories. Sweeping his arm for emphasis, Rivera indicated where portable bleacher seats and chairs had held the 1,500 American sailors.

Zander's breath grew short as they neared the ruined hulk. He couldn't imagine how anyone survived.

"The concert was originally set for indoors," Rivera said, his voice losing its edge. "But the audience was so large we moved the show outside. We assume the bombers never realized that, otherwise we would have had a lot more than 536 dead."

Tarps were suspended above the wreckage and where the bleachers had been to prevent rain from fouling the investigation. What was left of the bleachers had been bulldozed into three mountains of twisted metal and splintered wood. Zander noticed bloodstains on the ground and was sure that a lot more had already been scrubbed out.

Rivera asked him to wait while he ducked inside the wreckage. A minute later, Ned Nolan emerged wearing a miner's hat atop his round, appealing face. He was of average height, but with the short neck and husky build of a high-school wrestler. Wisps of gray hair escaping his hardhat suggested that he was well into middle age, but as he came nearer, his unlined face argued that he was barely 30. Zander took Nolan's sweaty hand. It was the grip of a strong but tired man.

"Dean Goodrich said I might hear from you," Nolan said, tossing Zander a hardhat. "If you don't mind I need to keep working."

Zander eased the helmet on top of his baseball cap and followed Nolan inside. "I had the impression this case was closed," he said.

"Not for us, it isn't."

It was hard to distinguish inside from outside. Most of the roof had been blown away, as had the entire side of the building facing the concert. A brick wall marked the left side of the path they took. Whatever once marked the right was gone.

Nolan stopped three-quarters of the way to the rear, pulled on a pair of nylon gloves, and began examining a small section of wall, going over it lightly with his hand. Despite the high sun, he still turned his helmet light on.

"What are you looking for?" Zander asked.

"Pretty much anything. Pieces of explosive—or the

vehicle used to deliver it. We've got most of it. I'm just going over the place one last time." He pulled a mountaineer's hammer out of his belt. "So how do you think I can help you?" he asked, extracting something with the claw.

Zander started telling Nolan about Penny's abduction, but Nolan interrupted him.

"Goodrich gave me the basics. Your girlfriend was snatched off the street in London. Dean wanted you to look up some bigwig here who could help you out? Have you done that?"

"The situation has changed since I saw Goodrich."

"How so?"

"I suspect that the guy Goodrich thought could help me—Ozbek, his name is—may be the kidnapper."

Nolan stepped back. "You're shittin' me."

"I wish I was."

"You've been to the police?"

"I'm told the police are in this guy's pocket."

"Christ. What about the consulate?"

"They say they're too busy with all this." He glanced around. "And I can't blame them."

"And Goodrich told you I could help?"

"I need official entree to the prosecutors' office or whoever the Bureau is liasing with."

Nolan slipped his hammer back into his belt. "Man, I'd like to help you. I really would. But I haven't been outside a 500-yard radius of this crater since I drove in from the airport two-and-a-half weeks ago. Even my hotel is just on the other side of those trees. Actually, you caught me on a *good* day. I've been on my hands and knees for so long I thought I'd forgotten how to walk. If you'd been here a couple of days ago I would have sent you to the Agent-in-Charge. Very sharp guy. Close to the director. But he's gone and so are his assistants. Only a handful of us are left. The Turks have treated us like fucking children. Let us handle the ballistics and forensics, but they didn't let our people spend five minutes with their suspects, which tells me it was all garbage. Regardless, we were 95-percent done a week ago. Most everyone blew out when the convictions came down."

Zander took a deep breath. He understood Nolan's situation and he appreciated his honesty, but it didn't temper his frustration. He was mulling over what straw to grasp at next when a GI ran up to Nolan.

"Sir?" the soldier said, handing a metal shard to the agent.

"Good work, son." Nolan sent the soldier away. He tossed the piece to Zander. "Part of the detonator." No bigger than a trunk key, the dull scrap looked like sandlot trash. "We've got virtually the whole thing now. Walk with me while I tag it."

Zander followed Nolan to the end of the erstwhile corridor. Nolan sat at a desk, jotted some identifying data on a plastic bag, and dropped the piece inside, making additional notes on some tablet computer he pulled from a drawer.

Zander berated himself for not contacting the FBI as soon as he got to Istanbul, but he wasn't sure it would have mattered. That could certainly have led to as dead an end as this. When Nolan answered his cell phone, Zander took his frustration down the pathway that hugged the flip side of the corridor wall. Small mounds of debris were piled against the base. A jewel-like aquamarine pebble atop one pile caught Zander's attention. He picked it up, thinking it might be the best substitute he would find for the pyramid he had promised his daughter, but was disappointed to see it was man-made: almost perfectly square, colored and silky smooth on top; white, rough and caked with mud on the bottom. He scratched some dirt off with a fingernail and held it up to the light. The blue was as brilliant as the water in a Hawaiian coral reef. An ancient tile, he decided. Better than a piece of soda bottle. Layla would like it. He ran his hand through the pile and found three others—two more in the same blue and one a vibrant yellow. He scanned the ground for anything similar when his eyes locked on the wall itself further down the pathway. A decoration of some sort was hanging there, though it was hard to see, since a narrow overhang of surviving ceiling shaded the near end. Zander craned his neck to get a better angle when it hit him like an electric shock. It was Linus Crane's mosaic.

He rushed to the near end and swept a hand across it in a wide arc, his fingers tingling over the glistening tiles and hairline indentures. He stepped back and inched along its full length. Hundreds of characters in a dozen different scenes on land and sea brought the entire wall to life. It was an entire world. He ran his open palms over the most intricate sections, as if he could absorb the energy of the colors, especially the shimmering sky of gold leaf. When he reached the far end he retreated to let his eyes roam up and down and around. It was easily 20 feet across and more than six feet high. He was puzzled at first because it looked more detailed than Penny's photos, but then he realized that her pictures included only the left half, which was actually the less complex of the two. The right side was packed with more figures, including an entire naval fleet. He understood Linus Crane's excitement. It was dazzling.

"That interest you?" he heard Nolan yell.

"You can't imagine."

"Well, I'd say take it with you, but it's a little heavy."

Zander walked back. "How the hell did this survive?"

"Luck," Nolan said. "This wall was in just the right place that it didn't take a direct hit from either the explosive or any falling debris. Beyond that, though, I think the picture was walled in, with either limestone or slate. Look at the bottom right. Some of the covering is still there."

Zander needed to know if Nolan could place Crane here. "Have there been any American archaeologists in here?" he asked.

The agent shook his head. "Not that I've seen, but I didn't get here until the third day after the bombing." "Is anyone around who was here in the beginning?"

"A lot of these soldiers have been digging 18 hours a day since the explosion." Nolan looked past Zander and waved over two soldiers.

"Sir?" Leo Metcalf, a lanky corporal, addressed Nolan.

"Were either of you fellas here right after the bombing?"

"Yes, sir. Both of us."

"Did either of you see a civilian by this wall?" Zander jumped in. "Thin, very young looking. A bit nerdish, maybe."

"I think you mean the professor, sir," Metcalf said. Finally! Zander thought.

"One interesting dude," said the corporal. "He was nearby when the bomb went off, having dinner, I think. Rushed in and helped for the first two days, carrying stretchers, clearing rubble, whatever he was asked. Pretty much non-stop. Then he saw this." Metcalf pointed to the mosaic. "And he just flipped. Pulled a ton of rock away so it showed more. Didn't see him much after that, but he was here for the dirtiest work."

Zander thanked the GI's as they left. He scanned the mosaic once again, still startled at how he'd stumbled onto Crane's trail just as Crane had stumbled onto the mosaic. "Nolan, what is this place?"

"It was Saint Eirene's Church. Built in the sixth century, if you can believe it. It survived fires, earthquakes, the Crusades, invading Muslim armies and two world wars. But one mother of a truck bomb took it out."

"What's gonna happen to it?"

Given how the Turks have buried the investigation, I wouldn't be surprised if they bulldozed it."

"When are you leaving?"

"Probably in the next 72 hours. If you need me," he said, handing Zander a creased and dirty card, "use this cell."

"Thanks," he yelled as he trotted out of St. Eirene's, ready to swim to Ozbek's island if he had to.

Chapter 11

The morning was slipping away but Helen hadn't stepped out of her room since Odysseus Simonedes escorted her back near midnight.

He'd seemed surprised when she appeared before him in the square outside the cistern, but happy as well. His back straightened, his jowls widened with a smile, and he reached out with his free hand. His terrier had reared on its hind legs to sniff her knee. She was still out of breath and quaking from her encounter in the cistern.

Her ordeal spilled out on their five-minute walk to Simonedes's building. Her new protector thanked God she was all right and insisted that anything like this would have been unheard of in his day. Istanbul was once the safest city on earth, he said, but waves of displaced peasants had changed everything. He took her arm and with surprising vigor led her up three flights to his apartment, past a fusion of dinner smells wafting from every door.

His place had the reassuring scent of heavy

furniture and drapes that had barely budged in decades. Overlapping threadbare kilims covered every inch of floor. Photos of relatives that Simonedes said had dispersed to every corner of the globe crowded walls and the top of an antique Bösendorfer. Small archaeological treasures—stone carvings, terracotta trays, a troop of bronze warriors—spread across the royal-blue velvet cover on a central table. Helen didn't see any television, let alone a computer; just an old Philips tabletop radio.

Simonedes brought her a cup of Earl Gray tea and a plate of butter cookies. His terrier went to sleep at his feet the moment he sat down with Helen. She appreciated that her host was kind enough to let her sip her tea and recover her balance in peace. After her skirmish with barbarity, she felt blessed to reach this outpost of civilization.

When Simonedes did finally speak, it was to suggest they call the police. But he accepted her argument that she had no time to file complaints or page through mug shots. She omitted that she simply didn't want to explain what she was doing in the Cistern of a Thousand and One Columns. She was not surprised, though, when Simonedes offered his own thoughts about the cistern.

"I have been there," he said, "and have examined every nook and cranny. Unfortunately, aside from the inspiration you might feel from the soaring vaults, there is little to recommend it."

"But I'm sure you've examined countless places. How can you persist? Is there any place you haven't looked?"

The old man sank back into his brocade armchair

and gently laughed. "If I could answer that for certain, I would give up," he said. "But I don't know where I haven't looked."

Helen nodded, almost dazed by the old man's devotion.

"The Athena still exists," he continued. I feel as certain about it as I do that the sun will rise tomorrow. And I have no doubt that she is here in Turkey. There is no other possibility. I will bring her home again. My life has no other purpose." He put his teacup down.

• • • •

Back at her hotel, without Simonedes to cling to, she once again felt shaken to her core. She took a long cool shower before downing two mini-bottles of Absolut and a Ambien chaser. Waiting to drift off, she opened her shoulder bag to see how badly the maniac's face had damaged her Nikon. To her surprise, the camera was untouched, as were her laptop, make-up kit, and sunglasses. The spine of her Blue Guide was bent, but she couldn't believe a paperback could inflict such pain. She could barely keep her eyes open when she turned the bag upside down and realized what had broken her assailant's nose: her ivory Nubian prince was shattered. "Oh no!" she moaned, grabbing the two largest shards. She was the least superstitious person she knew, but the good-luck piece had saved her life and was now destroyed. For the first time since being told that Jaffar Hazim had lost so much for selling her the Nubian, she felt a pang of shame.

Helen woke feeling no less sad and anxious as when she'd gone to bed. The memory of her scare in the cistern set her heart racing and she focused on her mission, which seemed more daunting than it had 24 hours earlier. She knew she was more likely to win the Irish Sweepstakes than to stumble on the mosaic her first day out, but she was discouraged that each site took so long to investigate. So while her list of buildings to visit hadn't grown, it felt much longer.

The view of the choppy blue Bosporus from her window reminded Helen of her initial misreading of the mosaic, thinking it depicted Jason's voyage. The Argonauts, she recalled, sailed through the Bosporus in pursuit of the Golden Fleece. She envied Jason, who had the gods' protection and guidance on his voyage. And despite everything, she realized she had absorbed Simonedes's faith.

• • • •

Helen's confidence was barely dented by visits to a handful of buildings that looked promising on paper but turned up empty. Today's search was easier, and she plowed through the Churches of Saint Theodosia and Saint Savior Pantokrator by mid-afternoon.

From her street map, she figured that the Church of Saint Eirene should be coming up directly ahead. She was perplexed when the bright sunshine seemed to give way to a black hole, instead of a church. Perhaps the road veered off at an odd angle, she thought; she'd been told the street maps of Istanbul were notoriously imprecise. As she got closer, though, she saw that the hole was actually a huge black tarpaulin. Two rows of saw horses intended to keep passers-by out of what she assumed was a major renovation were linked about 30 feet in front of it. A pair of Turkish policemen was standing inside the sawhorse barrier.

The neighborhood was full of shops—a butcher, a bakery, cheap dry goods. But the crowds fell away near the barricade. A bunch of adolescent boys shot in and around the sawhorses, taunting each other and daring the police to keep them out.

The whole scene energized her. Half by process of elimination and half by intuition, she felt this might be what she was looking for.

Helen stood opposite the two cops. "Excuse me," she said, "I need to go inside." The cop stood motionless. "Can I?"

"The area is closed," the younger one told her.

"I see that. But I am a scientist—an archaeologist—and I have come from the United States specifically to see this church."

"The area is closed."

"The area is closed," Helen mumbled to herself. She wondered if this idiot actually spoke English or had just memorized a single phrase. "I understand that, but I must get in."

The cop shook his head in silence.

Satisfied that no one was watching her, Helen pulled out her wallet and extracted a pair of hundred-dollar bills, splaying them in one hand like a magician. She watched the older cop's dark eyes widen and for a moment she wondered if he might arrest her. Instead he held up three fingers, like he was ordering beers in a noisy bar, aiming them first at himself and then at his partner.

"Six-hundred dollars?" She retrieved another four bills and slapped the whole pile into his hand.

The cops stepped aside. Helen ducked under the sawhorse and through a seam in the tarp.

The church's condition startled her. Her guidebook included a photo of St. Eirene's so she had an image in mind of what to expect, give or take some scaffolding. But here, it looked like a bomb had gone off...

Simply saying the words in her head were enough to make her grasp that of course a bomb had gone off. This was where the sailors were killed.

Helen noticed how quiet it was. Almost serene. The tarp was a damper to the street noise. The only people she could see were far off by some tents. She would go in, look around, and leave.

She headed toward the church. Before she had gone 10 feet, though, an American M.P. emerged from the far end of the building. His I.D. tag read "Rivera."

"Hello!" Helen shouted as he approached.

"Hello, ma'am."

Helen stopped a few feet from him.

"This is a restricted area, ma'am," he said in a calm but assured tone. "I'm afraid you'll have to leave."

"Yes, I understand that. It's just that I'm with the Metropolitan Museum of Art."

"That's very good, ma'am. But unless you're with the Department of Defense or the Department of Justice, you have no business here."

Helen tried to sound courteous. "But I do have business here. I've come all the way from New York to see the art in this church."

"Ma'am, if this church had any art, all it has now is dust. Now please understand, this entire area is a crime scene, plus you run the risk of a building collapse. You'll leave immediately on your own, or I will escort you out."

Helen was sure she could convince Rivera to let

her nose around for just a few minutes. "Come on, sergeant," she said, "we're both Americans. We can show a little trust. I'm not going to touch anything. I'll even put a hardhat on if you want." Helen smiled and walked toward the church on an angle, trying to give the M.P. a wide berth.

Rivera pulled his pistol and leveled it at her. "Stop right there," he ordered.

Chapter 12

Seeing the mosaic and hearing the soldiers' account of Crane's ecstasy at finding it helped Zander understand the chaotic events of the past few days.

He parked himself at an open-air cafe in the shadow of the graceful Blue Mosque. Everyone around him was apparently settling in for an extended afternoon of shamelessly tall drinks. He ordered soda water and was brought a liter of Trebizond in a bottle that looked like it had been in use since World War I.

All too soon, though, he felt his elation ebbing away. It struck him that if not for most people's ability to let small victories temporarily obscure their problems, the mental institutions would be overflowing. He envied the crowd rushing by. It would be so easy to melt in and join the holiday. Maybe order a beer and make an ass of himself by sending drinks to the three blondes a few tables over. Who cares if they speak English?

What did he know for sure? There was no question that a couple of weeks ago, in the midst of the project

Ozbek had funded, Linus Crane had stumbled across the glittering mosaic. He had apparently kept it a secret from everyone except Penny, and Crane was murdered just before announcing the discovery. Could Ozbek have demanded a full accounting, and been rebuffed by Crane? Meanwhile, the only other person who knew about the mosaic—however little that might be—had been kidnapped and brought to Istanbul. That could mean two things: either whoever was after the mosaic felt Penny could tell them where it was; or, if he already knew and wanted it for himself, he would want to silence her. Zander discounted this uglier possibility because Nolan said no one had been inside St. Eirene's except the rescue and forensic teams. Certainly Ozbek could have gotten in if he wanted to—but he hadn't, which meant he still didn't know what was there. As to how Ozbek had connected Penny to the mosaic, she might have hung herself by mentioning Crane's photos at the memorial service. Unquestionably, all roads led to Istanbul, though proof of Ozbek's involvement remained circumstantial. Still, Zander had to eliminate him as a suspect before looking elsewhere.

That meant getting to him. Zander figured he had two unappealing options. He could have Goktepe's press contacts arrange an introduction, billing himself as chief of the Los Angeles Police Department's Art Theft Unit and an esteemed member of the Cultural Property Advisory Committee of the President of the United States. This might tug at Ozbek's ego and even give the Turk pause, if he had indeed plotted to kill him. Most likely, though, Ozbek would offer some excuse for not meeting, or just refuse outright. Inviting your adversary to dinner and a game of billiards was a scene out of James Bond, not any investigation he'd ever worked. Besides, God knew how long it might take to make such arrangements. If Ozbek expected Penny to lead him to the mosaic, she was in deep trouble. Information was Zander's only currency and a deal could be cut based on what he'd seen this morning. But he had to confront Ozbek before anyone else found the mosaic or the building collapsed.

That left one other choice. He would go out there on his own. Ozbek didn't own the whole damn island. He'd take a ferry or rent a boat, check into a hotel and find Penny if she was there to be found.

He was finishing his Trebizond when his eyes were drawn to a short, well-dressed man striding across the square, his arms swinging like metronomes. Zander was dumbfounded for a few moments, suffering like many people from an inability to identify people out of context. But after closing his eyes and rubbing his forehead it became clear, odd as it was. Henry Demarest!

Zander picked up his bag, dropped a crumpled bank note on the table and took off. He had never seen the dealer so happy and heard him crooning from 30 feet behind: *"When I was fifty-nine, it was a very good year. It was a very good year for big-city boys of in-de-pen-dent meeeeeeans."* Directly across the square, Demarest walked into the Four Seasons Hotel.

Zander followed and stopped just inside the lobby. He watched Demarest nod to the desk clerk and step onto the elevator. Zander hopped on just ahead of the closing doors. Demarest pushed 8. He stood humming to himself, his shopping bags on the floor.

"Hello, Henry," Zander said, as if they had pulled

up alongside each other at a traffic light on Sunset.

Demarest's mouth opened, but nothing came out. It was now his turn to search for context.

"Yes. It's me."

"*Alexander*? What are you doing here?"

"Nice to see you, too. You didn't mention you were going to Turkey."

"Yes, well, some unexpected business."

The elevator stopped and opened. The dealer did not move. Zander grabbed the door when it started to close. "Isn't this your floor?"

Demarest didn't answer. Zander looked at his soft Italian shoes and watched him shift his weight ever so slightly back and forth, like a boy waiting in line at the urinal. "Are you getting out?"

Demarest stepped off only when the elevator started buzzing. He stopped as soon as the doors shut and pumped Zander's hand.

"Alexander," he said, "it was wonderful running into you. Come by the gallery when you get back. We'll have some lunch."

Demarest's anxiety only made Zander smile. He didn't actually care what the dealer was up to—though he was clearly up to something. They were far from home and Zander was happy just to see a familiar face. "Are you in a rush?"

"I've got some business to attend to, yes."

Zander decided that if Demarest was too troubled to spend three minutes with him, he at least wanted to know why. "Do you mind if I use your john?"

"What? No, no. The maid hasn't come yet and it's disgusting."

"I'm sure disgusting here is better than just-cleaned

in most places." Zander started down the hallway. "Which room is yours?"

Demarest followed. "I'm serious. The room's a disaster."

"What's the matter? You have a 10-year-old boy in there?"

"Of course not."

"I'll only be a second."

"Oh, all right." Demarest swiped his coded card through the lock. When the green light did not flash, he swiped it again. "You know, Alexander, this card wouldn't open before and they had to send a bellman up. Let's go to the lobby so I can get a replacement."

Zander snatched the card. "Let me try." The green light flashed as soon as he ran it through. "You were holding it backwards." Zander pushed the door open. "And it's already been cleaned."

Demarest pointed to a powder room just inside. "Here!" he said, still antsy as a first-time shoplifter.

Zander glanced at the bathroom but did not stop until he reached the living room of the sun-drenched suite. It was decorated with fine Bokhara rugs, Georgian English furniture, and a flat-screen TV thin as a dime but wide as a Ping-Pong table. "Some kinda room," he said, glancing through the picture window at the restaurant where he'd just eaten. "Breakfast included?" He stopped in front of a closed door. "This the bedroom?"

"Yes. And I'd like a little privacy," Demarest said, too late to stop Zander from pushing the door open.

A Sultan-sized canopied bed dominated the room. There were matching marble nightstands, a linen press posing as a dresser, and a large chest. But Zander's attention was fixed on the only thing that didn't come with the room: the cello case on the bed. "Henry," he said, his brief delight at running into Demarest flaming into anger, "I hope you've taken up an instrument." Zander leaned over the cello case and flipped its three snaps.

"Alexander!" Demarest screamed. "I'll give you $10,000 not to open it."

Zander laughed at the absurdity of the dealer's desperation.

"Oh, never mind," Demarest mumbled and dropped onto the bed. "I can explain."

Zander raised the lid and stared down at the ancient Anasazi girl. She looked none the worse for the trip. "How could you?" Zander asked, more disappointed than angry. "Not only did you break the law bringing this here, you busted your probation and you lied to me."

Demarest got off the bed. "I'm sorry, Alexander. But it was an opportunity to open a tremendously exciting account."

Zander was reminded once again that Demarest's notion of right and wrong was so twisted that he might be legally insane. "Really? Is that how you see it? To me it's an opportunity to send you back to prison."

Zander closed the case and walked across the room. He flopped down onto the arm of a leather club chair. "They told me the case arrived at UCLA. What was in it?"

Demarest's voice dropped to a whisper. "A cello."

Zander had thought Demarest's trip through the penal system had actually straightened him out. It made his disappointment all the sharper now and literally left a bad taste in his mouth. "Obviously you assumed I wouldn't find out," he said as he opened the minibar under the bedroom TV and grabbed a cold water. He hoped it would cost Demarest at least 10 bucks.

"I intended to procure a replacement before you got back."

"Of course. Who would know the difference? How much are you getting for it?"

"Money's not the issue."

"The fuck it's not. *How much*?"

Demarest stepped back, fear visible in his flared nostrils. "One hundred-and-fifty thousand."

"You greedy bastard," Zander snarled.

"The more important thing was finding something for a collector I've been after for years."

"Who?"

"You've never heard of him."

"Who?"

"You know I never discuss my clients."

Zander headed for Demarest. "Henry, if you don't tell me who the buyer is, I'm going to take the mummy out and stuff *you* in the fucking case. You hear me?"

"All right, all right! There's no reason to come unglued. His name is Bulent Ozbek."

The name hit Zander like a slap to the head. Was this possible? Was Ozbek at the hub of every wheel in Zander's life? He felt like slamming Demarest against the wall, but instead grabbed the dealer. He felt the dealer's fright through his padded shoulder as he led him back to the living room. "What else have you got here?"

"What do you mean?" Demarest asked.

"What else would you hate for me to find if I

ripped apart the rest of this place, which I think I might."

The dealer looked insulted for a moment, but then melted under Zander's glare. He leaned over to the nightstand, opened the drawer, pushed aside copies of the Bible and the Koran, and pulled out a Walther PPK pistol. He handed it to Zander, dangling the grip between his thumb and index finger.

"You didn't carry this on the plane, did you?"

"Of course, not. Some friends lent it to me here. Just for security."

"Right," Zander said, his caustic tone apparently unnerving Demarest even further.

"Alexander, look, I don't know what came over me. Just let me bring the mummy back to UCLA and I swear I'll..."

"Shut up," Zander interrupted him. "Just sit down and tell me how well you know Ozbek."

Demarest eased deep into one corner of the chintz sofa. "Why?"

"Answer another question of mine with a question and I'll have you sent to a *Turkish* prison."

"Sorry, sorry. The answer is I hardly know him at all."

"When did you see him last?"

"I've never actually met him," Demarest said. "We've only spoken on the phone. He was never interested in anything I offered before. But he knows my reputation."

"When are you meeting him?"

"Tomorrow morning. He's sending a boat to take me—"

"Out to his island."

"Right. You know where he lives?"

"Of course. Everyone knows where he lives. And you know what else?"

"What?"

"You're going to keep that appointment."

Chapter 13

Helen couldn't fathom that Sergeant Rivera actually believed she was a terrorist, even though he interrogated her for almost an hour. In the end, he accepted that she was what she maintained all along: a curator from the Met. If anything, Rivera seemed more upset with the Istanbul police guarding Saint Eirene's perimeter. As for Helen, he obviously just wanted her to disappear.

"Go back to your hotel, or visit some other church. That way we can put this behind us. Fair enough?"

But she couldn't walk away. St. Eirene's had become a crusade. There was something about the place. She sensed it. What's more, she was furious over being held at gunpoint and she let Rivera know it. She hiked up the sleeve of her blouse to reveal a contusion where Rivera had grabbed her. "I could sue," she said.

"I'm sorry, ma'am, but you brought that on yourself."

Helen pondered how to persuade this man to let her in, however briefly. No way he'd take a bribe. His honest character was etched in his face. But maybe a plea from the heart. "Just one minute," she said, her voice soft as cashmere. "Right in, right out. I promise."

She saw that her final appeal triggered an alarm in Rivera's head. "I'm sorry ma'am," he said, lifting the receiver from a red phone on his desk, "but you've got some kind of unnatural obsession that I don't have the time or the resources to deal with." He tapped in a number. "I won't have it on my head," he continued, waiting for someone to answer, "if you sneak back in here and get yourself crushed under a wall."

• • • •

Her final pleading proved fruitless, and Helen soon found herself in a holding cell at the Istanbul City Jail for Women, charged with trespassing, disturbing the peace, and attempting to bribe two Turkish police officers. The cell was beneath ground level, barely lit by a single hanging bulb. There was no place to sit but the floor, which was occupied only by those too sick to stand. Helen paced the damp concrete, breathing through her mouth to deflect the noxious chorus of piss, puke, shit, and blood. She examined the other women, particularly two with suckling infants. The rest— prostitutes and petty thieves, she feared—had drug-induced deadness behind their eyes.

Four hours later, Helen was finally permitted a phone call. She considered calling Odysseus Simonedes, but knew she needed more than a sympathetic ear. Instead, she reached Peter Sloan in London. Tears came flooding at the sound of his voice. But she managed to make her situation clear enough before a matron pulled the phone from her hand.

Helen cried again—this time with relief—when Gary Durkin arrived from the American Consulate 30 minutes later. It was too late to make bail, he told her, but he'd see the right people first thing in the morning. Helen cowered on her cot all night before she was taken to a makeshift jailhouse courtroom just after 9 a.m.

The judge had no interest in her account of events. She was getting out, he told her, only because, "Mr. Durkin, an esteemed member of the diplomatic community," had vouched that she had no history as a troublemaker. This, the judge added, left Mr. Durkin personally responsible for seeing that she leave Turkey within 24 hours.

Hearing this brought Helen to the brink of protest, but the look on Durkin's face told her that she would be tossed back into the pit if she said anything but "thank you." Hands balled into fists, she nodded when the judge asked her if she understood her sentence.

Chapter 14

Zander scuffed his soles along the deserted pier that reached into the Sea of Marmara, and leaned the cello case against a bench. Off to his left, across an aquamarine inlet where half-a-dozen pleasure boats were anchored, he watched Henry Demarest sip a coffee at the cafe where Zander had eaten lunch with the reporter Goktepe. They stared at each other for a moment, but when the dealer raised his right hand as if he might wave, Zander turned away.

A burnt-orange speck on the horizon caught Zander's attention. He watched it head straight for him, buzzing ever louder as it passed other boats, then stepped back from the pier's edge as the 25-foot Scarab pulled alongside, rocking in its own wake. A deckhand with requisite striped shirt secured the boat. Zander kept his eye on the pilot, a young woman who hopped onto the dock.

"Mr. Demarest?" she asked.

"Yes."

"I am Sherin," she said, whisking a metal detector

up and down his body. He took fair warning that Ozbek's world was both secured and paranoid.

"Okay?" he asked.

"Yes, let's go."

Zander handed Sherin the case and followed it on board, studying her sensuous mouth and the gentle slope of her nose beneath her oversized sunglasses. He was sure she never smiled.

She signaled for Zander to strap himself in, which he did, and she came about. He turned to catch a final glimpse of Demarest. The dealer was gone.

"The crossing takes 20 minutes," Sherin said, and brought the twin Caterpillars to bear. The boat lifted its front end and screamed out to the open water. Unable to hear above the roar, he settled into his solitude, wondering whether Demarest was right when he told him he was nuts to try this.

• • • •

"Here we are," Sherin said, as they coasted toward a lone pier about a mile from the town. "This is Heybeli, second largest of the Princes Islands."

Zander scanned the tree-covered hillside that rose sharply from the sea. A few large houses, all perched with spectacular views, poked out of the dense forest. "The islands have some royal history?"

"Yes, though it is rather dark. Whenever a new Byzantine emperor was crowned, he would round up any princes who might challenge him for the throne and ship them out here to rot. Sometimes their eyes were gouged out as an extra precaution."

"Interesting," Zander said, more eager than ever to get on with his business there.

"Until steamships arrived in the 19th century," she added, "these islands were quite remote."

"They don't look very developed now."

"You're right," she said as he stepped on shore and took the cello case from her. "No cars or trucks allowed. It's very peaceful." She pointed him toward a waiting carriage drawn by a pair of handsome chestnuts. "That's for you."

Zander watched Sherin rev up the engines again and blast off into the open water. It was one of the rare times he was glad to see a beautiful woman leave.

The carriage driver was a silent old man with a walrus mustache. Zander climbed on behind him and rested the cello case across his lap. He heard the driver grunt, presumably an admonition to "hold on," and the horses began trotting up a hard-packed trail barely wide enough to accommodate them. Zander opened the case, silently excused himself for reaching under the girl's bum, and removed Demarest's Walther pistol.

Chapter 15

Penny needed only minutes to retrieve the full story of Linus Crane's fantastic—and final—discovery from his laptop. Much harder was feigning frustration and failure while she bottled up her fear and tried to figure out how to stay alive. Ozbek had not returned since issuing his ultimatum, but his odious face invaded Penny's thoughts as his deadline neared. She had no doubt he would kill her if she revealed what he wanted to know. If he were capable of murdering the most celebrated archaeologist in the world, why would he think twice about disposing of her?

Linus Crane wore his genius lightly, but it had not surprised her when he explained that he had devised his own private shorthand at age nine and had used it his entire academic life. A friend of his at Cal Tech had created a neural network that understood his unique scribbling and was able, with 99.9-percent accuracy, to translate it into standard English. That program was buried on Crane's hard drive under the code name "Ventris," a salute to the brilliant young architect who deciphered the language of the ancient Mycenaeans. All Penny had to do was drag Crane's journal file on top of the Ventris icon and presto! Her search for Crane's London presentation proved fruitless—she imagined it was somewhere up in the cloud and beyond her reach—but the journal was explicit enough.

Penny was mesmerized but saddened to read Crane's account of his serendipitous discovery of the mosaic and his despair at the circumstances. He declared he had no doubt the mosaic held the key to uncovering the great gold-and-ivory Athena Parthenos. She wished he'd detailed his conclusion—God knows, he'd have demanded it of her—but she accepted his claim. She'd never known him to be wrong about anything important. Still, Crane made it clear that he hadn't found the Athena yet. He felt the medieval mosaic itself was an important enough discovery to announce at the London conference. His plan was to launch an expedition to find the Athena right after London.

This, of course, was what Ozbek wanted—what he had killed Linus for and would kill her for. She had no doubt that Linus's child-like naiveté—one of the things that she adored about him—had led to all this. Linus could never imagine how anyone was capable of murder. He must have dropped at least a few hints to Ozbek about the Athena, but then held back the rest and ultimately insulted the megalomaniac by suggesting he wasn't worthy of the goddess. She pictured Ozbek exploding at this. She wanted to believe she could stand up to him as Linus must have. But just imagining their confrontation drained her. She closed her eyes and pressed her fingertips against her forehead.

Some of Crane's comments were suggestive enough to understand. "BBC? PBS?" he'd written, which Penny took to mean he was considering bringing TV crews along to document the hunt. But other comments—"Beware Athena's favorite!"—was lost on her. Athena's favorite what? She was most spooked and saddened by two cryptic notes that Crane had written explicitly to her. "Message to Penny: Find your faith in the Country!" and "PST: MAPS LIE!" Why had he left a note directly for her? Did he worry Ozbek might come after him? And did his counsel about faith have anything to do with the Athena at all? Or just with her loss of faith in herself and his program, which she'd just abandoned? And what was the point of such a general comment about maps?

Her isolation only stoked her terror. Who even knew she was missing? What was there to hope for? The only person who might have an inkling was Zander, and for all she knew they'd killed him in London.

She looked over at Hikmet. When she had first opened Crane's computer, the tech whiz had waddled over behind her, presumably to check what she was doing. But she sensed him sniffing at her hair like a dog and she brutally shoved him away. After that he busied himself with illustrated books from the shelves and eventually took to dozing on the couch. She could probably overpower him, but what was the point? He phoned when he needed to get out, alerting someone to buzz the door open.

Elaborate meals were delivered to the office like room service at a four-star hotel, but she had no appetite.

They left her alone in her bedroom, but she'd barely slept. Both nights she was nauseated with anxiety, collapsing near daybreak and waking short of breath and with a pounding headache. She longed to see her family and friends again. She did not want to die here.

She returned again and again to the idea of pleading for more time. She thought she could convince Ozbek she was beginning to unravel what Crane was on to. Crane's stolen library had proved useful. Every so often Penny would complain aloud that she couldn't find some critical volume. "Tell your boss I might have some answers for him if these shelves were properly organized."

"You make it sound like you actually need all this stuff," Hikmet said, lifting his head from the cushion and gesturing toward the sagging shelves.

"If I'm ever going to find what he wants, I do."

"Really?" Hikmet said, stroking his dirty ponytail. "I think everything Mr. Ozbek wants is on the laptop."

She shook her head, though with little conviction. If even Hikmet sensed the truth, how could she fool Ozbek? What terrified her was that even if she broke down and told him, it wouldn't be enough.

Chapter 16

Virgin forest covered the last quarter mile to Ozbek's compound. Despite the languorous quiet—even the rumble of the surf was gone, replaced by the caws and whistles of exotic birds and the rush of animals through the underbrush—Zander gripped the case ever harder and felt his breathing grow more compact, as if they'd climbed 5,000 feet above sea level, not 500.

The carriage finally pulled up at a towering iron gate, and his driver placed his hand on a palm and fingerprint reader. Green lights flashed, motors kicked into gear, and the gate, the only break in an eight-foot wall of whitewashed brick, pulled open.

Inside, wilderness gave way to three stunning mansions amid the gentility and order of an English garden, with expansive lawns, tightly clipped bushes, lush flower beds, and stone-bordered ponds and fountains. Gravel trimmed with Belgian block replaced the dirt trail, and the horses seemed to step a little livelier, as if expecting to see their sovereign.

An armed man in military uniform stood in a guardhouse doorway and waved the driver on. Zander turned to watch the gate close. Sunlight reflected off rows of rusty metal spikes and jagged potsherds embedded atop the length of the brick wall. He unconsciously rubbed his hands at the cost of a hasty departure.

• • • •

Penny faced the courtyard windows in the rigid desk chair, her bare feet up on the sill, toes curling around the iron bars. She was scanning Linus Crane's old computer files; reading his memos, papers, and speculations brought him closer and lightened her sadness. She heard the door open, but did not turn around until the snoring Hikmet groaned and fell to the floor.

"Get up, get up, you piece of garbage!" Ozbek screamed, kicking Hikmet in the stomach. Penny watched in horror. When Hikmet managed to rise to his knees, Ozbek drew an arm back to punch him, but he covered his head like any nerd trying to survive another schoolyard beating. No doubt he'd had a lifetime of practice, Penny thought.

"Get out of here," Ozbek railed at his petrified lackey. "You useless swine!"

Hikmet scooted out, slamming the door behind him. Ozbek approached Penny.

• • • •

Zander climbed down from the carriage beside a wooden mansion painted the hue of an old-growth redwood. The driver departed and Zander stood alone, braced against the cello case, like the new marshal in Tombstone steeling himself for his first encounter with the Clantons.

He was still there when the door opened and a butler bowed low. Zander followed him inside, where the man gestured in a way that Zander understood as, "May I take the cello case from you?" Zander said no and the butler led him out to the slate terrace that overlooked the Sea of Marmara. A table had been set for lunch. The fine china, crystal, linen and wildflowers gave it the look and feel of an elegant but hip Los Angeles restaurant, perfect for Henry Demarest.

Zander wondered how he would explain taking the mummy back with him if it turned out Ozbek had nothing to do with Penny's disappearance. Meanwhile, a servant asked if he would like a cocktail. "Scotch rocks would be good," he said.

He put the cello aside and walked to the edge of the terrace. He noticed that Ozbek's brick rampart reached right to where the property dropped off to the sea and guessed that barbed wire had been laid to discourage uninvited guests. If Ozbek was as whacked as Goktepe claimed, the hillside might even be mined.

• • • •

Penny leaned back into her chair, still stunned by Ozbek's rage. "I'm trying to make sense of Professor Crane's notes."

"Trying?"

"Yes. Trying."

"You're a poor liar, Penny."

"I'm not lying. I'm just not a mind reader."

Ozbek sat on a corner of the desk. Her torso tensed.

"When I was at Harvard last spring," he said, chatting like a neighbor across a backyard fence, "Crane told me you were the brightest assistant he'd ever had. He said he treated you like a colleague, not a grad student, because the breadth of your knowledge was astounding and your research was more sophisticated than what any junior professor across the Ivy League was turning out. He was already angling to get you the next tenure-track appointment in the department."

"Now who's a poor liar?" she countered.

"You know it's true. That's why he insisted you be there when I handed him the check for the summer project. He told me you were crucial to his success, and he wanted you to share the glory."

"If he said any of this he was exaggerating. You don't even know I resigned last month."

"Of course I know. But Crane didn't take that any more seriously than I do. You were born to this and you'll never be happy doing anything else."

She suppressed her urge to argue. She felt ashamed even talking to him, as if it soiled Linus Crane's legacy. "You can believe what you want."

"What I believe is that you've already uncovered what I want to know. Perhaps you knew even before you arrived here. I don't care. The only issue is what you have for me now, because I have run out of time." He stood and stared down at her.

If he came close enough, Penny thought, she could smash him with the computer. Break his jaw if she was lucky.

"Well?" Ozbek asked.

The door opened just enough for Hikmet to stick his head in.

Ozbek turned. "What do you want?"

"Henry Demarest is here to see you. From California."

"I'll be right there." He flicked his head to send Hikmet away. "This will be brief," he told Penny. He walked to the door. "Linus Crane is dead and there's nothing you can do about it. I'd start thinking about myself if I were you."

• • • •

Zander was finishing his scotch when Ozbek joined him on the terrace. He'd only caught a glimpse of the Turk in London; now a second look found deeper lines, the beginnings of a second chin, and more gray. But Ozbek apparently thrived under the baking Turkish sun. He was dressed sharply but not flashily, like an entertainment lawyer out for 18 holes at Pebble Beach. A complex gold chronometer that glinted in the sun suggested an interest in precision more than ostentation. His eyes—deep, ravenous and unblinking—demanded compliance.

Zander offered an iron handshake and was met pound for pound.

"You're younger than I imagined," Ozbek said.

Zander wasn't surprised at the comment, given Demarest's reputation as the dean of Native American dealers. If he had worked out an appropriate response, it escaped him now. "That's southern California for you," he said. "We're all very into the health and fitness thing, you know. Plus," he lowered his voice to share a secret, "one of my best clients is chief of plastic surgery at Cedars Sinai. Top man. Does only the A-List. You let me know when you're ready." He slapped Ozbek on the shoulder. "I'll make a call."

"I see you've brought the prize with you," Ozbek said, eyeing the case. "Do you mind if I—"

"Of course." Zander handed it to Ozbek. "She'll be yours soon enough."

Ozbek laid the case down on a smooth granite table.

Ozbek's fingertips grazed her leathery cheek "She's... she's fantastic. So delicate... a sweet angel."

"Yes, it's a crime she was disturbed," Zander couldn't resist saying, though he tempered his words with a smile.

"Ah, but you shouldn't think that way. This little girl's body, beautiful as it was, was a mere cocoon." Zander arched his eyebrows, unsure where Ozbek was going. "That's putting an optimistic spin on it."

Ozbek laughed. "That is not my intent. When her body finished its purpose—when she *died*, as we would say—her soul simply departed like a butterfly. Perhaps to another life here on earth or, if she had attained certain knowledge, to a higher existence, free from pain or worries or wanton desires. An existence of pure, overwhelming love."

"Love?" Zander asked, surprised at the Turk's passion.

Ozbek pointed at Zander like a revivalist preacher. "Love that's far more encompassing and rapturous than anything we can imagine."

"But if she hadn't attained this knowledge?"

"Then she would return to another life on earth, as we all have."

Demarest had once told Zander that the secret to selling was helping the buyer talk about himself.

Besides, there was a part of Zander that wanted to believe. "And you can remember your previous lives?"

"Oh, yes. Many of them. But more important is that I've reached the end point. I have been told this is my final trip here."

"Who tells you?"

Ozbek laughed like he'd either heard the question before or thought Demarest was some sort of simpleton. "You'll know when your moment comes. Now let's eat and get to our business."

When a waiter placed a baked quince appetizer in front of him, Zander offered to answer any questions about the mummy. Instead, Ozbek launched into a monologue on Turkish history that ran all the way through coffee. Keeping to Demarest's rules, Zander let Ozbek lecture with only the odd question. "Come," the Turk finally said when dessert was removed, "I know your time is limited, and there are some things I want to show you."

Zander picked up the cello case and followed Ozbek to the museum mansion, inspecting every path they crossed on the way and creating a catalog of possible escape routes.

Once inside, Zander did not have to act impressed. He was. As Penny had told him, Ozbek's collection would stand out in the world's best museums. The tour wound up in Ozbek's gallery of death, with its sarcophagus and masks and petrified bodies. Zander thought that for someone who didn't believe in death, Ozbek couldn't get enough of it.

"This will be our little girl's new home," Ozbek said, sounding like a parent bringing home a foster child. "In fact, why don't you leave her here and we can take care of the mundane side of the transaction in my office?"

Zander tried to mask his discomfort with Ozbek's request. Leaving this mummy here would mean coming back to retrieve it. But how could he say no? "As long as you promise to show me the rest of the compound," he finally said.

"Nothing would make me happier."

Zander glanced around for video cameras as they headed out of the gallery. "You must have exceptional security here."

"Except for the guard by the front entrance, it's completely automated," Ozbek said, taking Zander into a small office by the front door that was filled with video equipment. "Every square foot is monitored."

• • • •

Penny ran the cursor back and forth across the laptop's screen, sighing heavily. It still upset her to be holding Linus's computer. In a sense it was his last will and testament. She forced herself to accept that it was better for the world to lose the uncatalogued brilliance the computer still held than to chance letting Ozbek break Linus's code. If Linus had surrendered his life to keep Ozbek from his discovery, she was not going to overturn his decision.

The computer beeped to highlight its warning message: *Are you sure you want to erase the hard disk? All data and application programs will be lost!* She pointed the cursor at the box marked *Yes,* tapped the trackpad, and put the computer aside as it swallowed itself up.

• • • •

The third mansion in Ozbek's compound comprised yet another world. From palatial residence to museum to office building. "You direct your operations from here?" Zander asked.

"Yes and no," Ozbek said. "We set and measure targets here, but I let the managers on the ground run things. They know their businesses better than I ever could."

Zander recalled the massive org chart of Ozbek's empire he'd studied on the journalist Goktepe's website, its tentacles interlocking around the world. He followed his host through a beehive of accountants and auditors, and up two half-flights of stairs at one end of the building. On the second floor, they stopped in front of a conference room set behind a wall of glass. Ozbek pointed to half-a-dozen men inside who were arguing via teleconference. "More important are the strategic planners and portfolio managers. I've got rainmakers here from the United States, East Asia, and all over Europe."

"They don't object to the isolation?"

"Any objections are overcome by their paychecks." Ozbek continued down the hallway, stopping outside another glass room, where Zander watched a dozen men, all younger than him, sitting in front of terminals and shouting into wireless headsets. "Our trading operation is tied into all the exchanges: equities, bonds, f/x, commodities, or whatever we need to purchase an opportunity."

Zander followed the Turk up to the top floor, which comprised Ozbek's office. A massive conference table, set against a wall of windows that looked out to the sea, dominated the near end. "This table belonged to John D. Rockefeller," Ozbek explained. "He used it for the boardroom at Standard Oil, before the Supreme Court decided no one man should have so much power."

Zander touched the inlaid walnut. "Competition is always healthy."

"Yes," Ozbek grinned. "So they told us at Harvard."

Ozbek pressed a button under his desk and a landscape painting behind him lowered to reveal a wall safe. Fingerprint and voiceprint readers were embedded in the steel. Ozbek placed his hand on the safe and whispered like he was trying to seduce it. The door popped open and he removed a black leather briefcase.

"One-hundred-and-fifty-thousand dollars," he said. Zander looked down at the cash, remaining blasé, as he thought Demarest might. Ozbek handed the case to Zander, and led him to a small elevator, which they took to ground level.

They rode in silence, Zander waiting for inspiration. There had been no sign of Penny. Someone said that behind every great fortune there is a crime. No doubt it was the case here as well, but Ozbek's crimes were out of his jurisdiction. He would take the Turk up on his invitation to tour the residence. But if nothing turned up, he'd collect the mummy and leave, inventing some story for nixing the deal.

As they stepped off the elevator, one of Ozbek's kitchen staff was waiting to ride down to the basement, carrying a plate of grilled salmon that had been barely touched. Zander's eyes widened, though, at the site of a tiny paper swan sitting beside a crust of bread, the product of a folded napkin.

Ozbek flicked the swan to the floor with his finger. "Not again!"

"Whose lunch is this?" Zander asked, his heart racing.

"A very rude guest," Ozbek fumed, turning toward the front entrance.

Zander stared at the plate headed for the trash and waited for the maid to disappear into the elevator. He kneeled down and retrieved the paper swan. "No kidding," he said. "I had a friend who used to make these. Her name was Penny. Penny Theobald."

The surprise that momentarily twisted Ozbek's face was all Zander needed to know he'd struck gold. He glanced over his shoulder to make sure that the accountants were secure in their cubicles before pulling his pistol from under jacket and jabbing it into Ozbek's belly. The Turk tightened from head to toe.

Ozbek tried to appear calm, but his halting voice betrayed him. "What do you want?"

"Just shut up and take me to her or you're going to die right here."

Chapter 17

Penny reflexively grabbed the arm of her chair when she heard the buzzer sound. Her jaw clenched for what she knew would likely be a fatal confrontation.

Seeing Ozbek being shoved inside and pushed to the floor was so unexpected it took her a moment to understand. She gasped when she saw Zander standing in the doorway, training his pistol on her prostrate nemesis.

"Zander!" she managed to choke out, and ran to throw her arms around his neck. Her eyes were closed and she felt for the first time in her life that her prayers had truly been answered.

"Everything's okay," he reassured her, closing the door behind them. "Did he hurt you?"

She wiped her eyes and held tight to his elbow. "I'm all right."

Ozbek slowly got to his feet. "You'll never get out of here."

Zander grabbed the phone from the wall and shoved it toward Ozbek. "Have the carriage brought to the front door."

When Ozbek smirked as if he wouldn't even consider it, Zander grabbed Ozbek's head and jammed the semi-automatic in his ear. Zander took the phone when Ozbek finished.

"Now get back on the floor, face down, hands behind your back."

Penny felt a surge of pleasure when Zander knocked him unconscious with the butt of the pistol.

"I need to fetch something before we leave," he said. "Come on."

• • • •

The same guard was stationed outside the museum and did not move even when Zander tried the locked door. "I left something inside," he said, trying to sound as casual as he could.

"I'm sorry, sir, but no one enters without Mr. Ozbek."

"I understand," Zander said, cursing himself for not holding onto the mummy. "But Mr. Ozbek sent me." When he saw that the guard wasn't buying, Zander pulled out the Walther. "Open it."

Even though Penny had seen the pistol just a minute before, Zander's readiness to use it startled her. He took her hand to calm her. The guard looked around, perhaps hoping either help or a distraction would wander by. Neither did, so he tapped in the code.

Inside, Zander extracted a Beretta from the guard's shoulder holster. He removed the clip and dropped the gun behind a display case.

They hurried the guard with them to Ozbek's gallery of death. The cello case was right where he had left it. He scooped it up, but one of the clasps was unlocked, leaving the lower section hanging open. Zander waved the guard back a few steps and reached down to shut it. But shifting his focus for half a second was all the guard needed to slap the Walther away and send it spinning across the marble floor. The guard lunged, slamming Zander to the ground like a sack of potatoes. His sore ribs screamed, but he still managed to roll twice and scramble to his feet without getting mauled. Suffering through the pain that accompanied each gasp for air, he circled and retreated a few steps, positioning the cello case between them in order to slow the line of attack. He caught sight of Penny off to the side. Though terrified, Zander saw her eyeing the gun across the floor. "Get back!" he yelled at her. The last thing he wanted was the guard to grab her and threaten to snap her neck unless he surrendered. He waved her behind a Roman sarcophagus. "Stay there!"

The guard now inched forward, his expression a mix of rage and disdain. Anticipating another blow to his kidneys he wasn't sure he would survive, Zander glanced around for a weapon among the priceless artifacts. But with everything either too bulky or under glass, he squared himself and waited, keeping his breathing shallow and his focus on the guard's mid-section. As he hoped, his adversary bulled ahead like a street brawler, giving him the chance to wheel sideways and drive a hard kick to his neck. Grabbing the guard's throat as he straightened up, Zander took the wind out of him with a straight right to the gut. With the guard doubled over and panting, Zander plowed straight ahead and hurled him back into a Hindu burial frieze. The sacramental stone hadn't survived 4,000 years for nothing, and so Zander knew that the crack ricocheting through the room was the guard's head splitting.

Holding her hand over her mouth in either awe or fright, Penny stepped from behind the sarcophagus and embraced Zander. He winced from the stress to his diaphragm, but still found holding Penny worth the pain.

"We have to go," he whispered as he retrieved his pistol and, once again, the cello case.

"What is that?" Penny asked, nodding toward the case.

"Long story," he said.

• • • •

As Ozbek had ordered, the driver was waiting outside the house with the carriage. When the uniformed guard stopped them at the front gate, Zander wondered if there was a standing order to keep Penny inside the compound unless Ozbek was by her side. He accompanied the driver into the gatehouse.

"Open it," Zander ordered, pistol in hand.

The guard did not hesitate to throw the switch and the gate slowly pulled open.

"Penny," Zander yelled out the door, "You know anything about horses?"

"If you mean can I drive this thing, yes."

Zander sent the driver and the guard marching into the forest, hands in the air, and climbed back on board.

Penny snapped the reins and they took off. She maneuvered down the narrow road as deftly as Ozbek's driver, but even at a moderate gait, the hardpacked road was rattling Zander's ribs. He slowly bent forward, wrapping his hands around his mid-section.

"Zander, are you all right?"

"I'm still sore from London." He forced himself to sit up just as the whir of an engine sent a jolt of adrenaline through his system. He spun around expecting to find a car chasing them, but relaxed when he saw a landscaper clearing brush with a chain saw.

"Zander, tell me what happened."

"Here on the island?"

"No. In the park, in London."

He pictured himself bounding down the steps of the Bertrand Hotel. It felt like another lifetime. He told her about the couple in the hotel tearoom, thinking how she might have disappeared without a trace if the old man hadn't piped up. He stopped for a moment, still incensed at the beating he took. "You saw what happened at the taxi," he said. "Next thing I knew I was in the hospital."

Penny held the reins in one hand and put her free arm around him.

"You drive like you've been doing this your whole life," he said, glancing back to assure himself that some new buzzing was only another chainsaw. He would have settled for a tractor. Instead, barreling down the horse path was a big yellow Hummer, its bank of fog lamps blinding even in daylight. "Christ!" he shouted, "We've got a few horses gaining on us."

"How many?"

Zander watched the Hummer roar toward them as if the carriage were standing still. "I'd say close to 300."

"What?" Penny glanced behind her. "Yaaa!" she fired at the horses and whipped the reins. The pair took off as if they'd burst from the starting gate at Santa

Anita. Penny seemed unaffected, her body moving in rhythm with the vibrating bench. Zander, on the other hand, was perpetually between beats. Pain rippled up his sides and he watched the cello case slide and shake so violently he was sure the mummy was turning to dust.

"Christ!" Penny screamed, spinning Zander around to see a teenage girl on horseback climbing toward them. They were on a straightaway now and the girl was only a few hundred feet off.

"Take my word for it," Zander said, "this trail isn't wide enough for us and that girl." He looked back at the Hummer again. He was shocked to see the guard he'd left in a lump on the museum floor at the wheel. If they slowed to let the girl pass, Ozbek's man would have them.

The girl had stopped. Zander couldn't tell whether the Hummer's driver could see her. While she was frozen with fright, her horse had enough sense to move to the trail's edge.

"Here we go!" Penny yelled. She jerked on the reins and the carriage ate up what little road buffered them from the woods.

Zander crouched down so the slapping branches wouldn't blind him. They flew past the girl, leaving her between them and Ozbek's men. The Hummer was wider than the carriage and barely fit on the trail by itself. No way it could squeeze by. Zander thanked God when the driver cut the wheel and the Hummer flew into the woods. He told Penny to ride to the town dock down the road. They tied up the carriage to keep the horses from bolting and headed for the ferry, vigilant for more of Ozbek's men.

Chapter 18

His physician pulled a stitch through the back of Ozbek's anesthetized head. Still woozy, the billionaire slumped on a leather divan in his living room, his white Henley shirt stained with iodine and dried blood. He was running through Kreisler's "Prelude and Allegro" in his mind to blunt the pain when Sherin hurried in.

"What happened?"

"That's what I want you to tell *me*," he seethed, flinching from the doctor's work. "That maniac forced me at gunpoint to bring him to Crane's assistant and then pistol-whipped me."

"He also broke into the museum. But only the cello case is gone."

"Of course it is. He came for the girl."

Sherin nodded. "Pamuk is in the village hospital."

"He should stay there," Ozbek said, lifting his eyes. "He can't stop them from breaking into the museum and then he can't catch a horse and buggy with a jeep. The impostor was the woman's friend from London, right? The American policeman?"

"I assume so."

Ozbek grabbed the doctor's hand. "Leave us, Ishak."

"I need another minute."

"I'll call you. Just go!"

The doctor pulled his work taut before stepping outside.

"You told me you eliminated him," Ozbek said.

"He was left unconscious in the gutter in London."

"Another problem I'll have to fix myself." He eased himself up. Black spots danced across his field of vision. "Too many mistakes, Sherin." He saw her body tighten like a fist. "Where were you?"

"None of your damn business," she snarled. "I'm not your bodyguard."

This was true. She was there only to handle those matters he had no stomach for. Still, her arrogance annoyed him. "You should be more concerned with my well being. Who knows what the Army or the police would make of your operations if I didn't keep them away."

"What I think," she said, jabbing a finger in his chest, "is that you're getting into a mess I may not be able to clean up—or want to."

He took her hand and lowered it to her side. "Please. Don't say something you'll regret. Just find them."

• • • •

They waited until the last moment to board the ferry, sharing a Coke while keeping an eye out for thugs Ozbek might have sent. If anyone was looking for them, it wasn't obvious.

"I thought I'd never see you again," Penny said as the ferry left the island.

A salty breeze tempered the blistering sun, letting them enjoy the upper deck. Unlike the rocket-propelled boat that brought him out, the ferry moved lazily enough for a school of dolphins to frolic in its wake. "Then we're even," Zander said. "I wasn't sure until yesterday I was even in the right country."

"How did you find me?"

Zander thought about the collection of people, leads, and connections he had followed from his hospital bed to Heybeli Island. He smiled at Penny, at her fine hair whipping in the wind and the soft pink of her lips, struggling to reconcile the intimacy of their shared misadventure with the fact that they barely knew each other. "It took a while to penetrate my thick skull, but a reporter I met here eventually convinced me Ozbek wasn't the saint you told me about."

Penny shivered despite the hot afternoon sun. "How could I have been so stupid?"

Zander watched her mouth turn down, the trauma of what she'd been through hitting her after the wild ride down the mountain. He put an arm around her shoulder and pulled her close. "The guy's a sociopath. You couldn't have known."

"He had Linus killed."

"Just for the mosaic at St. Eirene's?"

Penny pulled back to look at him. He watched his revelation dawn on her. "How do you know where it is?"

"I'd like to chalk it up to good detective work, but I found it by accident."

"Like Linus did," she breathed.

Now Zander was surprised. "How long have you known?"

"They gave me Linus's computer to figure out what he wouldn't tell Ozbek about his discovery. It was buried on his hard drive, but I knew where to look."

"Does Ozbek know?"

She patted his chest. "Thanks to the cavalry, no. But there's more to this than what you found. Linus was certain the mosaic is also a pictograph that would lead him to one of the greatest of all ancient treasures, a titanic gold-and-ivory statue of the goddess Athena. That's what Ozbek really wants. Linus refused to tell him about the mosaic because it would lead him to the Athena."

"And you weren't going to tell him either?"

"I want to go to St. Eirene's as soon as we get back," she said, clearly not wanting to dwell on what might have happened.

Zander nodded. He pictured the mosaic. If it contained some kind of puzzle, it wasn't obvious to him.

They resumed their watch as the ferry pulled into Istanbul. But no one stopped them as they crossed the crowded pier and flagged a taxi.

They had been at the hotel only long enough to deposit the cello case in Zander's room when Penny said she needed to stop into a boutique they had passed just a block away, since she had no clothes except what she was wearing. Zander was reluctant to head outside again so quickly, though he'd seen nothing to suggest anyone from Ozbek's island had followed them. Plus he found it essentially impossible to tell her no, which was a feeling he liked.

They almost ran the block to the store and Penny ducked inside while Zander stayed out front and called London. He did not want to leave her alone for long, but he felt obliged to update Scotland Yard. He dialed Norman Parrish and was transferred into voice mail, but Parrish's box was full and not taking new messages. The system switched him to the central operator. He asked for Graham Figgis, who answered after one ring.

"Hey, Zander, I've been worried about you. How's the hole in the head?"

"Still tender, Graham, but listen." He craned toward the boutique, unable to see Penny. "I'm in a rush here. I need you to tell Parrish I've got Penny and—"

"You've got Penny? " Figgis interrupted. "That's brilliant. Is she all right?"

"She's fine. Tell Parrish he can call off the dogs. And the same goes for the Crane investigation. I don't know the shooter's name, but the answer is not in London. It's down here with a billionaire named Ozbek."

"What are you talking about?" "Do you remember Penny had some photos Crane sent her?"

"The mosaic?"

"Exactly. Crane found it here in Istanbul and Penny says it's a picture puzzle that explains where to find some missing treasure."

"Jesus."

"I'll fill you in back in London." He retreated to the shop and poked his head inside. Penny was not there. He spun around in a panic, scanning the street for Ozbek's henchmen when a smiling Penny popped out from behind the fitting-room curtains and called him over.

"You all right?" she asked. "You look pale."

"I'm fine, fine," he said, startled by his own imagination.

. . . .

Special Agent Ned Nolan sounded happy to learn that Penny was okay. "But I need to impose on you," Zander told him over the phone. "We have to see that mosaic."

"No can do."

"It's gone?" Zander asked, thinking that Ozbek had somehow gotten to it. His question drained the color from Penny's face.

"Of course not. I'm looking at it right now."

Zander reassured Penny with a nod. "So what's the problem?"

"We're in a lock-down here. No one except FBI or DoD in or out."

"Why?"

"Some woman, an American, breached the perimeter yesterday."

"What was she doing there?"

"I have no idea. I only heard she was a wacko."

"How did she get in?"

"Flipped a couple of Turkish cops 20 bucks. So the Turks have been replaced by American M.P.s and the commander has barred all guests. It was the easiest solution."

"Christ."

"Don't get too upset," Nolan said. "We're all bugging out by lunchtime tomorrow. Twenty bucks will get you a ringside seat as soon as we're gone."

He hung up. "The mosaic's fine," he told Penny. "But we can't see it until tomorrow."

"Was there a problem?"

"Some mental patient snuck inside the security zone, so they've sealed it tight until the Americans leave. We'll get in right after."

"I want to take some photos to post on Facebook and also send some directly to Linus's colleagues at a dozen universities. Maybe UNESCO and some newspapers too."

Zander nodded, but a rush of anger was distracting him and Penny noticed.

"You don't like the plan?"

"It's fine. But even if the UN airlifts in an A-team of archaeologists, that sick bastard will still be getting away with murder."

"You think I don't know that? He was going to kill me!"

Zander saw he'd lit a short fuse.

"But we're in no position to destroy him," she continued, despair creeping into her voice. "He's part of the royal family here. The king-in-waiting. And you remember what Emerson said about kings?"

"It's on the tip of my tongue, Harvard, but refresh me."

"He said that when you strike at a king you must kill him."

"Smart guy."

"So maybe you should have shot him when you had the chance."

"Maybe. But there are other ways to kill a king."

Chapter 19

Zander and Penny found *The Express* in a 19th century commercial district clogged with warehouses, service bays, and machine shops. Goktepe greeted them at the door to the second-floor editorial office, above the printing presses.

"You look much better than most released prisoners," he told Penny.

"I didn't get out for good behavior."

They followed Goktepe to his corner desk in what looked like a dilapidated men's club. It struck Zander as an unlikely place to launch an assault on the state. The hardwood floor groaned with every step, and giant electric fans pushed warm air between the wide-open windows. Scratched and stained mahogany lined the walls. All 10 reporters worked at hulking oak desks, discarded long ago, Goktepe said, by a failed Ottoman bank. A pungent cloud of tobacco smoke hovered beneath the collapsing tin ceiling.

Goktepe sat at his desk and opened his laptop.

"Our circulation is small, but the right people read us. And of course everyone in the world will have access to the story after we post it on the web tomorrow morning. Perhaps some of the big sites in Britain or Germany, or even the U.S., will link to us."

Penny looked energized by Goktepe's words.

"It's been an interesting afternoon already," he continued. "Somehow Ozbek heard we were running an exposé and he's threatening legal action."

"You're printing the truth, right?" Zander asked.

"Yes, but my worst fear is that he wakes a corrupt judge at midnight who stops us from publishing until a court hearing that could be weeks from now."

"Is that likely?" asked Penny.

"I can't worry about it. The publisher told Bulent to sue us if he's so sure we're wrong, though he didn't put it so nicely."

"So what did your last source give you?" Zander asked.

"That a New York grand jury has subpoenaed Ozbek's accounts at Hanover Bank."

"Laundering?"

"Yes. Both his own money and for mobsters."

"So no doubt the IRS is asking questions," Zander said, encouraged that Penny and he weren't the only ones trying to tie a noose around Ozbek's neck.

"Why is this going on in New York?" Penny asked.

"Because," Zander replied, "the United States is still the safest place to park your money, especially if you've got a lot of it and need to move it around."

"*Yarim saat!*" a boy screamed from the center of the office above the din of the fans.

"He said we have half an hour to make the print edition," explained Goktepe. "Let's get to work."

Penny ran Goktepe through her trauma at Ozbek's hands like she was giving courtroom testimony. She made only a vague reference to the mosaic, not wanting the world to descend on Crane's discovery. Zander was hearing many of the details for the first time. He raged when she recounted how Ozbek slapped her to the floor.

Goktepe stopped her after 15 minutes to ask a few questions. "Until now," he finally said, "the dirt on Ozbek was dry, all related to business: bank and land fraud, tax fraud, money laundering, extortion and bribery. Terrible stuff, but it's hard to get people upset about white-collar crime. But what happened to you shows the true monster he is." He searched a contact list on his computer. "I just need to call Ozbek for his comment."

"I wouldn't want to hear that conversation," Penny said.

"I would," said Zander, almost understanding for the first time why people became journalists. "And I'd like to see the finished article."

"Then come here early tomorrow. I'll have the first copies and I'll translate while we celebrate."

Chapter 20

No matter how slowly Felix Maurer drove, every muddy bump and rain-filled pothole rocked the Mercedes Gelandewagen down to its bolts. He had told his bosses he would go anywhere to find the true bombers, and here he was, bouncing around the fringes of hell, otherwise known as Sultanbeyli, an unchecked virus on Istanbul's eastern fringe that had grown from an encampment of ethnic-Turkish immigrants in the early 1980's to a half-million people living in what he would generously call a garbage dump.

He had abandoned any hope that his long-cultivated network of spineless bureaucrats would deliver anything useful. He'd spent three years in Turkey planting seeds. All week he'd left explicit instructions for his assets at Justice, Interior, and Defense to report. But no one had shown at their drops, not even after he tripled the usual piece rate.

Much better to have a few well-connected friends—or, in this case, one well-connected friend. Bulent Ozbek had been so grateful after learning from

Maurer about that fraud Goktepe's so-called undercover investigation that he had arranged a private session with the Interior Minister. This allowed him to see the bombers' full videotaped confessions, not just the bits for public broadcast. He had expected—or maybe hoped—to find their common thread in Afghanistan, fighting against the Soviets. Or maybe even Iran, seeking collective enlightenment at some terror camp masquerading as a religious retreat. Rather, he'd been shocked to see the rumors were true. The background the five admitted to sharing—their leader Mazari had never broken—was terror training at the hands of Greek intelligence in the Aegean. This was not enough for Washington to turn against a supposed ally. Some of the training took place a decade ago. However it might be enough for the Turks to go to war. The government had already promised retaliation against whomever was responsible, and Maurer knew Turkish troops were being mobilized. If it turned out to be Athens, then Washington was looking at an unnerving crisis. Next to Britain, Turkey was America's best friend in Europe. No doubt Europeans would side with Athens and their Christian brothers in any sort of dust-up. Not only would NATO implode, but this would push the Turks further into the Muslim world. A dream come true for Islamic fundamentalists, who despised Turkey's accommodation with the United States and generally cordial relations with Israel. Having reviewed the crap that passed for facts in the lead-up to the Iraqi invasion, Maurer knew how easy it was to launch a war based on bad intelligence.

If the Greeks were responsible, then of course they had to be made to pay, not just by the Turks but also by

Washington. These revelations had bought Maurer a short reprieve from the chiefs at Langley. But it actually doubled the pressure to find the smoking gun. Who had actually commissioned the bombing, not just trained the bombers? The issue was now a shooting war in the Mediterranean—not just American pride—and he needed proof harder than the warhead of an ICBM. His boss was counting on him. And the Director was depending on his boss. And the President was relying upon the Director. The chain of command was sitting on his shoulders.

That's why he was here. He needed to know the truth, no matter where it led.

He was paying an unannounced call on Leman Mazari, mother of the terrorist who had succumbed to assisted suicide. He had met her outside the prison gates after officials told her she would never get her son's remains. Maurer knew this was bureaucratic bungling—the jailers, he assumed, needed more time to prep the brutalized body—and he had promised to help her. A day later, without any intervention on his part, she got her son back. Now, with his regular sources run dry, Maurer was hoping the terrorist's mother might yield something of value.

Rain from last night's drenching roared in fast-moving streams down both sides of the pitted dirt road. Shacks stretched as far as he could see: walls of mud, unmortared brick or cardboard, topped by tin roofs secured by rocks or string. There was no indoor plumbing, though TV antennas crowned most of the hovels.

He couldn't believe he'd made it this far. There were no streets, let alone street signs. An Israeli friend of his had sketched out a map that had turned out to be surprisingly accurate. The Mossad agent had been trying for years to get Maurer out to Sultanbeyli for some old-fashioned grass-roots intelligence gathering, but he had always begged off.

Maurer heard a bump and thought he'd hit a baby goat. He glanced backward and was relieved it was only a brick. He wasn't in the mood for an argument over reparations. But then a cinderblock building painted phosphorescent green that he'd been given as a landmark was upon him and he hit the brake in time to turn down what he thought was a footpath.

Shacks hugged the path so tightly that he would probably run down anyone taking a step out their door. Laundry flapped on ropes between walls, no doubt picking up the signature odor of all third-world slums: rancid cooking fuel, rotting refuse, and human waste.

He reached a clearing and got out. He asked a bearded young man where he could find Mazari's house. The Turk eyed him with suspicion, but gestured toward a rocky trail.

Fifty yards down, across the gully from a hovel pouring out disconsolate arabesque songs, a handpainted wood sign proclaimed "Mazari." Maurer knocked and a woman draped in black pulled open the makeshift door. She recognized him immediately, though he could barely see her eyes behind her headscarf. She grabbed and hugged him, but her dead son had murdered 500 Americans, and he barely draped his arms around her. Mrs. Mazari asked him to sit.

He now understood his Israeli friend's claim that the shantytown was not as bad as it seemed. He was expecting the same tumbledown filth as outside. But the inside of the shack wasn't a shack, it was a home: neat and clean. The few pieces of furniture had seen better days—or decades—but the rips were sewn up and the metal polished. The floor especially fascinated Maurer and he pecked at it with the toe of his workboots. It was hard-packed dirt, but not dirty. And the smell of Mrs. Mazari's just-baked bread displaced the stench outside. She spread a blue-and-white floral cloth on the floor and served bread and dried fruit along with tea, despite his protests not to bother. She joined him on the floor, pulling her scarf back and letting it frame her face.

Maurer thought she rarely had reason to smile, but below her small, intense eyes, broad nose and fleshy, sunburnt cheeks, her pursed lips were curling up. He knew from their encounter outside Bayrampasa prison that she spoke no English and he complimented her housekeeping in Turkish as she cut some bread with her thick, strong arms. He quickly asked her about the funeral. She told him it was small and private, at the police's insistence.

"Your husband was there?"

"He died last year." She had three other children, all grown and with families.

"You understand the government just didn't want any demonstrations."

"I only wanted my little lion to have a proper burial." Tears slid down her cheeks.

"I need to ask you some questions, Mrs. Mazari."

"Anything you want. You are a friend."

Maurer paused. Altruism was not in his vocabulary, but he wondered if he still hadn't done better by her than anyone else these past few weeks. "I take it you believe your boy had nothing to do with bombing the Americans?"

"Atilla was a good boy. He was not a killer."

"But the police say he fought in Afghanistan."

"Yes. But many did. To him it was his debt to Allah."

"Did he ever talk to you about it? About the friends he made there?"

She paused for a moment. "He said it was very painful."

"Do you know if he visited any other countries? Iraq? Greece, perhaps?"

She shook her head. "England once. To see friends, he said."

"Did you see him at all after the time of the bombing?"

"He came every week. He was a good son. My baby."

"Did he say anything to you about the bombing?"

She shook her head.

Maurer sighed, depressed by the woman's honesty. It had been a long shot, he reminded himself. "Perhaps the police were already after him," he said, throwing another line into a barren lake, "and he might have told you."

Mrs. Mazari got up and ducked into the one recess of the mud house. She returned with an Adidas shoebox, letting him see it was stuffed with papers. "Atilla left this on his last visit. He said he would come for it in a few weeks."

Maurer leaned forward, eager for a look. "Have the police seen this?"

"No. The police have never been here."

Maurer was astonished at such incompetence. "Do

you mind if I look?"

She put the box on the floral cloth. He flipped through it: a lot of correspondence, some in envelopes, some loose, some typed. A few trinkets rattled around.

"Have you looked through here?" he asked.

"Yes, but I cannot read."

He took the box. "I would like to borrow this. I will return it in a day or two at the most. I promise."

"You will tell me what is in it?"

"Yes, if you would like."

The promise of another downpour greeted Maurer as he stepped outside. He cradled the box like a starving man holding a feast. He wanted to devour it. But he set it down on the passenger-side floor, intentionally out of arm's reach, as he inched the Mercedes back down the pitted path. It would be too easy to overlook something, he told himself, if he ripped through the box now. And he had a critical chore to dispose of first.

Chapter 21

Helen forced herself to sit up and drape her legs over the side of the bed. Twilight filtered through the edges of the drawn curtains. She had no appetite, but the nausea had passed.

She thought about calling a doctor. There must be American physicians in Istanbul. Who do the diplomats use? They'd take her to the morgue before she'd let a Turkish doctor touch her.

The stench of that rat-infested torture chamber still coated her nostrils. She couldn't believe she'd actually slept a night in jail. No. Scratch that. She hadn't slept for a moment. Her feet hurt from pacing all night. The lice had been waiting for her to sit down. She would check into Lennox Hill for a complete battery of tests as soon as she got home.

She'd be on her way to London in less than 10 hours. She hated pre-dawn packing so she hoisted herself up and retrieved her suitcase. She couldn't wait for Istanbul to dissolve into a blur from 35,000 feet.

A glance in the mirror sent a chill across her

shoulders. She brought her face close to the glass and pried open her bloodshot, mascara-streaked eyes. "Christ," she mumbled, shaking her head in disbelief. Lennox Hill and then the Peninsula Spa.

She should call and thank Peter Sloan for sending Gary Durkin to spring her from hell. Maybe Peter could even re-book that hotel in the Lake District. Peace and quiet, fresh air, and bucolic vistas. And a few days with Peter might be necessary to ensure his silence. She wondered if the *Downton Abbey* house was near there. She stopped folding a blouse and felt content that despite everything she was coming home with the Sumerian necklace.

The hotel phone rang. Peter! she thought with a chuckle. He seemed to know when she was thinking about him. He said it was proof they were destined for each other. Durkin probably gave him the phone number.

"Hello, Helen?"

"Yes?" she said, the voice throwing her.

"This is Bulent Ozbek."

"Bulent! My God, I was just thinking about you."

Chapter 22

The cab had barely pulled into traffic before Zander and Penny moved perilously close to spontaneous combustion.

They floated from the taxi into the pension, arms intertwined. She suggested a nightcap, but Zander reminded her of their early appointment with Goktepe.

• • • •

"What can I get you?" Bulent Ozbek asked Helen.

"A tall glass of ice water would be wonderful." She sank into one of the overstuffed couches. "I'm feeling a bit dehydrated." She stared at the mural painted on the living room's vaulted ceiling: an aquamarine night sky filled with stars and constellations. "This reminds me of Grand Central Terminal."

"It should. The mural there marks the precise position of the stars the night that John Jacob Astor, the American rail baron, was born. Well, the sky here shows where the stars were the night *I* was born."

"Really?" Helen asked, but she couldn't imagine

Ozbek joking.

He handed Helen her Perrier, his laser eyes probing in advance of his words. "Now explain to me what you are doing in Istanbul."

Helen didn't expect the question so soon or so directly, especially after their roundabout conversation on the phone. She had told him that she was leaving early the next morning, and she didn't see how she could visit him and make her flight. She wasn't sure how he knew about her legal mess. But he made it clear, if indirectly, that he did.

"Don't worry about that flight," he had advised her.

"But—"

"Helen, sometimes the law grows too full of itself. Rest assured that no one is forcing you to leave Turkey."

He had turned oblique when she asked how he learned she was in Istanbul. "Because this is my city." She knew better than to try pinning him down. In the end she took his invitation. He had sent a car to shuttle her to the dock, where the Scarab was waiting. It was dark when the carriage entered the compound.

Ozbek joined her on the couch, cradling a snifter of Cointreau.

"I'm here for a short vacation," she said, seeing no advantage in showing her hand. "I was supposed to spend a few days on holiday in the Lake District after the conference."

"Really? Whom with?"

"An old friend at the American embassy. But he had to cancel because he was drafted, oddly enough, onto the team that's analyzing the Istanbul terror bombing." She wasn't sure how she'd come up with that, but it was logical enough.

"So you decided to pop down and inspect the bombing yourself?"

Helen would not be thrown so easily. So what if he knew about yesterday? He seemed discreet. "Actually I'm here because of you. Hearing you extol the wonders of Istanbul, I felt almost inadequate that I hadn't been here in so long, seen the city through adult eyes, as it were. So when my time freed up, I hopped on a plane."

"I'm hurt you didn't call me. I could have given you a personal tour."

"I couldn't impose on you. You're busy and I'm only here shopping and sightseeing."

"And not looking for anything in particular?"

Helen placed her empty glass on the lion-footed coffee table. "Such as?"

He got up to refill her glass. "Something rare and special."

"Well, that's what we're all looking for, isn't it?"

He handed her the refreshed drink. "Of course."

She could tell from the impatient curl of his mouth that Ozbek was not used to anyone's misdirection but his own.

"But you must tell me. Have you seen anything breathtaking on this trip?"

Helen stayed silent—another negotiating tactic daddy had drilled into her head. But her mind was racing like a NASCAR driver trapped against the rail.

"And what if I came across something truly special?"

"Then I would make it worth your while to share it."

"By that I take it you mean money?"

Now it was Ozbek's turn to show surprise, if his staccato laugh was any indication.

"Because money is not my motive," she continued.

"Of course not. You're a scholar."

"That's not it either."

"Then tell me how we can work together."

This was going better than she could have hoped. "You understand, of course, that I'm not speaking for myself. I represent the Met. And even though the Met is the greatest museum in the world—"

"Second to none," Ozbek concurred.

"Sometimes an opportunity is too big even for the Met. It's the way of the world today. Two studios produce a movie together. Two oil companies jointly explore a hazardous new territory. I'm sure you try to spread risk in your business ventures, no?"

"Of course," Ozbek said.

"Then," Helen said, I'd like you to consider a joint venture of sorts with us."

Ozbek's eyes widened and he sat back. Unlike most people, whose hearts raced when cutting a deal, negotiation seemed to put him at ease. "Even before I went to Harvard," he said, "I knew that half of something is better than all of nothing."

"Good. Then perhaps you know that before his death Professor Linus Crane came across something quite rare."

Ozbek downed the remainder of his Cointreau. "I have heard a rumor to that effect. What can you tell me about it?"

Helen smiled. She was considering what tidbit to dangle in front of him when she turned to see who was rapping at the door. The butler appeared. He handed Ozbek an envelope, which he opened and read. He looked at Helen.

"I'm sorry but my lawyers need me on a conference call. It is likely to last quite a while."

"We can pick things up in the morning?"

"Of course."

Helen didn't mind the recess. Let his interest grow over night. He'll be all the happier to see the mosaic photos and hear her interpretation.

Ozbek looked at his butler. "Show Dr. Vandameer to her room."

• • • •

Maurer flipped the tab on another Diet Coke. His tenth, at least. The euphoria he'd felt upon first opening the shoebox handed him by Atilla Mazari's mother had evaporated hours ago. He laughed nervously when he read Mazari's note to himself: "Atilla = Scourge of the Gods." This might be the highlight of his report to Langley.

He was elated at first to find the last two years of Mazari's personal finances. But the bank statements exposed only the details of a humdrum life lived just a hair above subsistence. What little money Mazari made—from teaching at an Islamist private school and some freelance magazine work, according to his personal ledger—was quickly spent. Travel was his only extravagance. From what he could tell, Mazari never had a credit card or owned any property. If there was any trail connecting this man to the bombings—or even any radical activities—he hadn't seen it.

At three in the morning Maurer opened a small

jewelry box. He thought it might hold an engagement ring. Instead he found a charm bracelet, along with a tiny vellum card wishing his mother a happy birthday. Silver animals: an elephant, giraffe, monkey, a hippo, and either a tiger or leopard, Maurer couldn't tell. He squeezed the bracelet until his hand bled.

"I'm fucked," he mumbled to himself.

Chapter 23

Zander was already in khakis and polo shirt when the wake-up call came. "Thank you," he croaked after hustling to grab it. The phone was only inches from Penny's ear but she was still as a corpse.

He was eager to see Goktepe again. Penny's eyes blinked open and he watched them dart around the room in panic. She calmed after focusing on him.

"Thought you were still at Ozbek's?"

She nodded. "Are you ready to go?"

Zander was brewing a cup of courtesy coffee when there was a tapping on the door. He figured that only the housekeeper or trouble would knock so early. He took the pistol from atop the desk and squinted through the peephole. He was shocked to see the bloated profile of Graham Figgis.

He threw open the door. "Figgis!"

The Englishman focused on Zander's gun. "Who were you expecting?"

"Not you," Zander said.

Figgis was wearing a banker's blue suit that looked

like he'd slept in it, which he had, he explained, on his flight from London. "I'm here to save you from yourself, my friend."

Penny opened the bathroom door in new shorts and T-shirt.

"You two haven't met," Zander said. "Penny, this is Graham Figgis.

They shook hands. "But how did you know we were here?" she asked.

"I called Scotland Yard to say you were safe," Zander said.

Figgis nodded. "Parrish wants the whole story, of course."

"He'll get it. But what are you doing here?"

"To tell you a story I wanted to tell you before you left London, but couldn't. When you called yesterday to say you'd freed Penny from Ozbek and that he'd arranged Crane's murder, I demanded permission."

Penny turned to Zander, looking at him for an explanation. He let her know with a shrug he was equally in the dark.

"Let me give you the bottom line and work back. You're both in danger and must get out of Turkey immediately."

"That's not news, Graham," Zander said

"I understand that, but here's the background. Our friend Ozbek has been the subject of a combined Scotland Yard-Interpol investigation for two years now. He's made a bloody fortune smuggling narcotics, arms, and antiquities, not to mention laundering all the proceeds and stiffing tax authorities in 30 countries. But most relevant to you, he's responsible for at least a dozen killings. His London townhouse and Yorkshire estate have been key transit points for his operations, so The Yard has taken the lead in what will be a multinational prosecution. I've been part of the task force from the antiquities end of it, but the entire inquiry has been top secret for political reasons. There are implications not just for Turkey and Turkish-British relations, but for all of NATO and the Middle East."

"And Linus Crane's murder will be part of the indictment?" Penny asked.

"Eventually."

"Thank God you're on to him."

"And Zander said you've learned more about the motive? This mosaic?"

"It's quite something," Zander said.

Figgis looked at Zander with surprise. "You've seen it?"

"Yes. Sadly enough, it's inside the church—what's left of it—that the terrorists blew up on July 4th. I saw it when I met an FBI agent there."

"Well, I'm sure you appreciate that Ozbek won't let your … uh… visit pass without evening the score."

"We've taken precautions—" Penny said.

"Please," Figgis interrupted, his tone taking an exasperated edge. "The only precaution is distance. You can't imagine the range of his network in Istanbul. No one can protect you here."

Zander couldn't contain his anger. "Goddammit, Graham, you couldn't give me a fucking clue about this before I came down here?"

"I thought you might take it this way."

"Is there some other way to take it?"

"I don't know, Zander. All I can say is that I'm here now. I wanted to tell you sooner—you'll have to take my word on that—but it was just impossible."

Zander still felt disappointed. But he didn't know what he would have done differently even if he had been warned in London. "So can you at least tell me when you're taking him down? You must have a boatload of evidence."

"My guess is within the next 72 hours, but I can't say for sure. You know how it works. That decision's being made well above my head. We need to ensure Ozbek hasn't an inch of wiggle room. To go against a foreign national of his stature, the case must be more than airtight. I'm meeting with local members of the strike force to coordinate final details. I put them off an hour to come see you."

"I appreciate it, Graham," Zander said. "And we understand what you're saying."

"So can you promise me you'll leave town?"

"We'll be gone today."

"And you're not playing Rambo again before then?"

"No," Zander said, looking at Penny. "The Rambo part of the trip is over."

• • • •

Zander put his arm around Penny as they set out for *The Express*.

"But I want to hit Saint Eirene's as soon as we leave Goktepe's," she said.

"Absolutely."

Twenty minutes later they were back in the factory district, the morning heat already reflecting off the blacktop. They turned down *The Express's* street two blocks from the office. Skirting a mountain of coffee beans in burlap bags, Zander froze for a moment and felt his chest seize up at the sight of thick black smoke billowing to the sky up ahead. Semis and dump trucks blocked his view, but he searched for the source. He grabbed Penny's hand and led her through a blocked intersection and into the midst of a crowd that was watching the newspaper's office burn to the ground.

Chapter 24

Helen sat in the gazebo amidst Ozbek's English gardens, waiting to be summoned to breakfast, regretting her stay on Heybeli would be so brief. Her room had been more sumptuous than a five-star hotel: a canopied Ottoman wedding bed, Louis XIV desk, tapestry rugs, a Degas bronze dancer.

She was pleased with her good fortune. Yesterday had started in hell and gone downhill. But Ozbek's call had put her back in the catbird's seat, as her father would have said. She woke up debating whether to hold back what she knew of Crane's discovery until Ozbek agreed to exhibit his collection at the Met, but decided against igniting a power struggle. Once they joined forces to find the mosaic she'd make sure he saw it was in his own interest to bring his collection to New York.

• • • •

Bulent Ozbek was making a few notes at his desk in the octagon library when his butler escorted the new guest inside. He stopped writing, shook his visitor's hand and motioned him toward a high-back leather chair. "Sit."

"Thank you. And thank you again for seeing me under these extraordinary circumstances."

Ozbek leaned back and held his hands as if in devotional prayer, "I was curious to meet the real Henry Demarest."

"As I was to meet you, if only to explain what happened."

Ozbek stroked the bandage atop his head. "I hope you can answer a few questions."

"I'll do my best."

"Good. Now the man who came here— "

"A police detective," Demarest almost shouted, "named Alexander Blake."

"How do you know him?" Ozbek asked while he put a check mark alongside what he'd already written on his notepad: *Alexander Blake, LAPD.*

"He handles art crimes. He's made a relentless pest of himself since I helped him on one occasion."

"And the Anasazi. That was the real mummy?"

"Oh yes. What he brought here was genuine."

"How did he get it?"

"He took it from me right here in Istanbul."

"And you agreed to let him impersonate you?"

"Agreed? No no. He threatened me if I didn't go along. With a gun."

"So why are you here? You no longer feel threatened?"

Demarest edged forward. "Because redeeming my reputation in the eyes of a valued client is more important than his threats."

"I see," Ozbek said, convinced that Demarest was

two-faced as a small-town mayor, but that he'd nevertheless consign some pieces to him for sale. "I'm still interested in the Anasazi. Do you have her?"

"No, I'm sorry to say, I don't. I thought perhaps it... or she... was here."

Ozbek laughed, struck that Demarest was more concerned with collecting a fee for the Anasazi than with his reputation. "Did the policeman tell you why he did this?"

"No. Except that he seemed to have some kind of grudge against you, though he never said why. It was crazy."

"I appreciate your candor, Mr. Demarest."

"Thank you. And if I could ask, as far as Native American pieces go, are you interested only in funereal artifacts, or can I think more broadly on your behalf?"

"The afterlife remains a priority. But I'm open to other works. Now I must ask your indulgence. I have another guest to attend to." He shook Demarest's hand. "Transportation back to the city is being arranged."

• • • •

Helen was spreading a piece of rusk toast with blackberry marmalade when Ozbek joined her on the veranda. A servant rolled out a cart with both their breakfasts.

"Did you wrap up the business with your lawyers?" she asked.

He spread his napkin. "Yes. Everything worked out." He took a sip of orange juice. "But getting back to last night, you and I were discussing the late Linus Crane."

Helen was ready to launch her gambit when Ozbek

answered his cell phone.

She could tell this was no social call. Someone was relating a story, apparently in English, which Ozbek, looking somewhat bored, was punctuating with an occasional "yes" or "go on." But all of a sudden, his face lit up.

"Are you absolutely sure? That's splendid. You've earned yourself a fat bonus."

Ozbek slipped the phone into his pocket.

"Good news?" she asked.

"Sensational." He reached out and gently grasped her wrist. "Helen," he said, "that call is forcing me to change my plans. So I have to ask you quickly. Do you know where Linus Crane's mosaic is?"

She offered him her coy smile. "Well, that's what we need to discuss."

Ozbek laughed, but then his touch turned brutal. "I don't have time for your mindless bullshit."

She tried to wrestle her hand away. "You're hurting me!"

He spoke with a cool rage. "I'm going to ask you again. And answer me directly or I'm going to break your arm. Do you know where Linus Crane's mosaic is?"

Chapter 25

"Oh God, no!" Penny cried, burying her head in Zander's shoulder as the second floor of *The Express* collapsed with a heart-stopping crack. Fire trucks and two-dozen firemen kept shooting high-powered hoses into the office, but Zander knew the battle was lost.

"What happened?" he yelled into the crowd, not knowing if anyone could understand him. "Does anyone know what happened?"

Zander watched a young man push back toward him. What he thought was a scruffy beard was actually soot. "We were firebombed," he said.

"You worked for the paper?"

"Yes, a reporter," he said, scrutinizing Zander. "You were here yesterday—in the office."

"To see Goktepe. We were supposed to meet him again this morning."

"He's dead." The young man's eyes dampened.

A scream caught in Penny's throat. "What?" she finally asked.

The reporter nodded. "He was upstairs, right where

the bomb smashed through the window, the police said. They took his body away—what was left of it—a little while ago. Two pressmen were burnt badly, but they were downstairs and managed to get out."

Zander instinctively draped his arm across Penny as the roof finally caved into the inferno.

"Do you have any idea who's responsible?" Zander asked.

"I could fill a page with suspects." The young man shook his head in disgust as mist from the hoses drifted onto them. "We angered a lot of people. Any of them could have done it, and I'm sure the rest will be happy to hear about it."

Penny cried into his shoulder. He thought how Linus Crane had underestimated Ozbek, as had Goktepe. And now he had as well. When she picked her head up again, she seemed startled. "What is it?" he asked.

Penny pointed. Down the block, past the crowd, one of the guard's from Ozbek's compound leaned against a car, nodding and speaking into a cell phone as he stared at the smoldering *Express*.

• • • •

"I should have known better," he told Penny as they hustled past a towering loading dock on their way to St. Eirene's. "Goktepe would be alive if I'd thought this through."

Penny pulled him to a stop. "Are you saying you're responsible for this?"

Zander snorted in disgust with himself. "Before Goktepe rewrote his article to include the stuff about you and Crane, Ozbek was only going to squeeze some judge for a restraining order. Goktepe told us that. But Ozbek obviously felt a murder charge would ruin him, so he struck first."

"You were trying to help him, Zander."

"Was I? Or was it just a selfish way to get at Ozbek?"

"Selfish? How?"

"Because it was risk-free for me, but hardly for Goktepe."

Penny shook her head. "It's just as likely that Ozbek planned to kill Goktepe all along. I've seen him up close. He's a monster. The legal threat could have been a diversion to get his guard down. And besides, Goktepe knew the risks."

"Maybe. Maybe not," Zander said.

"He seemed like an awfully smart guy to me," Penny said.

"Lotta good that did him."

The streets were swarming as they approached the city center. Just past the Blue Mosque, where a class of giggling schoolgirls tossed bread to a street full of pigeons, Penny suggested they cut through the park that paralleled the road. The short oasis from the smog and noise terminated at Saint Sophia, which was ringed by paramilitary troops obviously intent on keeping terrorists from striking the city's most familiar sight.

They hurried around the 1,500-year-old landmark and cut across a stretch of park to the bombed-out church. It was evident even from a distance that the Americans had left for home. The military encampment was gone. The grassy area was reopened to pedestrians. The piles of crumpled bleachers had shrunk by three-fourths, carted away in dump trucks that were finishing the job. The bloody pavement was scrubbed clean.

Most striking of all was the church itself. The tarpaulins had disappeared, replaced by a chain-link fence. Zander and Penny circled the perimeter until they reached the only entrance, a gate wide enough to accommodate heavy equipment. Two police officers stood together to one side, smoking and yawning.

Zander flashed his shield. "United States Federal Bureau of Investigation!" He pointed inside as if he was simply alerting the cops that he was going in, not asking permission. One shrugged his shoulders while the other waved them through. Zander threw them both a salute.

"Nice move," Penny said.

They were approaching the wreck from a different angle than he had before, but one pile of rubble didn't look much different to him from another. Penny seemed as chilled by the devastation as Zander had his first time.

He regained his bearings by focusing on some tall trees that Ned Nolan had used as a reference point, and they marched along the wall where Nolan had led him. At the end, near the point where the GI had handed Nolan some evidence to bag, Zander peeked around the corner. The indentations left on the ground by Nolan's evacuated desk looked fresh.

"You ready?" he asked.

"I think so," Penny said, clutching his arm. Zander led her around the corner. Penny looked up and down the wall. "Am I missing something?"

Zander stepped back. He wanted to believe they had taken a wrong turn, but he knew they hadn't. The mosaic was gone and he knew he'd been outfoxed once again. The rough gray wall announced like a billboard that while he'd won the odd skirmish since arriving in Istanbul, he'd lost the war. "No," he told her. "It was right here."

"Are you sure?"

He trotted to where the center of the mosaic should have been and leaned his cheek against the stone. "This section is a couple of inches shallower than the rest. It's been sheared off."

Penny brushed her palms against the sliced and pitted rock. "You're right, it's——. I hear something."

He heard it as well: voices, unclear how many, arguing in Turkish on the other side of the wall. A few seconds later, two hardhats in matching blue coveralls turned the corner. They stopped talking when they saw they were not alone, but did not acknowledge Zander or Penny. One lifted a stained canvas dropcloth off the ground, exposing a handheld power saw, some chisels and a sledge hammer big enough to pound railroad spikes, or, Zander realized, for splitting the mosaic from the wall. The men picked up the equipment and started back.

"Hey!" Zander yelled, stopping them. "Who are you working for?" The pair looked at each other. One motioned with his head and they kept on going.

"What do we do?" asked Penny.

"Follow them out." They trailed the workmen to a green Nissan pickup parked amid half-a-dozen trucks. A third man was standing by the open tailgate, securing a canvas that covered what looked to Zander like several stone slabs. The tool carriers tossed their equipment onto the bed and climbed in the cab.

"Goddammit!" Penny yelled. "He's got it."

"Ozbek?"

"Yes. That guy tying the canvas was one of the goons on the plane that brought me here."

Zander rejected the idea of trying to stop them. Who knew what they'd do to Penny. Instead, he pulled his cellphone from his pocket and snapped a few pictures of the crew, though he wasn't even sure why.

The driver threw the truck into gear and lumbered past them. Penny's kidnapper sat atop the priceless pile of stone, smiling at her. Her jaw clenched and her face turned crimson. Zander thought she was going to take off after the truck and hop aboard.

"I can't believe it," she screamed. "How did he know?"

Zander put his arm around her. "Let's go back inside."

She raced ahead of him toward the looted area. When he caught up to her she was inspecting the wall. He took more pictures on the chance they'd prove useful to Figgis's investigation.

"This close," she said, holding two fingers barely apart as she sat on the ground. "How did he even know to look here?"

Zander eased down beside her. "He could have gotten lucky, like I did. Or maybe some archaeologist came through yesterday and called him. We know he's got his finger in every pie in town. Or maybe he pulled something off Crane's laptop."

"No way. I erased the hard drive."

He was about to say that drives can be restored, but saw no point. Her disappointment was sapping her spirit.

"So that's it, huh?" she said. "He gets everything?"

He took her hand, trying to separate his desire to destroy Ozbek from the reason they'd come to St. Eirene's in first place. "If those gorillas make it to the island, then yes, he gets everything. We couldn't get near him again if we wanted to. But look, we came here to record the fact that the mosaic exists. If we get down to the dock before they ship it out maybe we can still get our proof."

"So if we get there in time," she asked, her enthusiasm reviving, "I distract them while you sneak in?"

Zander laughed. "I'm leaning toward a bribe. Maybe 50 bucks will get us a peek and some pictures." Once again he heard voices on the far side of the wall.

"Sounds like they forgot something," Penny said, "Maybe we can get our look now."

Four different men, all in jeans, t-shirts and work boots, turned the corner.

Zander could read their faces enough to see they hadn't returned to clean up. "Let's go," he told Penny, shoving her gently toward the way out. But before he could move, the front man rammed his fist into his kidney, doubling him over. Two others grabbed Penny and slapped handcuffs on her. A moment later two others straightened Zander up, pinned his arms by his waist, cuffed him, and stuck a pistol in his back.

Chapter 26

Wrenched upright but still gasping, Zander was led out of the wreck with the pistol jabbing his aching side. Penny followed right behind. A black Mercedes waited for them at the fence.

The car kicked up a cyclone of trash as it flew through Istanbul's cobbled backstreets. Zander and Penny faced one another. The limo stank from cigars and sported a stereo, TV, and wet bar. But far from partying, their abductors remained silent as Trappists.

"Where are we going?" Zander asked the apparent ringleader. He looked at Penny, sitting quietly, biting her lip. The prospect of being hauled out to Ozbek again obviously terrified her. "You've got the damn mosaic. What do you need us for?"

The man turned his buzz-cut toward Zander. "Why don't you shut the fuck up?" he growled in a drawl from somewhere between Kentucky and Tennessee.

The accent straightened Zander up. "You're American?" he asked. "On Ozbek's payroll?" The man, with the arms of an Olympic weightlifter, smirked at Zander but apparently had said everything he was going to say.

"I see water ahead of us," said Penny, squinting through the smoke-gray windshield.

"This is the Golden Horn," Zander said, as the limo crossed the Galata Bridge. "Ozbek's island is the other way. The only thing I know in this direction is the American consulate." Mentioning the consulate prompted the thought that he had to contact Durkin somehow. There was no one else left. Before he could even begin to imagine how, the Mercedes pulled to the curb of a broad avenue.

The ringleader removed their handcuffs and hustled them out of the car toward what Zander recognized as the street leading to the consulate. A Marine stood guard by a gap in a concrete barrier that diverted all traffic. Zander had no clue what was going on, but he wouldn't complain if they took him where he wanted to go.

"Soldier!" Zander shouted to the Marine.

"Shut up, asshole!" the ringleader snarled.

Zander glared at his keeper. He itched to take him down with a sharp kick to the knee, but restrained himself.

Penny rubbed some feeling back into her wrists while, to Zander's astonishment, the guard saluted the ringleader. Glancing back at the limo, Zander felt like they'd fallen down the rabbit hole when the driver snapped a stiff American flag to the aerial. The guard took down Zander's and Penny's names, home addresses, and social security numbers.

"Am I supposed to believe you're a Marine?" Zander asked the ringleader.

"Captain John Swanson."

"Then would you tell me what the hell you want with us?"

"And what gives you the right to force us to go anywhere?" Penny demanded. "You're gonna need a damn good lawyer."

If Swanson felt threatened, he didn't show it. "They're with me," he told a pair of Marines flanking the consulate entrance. He ushered everyone through a metal detector and brought them to a stop in the consulate's large foyer. He pulled a cell phone from his pocket. "If you two can keep quiet for three minutes," he said, his tone gruff but less antagonistic, "you'll get a full explanation."

The lobby was crowded with American officers in uniform, spillover from a noisy reception in the ballroom. A military band was playing Sousa. Zander wondered if their abduction was tied to Figgis and his investigation. His friend was obviously hamstrung in what he could say, but he had admonished them to stay away from Ozbek. It struck him now that the warning wasn't just concerned with what Ozbek might do, but of what the investigators might do if they felt their probe jeopardized. Figgis had been clear in describing the duration and scope of the inquiry. As angry as he was at Swanson, he felt foolish for misreading Figgis.

To his left, a Navy ensign sat behind a large table covered with laminated name tags. Zander peered into the festivities, excited to see Gary Durkin push his way into the foyer. "Durkin!" he yelled.

The diplomat took a step toward him when the band broke into "Hail to the Chief." The reception grew quiet and Durkin shouted, "One second," before turning away.

Halfway through the ruffles and flourishes, Swanson grabbed Zander and Penny. "Let's move," he ordered, and led them up a dim emergency stairwell to the second floor.

• • • •

Durkin turned to look for Zander as the President stepped behind a podium. He had helped the President's traveling staff write the remarks—making sure that key consulate staff got their Presidential kudos—so he didn't feel compelled to listen.

He wasn't surprised when the President decided to hijack the Defense Secretary's itinerary. The war on terror was a touchstone of his administration.

He'd thought it odd that the detective was standing alongside John Swanson. Was the Marine with Blake? If he was, that meant Maurer was involved, since Swanson was the station chief's muscle. He wondered how Zander had possibly become Maurer's latest target.

• • • •

Swanson opened "Conference Room A" and ushered Zander and Penny inside.

"Come," a voice said, its owner becoming visible as he emerged from behind two oversized charts sitting on an easel. "Felix Maurer," he introduced himself, "with the Department of State." He directed them to sit side by side at an oval conference table. "I hope your bags are packed."

Chapter 27

"Alexander Blake," Maurer read from printed notes. "Detective, LAPD. Member of the force for 18 years. Department specialist in fine art. Divorced. Two children."

He turned to Penny. "Penelope Summer Theobald. Ph.D. candidate and Lecturer, Harvard University, Department of Ancient Art. Assistant to Professor Linus Crane. Divorced. No children."

Zander was irked by Maurer's tone. He pictured him as a child, incinerating ants with a magnifying glass.

"Look, Maurer, I've had enough oddball encounters for one day, so let's skip the bullshit. We are not trying to derail your investigation. Running into Ozbek's chain gang was just bad luck. We were at St. Eirene's only to take some pictures. Believe me, nobody wants to put this bastard behind bars more than me—except probably Penny here. How about giving us pen and paper so we can write up our statements."

"The statement you want to make?" Maurer said.

"Let me guess. That a prominent Turkish citizen kidnapped Miss Theobald off the streets of London? Not, I suppose, that you came here to find your girlfriend after she'd dumped you?"

"What?" Penny cried out, looking from Maurer to Zander in disbelief.

Maurer continued, undeterred. "But even if I accept that you're not lying, the only other choice is that you're delusional. And that's a nice way of putting it. I don't have the power to send you for a psychiatric evaluation, though I can't say I really care what your diagnosis might be. You can visit the department shrink back home. But I can tell you plain and simply that there's no investigation of Bulent Ozbek. Why should there be? The man is an industrialist and philanthropist here and abroad, and a true friend of the United States. He shouldn't be investigated, he should be emulated."

Zander looked around the room while he ran Maurer's words through his head. "That seals it," he finally said. "Ozbek's obviously got a bigger payroll than the Yankees."

Maurer followed the edge of the table, letting his fingertips coast across the polished wood. He stopped directly across from Zander, pulled out one of the high-backed chairs and eased himself into it. "When I hear that sort of paranoia, I can only feel sorry for you. But let me ask you something else. Do you consider yourself a patriot, detective?"

Zander chafed at being talked to like a high-school student on a field trip to Washington. "No less than you," he said.

Maurer shook his head, splayed his fingers, and carefully placed both hands on the table, palms down.

"Then understand that while it may not be your intent, you and Miss Theobald are threatening the national security of the United States."

"Right," Penny snorted. "Zander and I are the threats to national security. Just how do you figure that?"

Maurer reached behind him and grabbed a large color photograph from one of the easels. He flipped it around for Penny to see. "You know what this is, Miss Theobald?"

"No."

"No reason you should. This is a photo taken from an American military satellite of the Turkish-Greek border. Not much further from here than you can spit. Even through some awful weather, our computers clean these up enough to see down to the shoelaces on a large massing of soldiers on both sides. That's normally what happens when a war's ready to break out."

"And this is all because of the bombers' confessions?" Zander asked.

"You got that right," Maurer said. "This picture was taken about two hours ago."

"So?" Zander asked.

"So by claiming that the Prime Minister's brother is a kidnapper—"

"And a murderer," Penny said.

Maurer glared at her. "By making such insane accusations, you are only helping to destabilize the Turkish government at a uniquely hazardous moment. A moment of peril for the whole world."

Zander's jaw tightened though he tried to check his anger. "*Insane accusations*, Maurer? Ozbek had Linus Crane murdered in London. And then had Penny kidnapped. Who's insane here?"

A vein throbbed on Maurer's bull neck. "Do you have even a shred of proof about Crane?"

"No more proof," Zander said, "than that he also had Yucel Goktepe, whom I'm sure was on your Enemies List, killed last night. But apparently truth is not the issue here. It wouldn't matter what proof I had."

"To the contrary, it certainly would. What have you got? Witnesses? Photographs? Video?"

Zander took a deep breath and rubbed his forehead. He had no trouble picturing himself in Maurer's shoes, where he might easily be asking the same sorts of questions. He could think of nothing else to say beyond a line he'd heard a thousand times himself. "Can you tell me what our motive would be for cooking this up?"

• • • •

Gary Durkin found John Swanson blocking the doorway to the second-floor conference room. "Is Maurer in there?"

Legs apart, hands locked behind him, Swanson did not budge. "I'm sorry, sir. Mr. Maurer is busy. He asked not to be interrupted."

"I'm sorry, too, but I've got an urgent matter to discuss with him."

"He said he was not to be disturbed under any circumstances."

Durkin stepped back in frustration. "Tell me something, Captain. Is Detective Blake in there?"

"I'm sorry, sir. I can't say."

"No, of course not. Let me remind you that this consulate is under the control of the Ambassador. He is entitled to be apprised of every single thing that goes on here, no matter which agency is involved. So if you think you can bully me and keep your damn secrets, you're dead wrong."

Swanson's tone was flat. "Yes, sir."

The diplomat pointed a finger at the Marine. "You picked a fight with the wrong guy," he growled, and pounded down the hall.

• • • •

Zander thought he heard Gary Durkin in the hallway. He tried to focus on the voice outside, but it was impossible to filter through Maurer's harangue.

"I've got critical matters to deal with, but you have managed to make yourself enough of a nuisance that I have no choice but to deal with you. But that's over with. Consider this official. You've both been declared *persona non grata* by the Turkish government."

Ozbek's work. Zander was sure of it. "If the Turks are so upset, how come we haven't been fined or arrested or told this in any official way by them?"

"Jesus," Maurer said. "You just don't get it. I'm doing you a favor here. We do this because the Turkish government lets us deal with American troublemakers. You want to be turned over to the Turkish authorities?"

"This is incredible," Penny said. "You should be defending us, not helping these creeps. And meanwhile, you're letting a murderer walk free."

Maurer's voice was cold. "You're really not helping yourself by repeating that. My only concern is American interests. And a stable, westernized Turkey is in America's best interest, now and forever."

"And the easiest way to insure that," Zander appended Maurer's thought, "is to keep the Ozbek government in place."

"You say that with a sneer, detective, but that's right. Now I'm not going to tell you the Ozbeks are perfect. No doubt they line their pockets like all politicians, and I'm not talking only about the Third World. But compared to some others we've supported over the years, they're a pair of Mr. Fucking Cleans. And even if it turns out they're humping underage goats, I don't care, as long as they let us base our B-2's here."

"Maurer," Zander said, "I know you think you're operating on some level we can't possibly understand. But let me tell you something I've learned from tracking criminals from one end of the earth to the other: the thugs here are no different than they are in Los Angeles. They cheat and steal and kill and sell drugs and launder money and anything else they can get away with. The only difference I can see here is they don't have to buy government protection, it comes for free."

"Ha!" Maurer said, pushing away from the table and standing in one motion. "With that crap, detective, you should be teaching at Harvard. It looks good on the op-ed page, but it's not the way the world works." He glided over to a large wall map. "You see this, detective? Miss Theobald?"

Zander walked near the map and read the legend aloud: "Islamic View." It was a map of the world with Jerusalem at its center. Moslem countries were inflated in size, everything else shrunken by comparison: the Americas, the Slavic world, and most of Asia. Greenland was invisible.

Maurer slapped the map with his hand. "This is the

world we're dealing with, Blake. I'm looking for things marked good and bad but I don't see them. What's on here are oil fields, and shipping lanes, and a few hundred million people who call America 'The Great Satan,' which might lead one to conclude that good and bad are relative terms."

"You're including murder as a relative term?" Zander asked.

"And this is all a crock anyway," Penny added, "because the victims here are Americans and you couldn't care less."

"That's not true. The whole point here is to make sure that when we count up the dead there are as few Americans as possible. And as we've already discussed, the notion that Bulent Ozbek is under investigation is nonsense, and your allegations against him are baseless." Maurer sat down again.

Zander hesitated on the way back to Penny, staring down at piles of papers alongside an Adidas shoebox. Zander ran his finger across a few loose papers.

Maurer jumped up, an anxious look displacing his arrogance.

"This belonged to the terrorist?" Zander asked.

"Yes," Maurer said. "How did you know?"

"His name's all over it. I read the news."

"I'd appreciate your not touching anything, detective. It's evidence. You more than anybody should understand the importance of not contaminating it."

Zander nodded but picked up the bracelet.

"This?" Zander said. "Have you looked at this?"

"That has to be returned," Maurer said, stepping toward Zander, apparently eager to ward him off. "It's nothing. It's a charm bracelet."

Zander flipped through the charms, then stared at Maurer. "There's a small key wedged into the back of one charm here. Have you looked closely? I've seen bank-box keys like this."

Maurer grabbed the bracelet and dropped it into its box, snapped it closed, and then scooped up all the loose papers and returned them to the shoebox. "I asked you to leave everything alone. Now sit down."

Zander felt his frustration ready to boil over, but he could see that Maurer was incapable of hearing him.

"I don't have any more time to waste. Like I said, the Turkish government has declared you both *persona non grata*—they want you out of their country."

Maurer took two envelopes from a desk drawer. "These are tickets on the 4:45 to London. That's in two hours. If you're not on that flight, then in addition to having arrest warrants issued, reports of your activities, detective, will be sent to the Chief's Office at the LAPD. I'm sure he'll love seeing that. And the Deans of the Faculty and Graduate School in Cambridge will also get a package, Miss Theobald."

Zander took the tickets. He itched to rip them in half. "You're a fucking disgrace," he said.

Maurer walked to the door. "Captain Swanson will take you down. You will be driven to the airport and put on your flight. Once you arrive in London you're on your own. But I suggest you wait until you reach Harvard Square to make any more trouble."

Chapter 28

"What an infuriating man," Penny said as soon as Maurer left them alone. "He makes me ashamed to be an American."

Zander paced the room in frustration. Of course it was possible that Maurer was fully aware of Scotland Yard's investigation and didn't care how clumsily he disposed of meddlers. But that didn't feel right. Maurer genuinely admired Ozbek.

"And I can't believe this is legal," she continued.

"You're probably right," Zander said. "But we're not going to see any lawyers before we're on that plane. Besides, who would we appeal to? The Prime Minister?"

Zander grabbed an eraser and wiped clean a whiteboard covered with a long list of place names. "Something that schmuck needed, I hope." He quickly sketched an animated group of figures against a geometric landscape.

Penny came over for a closer look. "I like it, but what are you doing?"

"I'm trying to recall the part of the mosaic that only I have seen."

"Really?"

"If I'd known I'd never see it again I would have taken some pictures myself, or at least made some notes—but I did take a hard look at it. Maybe we can recreate enough of it to decipher."

Penny pointed to one of the figures. "Can you describe this for me?"

The door opened and Swanson stuck in his head before Zander could answer. "Downstairs," he commanded.

"We have things at our hotel," Penny told him.

"It'll all be sent on. We go straight to the airport."

Zander erased the board and they followed Swanson down the stairwell. The lobby was even more crowded than when they had arrived.

"Wait right here," Swanson told them, and pulled out his cell phone.

Zander looked toward the densely packed reception, hoping Durkin might appear, but he didn't. He noticed that a few nametags remained unclaimed. He put his arm around Penny, suddenly feeling a deep sense of regret. "Sorry to let you down," he told her.

She snapped her head back. "What? I hope you're not serious. You've—" she broke off and gestured toward the reception.

Zander saw the distraction. The President was in the doorway, panning the foyer for someone.

A moment later the President headed his way. Zander looked behind him to see whom the President wanted to talk to. "Zander," the President exclaimed. "Nice to see you. I understand you've been doing great work on my Cultural Property board."

Zander sensed every eye in the room on him, compounding the surreal feeling of returning the President's firm handshake and staring into his warm but intense brown eyes. "Uh, thank you very much, sir. That's very kind of you to say… or even to know I was here." He noticed that a circle of presidential aides and gawkers, including Gary Durkin, had congregated around them, pushing Swanson back into the crowd.

"The President has eyes and ears all over," he said with a wink. "It's one of the perks."

Zander introduced Penny, mentioning her Harvard connection.

The President smiled, "I went to the Law School. Gary Durkin tells me you folks are on your way out. You're over here to inspect some antiquities?"

"Yes, sir, we are," Zander said, glancing at Durkin, who winked at him.

"There must be some wonderful things to see."

"Yes, sir. Many, many unique sights," Penny said.

"The First Lady would like to visit some historic spots, but it gives the Secret Service a coronary when either of us want to get out and about like that— especially here. Security and such, but I'm sure you know that, being a policeman, Zander."

"Yes, sir. I've worked a Presidential detail myself."

"Then I'll ask for you next time I'm in Los Angeles."

"That would be an honor, sir."

"You're getting out at a good time. The Turkish Prime Minister will be here any minute so we've got to put on our game faces, if you know what I mean."

"I know exactly what you mean, Mr. President."

"And next time you're in Washington for a Committee meeting, you get word to my staff and I'll stop by. I'd like to hear your impressions of Turkey."

"Thank you, sir. I will."

They shook hands again.

Zander couldn't see Swanson anywhere. Maybe Durkin had diverted him. Whatever, Zander wasn't waiting to find out. He took Penny's hand. "Let's go." Her astonishment at meeting the President promptly gave way to shock over escaping Maurer. But now, coming up the steps toward them, were Prime Minister Ozbek and Bulent, sandwiched front and back by Turkish Army officers.

Zander and Penny trotted down the steps while the Turkish delegation climbed. They passed quickly, but Zander watched Bulent's diplomatic face give way to rage at the sight of them. He winked just to rub it in.

"Where are we going?" Penny asked.

"Good question." He led her past the concrete barrier and onto the avenue, expecting Swanson but still not seeing him.

He looked down the line of BMWs, Jaguars, and the odd Bentley, advancing one after another to disgorge their VIPs. Junior Turkish Army officers were serving as valets.

Zander took Penny's elbow and started toward the third car in line, a jet-black Mercedes.

"We've got company!" she said.

Zander turned to see Maurer at the bottom of the consulate steps, scanning up and down the block methodically as a Terminator.

The lead limo drove off and the next car pulled up, but the Mercedes idled in place.

Zander tapped on the Mercedes' windshield like a squeegee guy demanding a tip. The driver's window lowered to reveal Henry Demarest's taught face.

"What do you want from me?" Demarest asked, his lip and brow covered with beads of sweat. "Haven't I done everything you asked? This is bordering on harassment, Alexander."

Zander looked down at Demarest. "We need a ride, Henry."

"He's on his way," Penny yelled, and ran over to Zander. She pointed to Demarest. "Is that...?"

"That's impossible!" the dealer said, as Zander opened the rear door and ushered Penny inside. She slid across the buttery leather seat and Zander yanked the door shut as he settled beside her. "I'm an Inner Circle contributor to the President's Re-election Committee, Alexander. The President is expecting me."

"I just spoke to him. He didn't mention you." Zander now noticed an attractive woman sitting beside Demarest. He was certain he knew her, but as usual no name came to mind, all the more so in this alarming context. "Dammit, Henry! Drive!"

"Hello," the woman said, leaning toward the back seat. "I'm Helen Vandameer. We met in London."

Demarest turned to argue when a loud bang shook the car. "Who the hell is that?" he shouted, watching in terror as Maurer again brought his fist down on the hood of the sedan.

"You won't get away with this, Blake," Maurer roared as the car jerked forward. "You'll wish you got on that plane after the Turkish police get hold of you!"

Chapter 29

Demarest drove to the Galata Palas hotel in silence. A herd of uniformed men surrounded the Mercedes as it pulled under the porte-cochere and helped Demarest out. Zander assumed he must tip like a sheik.

Demarest nodded to the doorman as he waited for Helen and Penny to enter, and then scooted inside, leaving Zander behind like a stray cat.

The hotel's lobby, warmed with plush carpets, vibrant tapestries and fresh flowers, reminded Zander of the Fairmont in San Francisco, where he'd gone once to arrest a film producer and reclaim a stolen Rubens.

Spots of chipped plaster and threadbare upholstery caught his eye, but Zander saw why the place appealed to Demarest. Its frayed elegance was inviting and comfortable, like a pair of old slippers. "How did you ever survive in the joint?" he whispered in the dealer's ear.

"Hello, sir," a desk clerk said, eliciting a quick

wave from Demarest. The clerk looked down at a computer screen. "Your suite is being cleaned. It will only be a few minutes."

They retreated to the hotel bar to wait.

"You changed hotels, Henry," Zander said.

"Yes," Demarest said as the waiter set their drinks down on the marble-topped table. "I was afraid you might come visit me again."

"Your luck is still running sour."

"That's clear, Alexander. But I'd still like to know how you found me."

Zander took a swig of his Absolut martini. "Your name tag was on the registration table so I guessed you were out there somewhere—fashionably late."

Demarest sipped his double Manhattan, neat. "And now there's an all-points bulletin out for me, but that's almost besides the point. I want to know why I am the one person whose single mistake comes with a debt to society that can never be repaid."

"As far as mistakes go, Henry, you were only *caught* once. God knows what you've gotten away with."

"I should sue you for slander, Alexander."

Penny slapped her hand on the table. "All right, boys. Enough."

"Easy for you to say, my dear," said Demarest. "That man wasn't glaring at you while he vandalized the Mercedes. He had murder in his eyes. Who was he?"

"Just some idiot from the State Department who forgot his Lithium."

"Are you certain?"

"He told us that himself," Penny said. "Not about

the Lithium," she smiled at Zander. "But he's only a Foreign Service officer. He can't arrest anyone."

"Thank God," Demarest said, exhaling in relief. "But what's he got against you, Alexander?"

• • • •

Felix Maurer rubbed his eyes, intent on focusing his attention on Atilla Mazari's shoebox of personal papers. He'd found nothing on the first run through. But he had no other leads.

He picked up a handful of index cards. But the difficulty of reading the jagged handwriting sent his thoughts back to the afternoon's fiasco. His nerves were still on a knife's edge. He would have taken a Valium if he didn't fear he might miss some clue. Instead he drifted over to his desk to pick at a smorgasbord of leftovers from the reception.

He popped the tab on a Diet Coke and stared at the screen of a laptop hardened for desert combat sitting atop his credenza. A pulsating green light at the center of a map offered some balm. He had managed to slap a transmitter on the car that carried Blake away. The laptop's GPS tracker, accurate to within 20 feet, showed the car was parked under the Galata Palas hotel. Maurer would have raided the hotel already, except that the Deputy Director of Counter Terrorism was expecting his report in his e-mail by 5 p.m., Langley time.

He couldn't help but dwell on his conversation an hour ago with his boss. He hadn't even planned to mention the shoebox. But when the Deputy Director confessed how tightly he was being squeezed, Maurer couldn't hold back. This was one of the few people left at the agency he admired. Not only did he mention the box, he said he was close to "the answer."

"Felix," he was told, "the President flies home from Incirlik at dawn tomorrow and expects the Agency's report on his desk when he reaches the Oval Office. He's already invited the Congressional leadership over to discuss the findings of his Special Board of Inquiry into the Turkish bombings."

Maurer wished he could just ignore Blake and his girlfriend. But they were not merely a distraction. The Turkish government was standing like a house of straw and the two Americans were doing their best to blow it down. They were his responsibility.

On top of sneaking away virtually under Presidential protection, Blake had to waltz right past *both* Ozbeks. Bulent was in his office two minutes later ripping him a new asshole and all he could do was sit there like a 12-year-old caught copying someone else's homework. "If Blake isn't out of the country in 24 hours, *you'll* be expelled," Ozbek had screamed on his way out. He shuddered at an image of *Time* magazine with his picture under the headline: "Who Lost Turkey?"

Maurer marched back to the conference table. "There's got to be something," he said aloud, and opened the box holding the charm bracelet.

Chapter 30

When Zander admitted he'd been declared an enemy of the state for crossing Bulent Ozbek, Demarest insisted they retreat upstairs immediately. The beleaguered dealer signed for the drinks while Penny and Helen made their way to the elevators. "So, Henry," Zander asked, "where did you meet your friend?"

Demarest took a moment, pursing his lips. He clearly felt that any question from Zander might launch an investigation. "On a boat this morning."

Zander couldn't say if it was Demarest's tone or his body language that invited skepticism. Of course, whatever credibility the dealer had accumulated since leaving prison evaporated the moment the mummy turned up in his hotel. "What kind of boat?"

"A tour boat. It takes you out into the harbor so you can gain a perspective on the city's architecture."

"Really?" Zander laughed. "I never pictured you as the tour-boat type."

"It wasn't the Circle Line around Manhattan,

Alexander. Just a small yacht for a select clientele."

"And she was on board?"

"Precisely."

"And..."

"And we struck up a conversation like any two intelligent people that fate has thrown together. Before long we realized we had a great deal in common. We had lunch after landing and I invited her to come to the President's reception."

"That's an impressive first date."

"It would have been," the dealer scowled.

• • • •

Demarest's suite shared the lobby's tattered charm and offered a splendid panorama of the old city. He opened a large bottle of Perrier.

"So," Zander said, taking the glass from Demarest, "Did you visit Ozbek after I left?"

Countless hours leaning against lopsided tables in stinking interrogation rooms had proven that there was often nothing more revealing than a direct question. But Demarest did not blink. "You can't be serious."

"Call him?"

"What?"

"Have you spoken to Ozbek on the phone?"

"No! How could I ever explain you showing up as me? You never even told me why you pulled that charade. You could have killed him for all I know. Though I trust you would have had the courtesy to warn me about that."

"Maybe I sell you short, Henry," Zander said, putting his arm around Penny. "As for the need to impersonate you, Ozbek kidnapped Penny in London and was holding her on his island. I needed a legitimate excuse to get out there."

Demarest's head snapped back. "My God."

This news apparently jolted Helen as well. She sank into a straight-backed wooden chair next to Demarest.

"And he was about to kill her," Zander added.

"I can't believe it," Helen said, in a tone that suggested she believed it completely.

Demarest loosened his tie and unbuttoned his collar, his shoulders slouching. "I'd heard he was eccentric, but is he some sort of psychopath?"

Penny glared at Helen. "Can you tell us? You know Ozbek, don't you? I saw you with him at the conference dinner in London. That *was you*, wasn't it?"

"Yes, of course. I can't deny we're acquainted. But I wouldn't say I know him, especially now that you say he's a kidnapper."

"Then can you tell me why you are in Istanbul?" Penny continued. "We saw you at Munstead's restaurant. You sat one table away from us and left me your card. And now you're here."

"I'm in Turkey looking for acquisitions," Helen said, taking the offensive. "If you're implying there's some connection between seeing you in London and again here, I'd like to know what it is."

"Is there some connection?" Zander asked.

Penny frowned at Zander, apparently disappointed with his evenhandedness. "Then explain what you're looking for here. Your card said your specialty is ancient Near East. Istanbul is no hotbed for that."

"I didn't say I was going on a dig. There are dealers here, you know, some of whom get first crack at the finest Near East pieces." Helen stood up and circled behind her chair. "You're still in school, so I wouldn't expect you to know the intricacies of the market, but getting an export license from a well-connected dealer is infinitely simpler than trying to send something home you uncover in the field yourself."

"Have you bought anything?" Penny fired back.

"Not yet," Helen said, her calm rendering Penny's accusations all the more overwrought. "But I'm sure I will. I never go home empty-handed."

Penny looked at Zander, who shrugged his shoulders. "I'm going for some air," she said, and walked out to the terrace.

Zander refilled everyone's glasses and laid out the entire saga for Demarest and Helen: from high tea at the Bertrand, to finding the mosaic at St. Eirene's, to the presidential handshake at the consulate. While Demarest listened closely, his face betrayed no excitement. Helen more than made up for it.

"And Professor Crane believed the mosaic was a guide to the Athena Parthenos? What a find that would be," she said. "It's almost unimaginable. You're going after it, aren't you? I mean, you have to!"

Zander appreciated Helen's enthusiasm. "Penny thinks we can try. And if it means keeping it out of Ozbek's hands, that's all the more reason."

Demarest nodded approvingly, which was what Zander wanted. The dealer had well-placed friends, and in a country where who you knew was clearly more important than what, he wanted Demarest's Rolodex at hand.

"But how are you going to do this, Alexander?" Demarest asked. "Ozbek has the mosaic."

"That's true. But I've seen half of it and Penny has studied the other half as well as Crane's journal. Between the two of us we think we can decipher it. And you're more than welcome to come along for the ride."

"Or to give you one, you mean," Demarest said. "But I'm going to limit my role to wishing you good luck and adieu. It's time for me to go home. For real this time."

Zander felt like he was trying to lure his kids to join him on Saturday errands. The right mix of cajoling, enticement, and threat was never clear. "I thought you'd enjoy the hunt," he said, opting to soft peddle his appeal.

"Only when there's at least a 1-percent chance for success."

Helen put her hand on the dealer's shoulder. "My God, Henry, how can you even think of not coming? This is the adventure of a lifetime."

Zander saw that if anyone was going to convince Demarest it wasn't him. "I'll be back," he said, and left to join Penny.

• • • •

Helen stood up to massage Demarest's neck. He sighed.

"The prospect of finding something special for the museum always puts me in a giving mood," she said, slipping off his jacket to massage his shoulders. "You're one big knot, Henry. You could use some time in the field, away from a desk."

"But Helen—"

"But, what? Legs not what they used to be?"

Demarest fell back against the couch. "It's not that.

I already spend more time in the field than most people half my age. And don't you think I'd like to redeem my good name by recovering something of this magnitude? Of course I would. But the whole notion's absurd. Monumental statues like this Athena were never just lost or hidden away. They were destroyed to make shields or bullion or even other statues. If you only knew how many times some bounty hunter or shaman has dragged me over mountains and deserts to King End-of-the-World's lost city. No one wants to think that this Athena was melted for spears, but you know as well as I that reverence for great art was almost unknown 2,000 years ago. And lord knows you don't have to go back that far to see Philistines at work. Think of what marauding peasants destroyed during the French Revolution. It could make you cry, but that's what history shows. Which is why the Athena couldn't possibly still exist."

Helen knew Demarest's argument was not just logical, but probably correct. He wanted exactly the kind of proof that, if she had it, she wouldn't need him around. She wasn't going to sway him with the few facts they had at hand. He'd have to be pulled along by his emotions—for good or bad. "You may be right. But doesn't the possibility intrigue you?"

"Coming from Alexander? No."

"Well, that's too bad." She sat down again. "Because you wouldn't want me to mention where we met this morning, would you?"

"You wouldn't tell him!"

"I really want to find out about this statue."

"So go with them. What do you need me for?"

"The detective's girlfriend isn't inviting me to

come along. But if you go then I'm your guest, not theirs."

Demarest took a deep breath. He leaned back to look up at her eager face. She left no doubt she was serious. "Okay," he relented. "But I don't get it. It's not like you're going off on your first dig. You know what's out there. Even if this statue has somehow fended off two millennia of barbarity, what in the world makes you think the four of us can find it? The more I think about it, the more preposterous it seems. I left the Greeks behind 35 years ago. You're closer to it, but it's not your specialty either. Penny is merely a student. And Alexander, my God, probably couldn't find anything unless it had a Lo-Jack attached to it."

Helen retrieved her bag from across the room. "You may be right, Henry. But don't call your airline yet." She opened the door to the hallway.

"Where are you going?" he asked.

"I'll be back shortly."

• • • •

Penny was basking under the star-filled sky. "What was that all about?" Zander asked her, offering his glass. "I thought you were going to deck her."

"I felt like it…. I still do."

"Why?"

"Because she's a liar. She knows about the mosaic."

"I just told her about it. I want Demarest's help."

"I heard. And it's fine at this point. But she knew before tonight."

Zander flashed back to his marriage. He wanted to sympathize, but more than that he wanted to lift Penny

out of her funk and tell her to forget about Helen
Vandameer. His wife said he never understood that the
end wasn't as important as how you got there. "It's the
process that's important!" she'd said so often it actually
ignited fights instead of resolving them. After a while
he just didn't care anymore. But Penny was worth
trying for. "How? You think she overheard us at
Munstead's?"

"More than likely."

"But even if she did, how did she get from there to
here? We didn't even know where here was at that
point."

"Do you think only the streets of L.A. are packed
with scoundrels? Universities and museums have their
fair share, believe me."

"But you're accusing her based on what?"

Penny hesitated for a moment. "Intuition, I
suppose. But she knows a helluva lot more than she's
telling."

Chapter 31

Helen shot out of the suite. She'd been on the brink of compromising her feigned ignorance about the mosaic and the Athena for an hour. It was suffocating. But with some luck she'd return with the help she knew they needed, especially if they were in a race with Ozbek.

She found Simonedes's building with no trouble. He was dressed much as he had been when Helen first saw him at the Archaeology Museum: in a well-worn double-breasted suit that gave him the look of a provincial mayor. He insisted she come inside, but she declined.

"I'm sorry to bother you so late, Mr. Simonedes, but I don't think you'll mind when I tell you why."

"Have you found something?" he asked, his eyes sparkling with curiosity.

"Some people I've met have come across a picture puzzle—something that hasn't been seen in centuries, I'm sure, that might be the most important clue ever found. But we need your expertise to decipher it. I'm sorry not to give you any warning, but it's sort of now or never."

"Give me just a moment," he said, and retreated to an upholstered club chair where he sat and struggled for a moment to tie his shoes.

Helen stepped inside to offer him a steadying hand as he pushed himself up again. Despite his excitement, Helen thought Simonedes looked older than when he'd rescued her the other night. His shoulders drooped and his hands shook visibly. Maybe she just hadn't noticed before, too consumed in her own terror after fleeing the cistern.

She put a hand on his shoulder just as he closed the heavy door behind them, his terrier barking its displeasure. "I must ask you something before we go."

"Anything, my dear."

"These people are not aware that I came to Istanbul looking only for the Athena, and—"

"You would rather I did not mention it?"

"That's right."

"If you would like it that way, then certainly."

Chapter 32

Bulent Ozbek trotted from the mansion to the guardhouse of his island estate. "Open it up!" he shouted to the sentry. The green pickup rumbled through the main gate and stopped alongside its owner. Despite Heybeli's ban on motor traffic, Ozbek had prevailed upon the local constabulary to let large pieces of artwork be hauled up to his property by truck. He patted the canvas-covered stone slabs. "Everything here?" he asked the driver.

"Yes, sir."

"Good. We're going to shed number 4."

Ozbek was frustrated at how long it had taken to get the slabs to the compound. They were far too heavy for the speedboat, so a cargo boat was chartered to carry the loaded truck to the island. Even after wasting two hours at the American consulate, Ozbek had passed the mosaic on his return to Heybeli in the Scarab.

There was little daylight left by the time his newest prize reached the compound. Ozbek walked alongside the canvas-covered treasure like a little boy having a pony delivered for Christmas. "Did anyone bother you?"

"No. But the people from London were there."

Ozbek pulled up short. "What!"

"The girl we brought here and the man in the park."

The news sent Ozbek reeling. The mosaic had already been hauled away by the time Maurer's bungling had let the detective and the girl scamper out of the consulate. Before that, Maurer had called to say he'd picked the pair up and was sending them to London, but he never mentioned where he'd found them. Ozbek needed to know whether he should care. "Were they there the whole time? Before you got there?"

"They arrived when we were leaving."

"So what did they see?"

"Nothing. It was already loaded on the truck."

Ozbek felt reassured, but it didn't last. "Could the two Americans have been there before you? Maybe you only saw them when they came back for another look."

The driver frowned. "I don't know."

Ozbek hustled back to the residence cursing Zander and Penny. Of course she could have had enough time to study the mosaic before his people removed it. They had left him no choice, he realized. They needed to be taken care of.

Chapter 33

"Where were you?" Penny demanded.

Zander looked up, startled by Penny's ferocity and wondering who the old man was alongside Helen. In his pinstripe with the overly wide lapels, and with a face as weatherbeaten as an old deck chair, he reminded Zander of an ancient Sicilian mafia boss, someone who might have hid the young Michael Corleone.

Helen glared at her nemesis. "This is Mr. Simonedes," she said, introducing him all around. "I asked him to join us because Henry convinced me we would need more help to decipher the mosaic."

"When did this become *we*?" Penny asked.

Helen ignored her. "The director of the state Archaeology Museum introduced Mr. Simonedes as a national treasure. He's an expert on Byzantium and, he tells me, deeply versed in the history of the Athena."

The old man bowed as low his rheumatism would allow. "Dr. Vandameer stretches the truth, but in the kindest way. She is trying to impress you. The fact is, the director of the museum thinks I am a crackpot who has wasted his life searching for something that was destroyed before Jesus was born." Simonedes faced Penny. "If you object to my being here, I will certainly leave. I do not wish to upset anyone. I only wish to help."

Zander wasn't surprised to see Simonedes's gesture melt Penny's resistance. Between his accent and the warm but tentative smile, he was everyone's immigrant grandfather.

"Dr. Vandameer informed me about the mosaic on our way here. It might put you at ease to learn that I knew Professor Crane."

"Really?" Penny asked with a touch of sorrow.

"I can't tell you how sad it made me to learn of his death. Such a tragedy. He was just a boy."

"When did you see him last?" asked Zander, wondering if he could conceivably know about the mosaic already.

Simonedes thought for a moment. "It was around Easter. He was here to make preparations for his stay in Istanbul this summer. We spent a long afternoon discussing our mutual interests. Despite his youth, few people understood the classical legacy of Byzantium as he did. And I believe he appreciated the insights that a lifetime here have brought me."

Penny turned to Zander, as if to see if he had any objections. Zander knew they could use all the help they could get—at least he could. "Let's get to work," he said.

Penny ushered him over to the couch. "Come join us, Mr. Simonedes."

Demarest turned to him. "Now Mr. Simonedes, why don't we get your opinion on what we've got. If you've been looking for this statue for as long as you say, then you've most likely already been down the road we're on and found nothing."

"It sounds like you're along for the ride, Henry," Zander said, satisfied that he'd delegated Demarest's recruitment to Helen.

"If there's a ride to be taken, yes." Demarest gave Helen a "happy now?" sneer, which seemed to please her. He turned back to Zander. "But I doubt I'll be going anywhere but the airport departures lounge."

"Do not worry, Mr. Blake," Simonedes said. "Mr. Demarest's comments do not offend me. He is more civil than most. But whether the Athena survives is not a matter of opinion. Hoping does not make it so. And dismissing the possibility does not destroy it. I believe it exists, but my opinion is worth no more than Mr. Demarest's. So why don't you tell me what special information you have. Perhaps I will learn something and maybe I can help you."

"I hope so," Zander said, and briefly filled out the story of Linus Crane's discovery beyond what Helen had already told him.

Simonedes listened intently, his glassy grey eyes trained on Zander, obviously amazed at the whole turn of events surrounding Crane's discovery. "Then you must tell me what you remember of this mosaic," he finally said.

Demarest pulled a drawing tablet from his attaché case. Penny opened it to a clean page and placed it on the coffee table between the matched couches. Demarest sat beside Helen on one couch, while Simonedes sat opposite. Zander stayed on his feet, moving about the room, wondering if he could possibly recall enough of the mosaic that only he had seen to give the others a fighting chance to decipher it.

Penny was either a born artist or had trained as one. A detailed drawing from her recollection of the photos and completely faithful to Zander's recollection poured out of her. Alongside her work, he thought, the sketch he started at the consulate looked like something a doting parent might tack up on a refrigerator.

She narrated as she drew, quickly rendering the Acropolis and the Parthenon, and then Athena herself, being hauled away by a small army of bearers. This must have been a contentious moment, at least in the eyes of the artist, who showed a band of men shedding melodramatic tears over the goddess's departure. A rival group—Christians, Zander wondered?—seemed to be saying good riddance. In a less-complicated second scene, Penny drew the Athena being loaded on an ancient ship. Her next segment depicted the boat at sea, heading into the rising sun. The other major element was a man, presumably royal, looming over the entire project like a supervising spirit. Penny suggested he was a Byzantine emperor, though her depiction of him was more freeform and less detailed than the rest of the drawing.

Zander glanced at Simonedes for his reaction and grew concerned. The old man, gripping the sofa arm in silence, was having some trouble breathing. Zander squatted beside him and asked if he was okay. The old man confessed he'd suffered from emphysema for years but he was fine.

Penny stood to look down at her drawing. Everyone turned to Simonedes, who seemed lost in his own world. Finally he reached out and tapped Penny's presumed emperor. "Can you tell me, my dear, if this man had any distinguishing characteristics. For instance, any facial hair?"

Penny thought for a moment. "Yes, he had a beard." She sat and drew it.

"Good," Simonedes said. "And how did his arms look?"

"His arms?" Zander saw her face brighten with recognition. "It's interesting you ask. It caught my eye when I first saw it but I hadn't thought about it since. The figure had only one arm."

"Good, good," said Simonedes.

"What's the significance?" Zander asked, wishing he could contribute more to the investigation than just his memory.

"It confirms that this is a portrait of the Emperor Zeno. He lost an arm as a boy in a gruesome accident with a lion."

"And what does that tell you?"

"That the story in this mosaic is plausible in that it does not contradict the accepted history."

"How so?" asked Helen.

The old man wiped his hand across a spot of stubble on his chin. "For the first two and a half centuries of the Byzantine era, from the time of Constantine through Justinian, the emperors issued orders every so often that notable public works of art— paintings, statues, mosaics—should be brought from the provinces to the imperial capital. While Athens remained a center of learning and scholarship, it was merely another province. It would not have been spared being stripped of its treasures. So the suggestion made in this mosaic that the emperor Zeno, who ruled half a century before Justinian, presided over the arrival of the Athena here fits with what we already know."

Zander turned toward the man who had become their guide through the mosaic and felt their time was running out. The glow in Simonedes's face had drained and his suit suddenly looked two sizes too big. His wheezing had grown more insistent.

"How are you doing, sir?" Zander kneeled down to hand him a glass of water. "Are you sure you feel up to continuing? Maybe you need to rest."

"Why don't you loosen your tie, Mr. Simonedes?" Penny suggested.

The old man drank half the glass before resting it on the cocktail table. He took a shallow breath and coughed, but then nodded to Zander. "You can tell me the rest of the story?"

Chapter 34

Ozbek's men had cut and dismantled the mosaic into four pieces, each roughly six feet square. Despite his insistence on speed, they had inflicted only minimal damage. Now the slabs were lined up against a whitewashed stucco wall inside the largest of the five outbuildings Ozbek used for conservation and restoration. Banks of bright but indirect lights illuminated the tesserae, he was sure, more brilliantly than since they were first put in place. The four slabs extended a little further than the wall they leaned against, leaving the last panel turned at an angle to the rest.

Alone now, Ozbek stepped back to take it all in. His eyes carried over and across, up and down the monumental work. The colors were alive, no doubt due to their unintended preservation under a blanket of plaster. The intricacies of the design, from start to finish, were astounding. The artist had not slacked off for a moment. Every edge was perfectly cut, every color perfectly matched.

He wondered where he would display it. He could put it in the mansion, but that would do it a disservice. A space as grand as the mosaic itself was needed. A new wing, perhaps. And if it turned out that the story in the mosaic was pure fantasy—and not a map to the grandest treasure—then maybe he would send it to London or Chicago. Let everyone know he was a collector without peer.

He was told over the shed's intercom that his expected guest had arrived. A minute later, his butler was holding the metal door open. Mehmet Oymen took two steps inside before the mosaic caught his eye and pulled him in like a magnet. The director of the National Mosaics Museum opened his palms and let them glide over the surface.

Ozbek gestured with open arms. "This is the piece I told you about. The one that's been buried in St. Eirene's for half a millennium. It was uncovered in the explosion."

"Praise Allah something good came of that tragedy."

"Indeed." Ozbek put Zander and Penny out of his mind and stepped back from the slabs. "Praise Allah. Now come over here. I want you to get some perspective on it. My interest for the moment is not esthetic. I want to talk about the story in the mosaic. There's a narrative here."

Oymen was dressed in a blazer and a boldly patterned shirt, open at the neck, as if he'd been on his way to a smart dinner party, which he had been when he received the summons from Ozbek.

The director studied the mosaic alongside his patron and recited the tale Ozbek had already deciphered himself: that the gold-and-ivory Athena Parthenos was being shipped from Athens to Constantinople.

"Ah, well this is fantastic!" Oymen exclaimed as he pulled a fine brush from his jacket pocket and swept some plaster flakes from one slab.

"Yes," Ozbek crowd. "Now where is she being taken?"

"Unbelievable," the director said, staring at the last panel as if lost in a haze. "Who would have thought?"

Chapter 35

"Wait," Demarest interrupted. "I have a simple question. Why didn't Crane take any pictures of what Alexander saw?"

"I wondered about that myself," said Penny. "But Linus wrote in his diary that he didn't want the full mosaic publicized until he could mount an expedition to find the Athena."

Demarest smiled like the devil come to collect a soul. "Well, it's all on *your* shoulders now, Alexander."

Despite his most spiteful efforts, Demarest couldn't add to Zander's burden. Penny's recollection had been superb. But if their search was going to get beyond the Galata Palas Hotel, he had to provide the direction. Simonedes and the others might interpret it, but he had to put it in front of their eyes.

Penny said she was ready to draw. Zander dropped down onto the couch beside Simonedes and closed his eyes. Without prompting, a dim version of the mosaic appeared before him. But he wasn't ready for it and slid back into his first visit to St. Eirene's, starting with his walk down the decimated corridor with Ned Nolan. He opened his senses to the rubble under his shoes; to the dust catching in his eyes and clinging to his forearms; to the sandy feel of the porous stone on his fingertips; to the smog from the adjacent streets that had infiltrated the hanging tarps. In his mind he turned the fateful corner and lingered by Nolan's desk. He could even hear Nolan's boom box playing Warren Zevon's *Lawyers, Guns, and Money*. Nolan must have had it on a loop because it repeated continuously the entire half-hour Zander spent there.

"There are three groups of figures, like panels in a cartoon strip," he began.

"Describe them one at a time," Penny's voice broke through.

Zander spoke quickly, concerned that the clarity of the vision might fade. "In the first segment, there's a long, oval stadium. It's big, like the Coliseum in Los Angeles. The Athena is there, set atop a pedestal at the far end, supported by a ring of columns. It's not the center of attention, though. There's some sort of track meet underway. The place is packed and runners are racing. Like the Olympics."

He opened his eyes at the sound of Simonedes clearing his throat. The old man hadn't moved, his head still lazing back into the sofa as if it were too heavy to lift. Zander wanted some feedback, even if just a nod. "So, the Parthenos was erected in the Hippodrome," the Greek obliged.

"Is that important?"

"Some have suggested it might have been raised there, and I admit I was not among them. But clearly it was. Fascinating."

"There were a lot of other statues in the stadium," Zander told him. "A magnificent team of horses in particular, but the Athena towers over them."

"What does the Athena look like?" asked Helen.

"Dominant ….defiant…. and gold. Bright gold, except for the head, which was white."

"Ivory," Helen said.

Zander looked at Penny's drawing. "That's good," he said. "But the statue's bigger in relation to the stadium."

He closed his eyes again, summoning the mosaic without effort. "The main feature of the next section is a map."

"That sounds promising," Demarest said.

"Actually, it's more an outline of the city, with a handful of buildings drawn in. The stadium is there, as well as some churches. Maybe palaces too. The view is from the sea, as if you were in the harbor looking ashore. And there are men on the city walls, looking out. Off the coast, in the harbor, there's a fleet of ships. Sort of like those paintings of the Spanish armada. The men on board are archers and knights dressed for battle, so it looks like an invasion force. Some are standing alongside catapults. In fact, a few ships are lashed together, packed with men who look like they're ready to scale the city's barricades."

"Where are the ships from?" Demarest asked.

Zander wondered how he was supposed to know. "Sorry, Henry. There aren't any names stenciled on the hulls. But some of them are more like troop transports, and they've got horses on board."

"Is the statue anywhere?" Penny asked.

"Yes. It's near the stadium, but it's lying flat, like

when it was moved out of Athens. Here it's on a flatbed being pulled by ox carts."

"Is the statue being taken out of the city?"

"That could be one interpretation."

"So it could be anywhere in Byzantium," Demarest said.

Once again Zander turned to Simonedes, but the old man remained limp, staring up at the ceiling. "Please go on," he said.

"In the last section, there are two people, a man and a woman, very similar to the emperor Penny drew from the first section. But this is a different man."

"And the woman?" asked Penny. "Any distinguishing characteristics?"

"Dressed like royalty. The Athena is between them, and they are presenting her with gifts."

Helen jumped up. "Like this?" Zander's eyes popped open. She pulled a textbook on Byzantine art from her shoulder bag and ripped through it until she held up an oversized plate for everyone to see.

Zander reached for the book and Helen handed it to him. She had the wide-eyed look of a student finishing first in a timed exam. The photo was so similar to his recollection he barely had to glance at it. "Yes. Same pattern," he said, happy to see his memories confirmed.

"This mosaic is inside St. Sophia," Helen said. "The Virgin Mary is flanked on one side by Constantine and on the other by Justinian, Byzantium's two greatest emperors. Each is presenting her with a gift.

"So this is what you saw?" Demarest asked, taking the book.

"No. It was like this, with the Athena flanked by

two people, but it was a man and a woman, not two men. And I can't picture what they were handing her."

"It would obviously be useful to know which emperor and empress we're talking about," said Demarest. "Unfortunately, boys and girls, the Byzantine Empire lasted a thousand years, so there's quite a list to choose from."

Simonedes sighed. "I hope you can tell me more, Mr. Blake."

Zander rubbed his eyes. He felt tapped out. "I'm not sure I can."

"Think about the ships in the middle section. The warships waiting to attack. Picture them and tell me if you remember any special markings."

Zander recalled the ships as best he could, but he came up empty. "Sorry."

"Perhaps you can picture a flag?"

"A flag?" Again Zander conjured up the fleet. "I think some ships have a flag. And it's... it's... it's red or maybe orange, with a lion on it. I think it's a lion."

"Good. Good. Now I would like you to think more about the man and woman."

"They both had two arms."

Simonedes gently laughed. "That wasn't my question. No. I have a good sense of who they are. What I must know is what they are presenting to the Athena."

Zander took a deep breath and exhaled sharply. He had surprised himself by remembering so much already. Any more might require hypnosis.

"As you may have surmised, the gift may be the key to the whole mosaic."

The old man sat up straighter now, as if even this

meager show of strength might push Zander along. Zander wanted a clue from Simonedes to latch onto, but the old man just stared at him, like a coach who felt you needed to push *yourself* across the goal line, that no one else could do it for you. Zander closed his eyes and focused on the emperor and empress's hands. In a moment he was back at the wall, brushing his fingers over the tesserae, dirt and grit adhering to his hand and darkening his nails while revealing vital colors: gold, reds, blues. He was right in front of the Athena, flanked by the royals, just as she was. They were larger than life-sized and he looked up at them. Their faces were purposeful and distinguished. The emperor was to his left. Zander focused on the unnaturally long and thin fingers. And they cupped... what did they cup?

"All right," Zander said, relaxing. "The emperor is holding a, uh... a woman.... It's a miniature of a woman."

"A woman?" he heard Penny's voice. "Describe her."

"Sheeee's... certainly not royal. A peasant, really. In a shabby, torn dress. In fact the queen is holding a small woman, too. Another peasant. I don't know if this helps, but there's a letter "C" next to the first woman and a letter "L" beside the other."

"Anything else?" Simonedes asked, his voice slipping again.

Zander forced himself back to the debris at St. Eirene's. Then, losing his concentration, he snickered.

"What's so funny?" Penny asked, smiling herself.

Zander fell back into the cushion again, laughter rippling across his cheeks.

"Come on," Penny nudged him. "What is it?"

"Okay. It's stupid, but I remember noticing it at the time and wondering what kind of weird shit those emperors were into."

"What do you mean?" asked Helen.

"Just this: the two women that the emperor and empress held in their hands —

they weren't women, if you know what I mean."

"No, Alexander," Demarest said, rolling his eyes. "I'm sure we don't."

"What were they?" Penny asked.

Zander turned his head and closed his eyes again. "The more I focus on it, the more obvious it is. These aren't women at all. They're in drag—and I don't mean togas; I mean dresses and make-up. But there's scruffy beards on both of them and they're muscular."

Zander heard Demarest scoff. "Like the Bearded Lady at the circus?"

"All right," Simonedes said. "You can stop."

"I'm sorry," Zander said, sure he'd embarrassed Simonedes and made an ass of himself. "Let me try again."

"That's not necessary," Simonedes said, just as he broke into a wretched spasm of coughing that shook his entire body. Zander hoisted him up straight against the cushion, and signaled for Helen to fill his water glass. It would be no strain to carry the old man downstairs to an ambulance, he thought. Another moment and he would have grabbed his phone, but the hacking ceased just as Zander raised the water to his lips.

Simonedes held his hand up and shut his eyes for a few seconds, which seemed to calm him. "I have to congratulate you, Mr. Blake. You have a superb memory."

"Thank you. You mean those were men in dresses?"

Simonedes smiled and held his head a bit higher, letting Zander relax about rushing to the nearest ER.

"Let me tell you what I believe the mosaic says," Simonedes started, his voice weak but steady. "We already know, because it was depicted quite plainly, that the Athena was removed from the Acropolis during the reign of Zeno, or roughly 475 of the Christian era. And there is, in fact, a first-person account written by a Greek who claimed he saw the Parthenos evacuated at that time."

"Proclus!" Helen blurted.

Simonedes' eyebrows shot up in admiration. "So the statue was brought to Constantinople, where at some point it was re-erected in the Hippodrome arena. But now we jump ahead approximately 700 years, as the mosaic does, starting with the depiction of the ships. There is no doubt that this was the Venetian fleet carrying the bloodthirsty knights of the Fourth Crusade."

"Why bloodthirsty?" asked Zander.

"Because," Penny broke in, "instead of fighting the Muslims for control of Jerusalem, which was the supposed reason they crossed Europe, they slaughtered their fellow Christians right here."

"Precisely, my dear," said Simonedes.

"Plundered the city," Penny continued, "and destroyed everything they didn't like enough to cart away. The team of horses you saw with the Athena in the Hippodrome has been sitting atop the entrance to St. Mark's in Venice ever since."

"Now, what the mosaic indicates," Simonedes

continued, "is that the Athena was removed from the Hippodrome while the Crusaders were still anchored in the harbor."

"Okay," Demarest spoke up. "Where did they take it?"

"The men in the dresses, I believe, will answer that question."

"How so?" Penny asked.

Simonedes reached for his glass of water and finished it. "The men resting in the emperor and empress's hands are Sergius and Bacchus, two very early martyrs for the Church."

"How do you know?" asked Zander.

"Both were ranking members of the Roman army under Maximian," Simonedes continued, "who were accused of being Christians. As punishment, their military uniforms were taken from them and they were paraded around in women's clothing."

"I can think of worse punishments," Demarest said.

"I'll bet you can," Zander said, picturing the dealer in his orange jumpsuit.

"Eventually," Simonedes said, "Bacchus was flogged to death and Sergius was beheaded. They were sainted—"

"And," Penny said, grabbing her pad and jumping out of her seat, "there's a church dedicated to them here in the city."

"Indeed," Simonedes said, his tired eyes sparkling. "The oldest church in Istanbul. Let me ask you one thing, Mr. Blake. Sergius and Bacchus are often represented carrying lances. Do you recall that?"

Zander nodded instantly. "I would have thought they were spears, but lances will do. In fact, they were both striking the same pose, like bookends, like they were aiming to throw them in unison."

"Throw them?" asked Simonedes, seemingly surprised. "At what?"

"Maybe there was something there. I don't know. But they were both pointed downward, toward about 4 o'clock."

Demarest clapped his hands to get everyone's attention. "So please back up a minute, Mr. Simonedes. Are you contending that the Athena is at this St. Sergius church right here?"

Simonedes nodded. "This is what I believe the mosaic is telling us."

"Perhaps," Demarest said, obviously not believing it for a moment. "But let me play devil's advocate."

"You never play anything else," said Helen.

"Sorry, but someone's got to keep their feet on planet Earth. Assuming the Athena was moved to this church 800 years ago, plenty of people must have seen it. So even if it was hidden in some deep cellar, how could it have been forgotten about? This isn't the middle of the Sahara here."

"That's an excellent question," Simonedes answered. "So let me suggest a scenario. The line of emperors who presumably removed the Athena from the Hippodrome was forced out of the city shortly afterwards and did not return for 75 years. By then the Crusaders were gone and the pretenders they had put in power pushed aside. The restored royal family, it is fair to say, would have waited for a period of stability before returning their treasures—what was left of them—to public display. However, the empire rarely knew stability again. If the Turks weren't threatening to overrun Constantinople, then the royal family was tearing itself apart. And, of course Constantinople fell to the Turks for good in 1453.

"And," Simonedes continued, "it is quite amazing what people can forget. You may not know that the Byzantines built huge reservoirs under Constantinople to provide fresh water for the city. As big as an underground stadium." He turned to Helen. "You are familiar with the cisterns, my dear?"

"The cisterns?" Helen realized Simonedes was talking to her. "Yes, of course."

"In fact, the largest of them still holds water. But after the empire collapsed and the Turks took the city, they fell into disuse. Over time, they slipped entirely from everyone's recollection. Then, 200 years later, a Frenchman named Gilles observed that from some houses in Istanbul you could fish through holes in the floor. People believed that Allah blessed these houses. But of course they were sitting above the forgotten cisterns. So things much larger than even the Parthenos can be washed from the collective memory."

"It also shows that they knew how to build underground," Zander said.

"Roman engineers used methods we still can't replicate," said Penny.

Demarest stretched his arms out. "Perhaps aliens showed them how."

"Shut up, Henry," Zander said, sorry to see that Demarest was still probably ready to pack his bags and go.

"But one other thing I don't get, Mr. Simonedes," Zander continued. "The Byzantines were Christians, right? This story of Sergius and Bacchus says as much."

"Of course."

"Then why did they revere this pagan statue?"

"Perhaps a simple love of beauty," Penny said.

"Or the fact that it was made of a ton of gold and ivory," said Helen.

"You're both right," said Simonedes. "The theologians of Byzantium saw gold as a symbol of truth and incorruptibility. Gold was light in its most concentrated form. But I would also guess that many emperors coveted the Athena because there was always a residue of belief in the old gods. Byzantium, after all, was the Roman Empire. Miss Theobald was right to mention the accomplishments of Roman engineering. We call them Byzantines but they called themselves Romans. The family that ruled the empire for the hundred years before the Crusaders arrived decorated their palace with mosaics from The Iliad, the Greek tragedies, and the triumphs of Alexander. Even Constantine, who made Christianity the official religion of the Empire, waited until he was on his deathbed to convert."

"Hedging his bets," Penny said.

"No doubt, my dear. The Hellenistic concept that arbitrary Fortune—and not a Christian god—governed the affairs of men was popular in Byzantium long after the time we are concerned about. And put yourself in the place of the people of Constantinople when they saw an army of Christian crusaders waiting to annihilate them. It must have made them wonder whether Jesus had forsaken them."

Penny ripped her drawings from the pad. "And why does it mean so much to you, Mr. Simonedes?"

"Because the Bright-Eyed One is meant to watch

over us, and…"   Simonedes raised his hand to make another point, but then shuddered, as if he'd caught a chill.

If anything, he looked even paler to Zander. "The Bright-Eyed One?" he asked.

"The goddess, young man. When a man obeys the gods, the gods listen to him."

Penny stood up. "We should stop. You need your rest, Mr. Simonedes. But you'll come with us tomorrow morning to the church?"

The question brought on another coughing spasm, even worse than before.

Zander took the old man's hand, which had turned clammy. "I want to call for a doctor, Mr. Simonedes."

"No," he said, sipping more water. "That is not necessary. But if you could call my son to take me home, that would be best."

Fifteen minutes later, a balding, middle-aged man was at the door. They had laid Simonedes down on the couch and Penny had draped a cool towel on his forehead. He'd fallen sleep almost instantly. Zander still wanted to call for a doctor, but he wasn't going to force one on Simonedes. The son went straight to his father without any introductions.

Father and son spoke quietly for a couple of minutes and then Zander helped the old man to his feet. The nap had restored Simonedes sufficiently to let him leave with only a steadying arm. "My son refuses to let me join you tomorrow. But you will call me?"

Penny took Simonedes's hand. "As soon as we know anything."

Part III

It is not down in any map; true places never are.

Herman Melville
Moby Dick

...do not seek to believe that you are equal to the gods...

Homer
The Iliad

Chapter 1

Zander wasn't surprised Henry Demarest pointed him toward the driver's seat when the valet pulled the Mercedes under the hotel's porte-cochere. Zander had half-expected the dealer to announce over breakfast that he'd changed his mind about the whole messy business and they should go on without him. Aside from his undiminished skepticism over the Athena and his clear discomfort at being seen in Zander's company, the country was sliding toward war.

Zander had switched on CNN after showering to learn that new evidence connecting Greek intelligence services to the Istanbul bombers kept surfacing faster than Athens could issue plausible denials. In the hotel restaurant, the staff huddled around a television to watch a Turkish general rant to a diffident newsman.

But Helen's hold on Demarest was unyielding—so much so that Zander wondered what she had on him. Still, just like he'd retreated to his office when the mummified Indian girl had first been brought to his gallery, it was easier for the dealer to keep his head down from the back seat.

"Just take it slow, Alexander. This car needs to go back in pristine condition."

Though just a passenger until now, Zander had grown accustomed to the shared insanity of Istanbul's drivers—darting between lanes like startled minnows; choking off intersections as if gridlock was part of nature's order; honking at the briefest delay. But unlike Goktepe's VW, the big Mercedes was a queen in this hive of four-cylinder drones. Traffic parted as he pulled away. Perhaps people suspected a movie star was lounging in the back.

Riding shotgun, Penny found the Church of Sts. Sergius and Bacchus on a map that folded out from Demarest's guidebook. The church, she said, had been converted to a mosque in the 17th century by the Black Eunuchs.

"The Black Eunuchs?" Zander laughed.

"Sounds like something you should know about, Alexander," said Demarest. "A South Central street gang, perhaps."

Zander imagined Simonedes rattling off the Eunuchs' undoubtedly peculiar history. He wondered if the old man had bothered to see a doctor, even if his son had to force him.

After crossing over the bustling waters of the Golden Horn, Zander sped along the coast road, which was named for President Kennedy. He marveled once again at this picture-postcard view of the city, which took them past Saint Sophia and the Blue Mosque and surviving sections of the ancient sea wall.

Penny read aloud from Demarest's guidebook, explaining that Sergius and Bacchus is known today as the Little Mosque of Saint Sophia because it resembles a miniature version of the city's principal landmark.

"Over there?" Zander asked, pointing toward a domed, sand-colored building separated from the road by a wide stretch of neatly landscaped lawn. He glanced at Penny when she didn't answer and understood why. Hugging the coast had brought them alongside the Sea of Marmara. Heybeli Island, topped by Bulent Ozbek's compound, stared straight at them. He tapped her knee. "Hey," he said. "We're here for Linus Crane. That monster can't hurt you now."

"I know," she said, returning to him. "I'm excited."

Hearing her say this made him realize he was too. Or he had been. The nearer they got, the more his enthusiasm gave way to an unexpected foreboding. It was like waiting to see if you'd gotten into college. All the build-up, all the anxiety, all the dreams, ready either to fly free or melt right before your eyes. Neither of them had talked about what they'd do if they found nothing. But now that seemed to him the most likely scenario. How could something as phenomenal as the golden Athena be waiting for them right in the middle of this megalopolis?

"That was it," Helen said, holding up her own guidebook with a picture of the church.

Zander took the next exit and cut through a park transverse. The Mercedes abruptly slowed to a crawl. It wasn't merely congestion, though. Police were diverting all traffic about two blocks away from the church.

He couldn't see any immediate cause. But living in an age of terror, especially in a city that had been repeatedly targeted, you never knew where security might disrupt things. Zander decided to turn away before reaching the roadblock. He pulled down a side street and slipped into a spot just vacated by a heaving dump truck.

"We can walk from here," he said.

Like every day so far, the morning had grown oppressive earlier than he would ever get used to. An ovenlike burst of noxious air swamped him as he stepped out. Each of the four doors slammed shut with a solidity that he knew was perpetually out of his price range.

Zander gently took Penny's hand. She responded by clutching his forcefully and locking their fingers together. As they'd seen at Saint Sophia and the American Consulate, concrete barricades were being hauled into position around the ancient church to prevent another catastrophe. Fifteen hundred years of easy access gone in a flash.

He winked at Penny and then glanced behind. Helen, in a striped linen blouse and a sharply pressed pair of jeans, looked probably as casual as she ever got. Her bouncy, determined stride couldn't contrast more with Demarest, who frowned like a teenager being dragged along on another dreadful vacation with his parents. Even he had dressed down, in a blue blazer and open collar.

The guidebook said the ancient church opened to tourists at 10. But that was 15 minutes ago and the doors remained shut. Visitors were permitted through the concrete barricade but were being contained behind a line of sawhorses about 30 feet from the entrance. Tightly ringing the building were city police and paramilitary troopers. Zander led the others into the crowd.

"What is it?" Penny asked. "A bomb threat?"

Zander looked up and down the police line. "I doubt it. They wouldn't let us this close if there was any immediate danger."

"Well, are they possibly looking for us?" Demarest asked, a nervous twinge to his voice. "Or rather you?"

Zander had already considered that, but wouldn't indulge Demarest's fear. He was turning to tell the dealer to relax when Penny squeezed his hand even tighter. "Oh God!" she cried.

Chapter 2

There was no question what had riled Penny.

Zander watched Bulent Ozbek march up the front steps of Sts. Sergius and Bacchus and confer with the police commander. The officer seemed to confirm something, and then rapped on the tall doors. Ozbek, accompanied by a wiry man in a loose-fitting brown suit, took a moment to scan the dense crowd.

Zander casually turned away, and saw that Helen and Demarest had both ducked down. Penny, meanwhile, stared intently ahead, almost daring Ozbek to confront her. "Hey!" Zander said, trying to divert her, but Ozbek and his aide disappeared inside.

"He knows," Penny said, clearly angry and exasperated.

Zander couldn't think of any other reason for Ozbek being there either. "He must have figured it out himself. He's got the whole mosaic."

"So what do we do?" Penny asked.

Zander detested the helplessness of the situation.

He yearned to whip out his shield, push the crowd aside, and follow Ozbek up the steps. He could tell from Penny's quivering lip that she would have been right beside him. But that was only a sure ticket to either detention or expulsion.

"I think we should go," Demarest said.

Zander and Penny ignored him.

"Do you have a plan, Alexander?" the dealer continued, his insistent chirp grating on Zander as much as a bawling baby on a six-hour flight.

"We're going to wait here," Zander said, frustrated but without a plan.

"Then what?"

Zander wheeled around and inched closer to Demarest, who retreated twice as far. "Then I'm going to hand you over to that psycho at the American Consulate. How's that sound?"

All around him, Zander sensed the crowd growing antsy in a dozen languages. Then, as abruptly as he'd arrived, Ozbek stepped back out onto the stone portico. He cornered the police commander, repeatedly jabbing his index finger into his own open palm. The commander nodded and then surveyed the crowd. Zander bounced lightly from foot to foot, anxious to know what had happened inside. Ozbek's expression was hard to read. Was he barking orders to find them? Zander turned away again, but managed to watch Ozbek's assistant take the full force of his boss's tirade as they headed off.

"I'm not going in there," Demarest announced.

Zander turned to the dealer. "For once I agree with you."

"I am," Penny said.

"Do you think he found something?" Helen asked, staring over the crowd at the ancient church.

"Only one way to find out," Penny said, her tone ripe with the resignation of a skydiver about to jump.

Zander was ready to insist that she at least wait 15 minutes. But before he could get a word out, Penny extracted a black silk scarf from the pocket of her jeans. She draped it over her head, tugging one end far longer than the other. She pulled the short end under her chin and up to her ear before clipping it to her hair, then quickly wrapped the longer end across her throat and shoulder.

"Instant hijab," Helen said admiringly.

Penny took a deep breath. "When in Rome."

She looked up at Zander. He knew he couldn't stop her, so he pulled the opaque covering a bit further down her forehead. "Just remember which direction Mecca is." She pointed off behind him and he had no doubt she was right. "We'll hang back at the edge of the grass. If you get spooked about *anything*, just turn and walk out. OK?"

Penny nodded and left them behind.

• • • •

The surging crowd almost lifted Penny up the stairs and inside. It was hard to believe the building had ever been a church. Every trace of Christian decoration was long removed or covered over, replaced with sedate and sparse Islamic adornments: tiles and some wall spaces painted with calligraphy or abstract decoration. No pictures. Vast oriental rugs covered most of the stone floor. She wished she could take a moment to let the soaring arches and columns transport her trampled spirit. Instead, she moved through the tourists and pilgrims, searching for access to the lower levels.

Chapter 3

Zander caught sight of Penny before she took a full step outside.

She found him instantly as well and stopped. It took only the slightest shift of her head for his stomach to ball up. Unconsciously he must have grimaced, for Penny responded with a shrug of her shoulders. She lifted her head just enough for Zander to see the despair in her eyes.

He told Demarest and Helen to wait at the car and both took off without a question.

Zander hugged Penny close. "It's always tough when your final lead turns up empty. There's a god-awful finality to it." She buried her face in his shoulder and he felt her convulsing, unleashing weeks of pent-up grief. "I have to admit that when Ozbek came back out of the Church, I wondered if he'd hit a dead end."

When she finally relaxed, it was as if a storm had passed. "I felt that too but couldn't admit it. I've been dreading this more than anything. Now I feel like we finally threw the dirt on Linus's grave," she said.

"I know," Zander said. "Chasing Professor Crane's dream kept him alive."

She stepped back and unwrapped her makeshift hijab, forcing a smile. "There's a saying in *The Iliad*. It was Linus's favorite. It says that a man will lose someone very dear to him, a brother born of the same mother, or a son, but he puts aside his weeping and sorrow, for the Fates have given humankind an enduring heart."

He embraced Penny again. "An enduring heart," he repeated. "Thank God for that."

• • • •

Zander was sure they'd turned the right corner. But where the hell was the car? An enormous Pepsi sign shaped like a bottle cap had been his landmark. But the Mercedes was missing, a Fiat parked sloppily in its place. But then he saw Helen near the brick warehouse where the car should have been. Even from 20 yards she looked dazed. Did Henry just abandon her? He grabbed Penny's hand to hurry her along.

"He's gone," Helen said, sighing and shaking her head.

"It doesn't matter anymore," Zander said. "Demarest—"

"No," she broke in. "Mr. Simonedes. He's dead."

The breath caught in Penny's throat. "What?" she asked, covering her mouth in disbelief.

"I just called to let him know what happened. Like we promised. His son answered the phone and said he died in his sleep last night."

Zander felt emptied by the news. "I knew he was worn down when he left the hotel. But still, if I sensed he was that sick I would have taken him to the ER myself."

Penny grasped his arm. "Could Ozbek...?"

Zander admitted the thought had flashed through this mind, but he dismissed it, given Simonedes's condition and that he hadn't mentioned any connection to Ozbek, even after he'd heard the story of Penny's abduction.

"Such a sweet old man," Penny said. "Maybe he was better off not knowing we struck out. He must have died hopeful."

Helen nodded, which struck Zander as the first time the two women agreed about anything.

"So where's Henry?" he finally asked.

"He sort of lost it when I told him," she said, rolling her eyes. "Said he had to get out of the country before it was too late."

"No great loss, but he's no dope. We should follow him out."

Like a reminder to heed his own advice, a line of three army trucks and half-a-dozen mobile rocket launchers rumbled by. Tanned young men—only boys, they seemed to Zander—sat rigidly on benches in the open trucks, clutching their rifles. Few managed even a tight smile. Zander was surprised to see Penny shaking her head. "No?" he asked.

"It doesn't make sense," she insisted.

Helen spoke above the smog-belching convoy. "About Simonedes?"

"No. About the church here."

"You think you missed something?" asked Zander.

Penny hesitated while glancing at Helen. Despite their moment of shared anguish, it was obvious she still didn't trust the Met curator, who sensed it.

"Look," Helen said, "I'll leave if you want. But I might be able to help."

Penny pursed her lips. Zander, with years of on-the-job training as a conciliator, felt more comfortable talking a jumper off a bridge than getting between these two. This was Penny's call.

"Yeah?" Penny said, as skeptical as a parakeet confronting a smiling cat, "then let's see how."

• • • •

Penny sipped an Orangina at the open-air café while Zander dropped a spoonful of sugar into coffee thick enough to pour over pancakes. Helen clasped her hands around her iced mineral water. The shade from the umbrella, emblazoned with a Panasonic logo, was the greatest relief. Zander dabbed a paper napkin across his brow.

He worried that foot patrolmen might be working the neighborhood with pictures of Penny or him, eager to make an arrest. He had picked a table far off the street but still surrounded by gangs of thirsty tourists.

"So what doesn't add up?" he finally asked.

Penny poked at the ice cubes in her drink, apparently gathering her thoughts. "I can't believe Linus was wrong," she said.

Zander took her hand, but she pulled it back.

"And I'm not saying this merely out of loyalty or grief. I can see that's what you're thinking. But we worked together for five whole years and he was too scrupulous and too smart."

"Even the best and the brightest miss the mark on occasion," Helen said. "And who hasn't succumbed to wishful thinking at times?"

"We all have," Penny agreed. "But Linus was certain enough to defy Ozbek even when he threatened his life. He would have known the Athena wasn't here."

Zander shook his head. "But you said he wasn't going to start searching for the statue until he returned here from London."

"Yes. But this was too easy to confirm one way or the other. He was in Istanbul for almost a week after he stumbled onto the mosaic. I'm sure he deciphered it quickly enough to come here."

"Ozbek could have been watching him," Helen said.

"Maybe."

"Okay," Zander said. "Assuming you're right and Crane knew the statue wasn't here, you believe he had some better idea about where it was—or is?"

"That's what I'm wondering," Penny said.

"You read his diary. Was there anything more than you've already told me?"

"No. But it's what I mentioned before that keeps running through my head."

"What was that?" Helen asked, her eyes dancing again with interest.

Penny folded her paper place mat in half, tucking the damp ring left by her glass underneath. Helen offered her a pen before she could even ask. Zander swept the zinc sugar bowl aside to make room.

"Linus wrote he had no doubt the mosaic revealed how to find the Athena Parthenos. And even though he encrypted the diary, he didn't spell out how. He must have been very deeply concerned about the diary falling into the wrong hands. I think he felt that anyone steeped in Byzantine iconography could make a serviceable interpretation."

Helen tapped the table. "And get themselves to Sergius and Bacchus."

"That's one possibility," Zander said

"You have another?" Helen asked.

"Sure. A simple one. That we're wrong. That we misread the mosaic. That none of us, including Simonedes, are smart enough to interpret the map."

"God," Penny said, "you're starting to sound like your friend Demarest."

"My friend?" Zander laughed, but realized it was true. With the dealer gone, he had somehow taken on the naysayer's role.

"But Simonedes was absolutely convinced," said Helen. "And given the depth of his expertise, I find it hard to dismiss his conclusion."

Penny took the pen and wrote across the place mat in large block letters: PST: MAPS LIE.

"What's that?" Helen asked.

"Well, PST is me, my initials," she said. "And this was a message Linus left for me in his diary. He didn't tie it explicitly to the mosaic, but when I think about it, it makes me question whether Mr. Simonedes was both right and wrong."

"Right *and* wrong?" Zander asked.

"Listen," Penny said, tapping Zander's hand, "you used the word 'map' yourself just now to describe the mosaic. Now, Linus didn't say *this* map lies, but maybe that's precisely what he meant."

"Then," Zander said, "you think it was correct to read the map as a pointer to Sergius and Bacchus, but that Sergius and Bacchus is just not where the statue is?"

"Exactly," Penny said, her hand balled into a fist that she held close to her chin and pumped several times for emphasis.

Once again, Zander felt like Demarest's stand-in. "Okay, but if it's actually someplace else, then we have to deal with the problem that the only one of us who might be able to figure out where died in his sleep last night."

He watched Penny's mouth turn down in disappointment and he felt wretched. "Of course," he continued, trying to find something positive to say, "Linus might have been toying with you again. His messages in the diary might be another test."

Helen tapped the place mat with her fingertips. "*Another* test?"

Chapter 4

"The other puzzle of his you showed me was an anagram," Zander said, "so why not this one?"

Penny nodded, but her thoughts seemed to be drifting. He turned Penny's place mat towards him, took the pen and started reordering the 10 letters, looking for combinations that made any sense at all. Should it be three words? Two? One? Helen pulled another pen from her bag and started scribbling combinations as well.

Zander worried about Penny, who stared blankly in silence at his and Helen's nonsensical dead ends, which soon covered most of the table: SPAM TILPES, I STEM PLAPS, MISS APPLET. Zander wondered that if there was anything to find here at all, it might not even be in English. And he doubted that the street-Spanish he'd picked up over the years would help. Helen shook her head and signaled the waiter to refill her glass. His pace slowed as they repeated their early misfirings again and again.

While Zander twirled his spoon through the muck

at the bottom of his coffee, Penny revived from her stupor. She rested her hand on Zander's forearm to get his attention. "Palimpsest," she said.

Helen sat forward. "Does that work?"

Penny took the pen and spelled it out. P-A-L-I-M-P-S-E-S-T.

"That makes some sense," Zander said, and folded his arms in anticipation of a pair of smug looks. "What? A cop can't know what a palimpsest is?"

"I have interns from Columbia who don't know what one is," said Helen.

Zander was enthused to show he could contribute more than just a good memory to the cause. "Last year a film producer who shall remain nameless called me in a panic. A private detective had delivered some very explicit snapshots to his wife of him going horizontal with one of his supporting actresses. The wife had yanked a few of his prized paintings off the walls, barricaded herself in his library, and was threatening to burn them unless he agreed to move out by 5 o'clock. She had a Cezanne and a Picasso and, for good measure, had grabbed this old English manuscript he kept in a vacuum-sealed glass case on his desk. The manuscript, he said, was a palimpsest because it had been written on once, and then partially erased and written over a couple of centuries later. I actually think he was more upset about the book than the pictures. He fancied himself something of a writer and claimed it was a fragment of the *Canterbury Tales* in Chaucer's own hand that been washed out and written over by a monk. Chaucer's words were still barely visible but an essay in Latin on God's designs for crop rotations was much sharper. And that, ladies, is how I stay ahead of the interns at the Metropolitan Museum. I did also talk the wife out of toasting it all, in case you were wondering."

"Incredible," Penny said.

"What? That I know about this?"

She shook her head. "No. That something so valuable could have been lost because some nitwit couldn't keep his fly zipped."

Helen tapped the place mat with her manicured fingers. "I applaud your intervention, detective, but I don't see how this by itself leads us anywhere." She looked at Penny, her eyebrows raised in expectation. "Did Crane leave any other messages for you?"

Penny nodded and spoke slowly. "'Find your faith in the country.'"

"Find your faith in the country? You think that's a jumble too?" Helen asked.

"No, actually, and I'm even less convinced it has anything to do with the Athena. I quit Linus's program in May because I was sick and tired of the whole profession. He called it a crisis of faith when I first let him know. I think this message was just his way of telling me to hang in there."

"I'm not so sure," Helen said.

"Why?" Penny asked.

"Well, this may be a long shot —"

Zander leaned his chair back onto just its rear legs. "Longer than any other shot we've taken?"

"Yes," Helen smiled. "Good point. But there's another very famous Byzantine church in Istanbul called Saint Savior in Chora. It's out near the ancient defensive wall, far from the city center, which is why it was given the designation 'in Chora,' which means *in the country*. I've been there and I know it's got a massive document collection."

"Yes!" Penny said, thrusting her chair back.

Zander was amazed at how completely Penny's anguish had lifted. "You look like Crane had mentioned this church himself."

"He didn't, but… there's just something very… uh…. very Linus-like about it. We need to get over there."

Zander folded his arms. He couldn't shed his new cynical hide. Looking at Penny, though, the reason was becoming clear. It wasn't that he'd tapped some new pessimistic vein of his own. Rather, for the first time in more years than he cared to remember, something precious had fallen into his life and he wanted to protect it—from both danger and disappointment. But the ominous anticipation in Penny's strained smile was all he needed to see. He understood now that this had nothing to do with art or gold, scholarship or celebrity. It was about a debt she owed Linus Crane. And her debts had become his. "Let's go," he said.

Zander threw some Turkish bills on the table and they stood to leave.

"What about the last message?" he asked. "There were three, right?"

"Yes. He also wrote, 'Beware Athena's favorite.'"

Helen took a last sip from her soda and dropped the pens back in her bag while giving Penny a quizzical look.

"I don't know either," Penny said. "Let's get to the church first."

Chapter 5

Helen hopped out of the taxi before it had pulled to a full stop across the square fronting St. Savior in Chora. "I was here a couple of days ago—it was a madhouse. A dozen German buses. A whole division, if you know what I mean. This is bliss by comparison."

Zander laughed at the image of the tourist blitzkrieg. In his seven years bouncing between low-life counterfeiters, middleweight dealers, and high-flying collectors, he hadn't met anyone quite like Helen. He wasn't sure what lay beneath the sophisticated veneer. She might easily fall south of even Henry Demarest on the ethical map, as Penny suspected. But she was certainly smoother. No way he could endure an hour with her alone, but Penny's lingering suspicions kept Helen's more obnoxious side bottled up, and so far she'd pulled her weight.

"Why were you here?" Penny asked.

"Uh... just touring. It's the most fascinating Byzantine building outside of Saint Sophia. I'm sure you could spend a year studying the mosaics inside."

"Another time," Zander said as they headed across the traffic-free square. Behind them ran the tumbledown remnant of a wall meant to keep ancient invaders at bay. It made Zander realize that the roadblocks that had been planted around most of the city's landmarks were absent from the umber-toned brick church, which, a billboard announced, was converted to Kariye Mosque five centuries ago. Not that security was lacking. An elite army unit ringed the perimeter of St. Savior. Judging by the way Penny slowed as she neared the heavily armored guards, each waving a high-powered Heckler & Koch assault rifle, they were far more intimidating than any concrete barrier.

"Thank God Ozbek's not here," Penny whispered, though they were well out of anyone's ear shot.

"He couldn't know about this," Zander said.

"I hope you're right. But if he's not smart enough to figure something out, he seems to get his way with brute force."

A flock of food and souvenir vendors were grouped outside the front entrance to St. Savior. Zander stopped to inspect a bronze model of the building, which sat among artists' sketches and photos of the church's pleasing mix of columns, graceful arches and airy domes.

A line of 20 overdressed French tourists waited to enter, slowed by a metal detector just inside the tall, heavily carved doors.

Stepping up and through the entryway, the air turned refreshingly cooler and smelled of ancient earth. Zander's jaw clenched when he saw a dozen policemen and soldiers huddled around the metal detector and behind the security desk. He wondered if Ozbek's absence had left them too bold. He realized now that he hadn't shaved in days and probably looked damn suspicious. Two sharp-eyed cops focused on him as he waited to clear the detector. Others glared at Penny and Helen, though Zander guessed that was just disguised ogling. Regardless, it was too late to turn around.

Helen handed her shoulder bag to a guard before stepping through the detector. Penny glided inside as well and waited beside her. Zander pulled his keychain from his pocket and stared down at it. He jangled the keys to his apartment and his Honda for a moment before dropping them into a well-worn plastic basket. He felt like he'd have to jump through a wormhole to use them again.

He cleared the detector and was reaching for his keys when one of the cops pulled the basket away.

"Identification," he ordered.

Zander took a breath and slipped his wallet from his back pocket. His police shield surprised the cop, who passed it to his companion. He extracted Zander's driver's license and compared him to his photo several times.

"Not a good shot," Zander laughed, unable to force a smile from his examiner, who was now typing his name into a computer.

Zander glanced over at Penny and saw she was frightened. He felt the hair raising on the back of his neck, wondering what database was combing for a match. Known criminals? Terror suspects? Outstanding warrants? Not knowing whether he was wanted by the authorities was maddening. His blood pressure spiked at the prospect of being arrested.

"Does the mosque have a library?" Zander almost shouted, breaking the cop's focus on the flashing screen.

The cop hit a few more keys but then abandoned his search. "Through the nave and right, back toward the tombs," he said, returning Zander's license and letting him scoop up his keys.

Zander appreciated how difficult it was for Penny to head through the church while barely glancing at the masterpieces clinging to virtually every inch of wall and ceiling. "It's been here a thousand years," he said, gently pressing his palm onto the small of her back. "You can see the rest another time."

"I know."

Reaching a windowless area that an old stone sign identified as the Parecclesion, Zander saw an office had been built into the most distant wall. "Archive" was written across a half-glass door that seemed like it could have led to Sam Spade.

It was locked, but a heavy young woman with a broad smile and dark, narrow-set eyes quickly answered Zander's tapping. She introduced herself as Merida, technically the assistant archivist, she said, but the *de facto* chief since her boss had retired three months ago. She invited them to sit, but Penny said they had only a few quick questions.

"We are looking for a palimpsest you might have in your holdings."

The archivist nodded vigorously. "You mean the Kapel?"

"Perhaps," Penny said, her voice half an octave higher than usual. "What is that?"

"It was uncovered here in 1908 by a Danish scholar

named Finn Kapel. He was researching his dissertation on Byzantine prayer books and detected some faint drawings and writing in one item from our collection. He eventually proved that a shortage of vellum had forced a 15th century group of monks to copy over a small secular manuscript and incorporate it into their book. The original manuscript—the underwriting—seems to have been the work of a 13th century emperor."

"What was in the older work?" Helen asked.

"Kapel only recovered a few fragments. The manuscript was removed from here during World War I and, I regret to say, either lost or stolen. It turned up in a Swiss auction house in the 1970's and mercifully we were able to reclaim it before it was sold. And as far as I know, the few scholars who have examined it since then have extracted only some repeated pagan references.

Zander watched Penny's shoulders jump reflexively. "Can we see it?" she asked.

"Unfortunately not."

Penny's eyes widened. She was clearly ready for a fight.

Helen jumped in, her tone insistent. "We are here as scholars. I am a curator at the Metropolitan Museum of Art in New York and I assure you we have vast experience handling rare documents."

"No no, Madame. That is not the issue."

"Stolen again?" Zander asked, glancing back at the glass door that any street thug could demolish blindfolded.

The archivist slowly shook her head, her lips hinting at laughter. "No. Nothing so exciting. I would be most happy to review your credentials and give you full access if they were in order. But the palimpsest is on loan."

"Where?" Penny asked.

"To Great Britain. At Oxford University."

Helen's head snapped back. "You're kidding. For how long?"

"It has been there six months now."

Zander sensed Penny's frustration, and slid his arm around her shoulder. Helen was still shaking her head in disbelief. "You look like you somehow should have known that," he told her.

Startled by Zander's suggestion, Helen took a moment to compose herself. "No," she finally said. "It's only that we were all just in England. So close, I mean."

The archivist nodded sympathetically, running a finger across her dry lips and clearing her throat. "However, I can show you a facsimile reproduction."

"That would be terrific," Zander said, knowing that high-resolution photos could be as good as the original.

The woman retreated to a low oak cabinet alongside her desk and pulled out a thin manila folder. She handed it to Penny, explaining that it held fourteen 8x10 color photographs. "These were taken earlier this year."

Penny opened the folder while Zander stared over her shoulder. He didn't expect to read whatever dead language the document was written in. And though he was excited to see that a quality camera had been used, the underwriting was virtually invisible. "This makes the Chaucer look bright as a neon sign."

"Even the prayer-book text looks washed out,"

Helen lamented.

The archivist pushed her tortoise-shell glasses higher on her nose and turned one photo towards herself. "I'm afraid the original is no better."

Penny shook her head with aggravations at every picture she flipped through.

"Is this your only set?" Zander asked.

"No. We have one more."

"Can I borrow these?"

"Zander," Penny said, slapping the file closed, "it's not worth it."

"She's right," Helen added. "No human being could read this."

"I know," he said.

Chapter 6

Penny's eyes burned into Zander's profile as he watched the Stars and Stripes flapping atop the American Consulate. Was she right? Was this insane? He couldn't deny that they were heading back into the lion's den, except that their personal lion tamer—the President—was gone.

Helen had encouraged him after hearing his reason for going, but then she'd taken off for her hotel, claiming a dozen critical calls needed returning. But she promised she and her car would be ready if needed.

"Felix Maurer, please," Zander told the receptionist, who seemed to remember him. "Tell him Zander Blake's here."

The thin-lipped Turkish woman tapped her keypad, whispered into her headset, and indicated Zander and Penny should wait on the black leather couches.

They moved to opposite sides of a sleek glass coffee table that held only a pile of unread consulate newsletters. Penny's smirk was starting to resemble a permanent feature, at least when she turned in Zander's direction.

"If you think this is so stupid," he asked, "why did you come along?"

Her expression dissolved into pity, the kind you might shower on a slow, middle child. "If you haven't figured that out yet, you're one shitty detective."

Zander was scraping for some snappy response when Maurer seemed to appear out of nowhere.

"Not much surprises me, but this does," the station chief said.

"Glad we could spice up your day. No goon to escort us up?" Zander asked.

"I'm reserving that pleasure for myself."

Now Zander was surprised. While not friendly—he doubted Maurer could effect any dictionary definition of friendly—this was a far cry from the madman who had pounded the hood of Henry Demarest's Mercedes yesterday afternoon. What's more, Zander was sure Maurer hadn't changed his clothes since then.

"Nice to see you, Miss Theobald," he said, accompanying his pleasant tone with a wink. When she didn't move even after Zander stood, he added: "I don't bite."

"I've got a deal for you," Zander said, seeing no reason to dither with this kinder, gentler Maurer, who might have softened only from sleep deprivation.

"I don't make deals. But come upstairs."

Penny finally loosened her grip on the couch and caught up as the elevator doors opened.

"A lot less crowded with the President gone," Zander said.

"A lot less than you can imagine," Maurer responded, pushing the *doors close* button. "All nonessentials flew out last night. This mess with the Greeks has reached the boiling point. And if *we* confirm that Athens had even a remote hand in the concert bombing, then all bets are off."

"You've got something definitive?"

"We should know today."

Zander and Penny followed Maurer down the hall and waited for him to unlock the same conference room where they'd faced off before.

"Is this your office, or some type of ultra-secure room?"

Zander had asked the question half-jokingly, but when Maurer earnestly responded, "It's not my office," the puzzle he thought he was piecing together took on a whole new shape.

"So you're not with the State Department?"

"Just sit down."

Zander's focus immediately turned to the objects Maurer had identified as the chief terrorist's personal belongings, now arranged neatly on the conference table. But more intriguing was what was beside them: several high-powered pistols, a small box of grenades, and two red-leather ledger books.

Zander glanced at Maurer, who was watching him study the weapons. "You're going to make me ask?"

"Since you're as responsible as anyone, no I won't. The key you noticed on the charm bracelet—Mazari's gift for his blessed mother—was, for lack of a better word, the key I'd been looking for. Friends in the Turkish Finance Ministry traced it to a large safe deposit box here in Istanbul."

Zander felt a wave of satisfaction, both that he'd helped implicate Mazari, and that he'd bested Maurer.

"And let me guess—the real jewels are not the arms, but those books."

Maurer nodded with an admiring look. "Right again, though they didn't give up their secrets easily. In fact they still haven't—not completely."

Penny cleared her throat. "Okay, enough. What are you two talking about? Those books and the guns belonged to the guy who blew up the American sailors?"

"That's right," Maurer said. "I retrieved them about seven this morning. The box was registered to Mazari himself. Those books that Detective Blake described as the jewels record financial transactions that underwrote Mazari's terror cell. Almost three years' worth. It wasn't apparent at first, but we found the source: a charitable foundation based in Zurich called the Foundation for Turkish Reconstruction. It wouldn't be the first so-called charity to pay a terrorist's bills. Naturally, the Swiss have been as obstructionist as possible. Assholes don't want to set any precedents they'll regret. But that's what I meant when I said I'd have something definitive soon."

"And you expect to find a Greek connection?" Penny asked.

"Most likely to some rogue intelligence operation, yes. The Turks have already convinced me that all of the terrorists trained in Greece."

"So you owe me," Zander said, leaning back against the table as if he'd just pulled a 21 at a high-stakes Vegas table.

Despite Maurer's huzzahs, Zander saw the words rankled. The station chief began chewing his gum like it was an iron bolt. "Much as I'd like to deny it, yes. Your catch was critical. That said, though, you're still being tossed out of the country, so you want to explain why you're here?"

"I didn't think our status had changed. And we can live with that. But I need your help."

"With what?" Maurer asked, tipping forward on his toes a bit, as if sensing the advantage shift in his direction.

Chapter 7

"Yesterday," Zander told the station chief, "you showed us some satellite photos of troops on the ground moving toward a fight. Crystal-clear shots from a high orbit through lousy weather. You've obviously got some incredible enhancement software."

"That's right," said Maurer. "State of the art—and top secret."

"I'm not asking you to tell me how it works. I just want you to run it."

"On what?"

Zander opened the folder of the palimpsest photos and handed one to Maurer.

"These are new pictures of an 800-year-old-manuscript that was washed, erased, and written over before Shakespeare was born. We need to know what the original manuscript says and I think the program that cleaned up your satellite pictures can tell us."

Maurer took the full folder. He flipped quickly through the pile, but his expression showed he was a quick study. "What's this about?" he asked.

How much should he say? Were they suddenly allies? Comrades in arms? Zander doubted it. The forces of the universe normally kept them light years apart, and he had no doubt their antagonism could easily resurface. But, for the moment, their orbits were in sync.

"I'm not sure you want to know," Zander suggested, testing how much of the charm bracelet's good will was left.

"There's nothing I don't want to know," Maurer said.

"Even about Bulent Ozbek?"

The station chief shook his head. "You're blaming him for erasing your manuscript, too?"

Not everything had changed.

When their host turned to Penny, though, Zander understood that Maurer would not demand a full accounting. "You're an art historian and archaeologist, right Miss Theobald?"

Penny nodded. "You've read my resume."

"Then tell me a story that leaves the politics out."

• • • •

Maurer picked up the phone. "Swanson, get in here."

Captain John Swanson barreled into the room, but pulled up short, his eyes bulging at the sight of Zander and Penny.

Zander couldn't suppress a low snicker. "Captain," he offered, though Swanson was seething. Zander could imagine what kind of shit he'd caught for letting them slip away yesterday.

Maurer slapped the folder and handed it to the

marine. "Take these down to Pollard. Tell him *deep* retrieval, right now, the whole set."

"Yes sir," he mumbled on his way out.

"Nice to have a gorilla on staff," Zander said.

"Swanson's no gorilla," Maurer sighed. "Gorillas are highly intelligent. Swanson's a brontosaurus." He held two fingers half an inch apart. "A huge body and a tiny brain. But he knows that one more screw-up and he'll be shouldering a rifle at the front gate."

• • • •

Zander was shocked when Swanson swept back into the conference room just 20 minutes later. He tossed the *Herald Tribune* sports page aside and huddled with Penny alongside Maurer so they could examine the results together. Clipped to each photo was a laser print of what hadn't been seen—not clearly at least—in more than 600 years. He couldn't understand a word of it, but whatever the technology had produced was stunning: crisp and clean text in a swirling calligraphy. A few spots on each page were blurred or blank, but the overall result was dazzling.

"This is beyond remarkable," Penny said, almost swooning as she collated the prints into a pile and retreated to read.

"Just a little NASA spinoff," Maurer said.

"A well-spent billion dollars, I'm sure," she said as she grabbed a pen, eager to start annotating.

"You're not complaining, are you?" Maurer asked.

She put her pen down and gave Maurer her full attention. Zander saw it was her way of thanking him. "No. Definitely not."

"What language is it?" Zander asked.

"Medieval Greek," she said, starting to scribble furiously in the margins.

• • • •

Zander was listening to Maurer catalogue likely Turkish-Greek battlefronts when Penny exhaled sharply. Zander turned to see her nodding her head in awe.

"It was there," she announced. "Just like Mr. Simonedes said." She smiled at Zander with a mix of amazement and joy before explaining to Maurer how Simonedes had helped get them this far.

"Do you mean *was* as in 'once upon a time,' or as in we missed it and need to go back?"

"Oh. I wish we could just go back. But it's long gone from Sergius and Bacchus. In fact, it was barely there."

Maurer cleared his throat. "And you trust this new source material?"

"That's a good question. This manuscript isn't signed, but it was certainly written within a few years of the events themselves by someone with intimate knowledge. I'd say only the emperor himself could know some of the details in here."

"And does it contradict the mosaic?" Zander asked.

"Not at all. The mosaic shows that when the emperor realized the Crusaders' intent was to sack Constantinople, he had the great Athena removed from the Hippodrome and brought to the church of Sergius and Bacchus. The manuscript says that a secret vault was being prepared to house it there. But then the real court intrigue took over. A prince in the emperor's own family—the document isn't clear on whether it was a brother or a son—conspired with a group of invading knights to bring the goddess to Venice. There was a horrible, bloody battle right inside the church and all the knights were killed, mostly burned alive. The writer even swears that Athena herself took part."

Maurer snorted. "Doesn't that sort of magical story make you question the whole thing?"

Penny cocked her head slightly. "I'll admit it strains credulity."

Zander's patience was waning. "So what's the bottom line? Does it say where the statue is?"

Penny held up a finger and smiled.

"Just listen. Remember when you were recollecting the mosaic last night, near the end you focused on the figures of Sergius and Bacchus?"

"I said they were posed like a couple of bookends, rearing back to spear something in tandem."

"Exactly," said Penny.

"But I said I couldn't say what they were aiming at."

"The target's not important," she said. "But the direction is. You described the angle they were throwing at."

Zander picked up a blue marker from the tray beneath the large whiteboard and quickly sketched a man flinging a spear.

"You'd call that southeast, right?"

Zander's nod sent Penny toward a map of the Aegean basin that covered almost an entire wall of the conference room.

"Don't bother with that," Maurer said. "That's not much more useful than wallpaper." He waved her over to his desktop computer. "What are you trying to find?"

"Can you set the old Imperial Palace here as the hub and show me what's a certain distance to the southeast?"

The station chief instantly brought up a map of northwest Turkey. He set old Istanbul as the center.

"What's the distance?" Maurer asked.

"150 miles."

"Precisely?"

"The mosaic said the Athena had been moved 150 miles."

"What?" Zander asked, wondering if she was just playing a game with Maurer.

"According to the mosaic, the Athena was taken away 150 miles as an eagle flies from the imperial palace. That's a little inexact because I know from some field work that the Byzantines didn't define a mile as rigorously as we do. It was often a little shorter, but it meant the same thing, 1,000 paces, from the Latin *mille passuum*."

"Wait a minute," Zander said, his agitation breaking through. "Where did you get that number from? I don't remember you mentioning it and I know I didn't."

"As a matter of fact you did," Penny said.

Zander didn't doubt her, but if the last 24 hours had proven anything, it was that he still had a damn good memory. "I don't think so."

"But you did. Remember when you described the figures that turned out to be Sergius and Bacchus?"

"The cross dressers?"

"What?" Maurer said, a lip turning up in distaste.

Penny waved her hand at Maurer. "It's nothing," she said, and turned back to Zander. "You said that alongside one figure was a letter C and beside the other a letter L, correct?"

"Yes," Zander said.

"Well, the manuscript explains that putting those letters together, CL, reveals how many miles the Athena was taken from here."

"150," Zander said, as if the sun had just risen behind his eyes.

"And the direction is revealed by the angle of the lances held by Sergius and Bacchus."

Zander gave Penny's elbow a squeeze. "How many dead languages do you speak?"

"Six or seven," she said, and looked at Maurer. "Now what's about 150 miles southeast of the ancient Imperial Palace?"

Maurer tapped a few keys and maneuvered the mouse. Zander stared at the screen. His recollection of the lances' direction might have been rough, but at the supposed distance nothing else was even close. A yellow line flashed between Istanbul and this end point. Maurer clicked on the town at the end of the line, turning it scarlet red. "Iznik," he said.

"Interesting," said Penny.

"Why?" Zander asked.

"Because it's an ancient city, much better known as Nicaea. In fact, I'm pretty sure the Byzantine court escaped the Crusaders there. Yes. It makes sense. The palimpsest could easily have been written there."

Zander needed more details before jumping through another hoop. "But the manuscript doesn't actually mention Nicaea?"

Penny folded her arms and took on her university lecturer face. "No, but that's the point. The manuscript is half of the puzzle, the mosaic the rest. You can't know where to look for the Athena without having both pieces. The mosaic gives you the data for where to look, but you can't interpret or analyze it without the manuscript."

"Like a fail safe," Maurer said.

"Right," Zander said. "But doesn't this raise another question?"

Penny nodded, evidently a step ahead. "How much of this did Linus know?"

"And how did he know it?" Maurer added.

Zander was intrigued by the station chief's interest. Perhaps he just liked puzzles. Regardless, they weren't getting out of the consulate again without his okay, let alone to Iznik.

"Then you agree this trail is worth following?" Zander asked.

The question brought Maurer up short, as if he knew Zander was trying to paint him into a corner. Maurer shrugged. "As much as anything else you've told me."

"All right then," Zander said. "We need a day."

"Ha! Are you nuts?"

"But you see what we've got," Penny implored. "We're not out to topple any government here. This doesn't even involve Ozbek anymore."

Maurer opened his arms like an evangelist advising his flock. "My friends, as far as you're concerned, everything has to do with Bulent Ozbek."

Zander felt his anger welling up. But he sensed also that Maurer wasn't finished. Pleading wasn't the right course, and neither was exploding. It was clear that Maurer felt an obligation and maybe he had the courage to pay up. Meanwhile, Zander saw that these seconds of silence were draining Penny's fight.

Maurer's right foot tapped to some unknown rhythm. "I'll give you 12 hours. You're back here tonight and you check in with me so I know you're back. And you're on the first flight to London tomorrow morning. That's not negotiable. Are we absolutely clear about this?"

Zander nodded.

"And let me warn you," Maurer continued, "though I suspect you've already guessed: a warrant's been issued for your arrest. The army may have it as well."

"We haven't done anything," Penny complained.

"That's debatable. And as the detective would tell you, also irrelevant, since I doubt you want to explain that to a judge, especially a Turkish judge. The fact is that you were ordered to leave the country and you skipped out of your detention. And your enemy isn't some small-town sheriff, it's the royal family. If the locals nab you, I can't help you."

Chapter 8

Maurer's cell rang just moments after Zander shut the door on his way out. The station chief prayed it was one of his sources tracking Mazari's backer, the Foundation for Turkish Reconstruction.

A search of the Agency's own databases revealed that FTR had aroused suspicions before, at least in Europe. French intelligence had labeled it a terrorist ATM posing as a Swiss-based relief organization. Just recently, German police had identified FTR as the source of funds used by a Frankfurt terror cell to travel to a terrorist training camp in Indonesia. Like similar groups, FTR was still operating because there was never enough evidence to gain an indictment, let alone convict in a public court proceeding. But Maurer wasn't looking for a conviction—just credible evidence of who filled FTR's coffers. The French seemed to have the best access, and his gut said they would blow through the dummy corporations and unveil the true operators, despite the best efforts of asshole Swiss bankers and regulators. The most troubling question still in his mind was how high in the Greek government knowledge of FTR ran. Aside from a war, which Maurer suspected would be far bloodier than many thought and would reshape the eastern Mediterranean for decades, Washington would deliver its own reprisals. God knew what they would be.

But Maurer's expectations deflated at the roar of Bulent Ozbek demanding an update on Zander and Penny. It wasn't the first time Ozbek had seemed almost psychic, and Maurer couldn't think of anyone he'd rather talk to less.

"It's under control," Maurer sought to assure him. "Because they just left my sight 30 seconds ago.... Look, they'll be out of the country first thing tomorrow morning.... They've gone to finish up some business in Iznik, after which they're leaving voluntarily.... Something up your alley, as a matter of fact: an antique statue." The silence from Ozbek's end was a balm. Maurer had never heard him at a loss for words and it didn't last long. "Yes, I'm serious. And I'm sure they were too.... What? You're kidding, right?"

• • • •

Ozbek slapped the phone down. He took a deep breath, still wavering over whether this was a crisis or a gift from Allah. On one level he wasn't surprised. These two Americans had unbelievable sources. But what in the world had put them on the trail to Iznik? Iznik, of all places. A wasteland since before Süleyman. How far was it? No more than 45 minutes by air. He felt energized as well for grinding his heel into Maurer. The station chief knew he was serious. If Penny and Blake weren't out of the country by tomorrow morning, then he'd see that Maurer got the boot.

• • • •

Maurer grabbed his aluminum briefcase and raced downstairs. Part of him—most of him, actually—was hoping they'd gone. But Zander and Penny were standing just beyond the security barriers, apparently waiting for the silver Toyota Avensis that just pulled up to them. Penny opted for the back while the driver moved to the passenger seat and let Zander take the wheel. Maurer jogged over and peeked inside. He recognized the other woman from the Mercedes yesterday. What was her connection to all this?

"Hope you've got room for one more," he said, and popped in alongside Penny before anyone could react.

• • • •

Ozbek tapped a speed-dial number on his cell. If it rang, he didn't hear it. "Sherin, have the helicopter prepped. We're going to Iznik. I'll let you know exactly when…. And is our new associate in town? … Good. Bring him along."

Chapter 9

"Sorry, but I can't afford a repeat of yesterday," Maurer said as he yanked the door shut. "Not that I think you're bullshitting me, but I can't spend my day sweating whether you're gonna fly the coop again." It was rude enough that Zander believed him. "Or would you prefer I send Swanson to hold your hand?"

"No!" Penny insisted, loud enough that she couldn't help but laughing, which thawed an awkward moment.

Zander knew he had no leverage, so he didn't bother to argue. "Welcome aboard," he said, pulling the car away from the consulate.

Penny returned to scrutinizing the manuscript photos while Zander introduced Helen and shook his head at hearing Maurer claim once again he was some plain-vanilla diplomat.

What did it matter, anyway? They had nothing to hide and he suspected Maurer knew the geography. If pressed, Zander would even admit to a certain comfort at having him along. Backup, if nothing else. Still, he couldn't help jabbing. "This has nothing to do with Ozbek?"

The question hit a sore spot. "Don't even go there," Maurer shot back. "This has to do with *me*."

"But didn't you say you were waiting for some critical calls?"

Maurer unclipped an oversized cell phone from his belt. "Satellite," he said, holding it aloft like a trophy. "No dead zones for this baby."

Maurer directed them out of the city without cracking a map. For a while it seemed there was no end to Istanbul and its concrete housing blocks, built to accommodate endless waves of villagers seeking a better life in the city. Zander tried to imagine how much worse things could be than these teeming, airless boxes.

Within an hour the highway had shrunk to two lanes of blacktop. The high rises had also given way to an ocean of tin shacks, spreading across shrinking hills of Judas trees.

If not for a stream of army convoys heading toward Istanbul, traffic would have been nonexistent. The country was clearly mobilizing. Zander lowered his window a few inches, tired of the icy conditioned air, and let the summer blow across his face. He imagined the troops crowded in the passing transports, groggy and sick from the heat.

Zander looked back at Maurer. "When does the shooting start?"

"Thirty-six hours, maybe less," the station chief said.

"And nothing can stop it?" asked Penny

Maurer shook his head. "Too late for that. The diplomats know they can't prevent it, so they're trying to contain it. What we really don't want is any other Europeans, meaning the French, deciding Christianity must be defended against the infidel."

"A helluva twist," Zander said, "if the Turks find comfort in the arms of hard-core Islamists when this is all over. Al-Qaeda couldn't have asked for more."

Maurer nodded. "They could have written the script. Our men and women are murdered, and the alliance that's supposed to stand strong against precisely that sort of thing ends up imploding."

• • • •

It was almost 4:30 when signs said they were nearing Iznik. Even with Maurer navigating, the ride had taken longer than Zander anticipated. The roads remained decent and uncrowded, but God help you if you were in a rush. Herds of cattle blocked the way twice. Marked police sedans idled off the shoulder every 10 or 12 miles and Zander knew it would be foolish—or worse—to get stopped. Maurer reminded him at the first opportunity that he couldn't fend off the locals.

They'd been hugging the shore of a calm blue lake for several miles when, cresting a rare hill, Iznik appeared in the distance. Motorboats, some pulling skiers, roared across the water. The sight of a floating dock, rocking with screaming kids, reminded Zander of summer camp. He felt himself sinking into a funk about their escapade and the long odds of success. But turning to see the amazement on Penny's face as she studied the manuscript buoyed him again.

Helen had been speed-reading a guidebook with microscopic print and sepia-tinted photographs that gave everything an antique air. "That should be the Istanbul Gate straight ahead," she said. "It will put us right on the main boulevard through Iznik."

Zander now saw that the city was built as a fortress, though its defenses had crumbled centuries ago. Spreading out on both sides of the arched Istanbul Gate, like broken wings, were the remains of stone defensive walls, reduced in some places to rubble and everywhere overgrown with shrubs and weeds. Zander guessed that Iznik stretched no more than a mile and a half across, barely bigger than a neighborhood in Istanbul. This was manageable, he thought.

Traffic slowed abruptly a hundred yards from the gate as the road narrowed and pedestrians pressed their way through, daring cars to hit them.

Zander knew they had no more than four hours until sunset, when Maurer said he was turning them around. He looked back at Penny, who had deflected his questions several times during the ride. She was still flipping through the manuscript. Now she stopped and closed her eyes, as if she were adding two huge numbers in her head. As far as he was concerned, though, the time for perfectionism had passed. "Penny," he said, more irritably than he intended, "Where are we going?"

"Right," she said, sighing as if she were exhaling a lung full of cigarette smoke. "I didn't quite follow this at first, but I think I've got it now."

"Let's hear it," Maurer said.

"Most of the early manuscript deals with the emperor's disillusionment and sorrow over the sacking of Constantinople."

"That's what Simonedes talked about," Zander

said, "when the Crusaders went berserk there instead of pushing on to Jerusalem."

"Yes, and what's fascinating is how the assault by these Christian warriors prompted the emperor's own spiritual crisis."

"Well," Maurer said, "he'd have to be dead from the neck up not to question everything he believed in."

"He more than questioned," Penny continued. "He abandoned his faith in Christ altogether and started searching for spiritual answers elsewhere."

"Like in pyramids and crystals?" Maurer asked.

"Not quite so New Age."

"In Athena?" Zander asked.

"Bingo."

"Okay. But where to now?"

"I'm getting to that. The emperor began to study and pray to Athena and grew devoted to the goddess in all of her incarnations."

Zander saw that Penny wasn't going to be rushed. He pulled off the road and cut the engine. "Incarnations?" he asked.

She put the manuscript down on her lap. "When we think of Athena today we usually imagine either the goddess of wisdom or of warriors."

"In full battle dress," said Maurer.

"Yes," she said. "But to the ancient Greeks she was the goddess and protector of many other things too. She looked after horses and artisans, especially weavers, and women who worked at home. Health and technology were her specialties as well, and even some more eccentric things, like trickery and craftiness. The emperor wanted to appeal to her in all of her guises."

The frustration on Zander's face was growing

visible, and Penny held up her hand like a cop bringing an intersection to a halt.

"I know. You want me to tell you this says the emperor hid the statue at the palace here, and that's where we should go."

"Only if it's true—which somehow I don't think it is."

"The emperor was consumed with distrust in the wake of being betrayed by his own blood once already. So he secured what he calls 'the golden goddess' and declared that only those worthy enough should see her."

Zander twisted around in his seat, facing Penny over the center console with a forced smile. "Seriously, do you have any clue where we should go?" He watched Penny bite her lip, clearly hesitant to drop whatever bomb was in the manuscript.

"The emperor laid out what he called *signposts of wisdom* around the city. To prove ourselves worthy, we first have to find them."

Chapter 10

Zander slumped back behind the wheel. He flexed his shoulders and rolled his neck, but nothing was going to help. His body had surrendered and tied itself in one massive knot. He stared at the tumbledown entry into the ancient city up ahead, the slow parade of cars and braying animals, the crush of shouting and sweating Turks. He wouldn't have thought it possible, but he longed to be inching home on the San Diego Freeway, listening to his daughter stump him through his Bluetooth earpiece with all the silly riddles in this month's *Highlights* magazine.

The notion that they were going to uncover a set of markers that had been placed god knows where around the city seven or eight centuries ago—and only then get a bead on the golden Athena—seemed absurd. Linus Crane, God bless him, was preparing to mount an international expedition with all the resources he might need—staff, publicity, money, and Ivy League authority—to accomplish what Penny and he needed to discover essentially on their own by sundown. Then they'd be gone, undoubtedly barred from returning to Turkey for at least as long as Bulent Ozbek had any claim to power.

He took a swig of Coke that had gone flat a good two hours ago and squeezed the fleshy ridge atop his nose, seeking to squelch an onrushing headache. "Assuming just for argument's sake," he said, "that I have enough brains to recognize a signpost of wisdom when I see one, please tell me there are at least some clues to finding these things."

"Yes," Penny said, her tone charged with encouragement, in reaction to Zander's slump-shouldered frustration, "there are. That's why I've been telling you about Athena and her different personas. The emperor became enthralled with Athena. These signposts—there are four of them—mark the end points of a symbolic cross. Finding them will let us calibrate the center of the cross, which is where, the manuscript says, the Athena will be found."

"A cross?" Maurer asked. "Doesn't that contradict what you said about him dispensing with his Christian God?"

Helen cleared her throat. "The cross is hardly just a Christian insignia," she said. "As a symbol of eternal life, which I think is intended here, it had meaning to Gnostics and Kabbalists, who took it from the Egyptians. You can even find it among early Buddhists in India. But..." Helen turned up the corner of her mouth.

"But what?" asked Zander.

"But I've been reading through Scott-Smith's and Lindy's histories of Byzantium, both of which have extensive sections on this period, and there's no mention of any Olympian idolatry. Not even a footnote."

"That should not be surprising," Penny said. "The object of their veneration was a state secret and I don't sense that this deviation, so to speak, carried over to the court's restoration in the capital. In fact, the rightful emperor's return to Constantinople clearly triggered a renaissance in Christian art and belief across the empire."

Zander was grinding his foot into the floor between the pedals. "Look, can we put the teachers' lounge theorizing aside? If we don't get a move on we might as well go home now."

"All right, detective," Penny said. "I'm willing to call it your case."

Zander smiled at her sarcasm, but he was eager to take the lead. "Okay," he said, "Given that the history books are absolutely no help, I think the only chance we've got of finding these markers is if the emperor made some logical associations between the city as it was then and these signposts. How does he describe the four of them?"

Penny was ready. Her finger moved down the page: "They recognize Athena Hippia, Athena Hygeia, Athena Promakhos, and Athena Ergane."

"Translate for me, kiddo. One at a time."
"Hippia. The horse. Athena as guardian of horses."

"Okay," Zander said. "The horse. What can we associate with horses? Was there a race track here?" He looked at Helen, who had her histories open on her lap.

"I don't think so," she said.

"A stable, maybe?" Penny asked.

"Hold it," Helen said. She flipped back and forth between pages dense with text and a gatefold map. "Yes."

"Where?" asked Zander.

Helen looked up at the Istanbul Gate, and then compared the antique map with a modern map in her paperback guide. "Go straight ahead. From what I can tell, the main drive through town is built right over the medieval high street."

Before putting the car in gear, Zander turned toward Penny again. "Do you have any idea what the signpost might look like? A statue? A shrine? A picture?"

She shook her head with a hint of regret that Zander waved off before inching back into the line of cars. Moving more slowly than he could walk, he soon saw that the slowdown wasn't just too many cars converging on a single lane. Inside the gate, jeeps packed with soldiers were eyeballing everyone passing through and ordering some cars and even pedestrians to stop and be searched. Zander would not be stopped. He lowered his window, slapped the side of the Toyota to catch one soldier's attention, flashed him a thumb's up, and swept on through. In a moment they were gliding down tree-lined Atatürk Boulevard, passing block after block of tidy apartments and crowded shops.

"Slow down," Helen pleaded, as she scanned back and forth between her maps and the street.

Zander hit the brake, but almost before he knew it, the car was nearing the stone gate at the far end of town, which was also patrolled by the Army. The ancient wall here was in somewhat better condition. Just left of the gate stood the remains of a guard tower,

15-feet high, topped with a fluttering Turkish flag. A makeshift police barracks stood near its base. "We're running out of Iznik," Zander said.

"Near here," Helen acknowledged.

With no place left to drive, Zander angled the car alongside a dumpster just off the square that fronted the gate. Like any back door, this end of town was less congested. He looked at Helen, wanting more details.

"The best I can say is that a royal stable of some sort was around here. The maps are hardly precise, though."

They were all eager to get out of the car. Penny and Helen took off in opposite directions along the dilapidated defensive wall. Zander assumed they had some notions of what they were looking for, telltale clues that would elude him. But if they found nothing they'd go back over his area. Maurer and he strolled together away from the gate, though Zander tried to keep Penny on the fringe of his vision.

Maurer and he scanned the square in silence. He felt like he was on the beach stalking some rare mollusk shell that his son had vaguely described to him. He was scraping his heel between two cobblestones to pull out a clump of weeds when Maurer nudged his shoulder and pointed to a street sign. "How's your Turkish?" he asked.

"Nonexistent," Zander said, reading the sign: "Meydan Arts."

"Well that translates more or less as 'Equine Square,' for what it's worth. Wait here a minute." Maurer trotted over to a leather-faced old man selling ice cream from a lopsided metal cart. He bought a vanilla cone, but then Zander saw the vendor vigorously shake his head and shrug his shoulders. Maurer wandered back.

"I asked him why this place is called what it is. He said he's lived here his entire life and it has always had this name, but he has no clue."

Seeing nothing that required even a second look, Zander felt they needed to try something else. He had decided to poke around outside the gate when he heard Penny scream so frantically he was sure she was being assaulted.

"Zander!" she cried again.

Chapter 11

Ozbek heard the helicopter approach Heybeli Island from the shed, where he stood watching one of his restorers delicately sponge bits of plaster and grime from the mosaic slabs. He retreated to the open doorway to watch his Bell Jetranger touch down.

"Keep working!" he yelled over the din of the slowing rotor. "I'll be back tonight." He headed out and across the macadam.

Sherin sat at the controls. Stepping awkwardly out of the rear to stretch his legs was a large, pink-faced man already sweating through his wrinkled suit.

Ozbek firmly grasped the man's beefy hand. "Good to see you again," he said, while holding a bank check aloft, which the man stared at for a moment before snatching. "Very glad you've joined us. Best decision of your life." The man examined the check for slightly longer than Ozbek thought well-mannered before slipping it into his jacket pocket. "The balance of what we agreed upon, correct?"

The man nodded his acknowledgement and

climbed back aboard at his new boss's instigation.

Ozbek strapped himself in beside Sherin and slipped on a headset. "Let's go," he said, and turned back toward his passenger. "This should be interesting for you, Mr. Figgis. You'll get to meet up with your old friend and earn your new pension all at the same time. I told you that neither Blake nor the girl could be talked into leaving Turkey. But I let you try. Now we do things my way."

• • • •

Penny was standing right where the police barracks abutted the tower, almost directly beneath the flag. Zander and Maurer ran over, reaching her just as Helen arrived.

"What is it?" Zander asked, catching his breath.

Penny pointed near the ground. Carved into a stone panel at the base of the wall were a dozen owls. "This?" Zander asked.

"Yes," Penny said. She was squatting down to examine the panel at eye level. She ran her fingers across the relief.

"You're sure?"

"Absolutely. The owl was the symbol most closely linked with Athena as the goddess of wisdom. We still make that association with owls, of course. They're fantastic, aren't they?"

Zander dropped down on one knee, but left room for Helen to duck in and take several quick pictures with the Nikon she fished out of her bag. The panel was about a yard wide and half as high. Two large owls dominated, with 10 smaller ones arrayed around them. All faced forward, bug-eyed.

"Like an intact family," he said, and then glanced behind at the sound of a bouncing basketball. Three boys, all around his son's age, had joined them, craning for a look at whatever was so interesting. The dribbler stopped when Zander caught his eye, though the boys didn't move on.

Penny paid the boys no attention. "It is said that a huge parliament of small owls lived on the Athenian Acropolis before any temples were built there, and that the colony was maintained for centuries afterwards."

"A parliament?" Zander said.

"Yes, that's what you call a group of owls. Like a congress of ravens or a muster of peacocks."

"A muster," he said, smiling and shaking his head, adding this to the list of ways she amazed him.

"What?" she asked.

"Nothing." He stood and offered his hand to help Penny up just as a policeman twirling a nightstick emerged from the barracks. "Excuse us, gentlemen," Zander told the boys, and led Penny, Helen, and Maurer away. He glanced back to see the cop questioning the kids about what everyone was looking at.

Back at the car, whose door handles were almost too hot to touch, Penny grabbed the manuscript while Maurer laid his aluminum briefcase on the trunk. He made it clear that he didn't want company, which irked Zander, who still managed to glimpse some type of keyboard—a hardened PC, he had no doubt—when Maurer opened the lid.

Waiting for Penny, Zander looked back toward the city center. They were only a few hours drive from Istanbul, as big and filthy and crowded as any city in the world, but this place—this end of town, anyway—

had an innocent serenity to it. He watched another group of boys, just eight or nine years old, playing soccer, racing up and down a dusty, farmed-out field. No fancy nets and crossbars. No adults either. Just some shirts tossed down to mark the goals. They needed a Turkish Norman Rockwell to paint them, he thought. Maybe small towns were the same everywhere.

A handful of storm clouds glided across the western sky, throwing them into shadows. A downpour was the last thing they needed. The sun emerged at that moment, forcing him to shield his eyes and reminding him that this wasn't just the sun anymore, but their own personal hourglass, and it was running down. He turned back toward Penny, who was still immersed in the manuscript. What was she looking for? "Come on, Penny!" he yelled, trying to sound good-natured. She nodded, but didn't look up. Past her, over the top of a grove of ragged cedar trees, he saw the ruins of a Roman amphitheatre. He tapped on the car to get her attention. "Any of your clues suggest that theatre over there?"

Penny glanced back toward it, but then shook her head. "Athena was many things, but nothing to do with the stage or spectacles. I think our next target should be Athena Hygeia, the goddess of health. A hospital would be an obvious choice."

"How about a public bath?" said Zander. "Or maybe a spring with healing waters,"

"A bath is unlikely," Penny said, watching Helen, who had buried herself in her histories and guidebook. "A thousand years earlier, maybe. But public baths in the true Roman sense had already disappeared."

"Did they even have hospitals?" Zander asked, unable to picture anything other than a comic, *Throw out your dead*!

"Yes," Maurer shouted as he slammed his briefcase shut. "Plenty of hospitals across Europe during the Middle Ages."

Helen nodded as if she'd found something she liked. "There was a monastery hospital here," she said. "And it looks as if the building was converted to a mosque that's still standing."

Zander looked back at Maurer to say they were going, but the station chief had already slipped into the car, stealthy as a shadow.

Zander and the others followed and they pulled away from the curb, following Helen's directions. They passed block after block of low-rise apartments, all with windows flung open and many with wash hanging out. He had not looked at the map, but an uneasy feeling grew as numerous turns took them near the old defensive wall by the city's east end.

"What's the matter?" Penny asked when she saw Zander shaking his head. "You think this is wrong?"

"I don't know. But if it's right it creates another problem."

"What?" asked Helen.

"If you take the modern street grid as your verticals and horizontals, where we are now is catty-cornered to the stable."

"So?" asked Penny.

"It means that it will be almost impossible to pinpoint the medians if we need to."

Chapter 12

Bulent Ozbek had never been to Iznik. Despite its proximity to Istanbul, its imperial role in Byzantine history, and its one-time notoriety as an artists' enclave, his parents never made a day trip of it and he certainly had better things to do as an adult.

With the town coming into view from the helicopter, the shimmering expanse of Lake Iznik was a pleasant surprise. Ozbek sensed it soothing the odd mix of anger and expectation he'd felt since speaking to Maurer. He understood what had drawn the first settlers 2,000 years before.

He was lost in the inviting swirl of the lake when the thunderous collision shook his soul and convinced him that the lake would be the last thing he'd ever see. He shot forward in his seat, held only by the shoulder belt, as Sherin struggled to regain control and bring the nose up. Over the horrific roar of the diving copter he heard Graham Figgis cursing and praying.

Down they went, faster than any dream, the water now a belligerent animal, ready to swallow them whole.

While terror froze his hold on the overhead handle for what he knew was the last moment of his life, Sherin bellowed as if she were lifting the helicopter on her shoulders, and their free-fall flattened, throwing Ozbek back. Then they were climbing, the sky surrounding them. Finally they leveled out.

"Are we okay?" he asked through gritted teeth.

She gave him a flinching nod, as if she couldn't believe it either.

Figgis slapped his shoulder. "Did you see that? Bloody fucking eagle. Came soaring up at us like a missile." Ozbek realized now that the splatter on the fractured windshield was a gory mix of guts and feathers. "I think it had a goose in its talons."

• • • •

Penny looked up from the manuscript photos. "Are you sure?" she asked. "There's no way to measure the distances and somehow compute the center?"

Zander wished he had an easy solution. "Not on a zigzag like this. We'll need a muezzin to let us peer down on the city from his minaret to even estimate the location."

"Not a concern," Maurer said, as definitive as an ayatollah.

Zander glanced at the rear-view mirror. "Why?" he asked.

"I recorded the first signpost on my GPS. I can fix the cross-point—assuming we find the other signposts."

Zander was about to ask Maurer for details about his positioning system when Helen shouted for him to stop. He slammed the brakes and followed Helen's line of sight to the right. He saw it at once and could tell from the gasps that everyone else did as well. Twenty feet off the street, through the dirt and dust kicked up by their short stop, and set like a cornerstone in a massive mud-colored stucco building, were the same dozen owls.

"Fantastic," said Helen, rolling down her window and snapping some shots of the new panel. "And look at the caduceus. It's still a hospital."

"A hospice, actually," Maurer said, "according to the sign over the door."

"Do you need to inspect it or can we push on?" Zander asked, thinking that maybe they could just figure this out.

Penny rocked in her seat, "Let's keep going."

Zander leaned against the door, staring past Helen at the owls. He didn't want to rush Penny. Her thoroughness had gotten them this far, but soon it wouldn't matter anymore. This wasn't a time for perfectionism. "What's next?" he asked.

"Give me a second," she pleaded.

Maurer, meanwhile, who had shared their exhilaration at finding the hospice plaque, was drifting back to his own world. He unclipped the phone from his belt to check for a signal, clearly frustrated that he still hadn't heard from his sources about the bogus Swiss charity. "Dammit!" he muttered, seemingly ready to crush it if it didn't ring soon.

Penny stayed oblivious to Maurer's frustration, flipping through the manuscript until she finally announced, "Promakhos! The warrior goddess."

"Okay," Zander said. "Goddess of war—"

"No," Penny cut him off. "Not really."

"Ares was the god of war," Maurer said. "Correct

me if I'm wrong, though I'm sure I'm not, but Athena's role was more of a guide and protector of the great warriors. Achilles, Hercules…"

"That's true," Helen said, "But Promakhos is Athena as a warrior, leading an army into battle, with armored breastplate and spear."

"So how about a battlefield?" Zander asked.

Helen shook her head. "There have been battles here, but none relevant to our time period. Major battles were either long before the court went into exile or long after they were gone."

"Then a parade ground? A barracks?"

Helen ran her finger across the maps. "How about an armory?" she asked.

Penny and Maurer both nodded.

"Anything else?" Zander asked. "A fortress?"

Maurer slapped his hand against Helen's headrest. "The entire city is a fort. This signpost could be anywhere around the perimeter wall—what's left of it."

"You might be right," Zander responded. "But we found the first plaque embedded in the wall. I don't know if that means the wall is a likely spot for another one or the least likely place. Let's check out the armory first. We'll have to split up to inspect the entire wall, anyway."

Zander drove off from the hospice. After a few turns at Helen's direction, he saw they were angling back toward the Istanbul Gate, down pleasant streets of well-kept white-washed houses. Barely a minute later, she was gesturing to pull over.

"Crap," he said when he realized where Helen was directing him. He didn't need to read the Turkish billboard to understand that this was the base for the local army garrison. From what he could see, it was spread across several acres, enclosed by a six-foot chain-link fence. Near the front gate, a Vietnam-era jet fighter, its grey metallic paint peeling in the relentless sun, was secured in concrete.

"Is that it?" Zander asked, pointing beyond the jet fighter to a tall and round stone building with a pointed roof that seemed as misplaced amidst the drab single-story barracks as a tiger in a pet store. It rose 10 feet above everything around it, but was mostly obscured by the other structures at ground level. Zander thought about the remarkable continuity of the Turks and their society—an ancient armory still used by the military, just as the medieval hospital was still treating patients.

"You're shit out of luck," said Maurer. "No way you're getting in there. Not with the country on high-alert."

Glancing up and down the base, Zander thought Maurer was right. What's more, the base seemed to be in lockdown. The guardhouse was empty and the front gate was secured. A handful of soldiers were visible in the distance.

"Let me have the camera," he told Helen, who fished it out of her bag and handed it to him.

"I'll be back," Zander said, throwing the door open.

"Zander?" Penny asked gently, as if he were a mental patient she didn't want to upset.

"Blake!" Maurer yelled. "What the fuck you think you're doing?"

• • • •

Ozbek's heart was still pounding as Sherin flew

low over quiet blocks of pastel houses. It reminded him of some Istanbul neighborhoods 20 years ago. He was sure he could buy up this entire quarter of the city for a pittance. Istanbul's new bourgeoisie would pay handsomely for weekend retreats this close to the city. Some restaurants and nightclubs, as well as hotels for day-trippers, would also earn out quickly.

The city was small, though, and they'd passed over it completely before he knew it. He told Sherin to circle around and put down on a patch of lawn by the lake.

"What now?" asked Figgis.

"We wait."

• • • •

Zander hurried across the street, peeking back at the car just once to see Penny following him with her eyes. He headed away from the front gate, hugging the fence and circling around the rear, which led him into a wooded area. He could easily scale the fence, but that wasn't his intention.

He laughed, though, when he imagined what Maurer thought he might try. It was one thing to go undercover to rescue Penny on Heybeli. Breaking and entering an army base was something else entirely. He was still a policeman.

He was surprised to find the base was shallower than it seemed. If that mothballed fighter out front was intended to radiate an expansive, muscular image, it worked. The armory was actually very close to the rear of the base.

He couldn't see the entire building. The side facing the street was obscured, but he had a good perspective on at least three-quarters of it. He brought Helen's

Nikon up to his eye, using the telephoto lens to get a close-up view. If the owls were here he'd see them.

He had just begun panning across the building when he felt the barrel of a rifle dig into his back.

Chapter 13

Zander soon found himself deep inside the old armory, which served as the base brig. He imagined that the walls must be three-feet thick, built to withstand battering rams and cannon balls. He sat alone in a musty, windowless interrogation room on a scratched folding chair, his hands shackled to a huge bronze eyelet that emerged from the center of the stone floor. He yearned to stretch his back, which also ached because the soldier who'd found him enjoyed jamming his rifle repeatedly into Zander's spine. The sentry, no more than 20, had also accused him of spying for the Greeks. Zander's protests that he was just an American tourist were ignored.

If they thought he was spying maybe they'd just start beating him. He pictured the Istanbul terrorists and how confessions had obviously been tortured out of them. His throat suddenly felt dry as sand.

He wondered what Penny and the others must be thinking. He'd been gone half an hour already. He could easily imagine being left here for a day to soften him for interrogation. Should he scream for attention and demand to call the American Consulate? Durkin could help, but perhaps he'd already been evacuated. Maybe he should ask to have Maurer brought in. But the station chief had warned him twice that he couldn't rescue him from the local authorities.

The door opened and the same soldier who'd found him stepped in, followed by an officer—ramrod straight, well dressed, two rows of decorations on his chest, sucking hard on a filter-free cigarette. He held Zander's wallet and Helen's camera.

Zander tensed his shoulders and lowered his head. He couldn't defend himself but he saw no reason to invite a boot to the jaw.

He was surprised but still suspicious when the officer ordered the soldier to remove the shackles. He rubbed some feeling into his wrists but stopped when the officer handed him his wallet, open for both to see his LAPD shield.

"I don't know what you are doing here," the officer said, his English husky but understandable. "But my country is in a crisis and I don't have time to deal with you. You're not Greek, and even if you were, I hope you are not so stupid to believe it is worth committing an act of espionage here."

"I told your soldier I'm just a tourist and I only wanted to see the armory."

"Yes," the officer said, clearly uninterested. "So you've seen it. Now go." He handed back the camera, the latched compartment hanging open, the battery and memory card gone.

• • • •

Penny was circling the car when she spotted Zander returning the way he came. He waved to keep her back but she ran to him anyway and threw her arms around his neck.

"Where were you? I thought… I don't know what I thought."

"I'm okay," he said, embracing her.

They returned to the Toyota. Maurer and Helen were sitting on the hood.

"What happened?" Maurer smirked. "You get arrested?"

Zander didn't want to give Maurer any pleasure or frighten Penny. "Let's just say there's no plaque on the armory."

"I'm not surprised," Penny said.

"*Now* you say that?" Zander asked.

"I decided we're going down the wrong track here. There's no denying Promakhos is the warrior goddess, but like I said, she was more the protector of warriors—Achilles, Jason, Hercules, Odysseus. This runs through all the literature. Through Homer, of course, but also through the playwrights: in Euripides and Aeschylus and—"

"Okay," Zander interrupted, "what does that mean for us?"

"I want to get back to the Roman theatre. It's the only place I can imagine we might find references to those heroes."

It seemed logical to Zander and he had no better idea.

They were piling into the car when Maurer's phone rang. Knowing what he was waiting to hear, the high-pitched tones took on an awful weight. Maurer looked straight at Zander, as if this was a last-minute call from the governor. Someone's life hung in the balance.

"Give me a minute," Maurer told them, and walked off.

Penny and Helen got into the car while Zander stood and waited. It took just a moment to see that Maurer wasn't hearing what he wanted.

"You're shitting me!" he growled. "That's not good enough!" He watched Maurer take a deep breath and close his eyes, the phone still clasped to his ear. Zander actually felt sorry for him. "Yeah, well, like every other important fucking thing, I'll get to the bottom of it myself." He slammed the phone into his open palm.

Zander didn't pretend he hadn't been listening.

Maurer ambled back to the car, his lips turned up in a small, cockeyed smile. "Nada," he confided.

"Nothing at all?"

"The Swiss are stonewalling. But it's not just them. We've hit one dead end after another. The paper trails from this Turkish Reconstruction foundation lead nowhere. But, of course, I'm still on it. I have no choice."

• • • •

It was almost 7 p.m. when they arrived at the ancient theatre. Everyone got out slowly. They were all tired, but Zander also sensed desperation. He felt it himself.

Though they followed a modern pathway that led them onto the rear of the stage, the theatre felt as though it had been deserted since the Romans left. Zander was surprised at the immensity of it. It wasn't the Staples Center, but it was far wider and higher than it had seemed from a distance. Grass and weeds grew from cracks in every row of stone seats. But there was still a graceful beauty to its symmetry and it reminded him of when he was a rookie cop and picked up some extra cash moonlighting security at the Hollywood Bowl—the closest he ever came to being on stage.

Zander started slowly up the center aisle, gazing up and down each row, when he noticed Penny running back to the car. Helen, meanwhile, was inspecting a series of ruined columns behind the stage, and Maurer had retreated with his briefcase way up top, parking himself in what would have been the cheap seats even 2,000 years ago.

Zander found no engravings or reliefs, but soon had a spectacular view of the lake and the city. Iznik was greener from up here, not as dry and dusty as it had seemed, with a dense cedar forest rising up in the hills that framed the lake's far shore.

He looked across at Maurer, who had his case open on his lap and was typing. He wanted to yell for the station chief to get off his ass and help, but then thought it best to leave him alone as long as he left them alone.

Heading back down, Zander saw Penny at the foot of the stage. She was cleaning some mud-encrusted reliefs he had not even noticed with a rag and a bottle of water from the car. As he got nearer he saw that some of the carvings were still sharp and deeply cut, while others had eroded to mere shadows. They were almost all battle scenes, with helmeted men brutally slaughtering each other with swords or spears. He was kneeling alongside Penny when she uncovered it.

"Ah!" she shrieked, loud enough to get Maurer's

attention atop the arena. He was on his phone but still waved his fist in acknowledgement.

A minute later they were standing in front of the third set of owls. The panel was set between scenes close to Athena's heart: Hercules slaying the Hydra and Achilles defeating Hector at Troy. "I know it's late," Penny said, "but let me grab the manuscript out of the car."

"Don't bother," Zander said.

The disappointment on Penny's face left him feeling like an ogre in a fairy tale. "Come on," she insisted. "We still have a little time. At least let's try."

"You don't understand," he said. "If you're right about these signposts being the end-points of a cross, we only need three. We can calculate the fourth ourselves."

Maurer hoisted his briefcase up onto the stage. "I've already fixed it." A map of Iznik glowed on the screen. The three pulsating spots were where they'd found the signposts. He hit 'return,' to show where they would presumably find the fourth panel. "And this," Maurer said, "is what you came here for." He hit a few more keys and, smack at the mid point of the virtual cross's perpendicular lines, a red "X" flashed.

• • • •

Ozbek ripped a sheet of paper from a small notebook and handed it to Sherin through the pilot's window. She was finishing a safety check on the helicopter's flight systems. "Can you get us to these coordinates?" Ozbek asked.

"Of course," she said and opened the security casing atop the navigation computer to enter the data.

"That idiot Maurer finally comes up with something useful," he said, laughing to himself. "And he doesn't even know it."

Ozbek had one foot aboard when a deafening crack of thunder sent his heart racing again. He stepped down and away from the copter to check the darkening sky for lightening. Not seeing any, he climbed aboard and strapped himself in.

"Let's go," he said.

Chapter 14

Zander pulled to the curb across from a stretch of crumbling 19th century apartments and shuttered shops, easily the bleakest patch of Iznik they'd seen. Only eccentric flower arrangements differentiated the low-slung buildings, some of which, Zander saw, were pockmarked with bullet holes.

Staring at the gravel-strewn lot beside them, Zander knew in his gut this was the place even before Maurer confirmed it down to the meter with his GPS. The scant remains of a stone building spread across the dusty block like architectural flotsam: fits and starts of a brick wall, messy piles of cut stone, shards of clay roof tiles, an apparently indestructible arch off to one side by itself. The melancholic ruin held each of them in their seats. Penny seemed especially shaken. The struggle to reach this holy place, confounding as it may have been, was finally over. They'd outsmarted and outdistanced and beaten aside every obstacle, but realizing that the prize had been so utterly and violently snatched away, it was like they were being mocked. By who? Invaders? The local peasants? God?

Despite his disappointment, Zander couldn't bring himself simply to drive away. He climbed out of the Toyota. Penny and the others joined him at the edge of the desolate acre. "What are we looking at?"

"The Church of the Dormition," Helen said.

A crow atop a rock pile gazed at them across the lot as though it owned the place. Add a few 17th century shepherds and it could pass for a Piranesi print, Zander thought, if Piranesi had bothered to include smashed beer bottles, rusty cans, and cigarette butts.

"You can't say you didn't try," said Maurer, who looked relieved to be reaching their journey's end, his obligation fulfilled, his debt paid. "You're just a little late. Maybe five or six centuries."

"Not nearly," Helen said. "The church was destroyed in 1915 during the Greek-Turkish war."

"No kidding," Maurer mused. "Given that we stand on the brink of a rematch, what could be more fitting?"

"The interior," Helen continued, "was supposedly covered with one of the finest and most extensive collections of mosaics in the world."

Zander felt a strange isolation as he scanned the pitted battleground. He put his arm around Penny and knew she shared his feelings. This was the miserable mess that Linus Crane had ultimately died for. It was almost a century since the church had been leveled, but he was filled with regret, as if they'd missed their chance by five minutes.

Scrutinizing the lot, Zander motioned toward the rear, where an area the size of a Dairy Queen was boarded off with 10-foot planks. Portholes were cut away to keep the curious from climbing over.

"Probably the only part of the church that wasn't pulverized," Penny said, chewing on her lip. There was a bitterness in her voice Zander hadn't heard before, but he thought she was entitled.

"Let's take a look," he said

Maurer cleared his throat. "Hold on. You've seen what you came to see. Now you've got a plane to catch."

"Not yet," Zander said. "We agreed to sundown. We'll keep our end of the deal so you keep yours." He took Penny's hand and marched off.

Maurer gazed at the western skyline. The sun was burning big and orange. Stringy clouds gathered beneath it. The station chief dug his hands in his pockets and followed a few paces behind. "Don't be stupid!" he yelled, pointing to a pair of electric-yellow Warning signs featuring skull and crossbones, plastered atop the enclosure.

Zander ignored him. He wanted to inspect a poster tacked to the pen. The sign explained in Turkish, French, and English that a UNESCO grant had been secured to restore the church, a project scheduled to last 15 years. "They're rebuilding," he said. "Then again, this proclamation is dated four years ago and so far they've managed to nail up a few boards."

He peered through one of the portholes in the plank bulwark. Six feet of crumbling brick wall and a small stretch of deeply scarred mosaic flooring was all he could see. If he hadn't been told this was once a church he might have guessed anything from a prison to a bathhouse locker room.

After glancing inside as well, Helen and Maurer wandered across the lot, he obviously waiting for dusk while she pocketed a few keepsakes.

"What's that?" Zander asked Penny, pointing at a huge block of stone he saw through the adjacent porthole. An elaborate script was chiseled across the entire top, which looked big enough for a circus giant to nap on. The far end rested flush against the brick wall, which had evidently insulated it from Greek and Turkish artillery. The sides were smooth, devoid of any design. The only serious damage was down toward the base, where a disk-shaped indenture was empty. Zander guessed that an aspiring art dealer had pried loose whatever had been there.

He stepped aside so Penny could peek through. He slipped his hands around her waist.

"It's a cenotaph," she said. "A monument for the dead."

"A war memorial?"

"Most likely, though I can't read much from this angle."

The enclosure's entrance was a few feet to their right. Zander ignored the padlock and pulled the pins from the steel hinges. The plywood door swung open lopsidedly.

"What are you doing?" she asked.

Zander looked at Penny, searchingly now. Somehow they'd reached an unspoken agreement not to mention the Athena, as if invoking the goddess was taboo. "I'm 7,000 miles from home and I don't want to leave feeling like I missed anything."

Penny nodded and followed him in.

He gestured toward the cenotaph. "More Greek?"

She studied the dense script, sweeping aside leaves and soot toward the bottom. "Yes, but mostly a list of names. Members of the court murdered by the Crusaders, or 'the Hounds of Hell,' as it calls them." She shuffled around the monument but pulled up short. "Ayyy!" she yelped and hopped to one side.

Zander brushed away the mound of twigs and dirt covering what Penny had jammed her toes into, exposing a half-buried stone with an abstract carving on the obverse. It was the missing disk, about 18 inches across.

Penny knelt and scratched some soil from the edge, revealing carved block lettering. "It's the emperor's name," she said. "Theodore Lascaris. The one I'm guessing who wrote the manuscript."

Zander dug at the hard-packed dirt like a dog unearthing a bone. He finally hoisted the stone, which easily topped a hundred pounds. He slid the base of the disk into the recess on the tomb and then rotated it back and forth like a spare tire, working it toward the rear until he slammed the top straight in with one hard shot. "Voilà!" he crowed. "Good as new." But before he even stood up, a crack like a rifle shot reverberated through the enclosure. Penny gasped and raised her hands to protect her head. Zander braced for the brick wall to tumble down on him, but nothing collapsed or gave way.

"What on earth was that?" Penny asked.

He was about to grab her and head for the car when he noticed that the engraved top of the monument had shifted two inches off the base in the near corner. It wasn't a solid block after all. Without even thinking he slipped his fingers inside and tried to pry it further. It wouldn't budge. He braced his feet and grabbed the far side with his free hand to gain some leverage.

A moment later, Helen pushed open the plywood door. "What was that noise? Did you find something?"

Zander shook his head and heaved. His face turned purplish and the veins bulged in his neck. Still, the slab held fast. Relaxing for a moment, he dipped his knees, grunted like a Russian weightlifter, and yanked, ignoring the pain in his ribs. The stone swung almost clear off the base. His feet skidded out from under him, dropping him to the ground. He looked up at his handiwork, which he could barely believe. He also noticed that Maurer had sidled next to him.

"Congratulations, Blake, you're now a certified tomb robber."

Penny leaned into the monument. "This is crazy," she said. "We need to file a report."

"On your next trip," Zander said. "Does anyone have a match?"

"Hold on," Helen said, as she rummaged through her bag and pulled out a silver Zippo that felt surprisingly heavy in Zander's hand. "Be careful with it. It was my father's."

A haze of ancient dust wafted up from inside the memorial, cutting Zander's visibility to less than the length of his arm. Still, when he reached the lighter inside he found the tomb was far deeper than the few feet it rose above ground. He expected to brush his hand against either the ground or maybe a stone slab, but instead only tapped blocks of stone at one end. He reached further down.

Chapter 15

"Stairs," Zander announced.

Penny's shock immediately gave way to curiosity. "I'm going with you."

Zander squeezed her hand, appreciating her eagerness. "Not yet. Let me do some quick reconnaissance."

"Wait a minute," Maurer objected. "You're going down there? Why?"

Zander raised an eyebrow. "Because there's no place else to go, Maurer."

Zander sat up on the corner and threw his legs over. He placed one hand flat on the wall ahead of him while he held the lighter aloft with the other. He could see only inches ahead, so he squelched the flame to make his way by touch. He expected the steps to be slippery, either from moss or condensation, but they were dry, deep and even. The air tasted muddy, and he fought off an image of rats scurrying up towards him. Twenty-eight steps down he felt he was on a landing and extended his leg. There were no other steps. He brushed against something metallic on the wall to his right, and lit the lighter to inspect it. A torch. The smell of pitch was still keen across the centuries. He lifted the tightly wound flax from the iron holder and touched his small flame to the top. It ignited with a gusty *wumph* that singed his eyebrows and momentarily blinded him.

"Zander!" he heard Penny scream.

"I'm okay," he hollered back, though he wasn't yet. His eyes adjusted and he stared down at another flight of stairs. It looked safe enough. "Anyone who cares to join me is welcome," he yelled.

"I thought there was an explosion," Penny said, after scrambling down. Helen and Maurer followed in line.

The second flight took them 28 steps deeper, where they reached another landing. Zander lit a second torch there and passed it to Maurer at the rear before leading the way down again. The air was noticeably cooler and the sounds from the street had faded away. Only the resonance of their own breathing and the shuffling of their shoes now broke the 800-year silence.

The stairs ended at a third level where Zander's torch illuminated a pair of towering wood doors faced with carved ivory panels. Penny surged up to them, her face glowing with excitement. It was becoming clear to him why people spent years digging in hundred-degree heat with spoons and toothbrushes.

Penny ran her hand across the high relief, which was broken into 20 scenes separated by raised frames of gold. Giving Penny room, Zander noticed the faint outlines of footprints other than theirs, and marveled that evidence from the last visitors might have survived nearly a millennium.

"Magnificent," Helen exclaimed, studying the carvings with a disconcertingly hungry look. Every segment portrayed a king or emperor in some act of mercy: feeding the hungry, clothing the poor, caring for the sick. Zander supposed it was the manuscript's author again.

He eased Penny away from the doors in order to open them, anticipating a struggle not unlike he had with the cenotaph.

"Be careful," she exclaimed.

Zander looked back, appreciating her concern.

"I mean for the door. It's probably extremely fragile and we don't want any more accidents. We really shouldn't be touching anything without recording it on video."

Zander turned around. "Are you saying we should stop?"

"No," she said, her eyes flitting to the doors and back to him. "Just go easy."

Zander nodded. He turned back to the doors and was sweeping a spider away from one corner when Maurer tapped his shoulder to get his attention. "Hey. Forget about the antiques for a minute. We need to be careful for ourselves."

"Why?" Zander asked.

"Nothing I've seen yet, but churches like this were often used to store dangerous materials—weapons of mass destruction in their time."

"Are you serious?" asked Penny.

"You mentioned it yourself," he told her, his shadow pulsing on the grainy wall, "though I don't think you understood."

Penny looked at Maurer as if he was confusing her

with someone else.

"In the emperor's manuscript, when you described the battle at that church in Istanbul, Sergius and Bacchus, you said the Latin knights burned to death. I'm telling you that was the result of incendiary devices stored in that church."

"He's probably right," said Helen, as a soft breeze from above sent the torches flickering for a moment. "Priests also safeguarded horrible toxins in the ancient world. The Great Plague that devastated Rome in the second century probably began when a Roman soldier broke open a sacred chest in a temple in Babylon that had been infected with plague as a security measure."

"Okay," Zander said, deciding to accept on faith anything Maurer said about WMDs. "Point made. Don't touch anything you don't have to."

He handed Penny the torch before planting one foot, bending low, and slowly forcing open the left door just wide enough to slip through sideways. A rush of almost frigid air blew by him. He moved along the wall lighting torches. Each flared up with an oily blast.

The flames revealed an immense, barrel-vaulted chamber, about 30 feet long and high. Penny followed inside and gasped at the sight of the long side walls, which were covered with mosaics framed in abstract ornamentation. There was no place for the eye to rest. Square in the center of the smooth polished floor, a sarcophagus rested on a marble plinth. Penny read an inscription at the base, confirming that this was the true resting-place of Emperor Theodore Lascaris. The lid was a life-sized relief of the recumbent emperor in regal robes.

Penny led him to the near corner and ran her hand

over the glistening tesserae while Helen and Maurer settled in front of another panel. She pointed to a few lines of script in the same style as the list of the dead covering the cenotaph. She translated for Zander: "The horrors which befell the Romans following the Fall of Constantinople." She looked up and down the wall. "This is like a documentary record of the siege."

The astonishment Zander felt moments before at the very magnitude of the mosaic room wilted before this graphic record of the Crusaders' rampage. Rape, torture, mass murder, and the annihilation of the city itself were depicted in vivid detail. Zander watched a consuming sadness infect them all, even Maurer, who stood open-mouthed before a rendering of 10 men being flayed alive, their contorted faces screaming for mercy.

Zander and Penny inched down the hall, drawn by some dark force to a scene of Crusaders destroying the high altar of Saint Sophia, smashing sacred icons, pulling gems from holy chalices, slaughtering horses and mules in the aisles, and installing a harlot on the jeweled throne. Elsewhere, piles of corpses littered the Hippodrome while babies were skewered like roasted pigs. Streets flowed with blood from severed heads and genitals. A raging fire consumed the grand palace, while burning women and children ran into the streets. Zander felt numbed from the volume of it.

The opposite side of the chamber proved a respite from the misery, but not the mystery. Two separate mosaics dominated the wall. The first showed a landscape view of a simple Byzantine church—a brick and stone treasure with a delicate red dome—set amidst a bucolic landscape. After a moment, Helen identified it as the Church of the Dormition.

"The one that was right here above us?" Zander asked.

"No question," Helen added.

The next scene was the most startling. It was the very room they were in. The entire mosaic of the pillaged city in reduced but spectacular detail covered one side of the miniature room. The emperor's sarcophagus was placed precisely in the middle. The wall they were then examining was there as well. There was one major difference. The rendering of the mosaic room had a pair of doors at the far end, above which was the same relief panel of a dozen owls they'd found three times around the city and had led them to where they stood now. The real room, the one they were standing in, had no such doors. The far wall was solid stone. Unlike the mosaic image, reality was a dead end.

Chapter 16

The misery recorded in the mosaics behind Zander would sicken any sane person, but there was something intoxicating about the miniature rendering of the very room they were standing in, and he couldn't take his eyes off of it. It reminded him of the toy trains he got one Christmas. He had spent countless hours examining the locomotive, amazed at the workmanship and detail. Now he couldn't help but glance back and forth between the mosaic and the larger room, searching for tiny features to test the artist's skill. He had to say that every aspect, every nuance, was precise, but one.

"There's no doors," Maurer announced. "Here, I mean."

Zander saw in Penny's eyes that she wanted to laugh, but she was better mannered than he was. "Nothing gets by you, Maurer," he said.

"I hope not." He approached the end wall cautiously, as if it were booby-trapped. Zander decided to follow him. While Maurer stood back and let his eyes roam across and around the wall, Zander sidestepped along its entire length and banged on it repeatedly, like a carpenter looking for a stud. But every inch felt as solid as the armory where he'd been held prisoner.

He turned back to Penny and shook his head. "If there's anything back there we'll need a jackhammer to find out."

Penny drifted to the wall now and also examined the seamless stone.

His own attention was once again drawn to the mosaic of the underground chamber. It was like looking into a trick mirror. He felt like the four of them should be pictured there as well. From this new angle, though, something bothered him. Once again he shifted his focus back and forth, searching for inconsistencies. Everything still seemed perfect, but on some other level, in his gut or subconscious or somewhere in between, something was off. His brain was registering it, even if his eyes couldn't see it. He asked Penny if she saw any difference, but she said no.

He was now only waiting for Maurer to announce it was time to leave. He didn't have any more excuses. No doubt it was dark up above. He rubbed his eyes and leaned back against the wall. From this perspective he could keep the mosaic in his peripheral vision while still seeing the entire room. It was what he needed to bring the problem into focus.

"Hey," he nudged Penny. "Look at the emperor."

She did, but didn't see what he saw. "What?"

Zander pointed to the mosaic of the room. "On the wall, the emperor's feet are facing us. Right now he's lying the other way—away from us."

Penny's eyes bounced between the wall and the

sarcophagus half-a-dozen times before she acknowledged he was right. By then Zander was standing alongside the emperor. "Come here," he called to her.

She followed his direction to stand behind the emperor's head.

Each of them took an end of the sarcophagus. At first it seemed absurd, but after jostling the huge block of stone, it began to revolve easily if slowly.

Helen and Maurer were staring at them in astonishment.

Zander heard a click as the emperor completed his 180-degree turn. Half a second later, it started.

The room shook as if a seismic fault beneath them shifted in response to what they'd done. Zander had lived through too many tremors—plenty more powerful than this—to think they were in trouble. Penny, however, ran over and held on to him for dear life.

The rumbling eased after a few seconds, giving way to a high-pitched squeal, like a braking New York subway.

"Look!" Helen yelled above the awful screech, though no one's eyes were on anything else. The wall at the far end began to sink straight down into the floor, revealing the doors pictured in the mosaic, topped by the familiar owl panel.

Zander glanced up at the mosaic and saw that the newly revealed wall was a perfect match. He edged forward, grasping Penny, who was as eager as a cat chasing a bird even if it meant leaping out a window.

The doors easily opened wide and they passed through together into a pitch-dark space. The air felt oddly humid and their torches revealed little, though

Zander could tell from their echoing footfalls that this chamber probably dwarfed the mosaic room. His sense was confirmed a few moments later. Apparently passing into the concealed chamber had triggered some mechanism to fill a trough along the circular wall well above anyone's reach with some form of oil that burst into flame. The bright and steady light revealed a surprisingly large rotunda, deep enough to contain a basketball court and perhaps 60 feet high. Simple pilasters adorned the plain marble wall every 10 feet. But there was no other decoration, nothing else to draw attention from the center of the chamber, where the sacred Athena towered before them.

It struck Zander that despite all they'd been through to reach this very spot, he hadn't considered the possibility of actually finding the goddess until this moment and it stunned him. She was golden, regal, and fearsome enough that he felt triumphant holding his ground. If this wasn't one of the wonders of the world, ancient or modern, he couldn't imagine what was. "Oh…my… God," he heard Helen mumble behind him, and he found himself nodding in agreement.

"I can't believe it," Penny said, shaking her head. "It's the most wonderful thing I've ever seen."

The square platform the goddess stood on, as tall as Zander and almost 10 yards on a side, was decorated with a sculpted relief of parading men and horses. Four intricately worked gold battle shields were displayed atop the base at its front, perhaps as offerings. Set back from the base by about 15 feet of lustrous stone, a reflecting pool encircled the Athena, broken only by a marble pathway that led directly to the front of the statue.

The goddess herself soared close to 40 feet. Her full-length gold robe was ingeniously sculpted to suggest a breeze wafting by. She was dressed for battle, with a thick mesh plate covering her shoulders and chest. She held an immense gold spear in her left hand, while her right rested atop a fluted column and held a winged victory. An oval shield leaned against her left leg, a snake curled at its base. Still, her carved ivory face was warm and open. Her sky-blue eyes showed a mother's concern. She had the implements of war at hand, but seemed wise enough to use them only as a last resort. Zander had no doubt she was grand enough to awe anyone who saw her, even an entire city. He would not have been surprised if she spoke.

With everyone anchored and mute in astonishment, the only sound was the gurgling of the pool.

Maurer finally broke the silence. "How has it survived in this condition?"

"The water," Penny said. "The pool keeps the humidity high, which prevents the ivory and the wood core from drying out. The Parthenon was constructed the same way."

"It's the find of the century, without a doubt," Helen said.

"The find of any century," Penny insisted. "Even if it was lying here in a hundred pieces. But to find it like this is overwhelming."

She led Zander ahead to get a closer look at Athena's shield. It depicted battles between gods and giants in one section, and between Athenians and Amazons in another. "If only Linus were here to see this, it would be perfect," she said.

"You're here for him," he said, though he still

shared her grief.

He was amazed at the detail, and it struck him that the statue was better off for having been lost for the past millennium, hidden from tourists and smog and souvenir hunters, not to mention invading armies. "How much gold do you suppose is here?" he asked.

"God knows," Penny said, shaking her head.

"More than a ton," Helen said. "My director at the Met will go into cardiac arrest when I call. We have to start documenting this—"

"Wait a minute," Penny said, putting a finger to her lips.

"What's the matter?" Zander whispered.

Penny pointed at the ceiling. Overhead he too heard the soft scrape of footsteps.

Chapter 17

"Quiet!" Zander hissed.

"Why?" asked Maurer.

"Shut up a second!"

Voices and footsteps echoed from the stairs and through the mosaic chamber.

Worry creased Penny's face. "How could he know?" she asked. "How could he possibly know?"

"Don't say that yet," Zander whispered, though he was asking himself the same question. He told Penny to stay back and headed back toward the mosaic room. She was right behind him, though, as were Maurer and Helen.

They were still 10 feet from the mosaic room when two men in similar sport coats and slacks slipped through the opened doors. The first was a stranger, though Helen gasped as soon as he appeared. Zander was certain he knew the second man, but fumbled to place him until the ghost entered behind him. Zander turned to Penny, who was now clutching his arm. She too looked like she was tumbling down the rabbit hole as she watched Odysseus Simonedes enter the chamber.

The second man, Zander realized now, was the tight-lipped son who had retrieved the ailing Simonedes the night before. The same one, presumably, who had informed Helen that Simonedes was dead. Helen, meanwhile, was standing with one hand covering her mouth and her free arm tightly cradling her stomach, as if she would collapse if she let go.

The mere sight of Simonedes was startling enough, but the vigor in his step was a further shock. This man was 20 years younger than the stooped emphysema patient Helen had introduced them to last night. Zander felt completely bamboozled and wanted to grab the old man to find out why.

Before he could move, though, Simonedes's two escorts pulled pistols from their jackets and quickly patted everyone down. Zander had left his gun back at his hotel, but the supposed son extracted a pistol from a holster around Maurer's calf, erasing any doubt about the diplomat's actual status.

"What's going on?" Maurer ranted. "You know these people?"

"I thought I did," said Zander.

Simonedes still hadn't spoken, but he swept past them all now, back into the shadow of the towering goddess. Prodded by his associates, everyone followed him in. He mouthed something to the Athena—a prayer, Zander wondered?—before turning to face them.

"You'll excuse me for any distress the news of my death—or my resurrection—might have caused. But I did not expect our paths to cross again, and certainly not here."

Helen, who kept eyeing the man Zander had never

seen before, seemed unable to shake the trauma that had overtaken her since Simonedes marched in.

"Who are you?" Maurer demanded.

The old man signaled for his protectors to holster their weapons. "My name is Simonedes."

"So that much is true," Zander snapped.

"That and much else I told you, Mr. Blake."

"But you're not some old fool who wastes his days looking for lost treasures instead of playing shuffleboard."

Simonedes shook his head. "No."

Maurer was clearly trying to control himself. "You work for your government?" he asked through clenched teeth.

The old man's son, or whoever he was, had heard enough. "Odysseus! No more!" and then continued angrily in Greek.

Just as Simonedes managed to calm his compatriot, Penny straightened up and pointed accusingly at the old man.

"Odysseus… Odysseus. Of course. Linus warned me."

The old man smiled, as if he wasn't surprised. "Did he?"

"Yes," she said, shaking her head. "But I didn't understand. *Athena's favorite*. When Linus said, 'Beware Athena's favorite,' he meant you, of course. Odysseus."

Zander was struck by the connection Penny had drawn, but wondered if she was reaching too far. "Didn't you say Athena had a whole posse she watched over?"

"She did. But she favored one above all others.

Throughout all the stories she stands by Odysseus and protects him like a mother because he is cunning and deceitful—just like her."

Simonedes spread his palms, as if to acknowledge Penny's hitting the mark.

"You knew that Sergius and Bacchus was a dead end, that the Athena wasn't there."

"Of course," he said, apparently intrigued that Penny was unraveling his pretense.

Zander pointed a finger at the old Greek. "And while we were chasing our tail there, you were on your way here. Those were your footprints on the landing from this morning."

"But why?" Penny asked, her tone angry but curious.

"Because it was never my intention that anyone should find the Athena except me. The fact that you are here, I must admit, is a great tribute to your abilities—but most unfortunate."

"But how did *you* get here," Penny demanded "if you'd only seen the mosaic? You of all people must know that wasn't enough."

"That's not what happened," Zander said "He already had the palimpsest."

"Correct," Simonedes said, "I had been working to decipher the palimpsest for 30 years. But without the mosaic it was worthless—a key without a lock."

"And," Zander continued, "you knew Linus Crane."

"Yes, quite well," Simonedes said. "And even though I had shared my work on the palimpsest with him over the years, he did not return the professional courtesy when he found the mosaic."

"Why not?" asked Zander.

"I have to say he did not share my vision."

"You mean he didn't trust you?" Maurer said. "Good judge of character, that one." His collar chafed against his taught neck. "What the hell's your motive for all this?"

"Motive? I do not even like that word, Mr.....uh.?"

"Maurer."

"Mr. Maurer. It sounds so criminal. My desire, if you will, is simply to return the goddess to her only rightful home—in Athens."

"But I still need to understand," Penny said. "Linus did not share the mosaic with you. Helen brought you to us. Is she working for you, too?"

The old man laughed.

"I can see why you would think that, but no. Very soon after Dr. Crane's unfortunate death, the fruits of his research became known to us in England."

Penny looked dazed. "But I didn't—"

"No no, it was not through you, my dear. Dr. Vandameer brought a photograph of the mosaic to a friend of my country, seeking guidance on how she might locate it."

Penny might have strangled Helen on the spot if Zander did not snag her hand. "I knew it!" she screamed. "I knew it that first day."

"This friend suggested she visit the Archaeology Museum in Istanbul, which is where we met."

"You were expecting her?" Zander asked.

"More or less. But Dr. Vandameer does not easily share secrets with strangers, so it was necessary to gain her trust. But after she had an unfortunate run-in with a thug in the city..." Simonedes indicated the first man.

Helen removed her hand from her mouth for the first time since Simonedes had arrived. "That was all arranged? And you were waiting for me outside the cistern?"

The old Greek tilted his head as if trying to soften the blow. "Not everything is what it seems."

"So what does all this lead to?" Zander asked. "What now?"

Simonedes turned to the Athena and then checked his watch. "In about three hours, a company of my country's most able soldiers will take the goddess home."

"Linus was right not to trust you," Penny said. "This undermines everything he worked for."

Maurer looked incredulous. "And it's an act of war, Simonedes. Don't you understand that?"

The old man nodded, apparently agreeing, but willing to pay the price. "Given the state of affairs between my country and this, we have nothing to lose."

"No," a horribly familiar voice boomed from behind. "You always have something to lose."

Zander spun around, instinctively stepping in front of Penny when he saw what was coming.

Having reached the doors to the Athena's chamber in total silence, Bulent Ozbek marched inside, trailed only by Sherin, whose cocked Uzi kept everyone at bay. Zander's attention was fixed on the pistol Ozbek carried, which he did not raise until he stopped five feet from Odysseus Simonedes and shot him through the chest.

Chapter 18

Ozbek did not flinch at Penny's scream or seem to notice that she had dropped down beside Simonedes. She tried to stanch the flow of scarlet across the old man's shirt, but it was no use. A few moments later, Penny lowered his lifeless head to the ground. She stayed frozen there until Zander helped her up.

Oblivious to everyone else, Ozbek stood back and admired the golden Athena as if he'd finally reached the summit of Everest. "I'd almost given up," he announced.

Zander wanted nothing more than to hurl himself at Ozbek, to pummel his face to an unrecognizable pulp, but Sherin was there, expressionless and unwavering, ready to cut him in half with her Uzi.

If Simonedes's comrades considered making a play for their weapons, it wasn't apparent. At Sherin's signal, both surrendered their pistols.

Maurer appeared to be in a daze. Ozbek's cruelty had clearly shaken him. The station chief had genuinely believed Ozbek was an ally worth defending. Zander fought off the urge to remind him how wrong he'd been. Maurer didn't need any prompting.

"You didn't need to kill this man," Maurer said.

Ozbek's eyes remained pinned to the goddess. When he finally turned to Maurer, it was as if he'd never seen him before. Then a look of distaste curled his features.

"You have been less than useless to me, Felix. Nothing will make me happier than to put you down alongside this goat."

Zander couldn't control himself. "You're fucking mad!"

Why Ozbek didn't kill him, Zander didn't know. He raised the pistol and let Zander stare down the barrel for the longest three seconds of his life, then lowered it with a nauseating snigger. Perhaps he had something worse in mind.

Ozbek approached Helen, who was still shocked by Simonedes's rebirth and sudden death. "You, too, continue to disappoint me, Helen. How have you fallen in with this crowd?"

"I haven't fallen in with anyone, Bulent. You asked me to leave your island. My interests have always aligned with yours, you know that."

Zander felt Penny's nails dig into his forearm.

"What I know," Ozbek answered her, "is that in this business it's often hard to tell who your friends are." He gave Zander a gloating smile before yelling out to the mosaic room, "Come in, Mr. Figgis."

Zander felt his gut constrict when Graham Figgis, puffy and disheveled, entered the chamber. His dark and sunken eyes were drawn tight.

"Detective Blake," Ozbek said, his hand extended toward Figgis, "Your good friend here has been quite helpful. He has kept me apprised of your every move since you left London."

Figgis continued to evade Zander's gaze. Zander wanted to hate him for betraying him, but he couldn't. He felt only pity.

"Frankly," Ozbek continued, "I was going to dispose of you before you left Istanbul this morning. I'm glad I didn't. It was so much easier to let you uncover the Athena for me."

"You mean you've been following us all day?" Penny asked.

"Of course not. I needed only your final destination, which Felix so graciously provided me."

Maurer seemed to be stewing in a hellish brew of rage and anguish. "I didn't know he was in Iznik," he told Zander. "Believe me, if I—"

"Is it really such a surprise, Detective? Surely, you don't think it was your charm that got you released from the garrison prison."

When Zander refused the bait, Ozbek gestured toward the Athena. He spoke as if addressing a crowd. "It's almost inconceivable, is it not, that this is the handiwork of a man? She watched over Pericles and she shall watch over me as I build this country into the power it deserves to be."

Something maniacal in the Turk's eye compelled Zander to try to keep him tethered to reality. "Perhaps you should have listened to the old man before you murdered him. A Greek assault force is going to storm this place in a few hours."

"A fool's errand. They will be annihilated the moment they cross the border."

Zander wondered how much to believe. Did Ozbek

have the Turkish army at his disposal? Had he really sprung him from the armory jail?

Ozbek's tone turned sharp. "Now! Everyone down on the floor! You can take your place beside the old man, Miss Theobald. You seemed fond of him."

"What are you going to do with us?" Helen asked, her voice quivering.

"Face down. On the floor! Now!"

Ozbek's command clearly disturbed Figgis. "You didn't say it was going to be like this. Nobody was supposed to get hurt."

"That's very noble of you, Mr. Figgis, but a bit late."

Figgis shook his head, as much to convince himself as Ozbek that this wasn't what he'd signed on for. He pulled the check Ozbek had given him from his jacket pocket, crushed it into a ball and tossed it aside. "I won't be party to this."

A slight nod from Ozbek, and Sherin's Uzi roared, riddling Figgis's body with a dozen bullets. The report echoed deafeningly as the force blew Figgis backwards before he crumpled to the ground. Zander made a move toward the body then checked himself as Sherin swung the Uzi in his direction.

The paper Figgis had discarded lay at Zander's feet. He scooped it up.

"Interested in how cheaply the police can be bought these days, Detective? Almost embarrassing, isn't it?"

Zander stared at the check for £50,000, drawn on a Zurich bank.

Maurer had been looking over Zander's shoulder but now snatched the check away. He gripped the paper with trembling hands while his neck grew tight and red with rage. Zander looked closely at the check and saw that the funds had been drawn from the account of some organization called the Foundation for Turkish Reconstruction.

Maurer was almost breathless. "So *you* are behind this?"

It took a moment for Zander to absorb the implication of Maurer's question. Was this the charity Maurer had linked to the terrorists? The idea was so barbarous Zander wanted to reject it out of hand. He glanced at Maurer, who was coiled and ready to pounce. Zander grabbed his shoulder to keep him from making a suicidal leap at the Turk.

"Of course," Ozbek said.

The station chief stared straight down, seemingly overwhelmed by Ozbek's gloating confession. But then like a bull whose eye has caught sight of a waving muletta, he lunged forward. Ozbek fired from the hip. The bullet took Maurer in the skull, dropping him to the floor like a marionette with its strings cut. Blood and pulpy scalp sprayed Zander's face. Helen shrieked and slapped at the gore that had spattered her arms.

Penny, numb with horror and disbelief, grabbed for Zander. Ozbek gestured at the ground with his gun and Zander pulled Penny down beside him.

"Hands behind you, on your necks!" Ozbek shouted.

Zander raised his head and saw Ozbek again admiring the Athena. He had no illusions that Ozbek planned to kill them, but evidently the Turk wanted them to agonize over it.

With Zander and Penny no longer a threat, Ozbek

pointed to the goddess. "Sherin!" he shouted. "Your reward, my dear. A shield of Alexander the Great. I dare say it is worth a hundred times anything you could imagine."

Sherin's smile showed a hint of surprise, though she did not move.

"Take it," Ozbek insisted. "You've earned it!"

Letting the Uzi dangle from a strap around her neck, Sherin headed down the stone pathway dividing the pool and lifted one of the four fabulously detailed gold shields at the feet of Athena. It was heavy, this gift to the goddess from the godlike Alexander, but Sherin raised it high to admire more closely.

Suddenly, a gush of yellowish liquid erupted from the space left vacant by Alexander's shield, drenching Sherin. The stench of petroleum and sulfur permeated the air. She cried out and the shield fell to the floor with a resounding clang. Sherin dropped to her knees beside the pool and splashed water onto her face to clear her eyes.

"My God," Penny said.

A moment later Sherin's hands and face burst into flames, and before she could raise herself to one knee, her entire body was engulfed in a roaring orange fireball. Shrieking, she threw herself into the pool but the water only seemed to fuel the flames. Within seconds she was roasted alive. A dark cloud of smoke hovered for a moment above the pool, then floated up and away toward the distant ceiling, like an escaping soul.

A gust of hot air blew past Zander, carrying the stench of burnt flesh, which coated his nose and mouth. He tried to swallow but his tongue and throat were suddenly so parched he only gagged. Penny turned her head away and coughed violently, her eyes bleary from the acrid fumes.

Ozbek had run up the pathway toward Sherin and now stood gaping at the black, bobbing corpse. Simonedes's two aides used the confusion to break for the doors. Ozbek turned and gunned them both down. His satisfaction lasted only a moment. When he glanced back at his captives he saw that Zander was gone.

Panicked, he bolted over to Penny and yanked her up by the scruff of her neck, almost dragging her toward the statue as he locked an elbow around her throat.

Now behind the Athena, Zander heard only the shots that killed the two Greeks, then grunts and scuffling sounds from the area where he'd been lying. He moved stealthily to one corner of the base but could see nothing. He considered scaling the sculpted relief along the base in hopes of blind-siding Ozbek from above, then thought better of it. Who knew what might trigger another spray of that jet fuel. Sherin's scream for help, mercifully short, was still reverberating in his head.

"Zander!" It was Penny. "He's going to shoot me!"

Zander's breath caught in his throat. Would Ozbek dare to just execute her?

"Get out here, Blake!" Ozbek yelled. "I'm counting to three.... One!"

Zander couldn't tell for certain, but it sounded as if the Turk was close by. He darted down the side of the Athena and peeked around the corner. Penny was standing in front of Ozbek, his arm locked around her neck.

"Two!"

Zander scanned the relief for any kind of weapon. The life-size sculptures beside him of men and horses in battle included shortened swords and spears. Zander tried to pull a sword free but it was fixed tight in the marble. And he despaired over what he could do with a sword, regardless. If he ran at him, the Turk would shoot him down and probably Penny as well. If he walked out, hands raised, Ozbek would kill him anyway.

He waited, hidden behind the corner, when the lights all around the rotunda flickered for a moment. Perhaps it was an illusion caused by the sputtering flames, but it seemed that the goddess's startling blue eyes glowed brightly for a second or two.

Seeing no reason to wait, Zander took a deep breath, flew around the edge and charged Ozbek, fully expecting to be shot. Though the Turk certainly heard Zander coming, it was as if a mist had descended over his eyes. Penny clearly sensed Ozbek's sudden disorientation, and she yanked his arm off her neck and spun out of his grip just as Zander barreled into him like a lion taking down a kill. Ozbek crashed to the ground, his pistol skittering away. Zander grabbed for it but Ozbek's sweeping arm sent it skidding into the pool, still fouled with Sherin's remains.

On top of him almost face to face, Zander grabbed Ozbek's forehead and slammed his skull into the stone floor as their entangled legs flailed. He felt the Turk's body seize up from the shock and thought he might subdue him quickly. He reached for the Turk's neck, then suddenly felt Ozbek's boots dig into his gut. The piston-like kick thrust him backwards like a rock from a slingshot, and he hit the floor hard.

He awkwardly lifted himself from the floor. As they squared off again, the stinging pain along his rib cage reminded him that he hadn't fully healed from the beating he'd taken from Ozbek's goons in London. His clumsy landing had also twisted his left knee, and he felt it almost give way as he angled sideways. He could tell from Ozbek's stance and movement that he'd spent some time in the ring. So rather than let the Turk size him up and pick his spot, he moved in quickly, snapping a left off of his chin, stunning Ozbek and leaving Zander close enough to crunch the side of his turned head.

The oddly angled blow shot needles up Zander's arm, but he was able to rest a moment as he watched Ozbek reel back and dab at the blood pouring from his ear. Zander's confidence rose and he felt his head clear when he glanced at Penny. But instead of slowing Ozbek down, the last blow only enraged him. His eyes flashed savagely and he charged Zander, growling like a wounded bear. Rather than take Ozbek's assault at full force, Zander dropped down and used Ozbek's momentum to flip him back over his head.

Zander's chest heaved as he tried to catch his breath, but Ozbek, relentless, came at him again, grabbing Zander's shoulders and forcing back toward the pool. He heard Penny gasp, and he was certain he was headed into the noxious water. But one of his feet slid on a damp spot, breaking Ozbek's grip and letting him slip back past the Turk toward the statue.

Zander now turned to fight. He barely sidestepped a quick right from Ozbek, but then took a painful left to the jaw that snapped his head back. He jabbed at Ozbek but the blow only glanced off his chin. Zander could see from Ozbek's expression that the Turk felt he had gained the advantage and that one solid blow would end it, so he was almost waiting for Ozbek's slow, roundhouse right and ducked harmlessly beneath.

Ozbek had put his full weight behind the punch, and the lack of contact threw him off balance. Zander shot his right fist into Ozbek's unprotected face and he felt the cheekbone shatter. He slipped past the stunned Turk and shoved him toward the base of the goddess. Not waiting for him to regain his equilibrium, Zander smashed Ozbek's contorted face with another right that sent him reeling back into the sculpted relief.

Then all was still except for the sound of Zander's own panting for air. Ozbek slumped against the marble relief like a broken doll. The Turk's eyes widened in shock, his body motionless. Blood bloomed slowly across his chest. He was impaled on an ancient marble spear, its brass head poking through his white shirtfront.

Zander recoiled as Penny rushed to his side, wrapping her arms around him and burying her face in his shoulder.

"It's over," he whispered, pulling her tight and hoping the words were as reassuring to her as they were to him. "It's over."

Epilogue

Zander was astonished to see Maurer sitting up. Helen had cleaned his bloody forehead with water from a bottle she had stashed in her bag and then bandaged it with a piece of Maurer's own shirt. Zander inspected the wound. Maurer was lucky. Ozbek's shot missed scalping the station chief by barely half an inch.

Though woozy, Maurer insisted on climbing alone to the surface, where he called Langley on his satellite phone.

Zander and Penny shared an exhausted, easy silence that proved unbearable for Helen, who ducked away and headed for the mosaics. Zander thought for a moment of calling after her, but the words didn't come, perhaps because Penny looked so relieved to see her go.

Even before Maurer finished relating the day's events to his boss, calls went out to the Greek and Turkish prime ministers. Both sides ordered their forces to stand down and announced that Washington would provide its good offices to let the adversaries negotiate a new and permanent nonaggression pact.

On his return underground, Maurer passed Helen in the mosaics room. With her camera now useless, she was hunkered down sketching on a small pad that was resting on her knees. From the rotunda, Zander could see Maurer loom over her, and by the way she was looking up at him from her crouch, Zander somehow knew she was promising him to leave the country immediately. She would be on a plane to New York the next day with a pledge not to disclose anything she had seen in Iznik in exchange for Maurer remaining silent about her rogue escapades across England and Turkey.

Then Maurer, still fondling the silvery sat phone, turned and strode over to Zander and Penny.

Zander extended an open hand toward the phone. "Do you mind?" he asked.

Maurer hesitated a moment, then handed it over. It was as sleek and compact as a Star Trek communicator. Zander marveled at the seamless, featherweight alloy. "This is what all the spooks get these days?" Zander asked, eager to hear what nonsense Maurer would cook up.

The station chief winked and snatched the phone back, but that was apparently as close as he would get to dropping his State Department cover. He slipped the device into his pants pocket and looked from Penny to Zander. "No hard feelings, I hope?"

"I don't think so," Penny volunteered after a brief but awkward silence, though she eyed Zander to confirm that Maurer's deceits and bullying somehow merited her understanding.

"None here," added Zander, surprised at the sympathy he felt for the station chief, at least professionally. "But I need you to answer a simple question for me. What the hell was Ozbek's motive for funding the bombers?"

"He was a sociopath," Penny insisted.

Maurer winced as he dabbed at his wound, which still oozed through the blue broadcloth. It clearly pained him even more to dwell on his connection to the Turk. "I wish it were that simple, but there was probably some very ugly logic behind this. You know Bulent wanted to succeed his brother as P.M., but it wasn't clear lately that his brother's government was going to survive long enough to give him a shot at the job. My guess is that he wanted to create a crisis for the country to rally around. And what better way than reviving an ancient animosity."

"So the Greeks had nothing to do with it?" Zander asked.

"Not in any real sense, no. The Greeks for a time did train anti-Turkish terrorists—we've known that for years. And the bombers were undoubtedly picked for the job in part because they trained in Greece at some point. What we'll find in the end, I'm convinced, is that Ozbek took factually accurate but unconnected events and whipped up a national frenzy by spinning a very compelling story."

Zander looked up toward the distant ceiling, which seemed to lack any depth in the poor light. "It just wasn't a true story."

Penny shook her head. "He's not the first person to pull that off."

"And he won't be the last," Maurer said.

Zander felt his side spasm where Ozbek had railroaded him to the floor, and he found himself moving toward Maurer as he tried to stretch out the muscle. "But why," he grunted, "do I sense no one is ever going to hear about Ozbek's connection to all this?"

Maurer gave him a knowing smile. "The world's news outlets will report tomorrow that Bulent Ozbek died on an archaeological dig in Anatolia."

"Suffocated in an ancient tomb?" Zander mocked.

"That works for me," Maurer said.

"You mean that's the *end* of it?" Penny shot back, throwing her hands up in agitation.

Maurer tried to placate her. "No, of course not. I'll have a heart-to-heart with the prime minister as soon as I'm back and spell out what really happened. We need to be sure he wasn't in any way complicit."

"And if he was?" Penny asked.
 Maurer swallowed hard. "I'll jump off that bridge when I get to it."

Zander kicked a loose chunk of marble hard across the floor. "It's not that simple, Maurer."

"And why not?"

"Because you can't just sweep this under some government rug. People died here. A lot of people, including people I knew."

"Nobody's denying that. But I'm trying to insure that a lot more people don't join them."

Zander thrust his arm toward Ozbek. "And letting people think he was a valued American ally is the way to do that?"

"You know it's a lot more complicated than that, Blake."

"My gut tells me it's actually a lot simpler than that, but I'll let you keep your damn secret under one condition."

Maurer folded his arms. "I'm listening."

"When you meet with the prime minister, you tell him that his brother's money—and I mean every last dime—is going to the families of the people he killed."

"I have no problem with that," Maurer said calmly enough that it seemed he liked the idea.

"Mostly the sailors. But some for Crane and some for Figgis."

"Figgis?" Maurer asked. "Are you sure?"

"Very sure. And a chunk to Goktepe's family and his newspaper."

A smirk revealed Maurer's waning enthusiasm.

"You and he have 30 days to make it happen," Zander said.

"That's too soon."

"No, it's not nearly soon enough."

• • • •

A detachment of U.S. Marines arrived within an hour of Maurer's call. The bodies of Ozbek, Figgis, and the two unknown Greeks were removed, as well as what was left of Sherin. Remarkably, Simonedes was still breathing, and a Marine surgeon managed to stabilize him. Though shot point blank, Ozbek's bullet had passed a few millimeters north of the old man's heart and straight out his back, nicking nothing vital along its way. And considering his age, the surgeon said his prognosis wasn't bad. Truly Athena's favorite, Zander thought.

On Zander's warning, the Marines isolated the source of the incendiary that had killed Sherin. Maurer said that tests would be conducted to analyze both the combustible fluid and the system that had fired it, but he was convinced from Zander's description that they had rediscovered Greek Fire, the most devastating weapon of the Middle Ages whose formula had been lost for centuries.

• • • •

Penny took Zander's hand and led him around the rotunda. He was eager to take one more look and sear this magical place into his memory. He felt he owed the goddess a debt and he paused directly below her elegant, sagacious face to admire her striking blue eyes. She remained as unchanging as a sculpture should, but he knew what he had seen before and he too felt like Athena's favorite.

Despite the horror and brutality they had withstood the past few hours, an improbable serenity had descended on him and he knew instinctively that Penny felt it too. Is this living in the moment, he wondered? He couldn't care less about any of the craziness that had gotten him here, and neither did he give a whit about where he might be tomorrow. How much of this was Penny and how much was almost being tossed into a fiery pool, he wasn't sure. He had seen more than once that people who survive a trauma together—a shootout, a fire, most any brush with death—are often bonded, and in his case, emboldened. "You know," he told her, "Harvard isn't the only place in the world to do whatever it is you need to do."

Penny cocked her head, as if a new angle would let her peak inside Zander's thoughts. "True," she said, lacing her fingers through his. "Only the best." They laughed and he felt her warmth envelop them both. His pains and bruises faded.

Zander led the way now, toward the rear of the rotunda, where the air was cooler. He stopped near a spot where the flaming trough had died down and the light was dimmer. "You'll take over Crane's work?"

She shook her head. "That would be like making a traffic cop the Chief of Police. They'll recruit a star out of Chicago or Princeton. They probably already have."

"Really?" Zander's tone lifted. "You know that even the wasteland where I live has its attractions. Places you might find worthy."

"Well, I have heard that California is the land of opportunity."

"Absolutely. There's UCLA, USC, the Getty. It's not the Ivy League. In fact I'm not sure ivy can even grow out there. But it has other charms."

Penny frowned and kicked him gently in the shin. "Is that the only way you think about me? Like my guidance counselor?"

Zander put his arms around her waist and pulled her close "Hardly," he said.

• • • •

About 24 hours later, with the explicit blessing of the prime minister, a convoy led by the U.S. Army Corps of Engineers rolled through Iznik on a special recovery mission. Using technology devised to rescue trapped miners, they opened the roof of the rotunda like a tin can, exposing the goddess to the warm July night.

Zander and Penny stood arm-in-arm on the ground above, edging close enough to the lip to peer down inside and see troops darting in every direction, boots slapping across the marble floor, disassembling in an hour what had withstood Crusaders, tomb robbers,

Mother Nature, and modern armies.

They had declined Maurer's offer to join him on a Marine transport back to Istanbul. Both sensed obligations to Linus Crane, to each other, and maybe to the goddess, that they could not leave before her.

Finally, amidst the fierce gusts and deafening swoosh of rotors from an angular, black helicopter that had emerged frighteningly from above, Zander and Penny fell far back from the chamber's rim. Marines dropped ropes from both sides of the hovering craft. It began lifting off just minutes later, raising the great statue into the open air.

For an instant the copter grew imperceptible against the night sky, and the golden Athena seemed to rise on her own, illuminated only by the lights recessed into the rotunda. The sight of the goddess against the stars seemed to Zander to transport her—and some part of him—back to a more ancient time. Zander watched her rise, his arm around Penny, and regretted that his time with her had been so brief. Still, she was the goddess of Wisdom, and maybe she had left traces behind.

The helicopter ascended stealthily into the night, its rotors whirring. The goddess followed upward, as though levitating to the heavens, becoming smaller and smaller, until she, too, was gone.

THE END

Acknowledgements

Several people helped drive this book down the home stretch, particularly Kristen Freethy and my friend Jessica Naeve. Heather McPherson of Raspberry Creative Type in Edinburgh, Scotland, designed the wonderful cover.

But a special, boundless thank you to Beth Franken for her editor's eye, encouragement, and friendship. There simply would have been no book without her.

About the Author

Ken Sonenclar has worked as a journalist (his byline appearing in *The New York Times* and *The Wall Street Journal Europe*, among other places), a technology consultant, and an investment banker specializing in media. He holds a Master's degree from the Fletcher School of Law and Diplomacy at Tufts University. He lives with his family in Westport, Connecticut.

For more about Bombs & Believers, go to
www.bombsandbelievers.com

www.ingramcontent.com/pod-product-compliance
Lightning Source LLC
Chambersburg PA
CBHW070751280626
47162CB00016B/59

* 9 7 8 0 9 8 8 8 4 2 3 1 1 *